EVERYDAY MERCIES

Evie Yoder Miller

BGP

Big Girl Press

Milton, Wisconsin

EVERYDAY MERCIES

ISBN: 13:978-1496152718

1. Intergenerational family relations—Fiction
2. Mennonite/Amish—Fiction
3. Organic farming—Fiction
4. Aging—Fiction

Published by: Big Girl Press
Milton, WI 53563

Also by Evie Yoder Miller

Eyes at the Window

To the memory of my parents, Bessie King Yoder and Herman Yoder, who gave me my first experiences of family

And to honor my daughters, Alice Christine Schermerhorn and Sarah Piper, for the ways they carry on traditions and establish new patterns of being family

If we had a keen vision and feeling of all ordinary
human life, it would be like hearing the grass grow
and the squirrel's heart beat,
and we would die of that roar
which lies on the other side of silence.

— George Eliot, *Middlemarch*

Generations come, and generations go . . . .
The sun rises and the sun sets . . . . The wind
blows to the south and turns to the north . . . .
All streams flow into the sea . . . . To the place
the streams come from, there they return again.

— Ecclesiastes 1:4-7 (NIV)

Chapter 1

Who's to say? Where, the peace that passes understanding? That passes reach. Forgive and then forgive again. What else is there? Martha tries to forget the sad times, tries to be glad for the good. Who ever gets fair? Daniel wanted her to be happy; she's sure. "Wipe away those tears; tomorrow will go better." Some days they *were* happy. Other days she put on the face.

No one really knew how he struggled. Not even Martha, not until that day. Not the extent. She had tried hard to make things go smoothly after his stroke. His maze of pills. The last thing she wanted was to make him more miserable. He had the strong leanings that way. Nothing she could do about it. Severe, some days. Some people's brains just cross over. The children never guessed; never let on, if they did. They must have thought: that's the way he is, quiet and withdrawn. The next minute, telling jokes. They never saw him extra bad.

He was a builder with his very own hands. How he studied that wood. So many beautiful things he made. The serving tray with the handles, the spiral candlesticks, the big wooden chairs that Charlotte calls Adirondacks. Their very own love seat with the wooden canopy. But he couldn't manage the swings of life. Sometimes he'd drag the toe of his shoe in the grass.

Momma had troubles, too; the diaries show it. Momma and Poppa Lloyd. "Call me Lloyd," he'd said in that voice that carried a cold wind. Martha tried to reassure her little sisters that he was their father. She didn't know why he wanted to be called by his first name. Why he insisted, "My name's Lloyd." Why they couldn't be like other families. It's a wonder, what children put up with. Little Clara, the one who didn't make it. Sometimes Martha and Irene called him Poppa in secret. "Poppa this and Poppa that," they whispered. *Shhh.* Always Lloyd, to his face. It was like he took on Momma as a down-and-out project; he knew she'd been taken advantage of. Six more youngsters. A hard, hard life. But she always kept to the strings.

Who's to say? You don't earn forgiveness. You don't say magic words. You're given it, if it's to be. And the forgiver never forgets, never mind the preacher. All those girls who had to get up in church; that was for spectacle. Three of them that one time. Gossip for the mills. Poor Momma. She didn't need to repent. She needed assurance that God had her under his wings like a mother hen. Impartial-like. Sure, Poppa Lloyd gave Momma another chance, but how many second chances did she give him? All those socks she darned. Those years, wearing the solid colors, strings on her covering.

No running water in Nebraska. The Broken Bow years. She never complained. Not really. Sold into slavery like Joseph. How many other women go willingly?

It's different now. They're still getting used to saying the twenty-first century. Charlotte gets her two cents in with James, makes sure her ideas get heard. And Carrie, she's the wanderer. As independent as they come. When will she ever come home for good? You can see the soft spot in her blue eyes, the way she looks at you, tender-like. Even looks kindly on an old woman. She listens, doesn't just say, "Uh-hum." It's a wonder in a young one. She looks like *she* could forgive.

Daniel forgave Martha, the time she smothered the chickens. Not that she meant to; it was an accident, an honest mistake that she forgot to open the chicken house on that terrible hot Sunday. And near the end, he didn't hold it against her that she needed to get out of the house sometimes. They ate store-bought cereal, when she could have fixed oatmeal. He forgave. It's no wonder, Martha never feels good enough, never finds the wherewithal. Sometimes she cries and frets when Charlotte's not around. But she has to believe she still has a purpose, still can be as useful as an everyday dress. Otherwise, what would ever make you press on?

Chapter 2

Carrie's dad was waiting for her at the Beloit bus station, just as she knew he would. How wonderful to be folded into his arms, into faint hints of sweat, the barn. She hasn't been that close to a man since Ryan left. Well, that time when Manager Milt jostled her; she was carrying a huge pile of clothes at Re-Use-It, and he tried to act like it was a joke. Now she's home at last. Wisconsin home. That never-ending bus ride. She's retreated to her bedroom—down the hall, last room on the left—glad for a chance to pull herself together from all the hellos. Her mom's hug, a whiff of chocolate on her breath. Grandma, tinier than ever, her bun secure at the back of her neck. The remodeled kitchen with its skylight and stainless steel appliances. A new bay window toward the woods. All this remodeling, then the barn fire.

Dad wore his plaid shirt—no surprise there—pale green with thin lines of maroon and white. When Carrie got off the bus, he explained that her mom was busy with food preparation. Last-minute cleaning jobs, too. Grandma almost came along but then decided to stay at home. So it was the two of them in the pickup. Their awkwardness. Long silences. She knew better than to rush in. It took a heifer in trouble to get him going. Last March, his cheeks had looked fuller—winter idleness, she supposes—but now he seemed in summertime shape. Short hair on the sides, some gray in his once-solid black hair that stuck out below his beloved Northrup King cap. Their halting talk in the toasty-warm pickup. Questions about sleeping on the bus, the disappointing fall colors, the unpredictable weather that had become predictable. Early November snow, now warmer again. She knew all that; Grandma had written it.

Carrie had gawked—the fields stretched wide, harvested and brown. Not the picture postcard the tourists want to see: green fields, red barns, dairy cows. They probably think it's all one shade of green, never see the dark evergreens in the middle of the silver and yellowish greens. That green in springtime that's actually a brown. She loved seeing the familiar curves, remembered the one she took too fast one winter before she knew she could end up in the ditch. Hills like little blips, compared with the tight mountains in Appalachia. Smaller than the foothills of southern Ohio where she lives. Her true home, here in Green County with the Sugar River savanna, once populated by huge, old oaks and prairie grass, tall enough to hide buffalo.

She asked if things had calmed down since the fire. "Oh, sure." He wanted to talk about his feed rations mixer, said he'd found a used Bobcat, went on about the convenience of moving large bales of hay, scooping manure down the center of the free stall. "Cow comfort." He kept saying that, then he'd grin slightly. It seemed a big deal that the cows weren't lying in their mess before they were milked. Then his sudden bombshell when she tilted her head back to empty the orange juice bottle: "Sometimes I think about selling my herd."

"You what?" She wiped her mouth and cheek with the back of her hand.

Of course, she knew how the USDA kept upping its standards for the required amount of open pasture. It was not news that they let the big guys get by. Dad kept rubbing his hand back and forth on his jeans. One collar of his shirt stuck out under his gray, fleece, zip-up jacket. She went blank, hadn't dreamed there'd be an opening this soon. What was she going to ask first? She thought she'd have to be sly, to cajole. "You can't do only grain," she said sharply, like he was trying to induce contractions. "Ethanol will bust when they develop other biofuels."

"Already happening," he said. And then his sarcasm. "Maybe I'll start a cottage industry like the Amish. Sell rocking chairs and jam." He's always been the super steady one, calm, as unchanging as Grandma. When he dresses up for church or a Farm Bureau meeting, he only shifts from jeans to Dockers pants, replaces his work boots with brown slip-ons. That day at Grandpa's funeral, he looked stuffed into a suit.

"Well, they've got a lot of it right," Carrie said. "The Amish don't pollute the land with chemicals, for one."

"Steel-rimmed tires? Goat farms? Outsiders think they must be doing something right because they look so quaint. Believe me, it can't be easy for them right now either, not even with eight youngsters helping." He scratched his forehead, readjusted his cap. "They keep buying farms, next county over. Neighbor guy, Jack Hasty, says they're everywhere, multiplying like ants. The latest row: some of them refuse to number their cows—sign of the beast or something. State wants to be able to trace every animal, know where it ends up."

She had managed to say something about regulation. He allowed that the government had its place—more head-scratching—but finished with, "Just let us farm, for crying out loud."

She's heard the rants before about the factory dairy farms coming in, acting like animals are machines. Now it seems like he's mad at everything. The government must be his Incorrigible Kid, the one who ruins the whole class and makes him want to get out. She couldn't think of anything useful or clever to say. All those years she'd loved to "work" with him, couldn't wait to be trusted to drive the tractor. He let her start on the International because she could reach the clutch. Mom even said she looked good on it, natural. And then one day it was, "Don't go out there and get all smelly again," like she'd just read an article called "Thirteen Danger Signs in Your Developing Daughter." The 4-H years had helped Carrie make it through. She was good at showing cows for the county fair; she trained them to back up, brought them forward again, just so. She power-washed them, brushed them, showed off their legs, their angles. All Mom cared about was how dirty Carrie's white pants were when she got home.

Now she changes into a green and black flannel shirt, finds faded black jeans. Where are her work shoes? She looks on the closet floor behind long dresses and blouses with pointed collars. *Get those out of here!* She needs to clear out this stuff from her teaching days; these shoes with the thick heels look obscene. Mom will know where the Goodwill is in Monroe.

"You never know when this might be your grandma's last holiday," Mom had written in an e-mail. But Grandma looks perkier than she did last spring, more settled with her move into Chad's old bedroom. Dad's the one—. Everything's the same and everything's different. Knick-knacks on Carrie's shelves: the replica of the Sears Tower in Chicago, the picture of her and Ryan that she left on the dresser in March.

Everything was fine back then. Kirsten had taken the picture when the three of them went camping in the Smokies. They had hiked up to Mt. LeConte Lodge and back down again in one day. They both look so carefree. Ryan has on his khaki walking shorts and hiking boots. His hair shows; Kirsten must have made him take off his cap.

Carrie sticks the picture in the top dresser drawer, tucks it under her old summer pajamas. *The roll of money.* She takes it out of her shoulder purse, flips through it quickly—it's all there: three hundred dollars in twenties!—and slides it under a stack of slips and camisoles. *No one will find it under these relics.* No one will enter without asking. Trudy can put this money to good use back in Ohio; her little girl, Spice, needs lip surgery again. The bus ride has brought clarity about that much.

But otherwise, what was she thinking? A short stay of four days to sow seeds for Christmastime. Make a proposal to move back home to raise lettuce and tomatoes. Everything lined up neatly last night on the bus ride. Even the Amish family climbing on board had seemed right, somehow. Two small children but maybe not a family exactly. An older woman with a thin but melodic voice; she likely sings when she hangs out the wash. But the elderly man with the hearing problem couldn't pick up the woman's whispers during the night. This morning Carrie had watched the little boy eat three bananas and pickle spears for breakfast. They passed sugar cookies with red sprinkles. And at daybreak when Singer Woman had gotten up to go to the lavatory, she looked directly at Carrie and smiled. Carrie suddenly felt exposed and looked away. The man's cane clattered again.

But now with Dad sounding so negative, she has to be cautious. If he's serious about selling, she'll look stupid, talking about marketing strategies for vegetables with a depressed grain and dairy farmer of thirty years. She had gotten off on the wrong foot with her mom, too. The house smelled of apples and celery, but her hunt for apple crisp came up empty.

"What time did you get in?" Grandma had asked, hanging on to Carrie's hand.

"Just a half hour late," Dad said.

Grandma had gotten confused about who was late. A timer screeched. "No trouble, Grandma. Wow!" Carrie had glanced past bread pieces mounded in a bowl. Mom's stuffing. "Wow. Some kitchen. Why'd you replace all the appliances? They all conked out at once?"

Mom hesitated only a second. "Look at this." She whirled and pulled out a narrow cupboard full of spices. "And I love having the washer and dryer closed off by these folding doors. Keeps the mess hidden."

"Nifty," Carrie said.

"Creature comfort, eh?" Dad grinned and joined the show-and-tell. "Here's my favorite spot." He pulled out the waste basket on a rolling shelf, hidden behind the cherry cupboard veneer.

"Why stainless steel?" Carrie had asked. "I mean, it's all right, but it looks cold." She folded her arms in front of her and walked to the bay window, gave the string of hot peppers a swing. The trees in the woods looked barren, except for a few pines.

"Oh, no, it's warm in here; I'm hot," her mom said. She fanned her face with her hand, pointed to the skylight. "Look up. The natural light makes everything warmer. Saves electricity, too. Stainless steel is very in today." She brushed at a tiny stain on her green and pink apron that said "Kiss the Cook."

"Not for me," Carrie said. "Cold, institutional. Did the cows foot the bill?"

Her mom and dad had stared at each other.

"Oh, that's right," Carrie said. "We don't argue openly." She had smiled at Grandma. "We come from the Quiet in the Land. Too nice to confront directly."

Ugh. Could it have gone any worse? She'll never convince her parents that way. It had surprised her: the remodeling. She hadn't realized it was so extensive. Grandma had barely mentioned it in her letters, only said something about beautiful cherry wood. But right now, if she stays in her room any longer, her mom will start asking questions. She needs to go to the kitchen and offer to chop something.

*　　　*　　　*

Carrie slides in on one side of the new kitchen nook, cozies up to the potted herbs on the ledge. Mom apologizes for the light lunch: cold sandwiches on plain bread, no buns; they need to use things up before the big meal. "It's good to be here," Carrie says. "I don't need fancy."

Mom and Dad go back and forth about the CD player not working in the Chrysler van, mention the bridal shower at church next week for Cliff and Nita's Debbie. Grandma asks about Carrie's teacher friend Kirsten, remembers that she's a Quaker. Dad mentions the neighbor in Kentucky—"big, heavy-set, friendly guy"—who had helped them load Carrie's large pieces, the day bed and dresser, on the truck when she moved to Ohio. "Didn't he have an uncle who was into cock-fighting?"

Mom blows lightly on her tomato soup and takes Dad to task for the hunters on their land. "It's posted, you know," she says to Carrie. Dad stays cool, says that Simp, the hired man, has friends who hunt around here. "That's no excuse," Mom says.

"I gotta keep him happy," Dad says. "He's helped me out a long time. It's hard to find places to hunt that aren't private."

"Just so no one gets hurt," Grandma says.

"Who feeds the new pup?" Carrie asks. She turns to Grandma. "I hear you were the one who named him." The round, four-month-old had sniffed at her socks when she got out of the pickup.

Grandma flips her hand down in dismissal. "Oh, it was nothing. A mistake, really. I said, 'The Word of the Lord sayest,' and Charlotte corrected me. I don't remember what we were talking about."

"'Therefore, the Lord *sayeth,*'" Mom says. "Most of the time it sounds like Seth."

"Yes, sayeth, not sayest." Grandma keeps her head down. "Although it depends."

"Just another moment of confusion among simple farm folk," Dad says. "Can't even get our Scriptures straight."

"Well, aren't you jolly?" Mom says. "Both of you," she adds, including Carrie in her glance. "I'm the one who takes care of Sayeth. On the porch mostly—Chad's too busy—I don't want Sayeth wandering off and getting in the way of some hunter who's not supposed to be out there in the first place." She pauses, "Has your dad been this entertaining all the way home?"

Carrie nods. "One belly laugh after another. I'm here to work on Dad's attitude. Transform his thinking."

The talk drifts to Mom's golf game, how it helps her keep the excess weight off. Next year she's going to work on her short game. She laughs about the time her ball rolled off the putting surface five times before it stayed up on the green.

"Forevermore," Grandma says. "That counts against you, doesn't it?"

"Every stroke," Mom says. "Too many lousy chip shots. That's my biggest problem. Sometimes that ball has wickedness written all over it."

Suddenly the conversation shifts and Mom brings up her old contention about the program at the school where Carrie taught in Appalachia. "At least you won't have to deal with that Christmas give-away program this year."

Carrie considers playing dumb. "You'll never forget that, will you?" she says. "Great idea to add celery to the soup."

"What's that?" Grandma asks. She rearranges a tidy pile of shaved ham, cheese, and a slice of green pepper, so it all stays put on her open-faced sandwich.

"School kids listed what they wanted for Christmas," Carrie says. "Then agencies in the community—they're going to give gifts anyway—knew what the kids would like."

"*Poor* kids," Mom explains to Grandma. "They need help, all right."

"The way it works—." Carrie pauses. Keep it simple and move on. "Each family that qualifies gets a standardized food box, but gifts for the children are individualized. A parent writes down the child's age, clothing sizes, needs, wants." Her eyes drift to the herbs. "Have you ever tried keeping arugula indoors, Mom?"

"Wants," Mom says. "That's the part that gets me." She tucks a stray piece of lettuce in her sandwich. "Arugula? No, I don't have any luck with that. Isn't that pot of parsley beautiful?"

"All your herbs look very healthy," Carrie says. She breaks off a tip of basil, holds it to her nose. "Uhm." She could specialize in herbs—ten varieties of basil—but there might not be market enough. She breaks off the whole basil leaf, then another, and slips them in her sandwich.

"Where do these programs come from?" Dad asks. His arm rests casually on the window ledge.

"Health and Human Services," Carrie says. No sign of baked apples cooling. Her nose must have betrayed her when she walked in the door.

"That's welfare," Dad says to Grandma. "Anybody want more mustard?"

"I see," Grandma says.

"That's what it used to be called," Carrie says. Grandma probably doesn't see; you have to be there, not look from a distance.

"I thought you said churches gave to these kids," Mom says.

"Some did, that's right," Carrie says. "It could be different now. I'm not there, you know. The good part is, the various funding agencies know each others' clients, so there's no overlap."

"Clients?" Mom raises both eyebrows. "Sounds like a business."

"Parents can sign up, Grandma," Carrie says, "but when they do—sign up so their children can get gifts—they have to surrender their pride. That wouldn't be easy." She takes a large bite of ham and cheese. "Uhm, Swiss cheese. Must be made locally."

"Surrender?" Mom asks.

"It's not easy to ask for help," Grandma says. "Daniel hated not being able to do things on his own. He lost his privacy."

"Don't they get used to it? Those people asking for handouts?" Mom asks. "That's my guess. I know some of them have had a rough time of it, but—. Pretty soon they come to expect it. I suppose anyone would."

"Entitlement," Dad announces.

Carrie swallows her milk slowly, such a different taste from store-bought skim milk. What's the point of trying to explain? "All kinds of red tape for people with limited resources to get substantive help from Congress. Politicians are too busy taking care of the oil and insurance businesses. Pharmaceuticals."

"Pfft. Why should the government step in and do what people can do for themselves?" Mom asks. "I guess I sound cold-hearted. I don't mean it like that."

"Maybe that's the question: can people do it for themselves?"

"Right, Dad. Let's see." Carrie taps a finger on her cheek like she's the drama queen. "Anyone around here know of any beneficiaries of subsidies?" She stares at the salt shaker. "Not that it's *not* needed. That's the point."

"That's different," Mom says. She eases her body out of the nook to get more water.

"Sure it is," Carrie says. "It's us."

Dad raps his fingers on the ledge. "We could be wiped out just like that." He snaps his finger and Grandma jerks. "Farming is one of the three most dangerous industries in the U.S. We're trying to get an insurance cooperative started here in the south central part of the state, so we don't have to each buy private coverage. Three years into the new century and still trying. As it is now, a premium can easily run to two thousand a month."

"Insurance means survival," Mom says. "How can you give a kid a DVD when what he needs is food? That's what gets me. I'm not against giving, mind you."

"No twelve-year-old boy is going to ask for a dinky plastic truck," Dad says.

"Huh?" Mom dips her bread crust into ketchup and chews slowly.

"A teenage kid wants to be like any other kid," Dad says. "That's all."

"You'd rather decide for others, Mom, what they need?" Carrie asks. "How do you know who deserves what?"

"How do *you*?" Mom replies. "Doesn't the Bible say the poor will be with us alway? Or is it always?"

Dad bumps his fist on the ledge like a metronome set at the slowest beat. "Just so no one gives that family any money for the grocery store. That child might beg for *corn* chips and get *fat*." He says words like he's pouring oil on a hot skillet. "It's *corn* that's evil."

Grandma makes clicking noises, then slips out of the nook. Her blue slippers squeak on the vinyl.

"Who's to say? Social, psychological, physical needs," Carrie says. "We're all poor in some way."

"My point is—." Mom fluffs her hair in front. "You don't die from wanting a CD and not getting it. You *can* die from not getting cancer treated. There's a big difference. Where did Mother go?"

Carrie sighs. She should have just kept quiet.

"Maybe no one deserves anything," Dad says. "We'd all be better off if we didn't expect anything." He stares out the window, his hand and arm still. "Just work your fingers to the bone. Hope to stay alive."

Grandma slides back into the booth, brochure in hand. "I wanted you to see this," she says to Carrie. "Service opportunities from the Mennonite Church. Some of their programs."

"Me?" Carrie asks. She looks at pictures of dark-skinned hands carrying a basket, other hands flattening tortillas, still others raising two fingers in the air. No faces. Only hands. Does Grandma want her to go to a mission outpost in Bolivia? Mexico? Hook up with Mennonites?

"Just to look at," she says. "I thought you'd be interested; that's all. Poppa Lloyd used to be taken up with the mission field. Back then it was something new. The Amish, of course, still don't go in for it."

"Oh," Carrie says. *What in God's name?* She unfolds the brochure: *Small loans . . . principles of self-help and free enterprise . . . the hands of the working poor.* "This reads like a seminar for a vegetable farmer wanting to start up." She can't resist looking at Dad. "'Missional'? What kind of word is that? Are these the liberal Mennonites or your kind, Grandma?"

She leans over to look and says, "Like the ones in Madison with more education. I thought you'd be interested. That's all. Oh, did I say that?" She hesitates, then adds, "I guess it's strange to traipse all over the world, when there are hungry people in Beloit."

Carrie nods. "That's what I've learned. Finally. If you're honest, how do you ever know whether you want to help or be 'the helper'?"

Dad motions that he needs to get out of the booth. "I'm heading into town to get a part welded for the combine. Want to come along, Carrie?"

"Oh," she groans. "I want to, but I don't have it in me to ride another mile today. Sorry, Dad. I still hear road noise. I want to go out to the corn crib when you get back." It hadn't looked as bad as she'd feared. The blue tarp must have covered the worst.

"Not a problem," he says, hitching up his jeans. "Just thought I'd ask. I'm getting all my equipment fixed up now, not waiting till spring."

Mom looks like she wants to say something but turns instead and carries the soup pot to the counter. Her brown hair layers smoothly in the back; she's always carried herself well. No middle-aged slump. And she doesn't look like she's put on weight; golfing must help. How many times Carrie's heard her go on about the weight she lost, only to have it come back.

Later with Dad out of the house, the table cleared, and dishwasher loaded, Carrie turns to her mom and asks, "Shall I roll out the pie crusts or is that all done?"

"Heavens no. Those pies need to be fresh tomorrow. Don't worry; I'm getting up early to bake them. I've got it all figured out."

Mom waves scraps of paper in the air. "I've got to get up to stuff the turkey, so I might as well bake the pies early in the morning. We have to eat by one o'clock sharp, so Chad can digest his food before practice. I'll take care of everything; you relax this weekend. You look tired," she adds.

It turns out that Chad has basketball practice on Thanksgiving Day. No joke. Mom isn't sure if it's a walk-through or a shoot-around, but it starts late afternoon. She goes on about the regular season beginning last night—some parents raised a stink about having a game during deer season—and it's too bad Carrie missed it because Chad scored eighteen points. Coach Lucey has big expectations for the boys this year. And so on. Carrie yawns and rubs an eye with her fist.

"You must be hot in that old flannel shirt," Mom says. "Roll up your sleeves, so you can breathe."

"I'm fine," Carrie says, tugging on her sleeves to lengthen them. She wanders around the kitchen, tries to make amends by opening drawers, commenting on the lazy Susan corner cupboard. "Gosh, Mom, do you have enough containers? Two drawers full!"

Grandma has moved from the kitchen nook to the small table with the blue legs in the center of the kitchen. "That nook sits as stiff as a church bench," she says. "I don't mean the chairs at your church, Charlotte." She studies a page lying open in the *Mennonite Community Cookbook.*

"But no one preaches at you when you're in this kitchen nook." Mom grins. "No one tells you to dress modestly and obey your man."

Carrie tries to catch Grandma's eye, but she's bending down, adjusting her knee-hi again. "They must have used cheap elastic when they made these stockings," Grandma says.

"You know knee-hi's are bad for your circulation," Mom says. "Whew! Plenty of coffee filters. I thought for a minute there—."

"Do you like the church services, Grandma, at Faith Community?" Carrie asks.

Mom looks up from chopping onion into fine pieces.

"They're all right," Grandma says. "I'm not one to make a fuss."

"Oh, Caroline, what I need you to do," Mom says, "is run down—sorry to interrupt—to the basement and get a couple jars of beans. Bring two jars from in front. I put up enough beans last summer to feed the whole county. I finally had to pull up the plants. Could you, would you, please?"

"Sure, I'll go," Carrie says. She's old enough to retrieve the home-canned beans. Mom will handle the important things for Thanksgiving like pies and turkey. How could Carrie have forgotten? It's happened again. When she's far away in southern Ohio, she regards her family with such warmth. Not that they're *tight*—she'd never go that far—but things sure feel better when she's away than when she comes home. Her memories of her mom have been wrapped in tissue paper. Carrie remembers the traditional three-layer cake her mom made for everyone's birthday. Chocolate, lemon, coconut—you name it; you get it. She's always been generous with food. So what, if she saves every Cool Whip container, buys a new set of blue Ziploc plastic?

"I didn't know you pulled up the beans early, Charlotte." Grandma's eyes return to the beige and navy floor pattern of the vinyl.

"Oh, they were practically done for. Scraggly looking, full of holes. It's not like I destroyed a human life." Mom laughs. "Somehow they kept on producing. No need to mention it to James, though."

Carrie goes to the side of the refrigerator, looks at the magnets: the winking Holstein, the putter surface with an oversized smiling face. A square blue magnet says: "Some people walk in the rain . . . others just get wet."

"Teresa and I give each other little gifts," Mom explains. "Whoever has the *low* score gives the loser a magnet. How's that for upside-down thinking?"

"Very cool," Carrie says, turning all the magnets sideways. Her mom is still the sports fanatic, plays golf religiously on Friday afternoons—Tuesdays, too?—with her "golf ladies." It always surprises Carrie, how important it is. What a contrast with most of the women who come to Re-Use-It, desperate for shoes for their children, scrounging for bargains. Her mom doesn't know what it means to worry about where her next beef roast is coming from. Or whether there will be *any* protein.

"Oh, Caroline, while you're down in the basement, would you check on Chad's room? Make sure it's straightened up." Belinda comes to the top of the basement stairway and cries pitifully. "I don't want that cat in the kitchen while I'm cooking." Mom nods toward the door.

Carrie's never been fond of animals in the house, never begged as a child to bring Sayeth's predecessor, Babe, inside. Babe's job was to bark at the cows and get them out of the barn; that's where she belonged.

"Go ahead, Mother, tell Caroline more. How you like our church."

"It's what you get used to," Grandma says. "Here's a dressing recipe I've used." She's kept a finger in Mom's spot while paging through the vanilla-stained cookbook, wetting her thumb with each turn. "Parsley, onion, sage. Daniel never wanted oysters. He was afraid I'd sneak some in. I don't know how he thought I'd disguise them. I told him oysters were a delicacy; rich people ate them."

"Oh, you mean stuffing, not dressing. You're going to love mine," Mom says. "Apples *with* the gizzards. And a secret ingredient. You'll absolutely love it." She's turned to cleaning again, stands on a chair to wipe dust off the top of the refrigerator.

"I couldn't always predict what Daniel would like," Grandma says. "Or do, for that matter. But he left no doubt about the oysters."

"How many gizzards does this bird have?" Carrie asks. Wasting an apple in the stuffing? Has her mom forgotten how much she likes apple crisp with milk on top? And Grandma—the big wooden cross hanging behind the pulpit must seem ostentatious. The flag in the sanctuary. Or maybe she feels out of place around women who get all gussied up to worship. Wait. Where is Grandma's covering? She always wears her head covering, doesn't she?

"You know what I mean. Giblets. Did you forget about the beans?" Mom turns back from the refrigerator, glances uncertainly at

Carrie. "You don't have to get them, if you don't want. I'm sure you're tired."

"I'll go," Carrie says. "Run down," she adds quietly. "Be Chad's sheriff." She pictures the beans, sitting in jars, floating in liquid, waiting to be devoured. Why do they need to be in the kitchen a day ahead of time? She opens the door to the basement, scoops up the whining Belinda, and flips on the light switch. Her sandals sound clumpy on the wooden steps. Carrie always hated going to the basement on errands. Her mom's servant. *Don't look in the shadows behind the stairway.* She'd never been enamored with the rec room either. Give her the rope swing on the big maple tree out front; let her spend time hunting for Mayapples in the woods. Tomorrow her mom will ask her to prepare the relish plate, slice the carrots in long sticks, arrange green olives with their eyeballs staring up. Mom will be the one to remove the delicate Jello salad from its heart-shaped mold. It's childish to complain. Why does Carrie start acting like a mopey teenager when she comes home? If her mom wants to have everything lined up ahead of time on the kitchen counter, that's her privilege. That's the way super-efficient people do things. Live by their lists.

Chad's new bedroom and bath are at the far end, down the hallway to the left, right under her own room. His door is tightly closed. *So be it.* She returns to the storage room where her mom's canned fruits and vegetables stand in neat rows with blue plastic labels taped on the front edges of the shelves. Perfect for those who can't distinguish a sweet cherry jar from a pear. Carrie picks up two dusty jars of beans. *Why not color-coded shelves?*

Upstairs, her mom and grandma are discussing whether or not to snip the ends of green beans before canning. Grandma holds out for cutting both ends; that's the way Momma taught her. Mom insists that if the beans are removed carefully from the plants and washed in cold water, neither end needs to be snipped. Certainly not the tail end. That would be a waste of time. And of nutrition, Carrie wants to add.

"I need to take a nap," Carrie says, as she sets the jars on the kitchen counter. "Chad's door was closed."

"Are you feeling sick or something?" Mom asks. She reaches for a wet dishcloth and wipes the jar lids. "Did you look in his room?"

"His door was closed." Carrie moves all the refrigerator magnets into a large oval shape. "I feel okay, just sleepy. Long night on the bus."

"Poor dear," Grandma says. "You're too young to be worn out." She makes clicking noises that follow Carrie down the hallway.

* * *

Her bedroom again. *Escape!* As much space in here as Carrie's combined kitchen and living room in Ohio—Acey Banger's double garage, upstairs apartment. As much room, if not more, than whole families share in tents or huts around the world. Stretched out on the bed, she closes her eyes, tries to block out the last hours. She *should* have gone to town with Dad. Maybe it was a mistake to come, period. It's a fantasy that she belongs to this family. This talk. Grandma insisting that peach halves be placed down when canning, so you can get more fruit in the jar. Carrie would bet anything those never-ending bean producers of Mom's were Carsons. The tragedies and triumphs of Mom's golf game: titanium, Big Bertha drivers, belly putters.

Not that domestic chit-chat is unimportant. Far from it. She could talk beans all day; raw purple ones are heavenly in salads. The ordinary *does* matter. But her family doesn't know how to talk about issues that affect people all over the world. Don't they care that people are still dying in the Middle East? That the U.S. goes along with political solutions that actually harm people? Leaders get by with whatever they want, because people won't speak up. Why did Carrie think she wanted to move back? Oh, right. A life with a working definition. How noble that sounds now. A place to feel welcome, where the work would feed her.

Mom and Grandma are probably talking about her right now. "She's too thin, needs some pep." "Needs a decent job." "If only Ryan—." Ryan? *Not again.* They don't know him. He's not the answer, Mom. But if he were here, he'd find some way to shock them out of their complacency. The Christmas gift program for Appalachian school kids would have made perfect sense, if he'd been here to explain it. Why is it, the things she cares about the most, she has the hardest time getting across? How can her family accept her, if they don't know who she is? *Her* wants. It's probably fatigue. Poor sleep on the bus makes her mind bounce.

Funny—she knew, or thought she knew, she'd feel this way. Adrift. From the minute she stepped onto the dairy farm—the James and Charlotte Lehman homestead with the black-and-white spotted sign out front—she knew she'd not feel at home. She'd tried to prepare. And yet, she wanted to be here. To give it a shot. She'd known excitement *and* apprehension. A yearning. The place where she could grow vegetables. Heartsick, if Dad shook his head. She'd been determined: find a way to fit in, even if her mom still called her Caroline, as if she were a princess or a president's daughter.

It's true; she went to Appalachia to get away. She'd pleased her mom by getting a B.A. and a teacher's license. That was perfectly acceptable. But then for two years Carrie had surrounded herself with warmhearted Kentucky people. Her mom had asked, "Why do you always need to be different?" as if she'd moved to a foreign country. She only wanted to know what it was like to be in someone else's world. Was that so wrong? She'd wanted to live with those less fortunate. Ryan had called her a sympathizer. True enough.

She didn't know if she'd been a mistake masquerading as a teacher, but all too soon, it felt like it. So what was the big deal? Teachers are supposed to help kids learn to spell, subtract, dissect frogs, no matter where they live. Why couldn't she? It looked so easy for Kirsten. What was so hard about teaching fifth graders their fractions? It had to be more than a bad case of Incorrigible Cody. As time went on, she had trouble carrying out her lesson plans. Her ideas seemed brilliant on Sunday night, but by Tuesday evening she'd either covered everything for the week or fallen far behind. She doubted herself. It snowballed.

People in her apartment complex had smiled and waved to her like she belonged. She'd wanted to earn their trust. But she never did.

They must have turned their backs at her naiveté, giggled behind closed doors. Her bewilderment at "Mash that button." They seemed clannish sometimes but maybe no more—less!—than the Amish. She hadn't meant to be condescending. Was she? Pollyanna-like? Only *two* years of teaching before she quit? What kind of investment in a bachelor's degree was that? A few graduate courses in education wasted, too.

She'd wanted to make the world better, to be a part of work that mattered. She'd wanted to know what it felt like to live with folks who were the butt of jokes: "Y'all hear about the mountain man who had three wives and couldn't remember their first names?" She'd wanted to see the real Appalachia, not the packaged media presentation. Now she knows a small slice of the picture. Is there no place on earth for her? Is coming back to Wisconsin a last resort, where the adage says they have to take you in? Is she coming back to jokes about the Amish who aren't supposed to know how to screw in a light bulb? What if she throws herself into growing food and then leaves again after a year or two? Gets tired of butting heads with her parents, or with the fast food system? Another huge investment down the drain. What did Grandma say about discontented people? Never satisfied. First they try one thing; then they go somewhere else. Tsk, tsk. *Heartsick restlessness.*

Every world Carrie has lived in has had too much *and* not enough. Emptiness *and* fullness. Beauty *and* trash. Why does she fall into the trap of thinking the world is one way or the other? Lovely or loathsome. Dependable or capricious. After the first enchanting months in Kentucky, she stopped taking pictures. When the trees lost their leaves, the extremes of wealth and poverty showed up along with the town's junk. Strip mining was right there, center stage. Right there on her list of things to be against, along with Cody the Kid. She began to stand apart while being present. Kirsten called her the Silent Observer. And yet, there was so much to like, too. Family values. The way the Hendersons took care of their elderly parents. The seasons. Gorgeous green mountains in the summer when the morning fog burned off. Stunning dogwood and mimosa trees. And in the fall of her second year, that brilliant red, followed by enough snow to cover the winter drabness.

How could anyone want to be a farm girl at the start of the twenty-first century? She should *want* to live in Chicago, if not New York City or L.A. That's where things happen, where cool people flourish. In Washington, D.C., she'd spell her name "Keri." And yet, she wants to *avoid* Chicago. How silly, to be glad the bus skirted the city. But it's true; she loves the afterglow of a sunset on a harvested field, wants to see the first sandhill cranes in the spring—their long legs, long necks—leaping for a mate down by the creek. *Such ordinary, country things.* Carrie turns over on her side, tucks her hands under the pillow. She's always had dirt in her belly button. *Give it up and get some rest.*

It was like this on the bus all night, shifting positions, stretching, getting a bagel with cream cheese when they stopped, sucking all the juice out of the apple core. The relentless question: what if doing good causes harm? The certainty: she was no Good Samaritan. The recurring image: a nameless, bony old man on the side of the road.

One of God's own. Someone's beloved. Rolled up like a stone, a mound cast aside. Her car lights had flashed briefly around the curve, picked up an object on the side. She drove by. Maybe it *was* just a black trash bag. Or a dog. Maybe it *was* too dark to see for sure. No room to pull over and get out on those narrow roads. *Walk back and see?* No way. In the dusk of her rearview mirror, it had looked like the mound became a stocking cap that rose slightly. A gloved hand tilted sideways. Yes, she *was* a woman alone. Kirsten had said to let it go. No point in taking unacceptable risks.

It's true, too—embarrassingly so—she went from Kentucky to southern Ohio on a whim. Kirsten had encouraged her when she was undecided about teaching for a third year: "Go see Ryan; he likes you." And now there she is, living in Athens; she'd *followed* a man like a crazed teenager. She'd never had a serious boyfriend in her life, preferred groups of kids. Oh, sure, brief flurries of passing notes in grade school, cheap bracelets exchanged. Kids' stuff. If she waits in Athens—yes, Mom, it *is* a dead-end job at Re-Use-It—will Ryan come back? *Shame, shame, to still hope.* Is that what it is?

They spent time together, learned to know each other over burritos in what turned out to be their favorite Mexican restaurant with school kids' art on the walls. *How could he walk away?* He'd pointed to a child's rendition of a father hugging his two children. "I wish I'd known that," he said. "Your father didn't love you?" she asked. "Oh, yes, he loved me. Too much. He told me everything I was supposed to do. Classic." Ryan had reached across the booth for her hand and said, "I don't ever want to do that." It must have been one of Casa's specialty beers that had triggered Ryan's touch. He could be as tight emotionally as Grandpa Ropp's millionaire of a brother-in-law who supported overseas church work in Tanzania.

Mom had snooped around—still acts like she needs to know—seemed relieved that they didn't share an apartment. *Well, heck no.* Carrie didn't know how to explain who they were, who *he* was for her. *People have to know.* What if there's no word for it? Best friends sounds silly, grade-schoolish. He offered companionship while he got his master's in international relations at the university. But yes, they were more than pals. Comrades? That sounds too political, although it's true: he said he liked the fire in her eyes when she zinged a one-liner. They'd egged each other on, made fun of the policy of telling people in a foreign country that you're killing them for their own good. Laughed their heads off, when it wasn't funny. How do you tell your mom that? She'd probably think "imposing democracy" sounded like a good thing.

Most of the time Ryan acted like a bro. He offered her security. Sort of. Not until he left did she realize how attached she was. Someone to hang out with, so she didn't have to go places alone. They spent nights on the Hill with a blanket, watching for shooting stars. Unconventional—their friendship. It's true; she had bought a lacy, black bra at one point. That was silly. At first, when his letters were infrequent, Carrie made allowances. She pictured him making the necessary adjustments to a foreign culture. The heat, an annoying, prickly, skin rash. Probably diarrhea. He was sketchy about where he was, how long it'd be before they took up a vigil at a different spot. Carrie thought he didn't give details because of security reasons. But doubts crept in, until she couldn't deny what must have happened. Mr. Disappearance.

No, Mom, *not meant to be!* That gives the wrong impression. Mom wouldn't like it that sometimes Ryan wore the same shirt three days in a row. And he wouldn't answer calls when he was studying for an exam. For all Carrie knows, Ryan might be a martyr already. *Get killed for the good of the world?* She thought she knew his mind, until he finished his degree and announced he was leaving for the Middle East on a peacemaking team. She'd nodded numbly, even drove him to the Columbus airport. Just like that—a matter of days—he was gone. She'd tried to slip her picture into a side pocket of his carry-on. Not likely to return, true to the '60s music they used to listen to on old LPs. Down that long corridor to take off his shoes for Homeland Security. She thought he'd turn and wave, but he never looked back. How could she have been so dumb? She'd followed a guy to Ohio and was left at Re-Use-It, looking for torn hems that needed attention before dresses were put on racks. Left waiting with a mom who expected an explanation.

Mom makes it clear; she expects Carrie to go back to teaching in an elementary school somewhere, soon. Settle into a job that carries respect, where she can be successful. For Mom, that means: make money. Do moms always think they have a right to draw a map for their children? Recently, she mentioned on the phone that her golfing partner, Teresa, had shown her—*flaunted*—pictures of her grandchildren. Her mom has no idea that Carrie browses ag-related websites, thinks about sustainability. Cold frames and high tunnels.

Irrigation drip lines. If Mom weren't so confident she knows Carrie, it'd be easier. Or maybe not. Mom only came to Kentucky with Dad and Chad that one time. She's never visited Carrie in Athens. "Where would we stay?" As if a college town has no motels in the area.

Carrie hears a door close. Probably Grandma's bedroom. How does she manage to live here with Mom, *her* daughter? Do they ever get into it? More than the dressing versus stuffing twit? It's probably not fair for Carrie to expect her family to talk about what's foreign to them. They tried, sort of. They tried to imagine what it'd be like to be someone else. A kid at Christmas with a dad who's out of work in the mines. Grandma might have brought out that brochure to show she cares about more than southern Wisconsin. Maybe Mom's uptight because of tomorrow. The Meal. She loves being extravagant, when it suits. She can sound so crass, but there's more to her.

Better to focus on Dad. Get him to consider alternatives. He's stuck thinking about corn and beans and hay with a little alfalfa thrown in. Be careful, though, not to take advantage of him when he's feeling down, unsure if he can keep on doing what he loves. But she'll need to be more direct, too. He has no idea she's serious about vegetables. That doesn't mean he's hopeless. She'll bring him along slowly. People need time to take things in, especially when a daughter reintroduces herself.

Chapter 3

Martha is relieved to lie down for her afternoon rest. She'll close her eyes a bit and then get up to read some more of the diaries. She doesn't need sleep in the daytime, but it helps to put her legs up awhile. She adjusts the blanket. Is the air conditioning on?

Martha doesn't know what to make of that school in the South and their plan for giving Christmas gifts to school children. She'd never heard of that, but if it helps someone in need, that's good. Charlotte's been mulling it over; you could hear it in her voice. She didn't need to be so hardnosed about it. Carrie doesn't even teach there anymore. Poor girl, tired and all. There's something a little off kilter, though. More than tired.

Life never turns out the way you expect. Not for Martha's children, not their children. Martha's boys will come with their wives tomorrow. Kenneth and Gloria will bring Meg and drive over from Janesville. They'll be at Charlotte's table to give thanks, but their Meg is no good at helping with the conversation. Maybe it comes from being an only child. Last year she sat there—in the middle of dinner—punching things on her cell phone. Gene and Sue will come, but not their girls. What ails this next generation? Momma would insist on some answers. Everyone has too many irons in the fire. Family sits on the back burner. The young are so afraid they'll be bored. And Charlotte overdoes it the other way—"Let's all play a game." She's old enough to know better. If she wouldn't need to win at everything, it'd be easier on everybody. She'll never get the best of Kenneth, though.

Life is never boring; that's for sure. Sometimes Martha's a little short of breath, but she does the best she can. Getting her shoes on and tying the laces can be a chore some days. But there's no good reason she couldn't be on her own, in her own house, the way she likes. She even had the front room painted after Daniel's hospital bed was taken out. She'd vowed she'd never live with any of her children, not be a burden. Now look at her. The boys called her "disoriented." *Discombobulated*, Daniel would have said. *He should talk.*

When Martha had a small kitchen fire—a hot pad got too close to a glowing stove burner—that was the last straw. That and backing into the fire hydrant on Gene's street in Sun Prairie. And she didn't take enough care with her hair there for awhile; her wave in front didn't seem to do right. Charlotte kept saying, "It's not safe for you, alone. You've worn yourself down with worry." She'd poke her nose in Martha's refrigerator, sniff, and say, "There's blackish-blue stuff in the sour cream." Martha had to relent. But it's only for a time. She never said forever. She's getting herself back together. Chad said she was "getting her legs back" and the boys thought that was funny.

She doesn't need nursing care; her blood pressure's been under control. Seventy-eight isn't that old these days, even with a heart flare-up. Her friend Ruby has it much worse: walks lame, shuffles along behind her walker, lost Delbert, has trouble reading the church papers. To be honest, James is the reason Martha agreed to live with Charlotte. Kenneth is too far away in Janesville; Gene would be even farther, but he made no offer. He would have been her first choice; he's the gentle one—that childhood accident with the scalding donut oil. He pats her hand when he comes.

But James is the perfect son-in-law, the calm one, except that he can't fix things. It's good he's getting help with that combine. The faucet in Martha's bathroom still drips. James replaced the washer, fiddled with the connections, and pronounced things fixed. But then the next day he didn't notice that it still dripped. Charlotte would never put up with a thing like that, if it were her bathroom. But Martha can't bring herself to say anything. This house is only thirty or forty years old, but they don't make faucets to last anymore. They don't make lots of things to last. Whoever invented that handle style, where "off" is in some unknown middle spot, exactly between hot and cold? Drip, drip, drip. And her children think *she's* the one with the hearing problem. It's always her fault. "Just keep it aligned," Charlotte says. Martha tries for the perfect spot, then places a washcloth in the bottom of the sink, so no one will walk past, hear the drip, and decide that a faucet is one more modern convenience she can't handle.

James makes up for his clumsiness with faucets by making other things bearable. Like thc way he explained things this noon. Sometimes he looks out for Martha. And he's perfect for Charlotte, "laid back," as the young ones say. He can ignore her bossiness—oh, such chatter and busyness—and get away with it. He knows better than to take a pliers to her connections. It was more Charlotte's idea than James' to leave the conservative Mennonites those years ago. Martha's sure of it. Then they went overboard and Charlotte turned uppity. If Martha were still in her house on Township Road and they hadn't hidden the car keys, she'd make the effort to go to her regular church. But she can't let herself dwell on what can't be. It does no good. She has to forgive. And Momma will have to understand. Now that Martha's gotten used to Faith Community, it's not so bad that the men and women sit intermingled. Your thoughts don't have to get sidetracked.

It's best to remember: Martha's a guest on this earth. Her daughter's in charge of this household, and it's no good to meddle. Charlotte thinks she controls everything. She comes on all full of bluster, but really she's just a fragile flower. A columbine. Martha should have been more tender with her, but she never thought about bending down to examine a grasshopper up close, or counting the buds on the peony bush. You didn't do that with Momma. But the preacher at this new church says to spend time with your young ones, like there's all the time in the world. Well, the reason she and Daniel had more than one child was so they'd have each other to play with. Martha had peas to shell and strawberries to pick, years before the children were much help. Still, she could have expressed more tenderness—the truth of what she felt—even on Sundays when Daniel was tired or they had company for dinner. So many ways she didn't measure up. It shouldn't have mattered when tiny Charlotte brushed off a kiss that time. And it's a poor excuse that Momma always went about keeping busy. "Work for the Night is Coming" was one of her favorites.

Charlotte hasn't figured out yet that things happen when she's looking the other way. Big deals sneak in when she's out golfing or shopping, not at a holiday dinner. Oh, how surprised she'd be if she knew. Surprised isn't the word. Too much thinking on it makes Martha nervous, but the pictures in her head don't go away. They've eased up, is all. How could Daniel leave her like that? Some things, you just know not to tell.

Charlotte says Martha repeats herself. Well, that's what old folks do. Doesn't she have the right? Martha was the one who watched Daniel get weaker and weaker. "It's too much," he'd cried. He begged her to clean him up. It was his bladder did him in. The leaking. Martha had to be right there with the urinal, more often than either of them cared for. Then he had to switch to a diaper. Charlotte had complained that his trousers smelled. Still later, Martha had trouble turning him. Even with all the weight he lost, he couldn't tilt himself right or hold on long enough until she could get the clean pad tucked underneath. Then he snapped at her. Then he cried for snapping.

When you're a baby, you don't feel shame like that. But he begged her not to put him in the nursing home. "I'll be good," he cried. The snot clogged his nose. He must have felt like his life was going down a long passageway. "Why can't I just die?" he'd asked. She didn't know what to say. "I don't know, Daniel; I don't know." She held his hand; she rubbed his hand. Martha never wanted to be a nurse, but she always ends up ministering, one way or another. The Home Health nurse came; that was a big help with the bathing and whatnot. Daniel never said it exactly, but he must have thought of himself as a burden, like Momma when she lingered. Martha put a cold cloth on his forehead when he worked himself into a dither. "You have to try your best," she said. So little she could do. *Still, she should have known better how to do.*

It's better for Martha not to mull, better to spend time reading the diaries. What a time Momma had—all that soul-searching—moving away from Arthur, Illinois, then back again. Never knowing. She must have felt soiled all her life the way some people treated her. Even during the good years with Poppa Lloyd. Not at Broken Bow, though; that was hard. Reading the diaries makes Martha feel closer. *Not much about The Child, though.* That was earlier, before Lloyd. And to think the diaries were almost lost, misplaced in a cousin's attic. Auntie Beulah's Marvel found them. Martha must remember to send her a card for her birthday coming up.

At first Martha read through all the diaries quick-like, skimming, hunting for any mention of her and Daniel. After his stroke, there was no time to read. No inclination really. Now whenever Martha can, she reads a whole week at a time from Momma. She sucks on a peppermint and savors every word. Sometimes at night she has to turn the light back on and read a week from a second year before she can get herself back to sleep. Right now she's reading all the years around Thanksgiving—*what a blessing, the diaries were saved!*—right when they were needing to decide about Nebraska. When Poppa Lloyd was deciding. If only Martha had asked Momma more about his zeal for mission work—did he want it for himself? Or for the Lord? Momma was more the homebody. She must have been half afraid the Lord would call Lloyd to India or somewhere far from everything. Nebraska was enough of a fright.

Momma's Diary - November 1926

Sunday

Mahlon had very nice sermon. Was much stirred. "Not try, but trust." Had a time with Baby. Brings to mind the Child. Esther Glick very low with bronchial.

Monday

Washed and scrubbed north rooms. Had awful headache. Lloyd is much to go. Think and wonder. Oh, just to know! And knowing, not to falter, fear, or question.

Tuesday

Tree blown over this morning. Cut out calico blocks. Blisters do not heal. At eventide it shall be light. Must open the wells. Dare not cling to Illinois if it is not to be.

Wednesday

What oh what shall we decide? I mean to wait upon the Lord. Want him to search and sift me. Oh, to be pure within. Much colder. Bells on the horses. Lloyd inside much of day. Must help him to stand and not faint. Nor to falter.

Thursday

Thanksgiving Day! Many and varied have been the experiences since last Thanksgiving. Brother Mahlon gave names of missionaries to whom letters are to be sent. Helped with young folks' singing at Uncle Ab's.

Friday

Started Baby's bonnet. Heavy rains. Esther remains poorly. Heard a very interesting talk by H. R. Summers about trip to Jerusalem. Cathedrals, catacombs, pyramids, valleys. It makes Lloyd wild to see such. Think it cannot be.

Saturday

Did Sat. work. Raked leaves. Cut out and sorted poems for scrapbook. Beginning to realize what it would be like for family to be scattered. Bathed. Not the best.

Chapter 4

Charlotte's upper arm shakes as she cleans the kitchen sink. Scrub *through* the dirt. No need to hold her left arm straight, like with her golf swing. She cleaned this sink two days ago, but so many food scraps have passed through since, that the shine is gone. She'll make it a quickie this time. No one's questions to bother her. James thinks Charlotte's a miracle worker, but the truth is, she just loves to fix food. Visualize things. That's the key, whether it's her golf ball going in the cup or a perfectly executed Thanksgiving meal. She's an artist when she adds a sprig of parsley atop the croutons, when she makes sure all is not yellow on the white china. Curried chicken, rice with saffron, corn with strips of yellow pepper? Never. Mother didn't teach her these things, but Charlotte learned, in spite of growing up with conservative Mennonite modesty. That was austerity, really. But she's an artist at heart, a lover of beauty. She makes the ordinary unforgettable.

She checks her list of Wednesday tasks. She needs to get this Jello out of the mold before Mother or Caroline come out from resting. Maybe even clean the celery, get it chopped ahead of time. She'd considered cleaning the oven of the blackberry cobbler spillover from last week, but there's really no point with tomorrow's turkey roasting. She loves to make things clean and sparkly; it's much easier now with the new appliances, never mind what Caroline thinks about stainless steel. Give Charlotte a Brillo pad and she means business. But she has her limits. Those stains on the old kitchen countertops had gotten so bad, bleach didn't work anymore.

What a relief to have the remodeling job done! It got to be a chore, dragging James in to decide on colors and styles. She was the one, had to stay on top of things, make sure they got what they ordered. No, they did *not* ask for laminate sheet gold-flake granite. And it's much better having a bank of lights above the counter where she does most of her work. The whole thing was more stressful than she'd expected. One night she dreamed a bunch of strangers came into her house—carpet layers, painters, whatnot. It wasn't even her house. A cathedral ceiling, for one thing. They marched right in without introducing themselves and had plans to disrupt the whole house. She finally had to chase them out, like they were stray cats.

Having Mother live with them still seems strange, even though it's going on six months. It took two months alone to finally convince her. You could see she was worn down from all the burdens of caregiving. Sometimes she even slept during the day; that was *not* like her. Well, she was in her room with the door closed; Charlotte knows that much. Sometimes Mother wore mismatched clothes, an aqua sweater that looked terrible with a light green dress. It was like she didn't care. Charlotte was afraid Father's death would bring on Mother's. You hear about that sort of grief. She didn't even go to church sometimes, although the Beachys would have been glad to stop and take her along.

It was fear that did her in. Late March, and she worried the furnace was going to blow. James checked about the strange noise; the furnace guy looked it over, too. Everyone said the furnace had always had that shimmy. "Not this bad," she'd said. There was no reassuring her. It's been okay to have her living here, a family arrangement Charlotte never would have anticipated. It was the only safe thing to do; both of Charlotte's brothers agreed. "Till she gets herself straightened out" is what they said. Right about that same time—well, James says it was earlier—Mother stopped wearing her head covering. She still wears it to church, just not all the time like she used to. Charlotte's been half-afraid to ask. You don't un-submit, do you? Some of the women in Mother's church have gone from big to smaller, or from white to the occasional black, or even to those little lace doilies. Charlotte can't keep up with the different groups, what they require. But to wear nothing? It's so strange. Well, it will all come out some time; these things do.

With winter coming on, it's certain Mother's not going anywhere any time soon, much as she talks about wanting to be back in her house. She takes care of her big fern—they made room for that in the living room—but she had to give the rest away. Charlotte won't have ten plants in every room. And Mother's furniture doilies can take a rest, too; she covers every wooden stand she has with some kind of crocheted something-or-other. She says that's the way her momma did it. Well, Charlotte's not being cruel; she knows people need things the way they're used to. But she's not having that kind of clutter. These Mennonite women, Mother's generation, for sure, are all the same. They look so meek, but when you get to know them, they're all spine. They have their opinions, too.

Mother was a trooper, picking out all those black walnuts for James. He always wants a black walnut cake—with bananas—about this time of year. There she was, hunched over the shells. He couldn't help teasing her about wanting to be a dentist. Now she worries that the renters on the home place didn't cut down all the perennials. But she won't call them and ask. It's not important; perennials can wait till spring. Charlotte took it upon herself to winterize Father's roses; she got them tucked inside the plastic cone covers. That was strange, too, feeling like an intruder, snooping around in Father's storage shed. And strange that Mother showed no interest, even though she used to brag about his yellow Peace rose.

She seems content enough with her needlework. She offers to help prepare food, but Charlotte has her own ways. She's not changing that. Besides, kitchen time is time to think, and there's no better way to bring pleasure. Teresa will drive out from Monroe in a second, if she hears there are fresh pecan tarts. It's no secret: you don't take shortcuts. When a recipe calls for lemon juice, you make sure you have fresh lemons. Chicken broth? You cook chicken pieces and use that juice. None of that stuff from a box. Maybe the canned, if you're in a pinch.

This Thanksgiving will be a test for all of them: the first holiday meal without Father. Fourth of July doesn't count because the Lehmans aren't patriotic in that flag-waving, hot-dogs-on-the-grill, fireworks-out-back way. Even though Charlotte and James don't belong to the Mennonite church anymore, they haven't bought into the red-white-and-blue fervor that can crop up around Borgmann. They'll stand for the National Anthem at Chad's games and James will sing along, but it's obvious there are problems in these not-so-united States. No blind allegiance from Charlotte. There's nothing she can do about any of the messes in the world—nothing came of all that turn-of-the-century frenzy—so why worry?

That's where Kenneth is so different. Her older brother keeps reminding her that they're to be "strangers and pilgrims," as if they don't belong here. He knows it irritates her. Her childhood was strange, all right, with its abundance of sermons about the wages of sin. Scare tactics, really. But strangers and pilgrims? It's like a holy mantra that's used to justify all kinds of weird behavior and self-righteousness. As if it's better to stand apart—a little following-Jesus snobbery. Well, religion is like everything else: it's better not to get carried away.

So yes, here's to Thanksgiving, even without Father. They'll do everything exactly the way he liked it: "Don't let that bird dry out." These celery leaves are still fresh; they'll be perfect for the stuffing. Three kinds of pie and singing around the piano afterwards. "Whaddya' mean, you're too full? Buck up." Father had such a beautiful baritone voice. He'll be with them in spirit, and they'll all move closer to healing. *No, Death, no sting from you!* Mother will finally put aside her fretting and show everyone she's gotten her appetite back. If it's anything they don't need, it's a chronically depressed matriarch. Charlotte feels a little nervous with all that's riding on the meal, but mostly she's proud—in a good way—and eager to pull it off. Oh, that aroma of turkey roasting in the house. It can douse anyone's dread of winter. Some years Charlotte's gone outside just so she can walk back in the kitchen and be lost in the wonder of it all.

James keeps saying that farm folks are supposed to be at peace with death and decay. *Farm folks.* That's another label she hates. He says it just to annoy her. So they're part of a cycle, huh? Well, it's not a part she cares to dwell on. Her father left them so suddenly those eight months ago, and no matter how you try to make it natural, death is not nice. She can't help it that Gene chose the profession he did. Or is it an occupation? Certainly more than a hobby for him to have three or four funerals a week. Charlotte's never heard Sue complain about Gene's work interrupting their family life, so everything must be peachy in their world of embalming fluid. Sure, it's unfortunate, Father never really accepted Gene's choice. When you die, you'd want to feel good about all your children. Well, when your father dies, you'd want him to feel good about you, too.

It's sad; the family doesn't get together like they ought. Charlotte's the one who has to make the effort. Even with that, Gene's girls won't be coming tomorrow. The next generation has its own interests, and you can't dictate. Charlotte has to do the interpreting, but

Mother doesn't understand. Even Caroline hasn't been home since her grandpa's funeral. She sent e-mails all summer, asking James how the crops looked, whether they were getting enough rain, even asked if the cows were keeping down the mosquito population. As if that's all she thought about. Caroline, the daughter Charlotte never could have imagined. So different from Chad. Life tricks you into expecting one thing and you get something completely different. But Charlotte has learned her lesson; she doesn't ask questions. Mothers get such a bad rap these days. Charlotte just accepts Caroline the way she is—even her claim that Americans eat way too much meat. You'd think she was a vegetable freak. She wrote about her tomatoes in southern Ohio—"No blight, Mom!"—as if they were her children.

Charlotte and James did what they could with both children, although Chad's still a work-in-progress. They made sure Caroline—such a beautiful three-syllable name—didn't grow up feeling bad about herself. *None of that wretchedness.* Charlotte and James had to make it through the "Shame on you" for this, and "Repent" from that, but Charlotte wasn't going to have her daughter stand with her arms crossed in front of her. She made sure Caroline learned to swim as a little girl; she could have taken ballet lessons if she wanted. Charlotte taught her to love her body, not be afraid.

Not that Charlotte goes in for tight-fitting clothes. She doesn't have the waist for it, for one thing; after two children, things just got away. And she's embarrassed about her varicose veins. Teresa is very forgiving when it's so hot that Charlotte has to wear shorts to play golf—longish ones, so they cover the worst bulge. But Charlotte still keeps up with the styles. No reason to wear pointed toes, if fashion says rounded. Or the other way around. These secondhand stores are always happy for gently-worn castoffs. There are always women who don't really care. It's hard to understand what Caroline sees, working in a place like that.

She is nothing, if not a mystery. For all their trouble, Charlotte and James got the shyest, most introverted teen in south central Wisconsin, grinning herself silly when she bottle-fed a sick calf, even begging to stay at home some Friday nights. Thank heavens she got into high school band, so she'd have a little social life. Well, you bring them up the best you know how, and then you have to throw up your hands. Otherwise, they'll drive you batty.

Right then, Charlotte hears a car in the driveway and a door slams. Caroline comes in the kitchen with her arms folded in front of her. "Oh, hi. Did you sleep?" Charlotte asks. "You don't look much better."

"It's still chilly in here," Caroline says. She walks over to the new bay window, gives the string of hot peppers a swing again, looks out to the woods.

"Oh, my no; your body temp must be off." Charlotte fans her face with her hand. "Are those the only shoes you brought?"

Chad bounces into the house, wearing a white T-shirt and blue shorts; his school jacket with the two basketball letters is flung over his back. Charlotte watches as Caroline stands on tiptoe to hug him. He puts an arm around her shoulder and hugs as best anyone can expect of a teenage brother. They stand there grinning at each other.

"So, how was practice?" she asks.

"Great," he says. "Short." He drops his backpack on the floor. "Too bad you missed my game."

"I know; I wish I could have come a day sooner."

Chad jumps like he's a rubber ball attached to a wooden paddle, tapping above the woodwork trim on top of the closet door. "I like your hair," he says. His eyes drop to Caroline's thick gray socks, bulging out of her brown sandals, then he does his jumping routine again.

"Thanks. Is that one of your drills?"

"That's enough, Chad," Charlotte says. "The jumping." He has so much energy; he doesn't know what to do with himself.

"No shaved head, I see," Caroline says.

Chad looks startled. "No way. Not with Coach. Or Mom. The Enforcers. No body piercings, no tattoos. What's to eat?" he asks, heading for the refrigerator.

"Make a sandwich, if you want. There's sliced ham," Charlotte says. "And be sure to straighten up your room before supper."

Chad grabs the mayo jar, balances leftover ham, cheese, and bread under his chin, bends a leg behind him to shut the fridge door.

Suddenly, James is at the side door, saying, "Want to come along?" to Caroline, as she turns the jarred magnets into three rows, upside down. "Simp's doing most of the milking today. Advance work for getting three days off. I need to make sure there's enough feed mixed."

"Sure," Caroline says quickly. "Unless I should help with something in here."

"Run along," Charlotte says. "I'm good." Then she turns to James. "Are you just getting back from town?"

"Yup," he says. She can't read the look on his face, can't tell if he was able to see the banker.

"There they are!" Caroline says, as if finding her work boots in the closet makes her day.

"Look at this," James says to her. He stops at the new computer desk by the side door. "Chad, your backpack is in the way. This will only take a minute, Charlotte." He grabs the mouse, clicks on the internet server, drops down his list of Favorites. "Look at all these farm websites. I can get the latest grain commodities, advice about trading for a used hay baler. Everything. Right here."

Caroline leans forward with her dad. "I've found lots of cool sites, too. Vegetable stuff. You keep all your records here?"

"My files for each cow are still out in the milk house," he says, glancing at Charlotte again. "The big wall chart is handier; better to have everything—the sire, dam, ID number, all the markings—right there if I have to look something up. Lately, though, I've transferred some of the data in here: vaccination dates, when a cow was bred, when the next one's going to be fresh. That's one good thing about the fire. I've made more duplicates, printed things out."

"Finally," Charlotte says. "Why are you looking up vegetables, Caroline?"

"All our farm expenses, house expenses, that's all here." James steps into his duck coveralls. "I tried to get Charlotte to record her recipes, but I don't think she did. Okay, yeah, we gotta go."

"Too much bother to type in all those fractions: half teaspoon, fourth of a cup," Charlotte says, rinsing Chad's milk glass. "Index cards are easier to read."

"You can wear one of my—; oh, you found your Badgers sweatshirt," James says to Caroline. "Back by six," he says over the running water at the kitchen sink.

And they're gone. Chad has slipped away downstairs. He likes it just fine to have his bedroom down there since Mother moved in. Too fine, James thinks. Chad can play his music louder, and Charlotte doesn't have to remind him so much about not jiggling when Mother's around. Okay, this is the perfect chance to finish a couple more salads for tomorrow. Chop a few nuts for on top of the carrot salad. Caroline acted like she was glad to get out of the house. It's never made sense the way she tags along with James. She can cook just fine—it sounds like she lives on baked potatoes—but she'd rather be outdoors.

That was years ago when Charlotte had to help James make ends meet. She'd worked odd jobs awhile, even when Chad was in grade school. And before that, those long days at the bakery when they were first married. After Caroline came—those were the worst years—Charlotte thought she'd never get pregnant again. She tried to stay on as receptionist in the law firm, but it tied her down too much. Too many things to juggle. Everyone was happier when Charlotte settled for keeping the farm books. Nothing online then, of course.

Now she still helps outside on occasion. James will call from thc barn and say he needs a hand. “Right now.” She knows what that means. She’ll hold a light, help keep the flap of skin up, so he can lift out the calf. It’s very exciting. They always want to see that nose first, know it’s in the right position. Sometimes they have to put baler twine on the front legs—make sure James has both hands free—so he can catch it before it falls out and hits the ground, all slimy and wet. Emergencies are more the exception, though. It’s better for James to hire help and Charlotte to stick to what she does best: feed everyone properly. Some day even Chad will look back and realize what fantastic meals Charlotte made.

Who doesn’t like to wake up to a fresh coffee cake with cinnamon streusel? Sometimes she can’t go back to sleep when James gets up to chore at four in the morning. He can’t simply *ease* his large body out of bed. So she gets up, too, brushes the frumpiness out of her brown hair—it never cooperates in the morning—pats her round face with the warmth of a washcloth, and lets those pores open up. The coffee cake—no, she doesn’t believe in boxed mixes—provides the stim for James’ appreciative “Uhmm” when he comes back in. They sit down together for breakfast, just like the pictures show. The modern farm couple without the pitchfork. Sometimes Chad joins them, though he’s more likely to grab a piece of coffee cake to eat in the car—he loves bagels with cream cheese—as he drives off to school. He runs late way too often. By the time he leaves, Mother is up and comes quietly into the kitchen, almost like a ghost in her blue slippers. She drags out taking her pills, as if she meditates on each one.

They may not be the usual family unit, but they've made it work. Now if Charlotte can finish this cranberry salad before supper—forego the nuts on this one—that will give her time to relax this evening. Just cook the sweet potatoes yet.

Chapter 5

"Let's see how Simp's doing," Dad says, heading for the milk parlor. "The guy won't wear a helmet." He points to the Harley-Davidson.

"What about the corn crib?" Carrie asks. "Wait. Christmas lights on the milkhouse?"

"Yeah, we left those up from last year. You didn't notice last spring? It was Charlotte's idea. She won't put this white kind on the house, but here, they're okay. Saves me some work, to leave them up. No juice, though, till after Thanksgiving."

"Look!" Carrie says. A pheasant struts along the edge of the nearest field, walks like it owns the place, head up, colors running down its back. The fields look muddy, but maybe by Friday she can walk them.

They go past the cows bunched up in the holding lot. This is the place she loves. The smells—a mix she couldn't explain to Ryan.

How do you describe corn stalk stubble and vegetative rot, mixed with crisp air? Today, though, there's humidity in this too-warm breeze that bends the tips of the cedars lining the ditch behind the old crib. "Any cows in heat?" she asks.

"Nope. No jumping around, no acting goofy," Dad says. "Things are pretty calm. Haven't had to ride any fences. Here, let's check out the mixer. Make sure there's enough feed." They step into the small building between the two blue Harvestore silos. "Here she is, the TMR, mother of all mixers." He slaps the red object that looks like a small cement mixer; his wedding ring clanks on metal. "Oops, forgot my ring. I've lost two already; Charlotte gets mad if I don't wear it, though, when I'm inside." He slips his ring into an inner shirt pocket.

Carrie remembers stories her parents told about walking around with a left hand in a pocket, until they finally were open about wearing their wedding rings, recalls how Mom said Dad looked so much more handsome when he could wear a tie instead of a plain coat. Now who wears ties? "So who gets this kind of feed?"

"My bulls and the heifers that haven't been bred yet. Had a bunch of them late last spring when I bought the mixer. They get this mixed concoction instead of the usual silage. My milk cows get the royal treatment, pasture land, so they're true, organic cows. Better feed, better production. Real simple. No antibiotics, no chemicals, no fly spray. With this mixer I measure everything on the scale: leftovers from bakeries, distillers' grain, what-have-you." He shows her a list of proportions for the byproducts. "Ethanol leftovers, too, they say. Cottonseed, that's in there; even waste candy."

"Waste candy?" A huge spider web covers half of one wall, swings over to the corner.

"Yeah, chocolate and gummy bears. Whatever would head for the landfill."

"What's wrong with it?"

"Got me. Nothing. Whatever the makers of candy or beer or bread deem unacceptable. Extraneous to their product, I guess." He flips a switch and an auger blows silage down the chute into the mixer.

She can't read him. Does he really think this is safe? Heifers dining on chocolate? It doesn't sound natural at all. She scuffs her boot through a pile of cottonseed. That line from college days: "Whatever you touch, touches you."

"Cows are doing great, even with the beer contamination." He grins and settles on an overturned five-gallon bucket in front of the scale.

"Creature comfort, I suppose. Whatever happened to the idea that the earth is a system?"

"Can't hear you," he says, cupping an ear.

She shrugs, leans down. "Will you cut down on grain next summer?"

"Don't know yet." He takes off his cap and scratches his head. "One of these Holsteins eats—what is it?—ten times her weight in grain each year. You're the teacher. If a cow weighs between twelve hundred and two thousand pounds—. I've got seventy cows right now. You figure it out." He stands to make sure the auger's moving everything out to the far trough, scratches his back inside two layers of clothes. "We can get the figures on Madison's Dairy Science website." He props his foot on the bucket, talks loudly. "I'm trying some winter wheat this year. It's making a comeback; good cash crop. I can use it for bedding, too. I'll be all right as long as we don't have too much freezing and thawing; that's a killer."

Suddenly Carrie swings her head, shields her face. "Bats?"

"Put your hood up if you don't like it. I use about eight to nine thousand pounds of feed a day. I can't grow that much." He spits sideways into the straw-covered floor.

"Wendell Berry says to let the land be grass for a year or two."

"A farmer can't always afford what's ideal."

"How can we not? It's the only land we have." She hesitates, decides to push on. "It's like cheap food. Cheap food isn't cheap food." Her voice sounds strained. "Not when you factor in taxes to clean up polluted surface water, health problems from consuming foods that don't have much nutrition."

"This isn't an ideal world, Carrie. Sometimes you have to compromise." He looks at his watch and shuts off the mixer.

"Whatever happened to the cowness of cows?" she asks.

"What's that?" His eyes stay on the auger.

"Nothing," Carrie says. "Cowness of cows. We can talk about it later."

"Another thing." He seems to weigh his words. "Your mom can be difficult—that mess this noon about Christmas gifts for school kids—but you know she's got a good heart. Just a little sharp around the edges. She hates being taken advantage of."

Carrie nods weakly. "Sure, I know." She's never understood why couples are attracted to each other. What did her parents see? The wedding pictures show good looks on both sides. Above average height for both. Maybe it was divine leading—genes for an athletic son?—a lightning strike to the heart. No one said love has to make sense. You see what you want to see and ignore the rest. Make excuses if necessary.

"The push today is for a cow to produce huge amounts of milk but only for three or four years. Maybe five. Then it's hamburger."

"Hey, I'm not a Fresh Air kid from Chicago." Don't talk down to me, she wants to say. Don't act like Manager Milt at Re-Use-It and give the promotion to Eddie Ruble, the laziest office Boy Wonder ever. She has to win her dad's respect, get him to believe she knows what she's talking about. Not put him in a spot where he treats her like a know-nothing girl.

"Everything's skewed toward agribusiness." He shuts off the auger. "Forget about a fair, competitive marketplace. The big dairy factories get all the exemptions. Guess I repeat myself as much as Martha." They both stare at the mass of cows' rumps moving toward the milk parlor, pushed slowly by the crowd gate. "Charlotte's right; it *is* hard to get to events in the evening. She says we don't have a life."

"Is it still hard to get good help?"

"Yes and no. Simp helps with the milking; enough guys were looking for extra work during busy times with the crops this fall. Eleven or twelve bucks an hour. Simp's often late; that's what bugs Charlotte. But I hate to have to train a new guy."

"So, what are you going to do?" she asks, her hands jammed in her sweatshirt pockets. Maybe it's inevitable: every farmer, stuck in routine, thinks about getting out, hates the thought of change.

"Do what I've always done. Follow where there's a little bit of money. Right now it's in milk. Let's go." He pulls on the light chain and steps outside. "I don't violate the land; I treat my cows well."

"Yeah, I know; no confinement."

"I've tried to simplify. Only do some chisel plowing. Break through the soil but not turn it over. Nothing like the moldboard. Strictly no-till for the beans."

"I rode with you the first time you planted corn right over the previous year's stubble. Remember? How many years has it been since you stopped using the corn crib to store corn? You're not going to dismantle it, are you?"

"I can't bring myself to do that. Charlotte says it's an eyesore, said that *before* the fire. For me, it's the family farm right there. That and the red barn. How could I take either one down and say only the lumber is worth anything?" He stands in the day's waning light, shakes his head again. "Barn needs paint, but there's no money for that." He blows out his lips; his cheeks billow, sag.

Where's his passion? He's the one, taught her the farm routines. He *showed* her the beauty of the ordinary. Every day was sacred, not just Sunday. Farming gave him something to shoot for: a higher yield, pest-free crops, contented cows. He used to sing when he went outside. Well, it bugged Mom inside the house. He'd sing when he was fixing fence. *I've got a home in Glory Land that outshines the sun.* Maybe it just seemed he was happy because *she* was. Outside, with him.

"You going to just stay there in the dark?" he asks. "You said you wanted to see the crib. Simp gets edgy."

The outside air has turned cooler as the sun's light disappears. Carrie flips up her hood, tugs on the drawstrings. It's going to take time. She has so little to bargain with: a lot of theory, not much know-how. He might be looking for *more* acreage, not ten acres less. He might not want to hear *diversify;* might say vegetables are for sissies. That crease between his eyebrows has grown deeper; she's sure of it. She'd have to borrow some of his equipment, use his muscle and experience. She'd always be indebted. But she could help him out with crops when he was in a pinch.

Dad picks up his pace, cuts across brown grass toward the old crib. The blue tarp covering the top center bulges whenever a breeze catches it. He's still muttering. "Archer Daniels comes out just fine. Bloated Bully."

Carrie half-runs to catch up. Agri-business, centralized farming—dirty terms from Dad's perspective. He's right, though. Industrial agriculture squeezes the little farmers till they cry and give up. The big boys gloat like arm wrestlers. *Had enough yet? Say when!* Does Dad understand, though? *He's* a big boy, too, by some people's standards. She knows what a typical farmer's set-up looks like in Appalachia. It all depends: whom you compare yourself with.

He waits near the crib, points a thumb at smoke-singed shingles. He leaves the front end open, so they can see inside; the blue tarp has darkened everything. Eerie. They walk past the old tractor, the plow and spreader, lined up like always in the center, looking like undeserving survivors. Relics. Like a makeshift morgue for farm equipment. There's a bad smell of leftover smoke, even with the door open. A water-soaked dirt floor. "Here's the worst side. I had a bunch of stuff stored at the back. Charlotte called it 'old junk.'" He shakes his head. "No way to replace Grandpa's horse harness."

"You used to keep bags of fertilizer here, leftover seed corn. That's all gone?" She steps gingerly.

"Yeah. Till I got out here that night—yelled at Charlotte to call 911—this side was all smoke. I wasn't much of a hero."

"Dad, it's not worth putting your life in danger. You didn't know if it was going to explode or what."

"There's nothing to explode, but it could have been a lot worse. Your grandma said, 'The Lord is good.' Act of God, I guess. The lightning."

"Or nature."

"Uhm. Percentages. My turn, I guess. So it goes." He kicks at the tires on the old Case. "Maybe it's a sign."

"Sign of what?"

"I don't know. Sign of whatever. Maybe it'd be easier if the whole thing had burned down."

"Dad!"

"Sign of whatever you want it to be. Sign to get out. Sign to go sign on for more debt. Even if I replace it with only half the size, the cost of another pole shed like where I keep the combine—?

Prohibitive." His cheeks fill again, sag. "No point in fixing it. Numbers don't come out. A corn crib is only good for nostalgia. And I'm just another expendable farmer. A statistic."

"Sometimes you have to think outside the box, especially when the box is a cow."

He turns away sharply. "I'm not going to supplement my dairy by going into breeding like Smithers did. And I refuse to switch to goat farming, if that's what you're thinking. Can't help it that goat cheese is a big seller right now. All of a sudden, people have allergies and digestive systems that need pampering."

"Actually, I've got a different idea." She waits.

"What's that? We gotta keep moving. Simp probably thinks I skipped out."

"Rent ten acres. To me," she says. "For now. I'll pay you." He keeps his back to her, acts like he can't move. "Don't dismiss it, Dad. Hear me out. You could make the shift—say three years—to organic vegetable farming. But that would be my business. You could ease over if you wanted. Don't say you're expendable. You could still have cows." She's afraid to look as he turns to her. "Forget corn and beans."

"Do you have any idea what you're saying?"

Their eyes meet and she sees his disbelief. She can't stop now. "They say it takes about three years to get the chemicals out of the land. I'm going to need backing for lots of small equipment." He looks like he's being forced to swallow a quart of sour milk without stopping. "No, really. All I'm asking is ten acres. To rent. Six, at the very least, for now. I'll need to borrow your name to get loans. Your reputation."

He takes off for the milk parlor. “I’m not stupid.” He finally stops outside the milk house. “Know what Jeb Moeller does? Two miles south of Monroe. Puts in his crops, then drives a semi cross-country for four months. Comes home and harvests what’s there. Trucking. Now what kind of farmer’s life is that?”

“A realistic one, I suppose. People just want their Toasted Popovers for breakfast; they don’t care where they come from. Or how.” He won’t look at her as he steps into the milkhouse, bangs on the side of the bulk tank. The booms reverberate. She’s making a fool of herself, but it’s too late to stop. “We have to educate people. Get people to buy locally. Vegetables in season. That kind of thing. Then a small farmer has a chance.”

“You *are* mad.”

“Listen, Dad. It’s not just economics. It’s—.” The metal door of the milk parlor sticks and scrapes on cement. Carrie’s words, “People need to get over their convenience-fix,” are lost in the heavy slap-slap of Dad’s boots.

“How’s it going?” he asks, walking down the steps to the lower part.

Carrie follows, catches the heavy door, so it doesn’t bang. Dad sounds relieved to see the hired man. Someone sane. It’s probably good she had to stop. *We’ve lost our soul* was coming next. She has no idea if it would work to be partners with Dad in *her* enterprise. That’s how older generations pass on their land, isn’t it? First, partnership, then sole ownership. It *is* crazy to think he’d consider letting her be in charge.

"Simp, you remember my daughter, Carrie?"

Simp's nod covers most everything. "Good," he says. "How's you?" He throws a used paper towel at the bucket but misses. He might be in his forties but could be ten years younger, or older. He barely glances at Carrie from under the bent brim of his Badgers bill cap. Then he looks out into the holding lot and raises seven fingers, grins, and hunches like he's sighting through a rifle. "Seven cows away from three days off. Gonna get me a big one."

"Been practicing with your scent bombs?" Dad asks, picking up the errant paper towel.

"Hnnh. Got my camouflage packed, enough beef jerky to last me the duration."

"It's going to be tough without a snow cover," Dad says.

"All the better." Simp slaps one fist into his open hand. "I've been practicing that since I was ten; the first time I field-dressed one, I was only thirteen."

"Just remember: you promised me deer sausage."

"Gotcha. Too many freaking deer running the place; I'm gonna make sure there are fewer car wrecks. At least two."

"You mind finishing up?"

"Easy-schmeezy," Simp says, clomping in his high rubber boots with the loose buckles. He squirts a quick stream of milk before putting the milker unit on another cow. Then he looks directly at Carrie. "Gotta sanitize these titties," he says.

She stares back at him and then looks away, studies the two rows of milk receiver jars, watches the foam slosh on top.

Dad points to his watch as if that's a shared code for domestic expectations. "See you Sunday evening."

"Have a good one," Simp says.

"You, too. I'll come out later, check on things."

Carrie and her dad head slowly toward the house. "So it's *his* hunting buddies you can't throw off the land?" she asks.

Dad ignores her, methodically wipes his boots on the grass.

"What about the new Bobcat?"

He looks at his watch. "We've got to get inside. Charlotte—. We'll have to save the calf barn for tomorrow, too. You probably want to see—."

"Look!" She points toward the row of cedars. A hawk pauses in pecking at its prey, its feet firmly planted on top of a still body. "The pheasant," she whispers. "Oh, no."

They watch silently as the large brown hawk picks at its feast. "The natural order of things," Dad says.

"The hawkness of the hawk," Carrie says.

Chapter 6

What can you do with a daughter like this? Charlotte had planned a simple meal for the night before—no need to eat big when tomorrow's feast is coming up—but Caroline made everyone testy by jumping on James over his definition of lowly. She liked the mac and cheese—"endless elbow" as Chad called it—and the salad greens. And Charlotte's homegrown carrots, she had seconds on those. Oh, the miracle of a brown sugar and butter glaze. But does every meal have to produce an argument? Practically the same topic, too. Charlotte had to shoo them all out of the kitchen. She needs time to straighten things up again; she forgot to scrub the burner pans this afternoon.

The nook worked fine for the five of them, but they should have put Chad in the gopher chair. Mother almost got smacked in the face when he had his windmill going. It all started when Caroline wasn't impressed with the story about Charlotte getting stuck in the makeshift clinker for this fall's fund raiser at church. Charlotte hadn't minded being a volunteer—a good cause: the youth group's mission project in San Antonio—but she hadn't known she was going to be stuck in fake handcuffs in the middle of town. James was a good sport, bailing her out, once she got hold of him on her cell phone. But this evening Chad ate it up all over again. "Not just a common criminal," he said, clapping his hands big and swinging his arms around, "but a corporate executive with major fines to pay."

The real jabs started, though, with the last of the chocolate cake; Caroline poked around, seemed miffed that there weren't apples in it. Money came up. James said very innocently, that he thought money, when earmarked for missions, should feed the poor, "the lowly." It was *that* word. Caroline asked James if he meant people in Appalachia. "'Feed my sheep.' That kind of lowly?" What is it with her? She takes everything wrong. "Lowly" doesn't have to be a putdown; James doesn't have one arrogant bone in him. But you don't flat out give a wino money. You don't *throw* money at a problem willy-nilly. Just because Charlotte's a responsible person, doesn't mean she's hard-hearted. It didn't help that Mother chimed in about the old city mission philosophy: make the street men listen to a sermon before they go through a line to get soup. Caroline, of course, had to point out that they're not all men these days. That just added to the loose ends, and Mother backed off, said something lame about never knowing for sure when someone is ready to listen to the Gospel.

If Mother hadn't been around, Charlotte would have made it clear: *she* knows what lowly feels like. It wasn't from lack of money. She had nice enough skirts growing up, not made from feed sacks like some of the older girls at church. But twice a year, you were supposed to feel bad about yourself. That's not really what's intended with Communion, but how could you *not* feel like a worm when the preacher finished running through his list? Who didn't get nailed during preparatory service? Mother never seemed to notice how women always got singled out. Too much attention to adornment; stay away from those shiny hair clasps.

Okay, that's an exaggeration, but her school friend Lily's indiscretions weren't a joke. As if Lily hadn't had a partner. Oh, no, Lily had to take all the blame on herself. If it would have happened to Charlotte, she would have run off and gotten an abortion. Not that she had any idea where she would have run to, or how money would have dropped from the sky to pay for it. She knew it was wrong—all killing—but she felt so bad for Lily. The humiliation of men making decisions about Lily's body, making her feel cheap. There had to be some other way than for Lily to have to stand and confess in front of the whole church. And Roger—the toadhead—he could disappear. If Chad ever gets in a mess like that, Charlotte will make sure he takes responsibility.

Things are better for them now at Faith Community, but back then, anything you did was subject to someone's scrutiny. Anything you said, even when you didn't know better—"Sally has big zits"—was flung back at you. Fearmongers who wanted you to feel wretched with their gloom and doom. How could you help but go forward at the next revival meeting? And then, the way adults covered for themselves. The week before Communion, all the women said they were at peace with all the brothers and sisters, and all the men said they held no enmity. But really, the men were jealous of Sam Yoder's per bushel yield, and the women thought it unseemly that Mandy Beckler had ripped out her long row of bridal wreath shrubs and replaced them with showy perennials from the nursery. How many times has Charlotte told James, "Sing me a song about a God who's not stern, a God who loves me the way I am"? James reminds her: they've all changed, even her mother. He's right; it's not something to dwell on. But he can be exasperating the way he dismisses things, especially church conflicts. She's left to wonder alone what her life would have been like if she'd escaped those times of feeling like she counted for nothing.

It's irritating to hear Caroline insist that Charlotte hasn't seen the real Appalachia, only looks on the surface. Well, those *were* satellite dishes in front of trailers that time they visited in Kentucky. What makes Caroline think *those* people have their priorities straight? James will never buy a dish; that's for sure. If those mountain people aren't a mission field, then who is? Sure, there are good people there; there are good people everywhere. Some are lowly and some put on airs. Charlotte knows Appalachians have their strong families and go to church; they have fun on a shoestring: singing, dancing, storytelling. She's said all that. They're people. Caroline doesn't have to get all high and mighty, telling Charlotte she's making classist judgments. Of course Charlotte judges. Everybody does, especially those people who claim they don't.

Sometimes it's hard to remember when Caroline was their little bundle of joy. She seems so argumentative. Maybe she's just overly tired and crabby. She even looks like a worn dissident. Is that really how she's wearing her hair? That short haircut makes her face too thin; she's always been such a beautiful daughter. James used to tiptoe into her room and stick his head over her crib, make sure she was sleeping. *Make sure she was breathing* is what he meant. Of course, they never mentioned SIDS. They both knew: if you talked about things that could go wrong, there was a much greater chance that they would. Kenneth has a fancy word for it—opposite of placebo. Or he'll say, "Self-fulfilling prophecy." It's like Mother worrying too much. Half the things she frets about never happen. But she's giving the goblins permission to enter, fixating on a fungus and then wondering how it took control of her toenails. Sure, bad things happen; there are odds. But you don't need to act like you *expect* something to spoil all the pleasure that's out there, like you're scared to death.

* * *

That evening everyone gets crosswise. In a family that dotes on orderliness it only takes one member's slight shift to bollix the whole works. Not that the mantel clock chimes before its appointed hour, but everyone gets called on to make adjustments.

Carrie hears a phone ring in the distance. What has gotten into her that she naps after every meal? Not really sleeps, but escapes. The long bus ride threw her off more than she expected. It was too dark after supper to take a walk, and the chill on the screened-in porch with Sayeth nipping at her took away any desire to ride the exercise bike very long. Still, she needs to be sociable. She runs a hand through her short hair, makes sure the roll of money is in her dresser. In the living room she hears her dad say, "They're not coming."

"My, my," Martha says. She smooths the tea towel she's embroidering, considers going to her room.

James sits in his recliner, rubs the heel of one gray-socked foot against the other. "Business came up. A death, I guess. It sounded unavoidable. Complicated."

It takes awhile for the full impact to soak in for Charlotte. Surely Gene and Sue could come for part of the day, the meal at least. A bereaved family can't need counseling all day.

"Something about something near-death something," James says. "Gene had given his assistant the week off. They get Christmas. Something like that." There's no explaining it. Next time he'll get up and hand the phone to Charlotte.

"Oh, for crying out loud," she says. "Why didn't you—? What do you mean, 'complicated'? Undertakers don't wait around for death." Her dinner seating arrangement is out the window. Ten is the perfect number: enough people that no one can dominate, but not so many that someone's elbow puts your gravy at risk. "It's not like someone's going to steal a body if they lock up the house." Charlotte pulls the sheers all the way shut. She's thought before that Sue was too quick to use funeral business as an excuse.

"It's not up to us to change their minds," James says. "Gene seemed a little shaken, out of breath. I couldn't follow everything. Something about near-suicide. Or might be."

"Forevermore!" Martha says.

"I'm only repeating. Trying to." James sits up straighter. "'Need to get to the bottom of this.' That was part of it. You know how he talks so quiet. Seemed in a hurry, too. The point is: they need to be there in Sun Prairie. Can't we be reasonable?"

"It must be a very hard case," Martha says, "for Gene, I mean." She had planned to ask him about that new mailing from Medicare.

"How can there be a question? Either it's a suicide or it's not," Charlotte says. She flounces on the couch. James doesn't even know if the guy left a note, then says he's sure it was a female. Be reasonable? This is what happens when she tries to create a special family time now that Father's gone. Something comes along.

Carrie sits down on the couch, a Johnny's Seed Catalog in hand. She's put on a bulky, green sweater over her shirt.

James is the misguided one who suggests maybe they should go to the service at church that night. He tosses the TV remote back and forth in his hands and says, "Maybe it's a sign." Carrie whips her neck to look at him.

Charlotte quickly puts that to rest. "What's gotten into you? You told them you couldn't sing in the quartet." Then Mother gets confused about what time the hymn sing starts, and Charlotte has to set that straight. The mantle clock dings seven times as if to back her up. They're not going anywhere in less than a half hour.

When Martha gets a tickle in her throat and reaches for a butterscotch candy to suck on, everyone stares until she stops coughing and her platform rocker moves smoothly again. She's happy to stay at home with her sewing; if things go well, she can work on the yellow border to frame the fruit on the tea towel. Momma taught her to do that, the finishing touch.

Carrie doesn't know who she'd want to see at Faith Community; most of her school friends have moved on to Platteville or Madison. Maybe Dad was trying to be considerate. It's not a good *sign* for the evening. The family biggies: what time something starts, who said what. Mom goes to the kitchen to check on the sweet potatoes cooking, says she doesn't want help.

James starts singing, "*Come, ye thankful people come.*" He pauses to see if there's a response from the kitchen, blows dust off the buttons of the remote, and explains that the Harvest Sing worship service is for people to give thanks for the bumper crop. "Price of farmland has gone up so much, big farm operations may be the only ones that can afford to buy land."

"How many people in church have anything to do with the fall harvest anymore?" Carrie asks.

"Good question," James says. "There aren't more than six families still in ag: the Benders, Urquharts—John and Marvin—." He holds up his left hand to count on his fingers, "Charlie Hall and Ed Manson"—adds the thumb on his right hand—"us. That's what I thought."

Chad suddenly pops up from the basement, wearing his white Tar Heels cap backwards and carrying Belinda. A baby blue T-shirt sticks out beneath his favorite dark red Abercrombie and Fitch shirt. "There's a party at Justin's. Gotta go soon."

"What's this?" Charlotte asks, coming to the living room, wiping her hands on her apron.

"Just a minute, young man," James says, moving his recliner to an upright position with a bang. "You still have curfew. Just because you don't have school anymore this week—."

"I know, I know," Chad says. "Eleven o'clock." He jumps high and touches the wall above the opening to the living room, bends low and pretends to dribble a ball through his legs. He fakes left, jerks his head to the right. He hates curfew.

"Tell me what you did to straighten up your room," Charlotte says.

"What kind of party are you talking about?" James asks, his hands gripping the chair's arms.

"Just, you know, hanging out," Chad says, hands waist high, moving sideways. *Lateral, lateral. Move it. Sideways. Slide.* Coach doesn't allow slackers.

"That's an answer?" James asks. "Come back here. Are Justin's parents at home?"

Chad stops and twirls the clump of bananas on the kitchen counter. "Just kids from school. I said, hanging out. Stuff like that. I suppose they're home. I'll make my bed first thing in the morning, Mom. Promise." His parents are way too uptight, act like he's going to be an alcoholic, if they find out about a party he went to.

"Not so fast," James says. "Your sister's home, only a few days. Sit down."

Chad and Carrie shrug shoulders at each other, grin. "I'll be here tomorrow," Carrie says. "And the next day." She opens the seed catalog, pages toward the herbs.

"Cool," Chad says, heading once more for the kitchen. He has a little time before things really get going. "Don't we have chips?" His parents don't need to know. Justin's parents have gone to Milwaukee; he convinced them he couldn't miss tomorrow's shoot-around and promised there wouldn't be any trouble. Chad's friends don't need to drink to have fun anymore. That was pointless, freshman year stuff, that time Justin got sloshed. Some parents are way cool about things like that.

"Up higher," Charlotte says, "to the right of the stove. We just finished supper." There's no filling up that boy. Okay, sweet potatoes need to simmer longer. She wishes she hadn't bought such big ones.

Chad takes a can of soda along to one end of the chocolate suede couch. "Watcha reading?" His fingers beat out a rhythm on his legs: buh, buh, buh, bum, bum. Belinda stretches her perfectly white paws in front of her.

Carrie holds up the catalog, her chance to show and tell. "It's never too early to choose vegetables for next year."

"Are you ready to spend an afternoon with your Aunt Gloria?" Charlotte asks, watching Chad's Adam's apple bob with each swallow. She'll get everyone in a good mood again; Mother doesn't need to sit there, frowning at the embroidery hoop. And why does she stretch her neck forward like that? "Don't spill, Chad. Maybe your Uncle Kenneth will let us in on his latest money-saving device. He's always loved to save: shiny quarters from all the states, unused envelopes that have good stamps, time."

"I'm psyched," Chad says. "If I can hold off Old Glory. Aunt Gloria. Last time, she gave me a hug like a leech."

"Don't exaggerate, son," James says. Belinda has settled on his legs, eyes closed.

"I'm not kidding. How are you supposed to hug someone, especially an aunt?" Chad asks. "An aunt with a goofy smile."

"Chad," James says, jerking his head in Martha's direction.

"Very carefully," Charlotte says. She pinches her nose with her thumb and index finger. "Gloria comes from a more expressive family. Last time they were here, she told me she loved me."

"Gloria said that?" James asks.

"You have to stoop down to the rest of us, don't you?" Martha says to Chad. "How tall are you now?" A fat, yellowish-orange peach begins to emerge from the stenciled tea towel, right beside the apple. Last year she gave sets of matching pillowcases; everyone acted like it was a nice gift. She'll be glad, though, to put the needlework aside tomorrow; it gets to be a strain on the eyes. She needs to remember to take her sewing basket to her room tonight, so it's not in the way when company comes.

"Six-one. Definitely six feet. Without my sneakers," Chad says. "Coach says I'm still growing." Chad cracks his knuckles. He's one of the coolest juniors at Monroe High School, loves cold weather and khaki cargo pants, wears T-shirts all year, layers them, sometimes adds a flannel shirt in the dead of winter. His mom doesn't need to know how low on his hips his jeans ride at school.

"Use some common sense," James says, rousing the cat as he crosses his legs, "with Gloria or anyone."

"No problem with Uncle Kenneth draping himself on you, is there?" Charlotte says. "You did straighten up your room, didn't you?"

Martha rustles in her sewing basket for more of the pale orange thread—salmon is what they call it—settles back on her wooden rocker with the deep purple cushions. The boy asks such strange questions. It's not natural. And why must Charlotte always put Kenneth and Gloria in a bad light?

"Last time, he gave me a fist bump; that was cool," Chad says. "But he calls me 'Kid,' even though I've looked down on him for three years." Chad cracks the knuckles on his other hand and adds, "Nobody's going to see my room."

"No one looks down on Kenneth," Charlotte says. Sometimes it feels like he's still laughing at her. Maybe because she never finished college. He throws big words out there just to agitate. What was that one? Puissance. And nocebo—that's what she was trying to think of. James calls it sibling rivalry: the two oldest children still vying for attention. Easy for him to say; his parents have been gone for years. Oh, Charlotte knows she should get over it, but it's so easy to take it out on Kenneth's wife. She's such a sweet thing, a goose really, if the truth be known. A stranger and pilgrim goose.

"So what did you say when Gloria told you she loved you?" Carrie asks.

"What are you supposed to say?" Charlotte answers. "You have to be polite. That reminds me. Let's all agree: everyone needs to be relaxed tomorrow. Caroline, get some sleep tonight. No interrupting." She pauses. "Is everyone listening? No knuckles, Chad. Okay?" She waits until he looks at her. "Act interested."

"What about me? Was that the part about being polite?" James asks. His role is to keep Charlotte loose. He pitches in when she calls: an extra board for the dining table, a straight chair retrieved from the basement. She chooses the food, handles the entertainment. No need to hear her pooh-pooh his suggestions.

"Mom's telling me not to bring up money," Carrie says, "or 'lowly'."

"Kenneth's father—*your* father," Martha says, pointing a needle at Charlotte, "was never demonstrative. Not a one of them in that family he came from. If you're looking for family patterns, or whatever you call it." There were nights when she had to coax Daniel to put his arms around her, long before he got sick and turned, before he became clingy.

"Kenneth sure found his opposite then," Charlotte says.

Chad makes eye contact with his grandma. Sometimes she seems so sad. They got close last summer when his mom was golfing or away doing something with her lady friends. He'd convince his dad that Grandma needed company in the house. She'd make him fried egg sandwiches with melted cheese. Super quaint, but sweet. Long ago, when she and Grandpa lived a few miles away on Township Road, she brought him orange candy whenever they visited: circus peanuts, corn candy, then those candy orange slices with white sugar. She loves shopping at Troyer's. But these days she's given him a major assist; basement freedom is no small thing. Not that it's easy having Grandma in the house; he hears "Shh, not so loud" way too often. But it's so much easier to slip downstairs. And Mom's such a pushover if you treat her right.

"Back in Grandpa's day, men weren't supposed to show emotion, right?" Carrie asks.

"It wasn't expected," Martha says, "but sometimes your grandfather couldn't help himself." It feels like she has a seed stuck in one of her molars, and her tongue can't dig it out. "When he got sick at the end, it was too much."

"How come you don't ever show emotion, Dad?" Chad asks. "Except when you're mad." He brushes oily chips from his fingers, rubs a hand on his jeans.

"What do you mean?" James asks, looking up from the latest *Hoard's Dairyman*. "Now some bright guy claims he can make a mint from cow manure, has this brainy idea of a digester that makes methane gas as renewable energy."

"Cows are nasty suckers," Chad says.

"There's nothing wrong with an arm thrown around a shoulder," Charlotte calls out from the kitchen.

"That minister at your church gives me the warmest handshake," Martha says. "Like a caress." She looks at her hands, rubs one inside the other. Then she looks up and says, "Is that the wind I hear? There's been so much stormy weather." It's hard, being away from her home place. She hears the wind moan at night and wonders if a tree has blown over in their orchard.

"So I should drape my arm around Uncle Kenneth's shoulder?" Chad asks. "Give him a little neck squeeze?" He jumps up, throws the chips can on the couch, plants his feet and stretches his right hand high like a policeman, left hand like a claw at his waist, daring an opponent. Belinda raises her head: the disdainful tiger cat that wandered into the barn years ago, found the milk James always put out, and converted to an indoor sweetheart.

"Use some sense, Chad," James says. "A hug isn't just a hug. Watch what others do."

"When did Father show too much emotion at the end, Mother?" Charlotte asks, taking a seat again. "Is that what you said? He never hugged *me* when he was sick. It was always up to me. After he rallied, I didn't realize how weak he still was." She shudders and tugs on her nose again. "It almost seemed like he didn't *want* to be cheered up. Like he gave up. That's not *too much* emotion."

Martha's lips form a severe circle. "Your father's father, Charlotte, had a handshake like a vise grip. Zeke was a hard, hard man." She rests the tea towel on her multicolored lap robe, searches for the right shade of green thread. "Would someone please thread my needle? The orange slipped in easily, but sometimes I can't see for trying. This light is no good anymore."

"Here, I can," Chad says, untangling his long legs. "Even a camel would have trouble squeezing through this hole. Right, Grandma?"

"By the way, Charlotte," James says, "you didn't make that cranberry salad that runs all over the plate, did you?"

"No, I did not. Please don't make crumbs, Chad; you know better than to brush things off. Everything is clean." Charlotte will check his room in the morning when she goes downstairs to use the extra oven—make sure. She'll write herself a note. "Did you hear that Gene and Sue aren't coming?"

"No way. Really? Bummer," Chad says. "Meg's still coming, isn't she?"

"As far as we know," Charlotte says.

"Gene's the best; he doesn't bug me," Chad says, bouncing one bare foot, crossed on his other leg. "Doesn't ask a million questions like Uncle Kenneth." Bum, buh, bum, buhh.

"That's because morticians practice formality and distance in their work," Charlotte says. "They know what's appropriate; they don't snoop. I couldn't have two more opposite brothers. You're sure they're both yours, Mother? Just kidding."

Martha rocks slowly, begins the outline of the peach leaf. Now she's sure she hears the wind rattle the big picture window behind Charlotte's insulated beige drapes. "You're awfully quiet tonight, Carrie."

"Oh." Carrie sits up straighter on the couch. "Just listening." So much for thinking she'd say more about her vegetable farming proposal tonight. The mood's not right at all. No one shows the slightest interest in her seed catalog.

"Gene cracked up, the time we pink flamingoed their front yard," Chad says. He crunches the soda can in his hands, taps on it. That was the same year he did cheerios for the first time in the school parking lot. That's lame now, compared with car surfing. Very cool.

"Very foolish," James says, closing the magazine. "All that distance you drove. Sometimes you kids don't think." Chad has a nose for trouble that makes Carrie's attraction to vegetables look like a blessing. These kids and their parties. James is sure Chad never came clean about that choking game this fall.

Charlotte puts on her oval-shaped glasses—they're a nuisance, but she needs them to read—pushes back her hair, and laughs. "Four yards in one night. I still don't know where you found all those flamingoes." She needs to check the pie recipes again. She's looked at the ingredients before, of course, but if you want things done right, you can't look too often. That's the key. Things have a way of disappearing right off your shelves if you're not careful. "Everyone listen up. I need all the apples left in the crisper. For pie and the stuffing. No one is to touch them."

James points at Chad. "Gene should've reamed you. What if he'd had a family coming in to make arrangements?"

"Oh, we checked his website," Chad says. He bites on a fingernail. "Gene's not stuffy. I'll bet he doesn't even own a black suit. And that silver hearse—way cool. I'm going to get me a Dodge Magnum some day, low to the ground like a hearse. Big wheels, 425 horsepower makes a huge rumble with its Hemi V-8."

"Gene has a lot of his father in him," Martha says, "quiet on the surface. Both boys like their practical jokes, but Kenneth is more clever with words." She tugs against the knot with her needle and thread. "At the end Daniel needed tenderness when the world turned against him. 'Why can't—?'" She stops, her eyes spread wide.

Charlotte and James stare at each other; that's the same unfinished question Charlotte's heard before. It's pitiful, how much Mother repeats herself, doesn't finish sentences. "Of course, Gene has black suits," Charlotte says to Chad. "And hugs aren't meant to be sensible. Remember that. If they were sensible, they wouldn't be hugs."

"Lots of people think the world's cruel, long before they get to be seventy-six," James says.

"Seventy-seven already when he had his stroke," Martha says. "I told him—."

"Sorry," James says. "Like the people you met in Appalachia, Carrie; it sounds like some of them start with one foot in the grave." He takes one look at Charlotte and hits the POWER button on the remote. College basketball on ESPN—the Alaska Shootout tonight—can get him out of this jam. It's crazy, the way there are games to watch any time—late at night, reruns in the daytime. He'd find plenty to do in the house, if he let himself.

"I told him he had to make the best of it," Martha says quietly.

"What do you mean? It's like you talk in riddles sometimes," Charlotte says. "'Father needed tenderness at the end.'" Mother tells some of the strangest stories. That one where she claimed Father took a bucket of grapes—she'd picked them off the stems for him—took the full bucket to the basement along with a big bag of sugar. He wouldn't say what he was up to. "His last days were peaceful enough. I know he suffered—everyone does—but he kind of joked around about wanting to die. Then I told him—I remember this distinctly. I said, 'Oh, you don't mean that,' and he closed his eyes. James, please put that on MUTE."

"I wish I had a couple more inches on me. Six-three would be sweet," Chad says. He lowers his head and bites on another finger. "Uncle Gene says I've got it all—the build, the moves. He says he'll come to Madison if we make it to State." Chad will go to any basketball camp that will take him; he wishes he could play AAU ball next summer. Anything to avoid farm work. Mom convinced Dad that a high school junior doesn't have time to help with chores during the school year. Sweet. He hates shooting baskets in the barn; no matter how much he sweeps it ahead of time, he stirs up all that dust. Grimy old hay bales. The only thing halfway fun about farm work is getting to pee behind the barn. Well, it's cool, too, when the breeder guy comes to get semen from a bull. He pulls out that long thing that looks like a radiator hose.

"Daniel couldn't handle getting old," Martha says. "I've told you that before. He said it wasn't fair, the way his body gave out. 'Why can't I—?'" She looks down quickly at the stenciled shape of the leaf.

"He never got over his popcorn withdrawal," Charlotte says. "Please stop picking at your fingers, Chad. Father's favorites: ketchup on everything and popcorn. Remember that time, James—New Year's

Day—when I made you go to Leroy's Bar to beg for some ketchup? After that, Father started carrying more food items at the store."

"Moocher," James says. "You made a moocher out of me."

"Popcorn was the least of it," Martha says. "Losing his faculties, needing help for everything." She makes clicking noises. "'Help me get up. Help me sit.' Wherever he wasn't, that's where he wanted to be." She'd helped Daniel walk from his bed to the chair; he'd moaned and said, "I hate this." If only she can be spared. *Please, Lord, look down in your mercy. Send your sweet dove, if need be.*

"You want emotion, Chad?" James asks, clutching his dairy magazine again. "Check out the ten-year farm outlook. Grain prices—who knows how long ethanol will last. Fuel prices? Out of control." He slaps the arm of his chair. Belinda jumps off his legs and looks back at him, her ears pointed. "I heard the other day, there's a soybean fungus, Asian soybean rust, hitting the South." He shakes his head. "Always something."

"Isn't that the truth," Martha says. "It bothered Daniel when he'd repeat himself. 'Did I already ask—?'" Martha spreads out her hands in front of her: thin, wrinkled, large blue veins. Nobody said so, but she's sure they all thought she'd be the first to go. Her heart spell almost ten years ago. First, they said fibrillation, then flutter. Then back again. All that fuss. And here she is.

"What about you, Mom? Does your life suck?" Chad asks. He flips his right wrist like he's shooting multiple free throws. No one can stop him when he runs the break. It's not fair that small guys have such a tough time making it in the NBA.

"Watch your language, Chad," James says.

"Oh, I wouldn't say that." Charlotte glances at her mother. "There's lots that's good about life." It would sound silly—Mother sitting right there—to mention how embarrassed she was to wear long brown stockings to school; she'd roll them down till she got home again. But there's lots worse today: James and his farm problems. Kenneth never tires, asking about the Death of the Family Farm. It's like he's keeping vigil or something. "I've got this flab in my upper arm," she says. "My biggest handicap, Chad." She interlocks her fingers around an imaginary putter. "Just kidding."

James can't begin to name all the parts of his life that hang by a thread. So many people he's dependent on: neighbors, hired help, Mr. Starling at the bank. Carrie can't be serious; she'd muddle things up, big time. "We never know when our time's up," he says. "Then it's too late. The bell tolls."

"Pfft!" Charlotte says.

"A cow bell, right?" Chad says, scooping up Belinda. His dad only thinks about the farm, never has time to do anything fun. Sure, he makes it to Chad's basketball games, unless some two-thousand-pound sweetie is sick. But Chad used to beg his dad to restore an old Camaro like Justin and his dad did with that '68. Not a chance that'll happen. New full rear quarter panels, wheel wells, spoilers. They rewired everything, rebuilt a 350-cubic-inch-displacement V-8.

James has followed Charlotte's eyes to Martha. "No, I mean any one of us," he says. "How much time we have left. None of us knows, even though we act like we're going to live forever. We forget that our bodies are made to disintegrate." He stares at Charlotte and says in a high-pitched voice, "It can't happen to me."

"You rock, Dad," Chad says. "The big GR. Screws you, huh?" His long fingers run through Belinda's gray and white coat; she settles back, closes her great cat eyes.

Martha stares at the drapes. "GR?"

"I told you to watch it, Chad," James says. "Grim Reaper," he mutters. *That's one thing his old man would never put up with—a cocky kid.*

"It's not something we need to talk about," Charlotte says. Why can't James see he's only egging Chad on? They're always at each other. "If I were constantly on the lookout for death, I'd never get anything done. Worries aren't worth the bother, are they, Mother? I say: if things go wrong, they go wrong."

"Screw is good," Chad says.

"What is it with you?" James asks. "Shush."

Charlotte leaves the living room, absently pokes at the turkey in the refrigerator one more time, squeezes a bluish leg—yes, it's thawed—hears Chad say, "That bites!" He can be so obnoxious at times. But when he irritates her, she pinches him playfully on the cheek and he shapes up. The less said, the better. If only he didn't chew on his fingers. She and James will stick this out: no rigid boundaries like they grew up with. Last year it almost backfired—kids are going to be kids—but things settled down once Chad got reinstated on the team. What can you do in Wisconsin where alcohol runs like a river? Chad's just a harmless teenager with a driver's license, too many hormones, and a mouth that runs faster than his head sometimes.

She hears James tell Chad he's a mega-sized pain. Chad says something about always getting yelled at. The word "freaking" is in there. It sounds like he's leaving; "running late," he says. Father never took any lip from his boys; the worst Charlotte ever heard from him was "Jeepers creepers." One time she and Kenneth sat on the porch swing, though—must have been a rainy day—and practiced saying lots worse than "darn" and "dang." But Chad hears dirty stuff all the time. You can't protect kids these days, not with TV and friends. Of course, he has to see what he can get away with.

Charlotte follows him to the side door, puts a hand on his arm. "Be careful, please."

"Keep it between the ditches," Carrie calls out. "That's what you used to tell me," she says to her dad.

They listen to the high whine of Chad's Geo, his sub-compact going swiftly out the driveway, shifting into high gear on the hardtop road.

"He drives too fast," James says, reclining again.

"He knows to be careful," Charlotte says.

Martha sighs and reaches for more of the green thread. Charlotte lets the boy go out without a jacket.

*　　　*　　　*

What can you say about the rest of the evening? Charlotte would rather forget it. Not that anything bad happened, but things got more confusing. Chad has a right to show up with a new girlfriend, but it came as such a surprise. Charlotte thought he was still in between girls. She's a beauty, all right—that dark brown leather jacket over her pink cashmere sweater. And beautiful, long black hair. Chad usually goes for older girls, but Nicole is only a freshman. A knock-out with those dimples. Charlotte had to repeat the last name for Mother: Martinez, not Martin.

Why these things happen when Charlotte is tired and discovers a spot on her pale yellow blouse—well, she should be able to laugh about it. Caroline was full of surprises, too. Mother tried to make a missionary out of her, asking about her teaching days in Appalachia. But Caroline would have none of it. She said she mostly dropped the ball. It's never made sense why Caroline gave up teaching so quickly, but apparently she let one kid do her in. How could teaching math be fun and most of the students be cooperative—except for the ones who couldn't sit still because of learning problems—and yet Caroline quit?

It obviously bothered her to talk about it because her voice got shaky. "I lost control one day. This kid walked around the classroom and all the other kids went wild. I didn't know what to do. I didn't really understand Appalachia."

Why didn't they have a mentor for her, fresh out of college? No wonder she looks worn out, if she's still thinking depressing thoughts from a year ago. She said all the extra money in the system goes for coaches' salaries; she claimed they get jobs as principals when they don't have a clue how to run things. Pfft. She showed no interest in talking with Kenneth tomorrow about getting a job back here, just shrugged her shoulders like she's determined to stay away. "Kenneth can't get me the kind of job I want," she said. How does she know? That child makes no sense. If she would just accept that it's a man's world out there, she'd be a lot happier. She kept talking about the old boys' network and some other word. Nepcrosis, neptitude—something. There she sat, twenty-five years old, a good education, and staring at the world like it could be fixed.

Then Mother took Caroline's side and said too many women let themselves get walked over. Well, duh. Mother even admitted that Charlotte's been right; women should speak up more. And then, some of the things Caroline said about Ryan—very confusing. She insisted she didn't know where he was—"the Middle East somewhere"—and acted like it was over between them. She's letting a good man walk away, just like that. Charlotte had to ask her point blank if she knows what she's doing, and she had the nerve to say, "Who's to say what's good?"

James was no help: he sat there clicking his ballpoint pen. He gets restless when things turn tense, so he excused himself to check on the cows. He was still outside when Chad came with Nicole. It seemed like James' barn smell was stronger than usual when he joined them again. Maybe Nicole didn't notice. Chad is such a tease, not breathing a word about Nicole to Charlotte. He said he wanted her to meet Caroline. If only he could keep his legs still; they were on the move the whole time, opening and shutting like a gate. His Nikes—one of them balanced on its edge—looked huge compared with Nicole's tiny black shoes with their thick heels. And they kept passing Chad's cell phone back and forth, whispering and snickering.

The nook would have been perfect if Charlotte could have gotten everyone to play a game. But James seemed preoccupied—he took no initiative to make popcorn—and Mother kept her needle moving, studying that apple like she was Adam's assistant. No, it was the yellow border by then. Chad said they couldn't stay long, but they did! Small talk, that was it mostly. Weird topics: Illinois drivers and bumper stickers. "Honk If You Are Amish." Caroline thought the one she saw was funnier: "Honk If You *Are* Jesus." Mother gave an elaborate explanation of how Father was a farmer before he went into the store business. But then when Father sold to Jim Henry, the bank didn't keep tabs like they should have. That made James pipe up about how afraid he was, starting out, that the bank wouldn't carry collateral for them. Like Nicole cared about any of this. Everyone was simply trying too hard.

Caroline mentioned that some Amish people got on the bus at Indianapolis and got off again in Illinois. She thought maybe they were going to Arthur and went into a long description—for her, anyway—about the elderly man who had trouble hearing. Nicole picked up on the Amish reference and asked about the little white caps, the different shapes and sizes. That's where the worst started. Mother took it upon herself to explain that her momma came from Arthur, Illinois, where they wore strings on their coverings, but Poppa Lloyd grew up in Buchanan County, Iowa. Like *anyone* cared.

Imagine! Explaining head coverings to Nicole. She was wearing a gold cross on her necklace, but why Mother chose to elaborate—it goes against any good sense. She said if a woman wants to publicly show she listens to her husband, she has the right. And, of course, the covering means you're submitting to God and the church. Nicole nodded like it all made perfect sense. All Charlotte could think about were her own teenage years when she couldn't wait to pull the straight pins out of her lid as soon as she walked out the church door.

It was mind boggling the way things went. Charlotte sat there, stunned. Trying to change the subject was like trying to turn a steering wheel in snow when your tires are locked. James and Caroline felt it necessary to name all the different groups of Mennonites and Amish in Wisconsin; Caroline suddenly acted like an authority. She claimed there were over forty groups, just of Mennonites, in the United States. Poor Nicole—. It's confusing enough for those born into this mess. She was polite and acted interested, but then she got into trouble with Caroline. It was uncalled for.

Nicole said something like, "It's too bad so many Amish young people go wild."

"Wild?"

No one can pounce like Caroline.

"Yeah, experimenting with drugs and sex." Nicole twirled her beautiful hair and looked at Chad for help, but he stayed focused on his phone.

"Where'd you get that?" Caroline pulled herself up straighter and leaned forward.

It turned out Nicole had seen a movie and been reading books about the Amish. "Those book covers always have young girls with caps," she said. "Chad says you call them coverings."

"Fiction about the Amish?" Caroline asked. "Where everything works out just right, especially when it comes to romance?" She might as well have snorted.

But Nicole stood her ground. "Yeah, I love those books. My sister and I pass them back and forth. You know exactly what the girls are thinking, how they're looking for the right man."

Caroline sat back and looked half-sick. James had closed his eyes.

Charlotte couldn't think how to get Nicole to stop. Poor child, she didn't know any better.

"I see them around," Nicole said, "at Wal-Mart and other grocery stores. They're so cute, especially the young girls and the little Amish boys. Their horses and buggies are everywhere on the county roads."

That might have been when Chad poked her and showed her something on his phone. They giggled and Charlotte thought it was going to blow over.

But Caroline couldn't keep quiet, made a speech out of it. "There's not one of us lives such an exotic life, knows such enchanting love, even though we have relatives who are Amish and parents who grew up Mennonite. We're just us. Ordinary people—farmers and such—doing the best we can every day, trying to ignore all the misconceptions out there."

Charlotte was sure she was going to scream; there was so much pressure. In her usual, befuddled way Mother came to the rescue by throwing in another long story. How Father was a generous man and gave out yardsticks at Christmastime. Like someone was questioning it! She said he used to pay for filling the five hundred gallon propane tank of that Fortwright neighbor whose wife shot herself in the backyard. You can bet that got Chad's attention; he was all ears. The woman had draped herself over her laundry basket.

Charlotte remembers all the talk, but according to Mother, it made quite an impression on Father. He boo-hooed in her lap, carried on like the woman was his grandmother. "Such a bloody way to go" he kept saying. "She must have been *very* disconsolate." Charlotte hates that word. Some words just sound ugly. Fatalistic is another. But apparently, Father couldn't get over the ordinariness of that laundry basket. Maybe he didn't know a woman could be anything but meek. But he surely came across some tough customers in his store; they wouldn't all have been men. Still, what a mess that must have been to clean up. Or like Chad said, "What a surprise to find an eyeball in the overalls!"

Finally, Chad and Nicole were gone, almost as suddenly as they came. He pointed to his phone, grabbed her jacket, and they hurried out. She promised to come again, but Caroline didn't even stand to say goodbye. She just leaned forward and waved. Driving off, they must have had lots to talk about. And laugh over.

All Mother could say was something about "another morning and evening," like it was no big deal. Charlotte was so tired she could hardly check her lists again. It was weird, feeling embarrassed about her Mennonite background; she thought she'd moved past that. Once she gets some sleep, she'll be on her toes again, determined to keep things on track. She makes a note to remind James to turn down the thermostat tomorrow. With people coming and the oven on, it can get much too hot in here. For now, though, it's best to just turn off the kitchen stove light and know that the sun will come up on a whole new day.

Chapter 7

Carrie wakes during the night and reaches for her stomach. Her hands reassure her, she's not six months pregnant. She's never been pregnant, but the dream was so real. She was large enough that everyone knew. Where was she? No, not the work room at Re-Use-It, but yes, pulling zippers out of pieces of clothing, throwing what was left onto rag piles. Others were doing the same. There was an urgency. A need to complete the task, to watch for the vehicle leaving. Not a boxcar, but something ominous. A horse trailer? Whatever it was, she couldn't afford to be left behind. People she didn't recognize were grabbing stragglers. In spite of watching, she missed the truck.

Now fully awake, Carrie doesn't want to interpret—what did Jung say about dreams? The images keep coming back. Zippers? A wasteland and barrenness. But flowering, too. We dream to balance ourselves; that was it. To correct our subjective viewpoint. She had felt overwhelmed. Real people in real misery. Like looking at old photos of

Johnson's War on Poverty. Only worse, and the misery was hers. Theirs. Nearly everyone's. Far beyond kids throwing paper wads, marching around the classroom.

She hears a movement in the hallway; a door closes. It's probably Grandma, using the bathroom. What might waken her besides bodily needs? Does she know what she was saying tonight? Sometimes she separated herself from her mother, the usually revered Momma. Not putting so much faith in rules anymore, in God-as-policeman. What if she had defied her momma long ago, cut her hair, jumped on a train to San Francisco and joined a worker's union? A rebel dish who ran away without the spoon. Crazy. That wouldn't be her. If that were Grandma, Carrie would be someone else with a far different mom, surrounded by completely different norms.

Grandma talked about Grandpa with such devotion, like none of them knew him. His generosity. Something was bothering her. What had life been like for them behind closed doors? Had she been happy? Or did they feel trapped in their little nuclear family? In love *and* in habit? Grandpa's dying must have been horrible. Does she see him walking on streets paved with gold or strolling among his roses? His head looked strange from the back: almost flat, no curve, hair cut short. He was always old, blond hair turned whitish—his nose hairs! Sometimes Grandma looks—how to say?—not wild, and not frail exactly, but scattered. Is it uncertainty that makes her say what she does? Blurt things and contradict herself. One minute, she apologizes for finding fault and says she's no good; the next minute she says she should have stood up for herself more. She still must be grieving.

Grandpa cried. They say we're more stunned by a random shooting than a military body count in the thousands. Had Grandma soothed his face with a wet cloth? Had he gone to work like usual the next day?

That talk earlier about men and their emotions. When Dad's upset, he gets woodenish—looks like he's lost five cows in three days—but she's never seen him break down. Malaise, yes. Teetering between having no energy and being ready to sell the herd. And Manager Milt—if he has problems, he solves them by promoting Wonder Boy and letting the females flounder with reduced hours. Chad's world is far from heartbreak—unless he'd be looking at a wrecked Geo. Didn't Mom see how disrespectful he was? Carrying on like that with Nicole in their own little world. Maybe Mom was just glad to have them at home, not out at a wild party. Is Nicole the daughter she wants? The reader of romance? Her long hair swishing between Chad and everyone else. She has no clue how insulting that is to make generalizations about *rumspringa* and Amish youth.

And what's Mom's problem, implying that Ryan was Carrie's only chance? Does she ever think before she speaks? Her questions have stirred up old memories. On the way to the airport Ryan told Carrie that his thesis advisor had said, "The Middle East? That's a long way to go to get shot at." No, things certainly didn't "fall into place" for them. Was that the truck that left? The only tangible object she has left is a smooth, river stone Ryan gave her one time. Beautiful shades of brown and gray, worn by the rush of water. For awhile she carried it in her pocket, liked to find it there with her car keys and imagined it meant something it didn't. If Carrie never marries, her mom will be mortified, her reputation damaged. No male found Carrie attractive; no male wanted her to carry his child. Mom must think finding completion in another person is universal.

Carrie knew Ryan hated all institutions, including marriage. He'd said he had to swallow his pride to join up with a peace group; any group would have its lame rules. Maybe he was just scared. Had she pressured him? Gotten too serious—needy—without realizing it? She'd offered to help him put his resume´ together; she meant it only as a return favor for him having set up her used computer. Surely he hadn't left because of her, hadn't needed to *get away,* rather than needed to *move toward* something. Sometime she'll check with Kirsten, but right now that feels like it'd still be running after him. E-mails into the void.

Is that someone crying? Carrie holds her body still, flat on her back. Someone sighs, mumbles. It must be her imagination. Someone spits. Too soft for Dad. Grandma's body, too slight. No, there it is again. A sigh turns to a groan. Carrie must still be dreaming. *She missed the truck!* If only Dad would say, "I believe in you, Carrie. Right now, not just when you were a baby in my hands and I imagined your future. Follow your heart." *Stop it. He doesn't ever say things like that.* He'd probably be happy if she wanted to come home and take care of the calves. He'd respect that. But otherwise, she's too young to know anything.

Carrie hates her own crying—Kirsten called it self-loathing—those moments that turned into days when her insecurities took over. One day last week Carrie called in sick at Re-Use-It. She looked horrible: her eyes red and swollen, her cheeks puffy. She felt worthless, couldn't do anything right, turned people off. But crying was ineffective, a sign of weakness, something to be ashamed of. Long ago, Carrie had climbed onto her mom's lap atop the red-and-brown plaid couch, tried to look into her eyes, and asked, "What is it?" Her mom had hugged Carrie, and with their cheeks squished together, had whispered, "Mommy feels sad, but she'll be all right. Go on and play." That was Carrie's introduction: grown-ups had problems. Her mom had stayed slumped on the couch, as if she couldn't get up. Finally, she grabbed her pile of soaked blue tissues and rattled pots and pans in the kitchen. Had a truck taken off without Mom? Does she ever want something so badly, even if it's outside the norm? Something more important than another basket from Central America for the screened-in porch?

Coming home reminds Carrie how spoiled she's been, how much she has. The luck of her birth! That was so much fun when they used to invite the neighbors over for homemade ice cream. She took it all for granted, as if she deserved it. Now she knows: one person's fortune comes at another's expense. Some people do start out with everything against them. It could be in Appalachia or in Milwaukee. But with the way things are going in the U.S., if they all go down—was that the truck leaving?—lose everything because of imperialistic greed, will Carrie be doing what she most wants to do? She can't just be against war and sexism and discrimination. She needs to be *for* something.

Native Appalachians complained about outsiders who wanted to change everything and only made things worse. They had a point—those early VISTA workers. The coal companies that stole land rights with their bags of tricks. Carrie had tried to cross cultures; she had big hopes to connect. She was a do-gooder. Oh, sure, those fifth-grade girls who sat in front and wanted to answer every question her second year—they liked her. But she must have looked as silly to her southern neighbors as a tourist trying to sell an Amish man equipment to modernize. As disconnected as Chad's stereotypes tonight. He talked about driving behind a hillbilly in a rattle-trap truck, admitted he wanted to go deep in a coal mine.

So what had her two years amounted to? Some of her college loans got deferred. But how could it have been important to go away to Appalachia, if it didn't matter if she came back to Wisconsin? And what's she to do now? Forget about being part of a scheme for people to buy locally? People seem hell-bent on ruining the earth, so look the other way. Blame fast food and corporate greed. Realize she's only one, insignificant person. She'll be a vagabond, a bus junkie. Head south from Indianapolis, go through Kentucky, follow Interstate 75 down to northern Florida, drift west through Texas, drop into Mexico from El Paso. Get away from it all.

No one at work wants to talk about increased animosity toward the U.S. "Lock your door; a bunch of crazies out there," Trudy says and walks away. Manager Milt laughs about climate change—"Made-up stuff," he says. So stick to reality shows. Fantasy football, where no one gets hurt. Pretend that a mother's reality matches your own. That the balance of power remains with the U.S., and other countries respect that. Believe the big boys' mantra for the 95%: "Keep 'em down. Keep 'em afraid. Keep 'em demoralized." After all, the most power in the world goes to those who create reality for the rest.

Attitudes here in Wisconsin would have to do a three-sixty for her to fit in. Some people aren't meant to have close friends *or* family. Miss Outsider with nary an Insider bone. *No place. No home.* No running back to Daddy. No freeloading. Other young adults can go back and live with their parents. Not her. There's no way she could move a trailer onto the property. Mom wouldn't let Carrie put up a clothesline, not even behind the house. Dad knows to protect himself from catastrophe. He'll never tell Mom about the vegetables.

Carrie can't make others see the world of disadvantage she's seen. Can't *make* Dad change his view of farming. Mom's probably still labeling Carrie a scary feminist. Get back to sleep; put away self-absorption; stop the pity-poor-me syndrome. Just get through tomorrow. She can't afford to be crabby at her mom's party.

*   *   *

Martha doesn't want to throw back the covers and feel the cold air go through her warm flannel nightgown sprinkled with the tiny pink flowers. But she won't be able to get back to sleep until she uses the toilet. Daniel would say: the old bladder ain't what it used to be. That was on one of his good days, when he could laugh about it. Heaven spare her the humiliation of a diaper. Depend. What a brand name! *Who will take care of her?*

Martha doesn't want to die in a hospital. Still today, she hears others tell how a loved one got admitted and the doctors did every test under the sun. Her children need to know not to allow that—sometime when they're all together—so there's no squabbling. Daniel knew her wishes, but he's no help now. *When it's my time to go, don't hang on for me. And don't let me die all hooked up.* That's what she'll say.

Charlotte's house is too quiet. It's always quiet in the middle of the night, but this is a quiet that sends out little zigs in Martha's back. Sharp tingles, right around behind on the left. No pounding rain like last night. Thank goodness, the wind has settled down. Is Chad home? He picks up on a lot more than he lets on, even when his thumbs are flying on that phone of his. Could Carrie be awake? Their bedrooms are back to back and they share a bathroom. What a surprise, if Martha headed there and found Carrie. The poor child hasn't had a chance to settle in yet, catch up on her sleep. What an evening they had. Talk, talk, talk. Martha was so afraid someone would agree to play Dutch Blitz. She's never quick enough with those slippery cards.

As far as Martha knows, people don't dream in concert. Oh, it *could* happen. A married couple might dream the same dream at exactly the same time of night, or identical twins could have a duet dream. When she was little, her nightmare was being chased by a bear. Much later, a stately buck turned into a bear that smothered her but didn't mean to hurt her. The mind plays tricks on people. That dream where Daniel was popping grapes in his mouth, one right after the other, so fast he had trouble swallowing. He never told her any of his dreams, even though she asked when his body twitched more than usual.

She slips out of bed, puts the top quilt back in place so her flannel sheets will stay warm. It's reassuring to put her feet on the solid floor. Her legs still work, but oh, her joints. Her balance isn't always the best; some nights she bumps into the doorframe. Martha sits on the toilet longer than usual. The cool air makes her shiver, but she's not eager to go back to bed and lie down. It will take time to push away the dream. She tucks her nightgown down over her skinny knees. Daniel loved her poor, bony body. How nice that would be, to be touched warmly again.

Has Martha strayed? Putting aside the covering, except for when she goes to church. For years she hardly questioned anything. Momma called it faith, to keep to the old ways, the strings. But Daniel's health problems put things out of kilter. The certainties crumbled. Knots and snags—*ziggles*—where there should be smoothness. Ruby hasn't been as friendly lately. She has Delbert to grieve over, but it's like she's put two and two together—what happened with Daniel. She looks at Martha with pity. Tut-tut.

Martha tries to be detached from the things of this world. She dare not clutch. She's separated by circumstance from her own church, hears rumors there's talk of another deacon. She tries not to comment about what's for breakfast. Charlotte never asks—seldom ever—what Martha would like. Far from her house on Township Road, that's the hardest to be away from. There ought to be a verse: Cling not. She can't have everything ripped away. *Oh, Lord, please no, not her house, not forever.*

Martha shuffles back to her bedroom, slips into bed, pulls the covers up, and tucks the sheet under her chin. The dream that woke her up. All right then, if she must. The house from her childhood, the second house in Illinois, was being moved. A squarish, wooden frame house with a back porch where Momma butchered chickens and shelled peas. The outside boards were gray and needed paint. Momma, Poppa Lloyd, four girls, and two boys. Clara, the one who died when she was only four. Something was not right with her eating; she never made adequate gain. Two bedrooms, a kitchen, a sitting room, an open room upstairs for the boys. Each bedroom had a covered pot for nighttime. That was the house in the dream.

Men, both Old Order Amish and Mennonites, wearing go-to-church hats, stood around, drilling into the ground, testing equipment, jacking up the house, motioning for "a bit more over here," then yelling a sharp "Whoa!" to a movement that went too far. No one said why the house had to be moved. Poppa Lloyd looked the way Martha remembered: bib overalls, long-sleeved shirt, full beard, toothpick in his mouth. But wearing a go-to-church hat? No sense there. He kept saying, "Over there, there's daylight underground." Martha, the little girl in the dream, was too young to dwell on confusion, but she was scared. Wouldn't too much moving upset the oceans underneath?

She was jittery, hopping around on one foot, like when the tramps came wanting food. Poppa called them old codgers and insisted they were harmless. Momma gave them leftovers, anything they wanted, the scraps that were too good for the hens. Sometimes they were allowed inside with the family. Their heads down, they ate like starved black crows. Pick, pick, pick, shovel. One fellow went after a pork chop with two hands like it was a harmonica. If they took a notion, they might sleep in the barn overnight, stay for breakfast, and then drift off. Sometimes they chopped wood to pay a little something.

The gypsies in Nebraska were even worse. Momma's eyes filled with fright when she told the cousins—one Thanksgiving when they came to visit—about the gypsies. They came in covered wagons and asked for hens to butcher. They camped along the way—sometimes a couple wagons traveled together—and wanted water for their horses. The women wore strange head gear: black scarves wrapped around their heads. Years later, when Martha saw pictures of Hutterite women, she had to catch her breath. They weren't the same at all—navy blue scarves and bobby pins—but enough to give a start. The gypsies wanted eggs. And children. That couldn't be true; Momma must have stretched it to teach a lesson.

But the dream wasn't about tramps and gypsies. It was about the house being moved. Suddenly, the house jerked out of the ground. Everyone raved about how good it looked. Men slapped each other's backs and shook hands. In the dream little Martha felt a sudden chill. She dashed into the house before Momma could stop her, snatched her pale blue sweater, and ran back out again, leaping over boards that propped up the foundation. It's bad if you make no effort to avoid being bad. But it's very, very bad if you intentionally want to be bad, even do wild things.

Then there was more drilling. Suddenly the house slipped awry, tilted, about to pitch on its side. Men waved their arms and yelled loudly. How could this go so wrong, when all had been smooth? Everything in the house would have to be abandoned. Momma looked straight ahead and put her hand on Martha's shoulder. The dream stopped. The hand on the shoulder must mean that the house-tilting wasn't Martha's fault, even though she'd run back in the house for her sweater. *No, it wasn't her fault.* But someone had to have made a mistake. Why hadn't Momma tried to stop the men? Poppa Lloyd was right there and did nothing.

The dream stays a jumble like this evening's talk. Martha tried to enter in. So many stories she could have told for the edification of the young. But young ones want swift answers, not mystery. Chad will have to find things out for himself. He won't amount to anything, though, if he never learns to work. But with Carrie, there's more there. She pays attention, and she knows about *the least.* Something good burbles up inside her but puts on the look of trouble. More good than bad had to have happened during those teaching years.

Martha can't follow Carrie's political talk, though. Something about a new economy. And saying we pretend all the time. If we have money in the bank, we think the world's the way we want. We think we're in control. She even used Charlotte as an example: she thinks we'll have a big dinner tomorrow. Well, of course. Carrie added that she expects to get on the bus on Saturday. She admitted: we might not accomplish anything if we didn't anticipate what's to come. Charlotte went right back to her own business. All she wants is cheery. So different from Daniel's: "Expect the worst. If it happens, you're prepared. If it doesn't, you'll be thrilled to death."

Long before Martha married Daniel, she'd learned to blame herself for troubles, to know she was the heart and soul of most every misstep. Just like Momma. Martha was supposed to stand with Daniel, not lead him to looseness. But sometimes she made it difficult for him to obey the church's teaching. She'd wanted each of her children to play a musical instrument. Now she's determined to safeguard Daniel. The bad must have come to look like good to him. Maybe he had time to ask forgiveness; even a split second might have been enough. "We'll Go an Extra Yard for You" was his yardstick slogan from the store. She wants her family to remember him that way. They don't need to know the whole. Not anymore than anyone needs to know about Daniel's half-brother, a chip off Zeke's hard block, lost to the world's evils in New Jersey with gambling and such.

Martha doesn't need to talk about Daniel's tiffs with his father, either. The farming business—whether to rotate crops or not. It was good Daniel got out when he did. Zeke had a conniption when he found out about the gift of heating oil. He told Daniel to take care of his own family, not throw money away on a man who couldn't make ends meet. A rift in the family over being neighborly. Zeke had to drag in church people, too.

It's better to protect those we're closest to, not fail them. Momma's missteps before Poppa Lloyd came along. The Child. The fatherless toddler buried at the far end of the cemetery. No one needs to know. That day when Momma told Martha about it. Hush-hush. *"Now is not the time."* After that, she felt an odd fear around Momma, that it might have passed on to her as well, running loose in the blood. How Momma prayed when she lingered, asking for room at the Mercy Seat. Martha wiped drool, like tears gone astray, from Momma's chin and neck. There was little place for deviation in Momma's world. The bishop had made his determinations about what was right and wrong; everything else must fall in line.

Those hard, hard years, the late '20s when Momma and Poppa had moved the family to Nebraska. Momma was heartbroken to leave behind all the relatives in Illinois. Martha hears the soul-searching in the diaries. How she wishes she'd asked more questions. But when a person's passed on, it's too late. Poppa Lloyd had to scratch his itch to see more of the world. The whole family packed up and went to Milford, then on to Broken Bow and its cattle country. There may have been church trouble, too, forced the move. Who knows? Then one day Poppa Lloyd deposited the grain check and the next day they lost everything. After that, he wanted to move the family farther west to Kansas. It's a mystery what shook loose, what made them finally troop back to Illinois.

Did anyone really hear Martha tonight? She said it's mercy that people need, not more rules. Carrie perked up, but Charlotte probably passed it off as confusion. Martha's been muddled—she'll admit that—but not tonight. She's come to understand that when Momma got rigid, it was because she'd forgotten the story about the bent woman. How Jesus went about setting people straight when they held on and held on to how things had always been. The authorities gave him trouble for breaking the Sabbath. But when he saw that bent woman, he knew to call forth her straightness, never mind the day of the week.

Daniel was a strict one, too. He followed the church's order of things, the chain of obedience: God, man, woman, child, cow. Some days the cow came right after the man. Law before grace, until it became too much for him. *Oh, there's never enough grace in this world of woe. Not in the Church. Not for Momma and her Child.* Daniel started to see, back when that Fortwright woman shook up his world. No, he didn't know her from Adam. Charlotte tried to make something of it but couldn't even keep her name straight: Farnsworth, Forthwright. Martha doesn't judge the woman, either. Not that what she did was right. But Martha doesn't know the why. When people are gone, the what-for stays under the covers.

From then on Daniel apologized that he hadn't treated Martha better, not to the extent he wanted. He tried with the washing machine; he bought things when he could. He showed more tenderness with the youngsters' scrapes and falls. And still, he couldn't do it, not the extent. Martha was his woman: someone to make the beds and wash the clothes. Man before woman. And Martha bought right into it. She can't blame him alone. She did her duties, followed right along. *Someone* had to fix dinner. *But they both knew better.* And still they couldn't change.

Martha didn't mean to talk in circles tonight. Oh, that her frail words and works might not be in vain. No human being can ever be good enough, because no one can be perfect like Jesus. But you have to try, and then not take any credit. Momma always said, "It's bad to think you're too good, to stand apart." If the mashed potatoes come out right, that's good for only that one time.

For now, Martha will content herself with more of the diaries. She'll try to ease back into sleep. She reaches for a wintergreen to soothe. When she stopped reading this afternoon, they were getting close to making their move.

Momma's Diary – November 1927

Sunday

Special meetings tonight. Quite a number (11) went forward. Good talks on how marriage and the home bring solace. After thinking Lloyd understood about waiting till spring, we are going ahead. Are not to drag feet. Listen and obey. Can it be God's answer in the affirmative?

Monday

Big wash. Cannot believe we will leave Father and the cousins. Think and wonder. Are not to worry or doubt. The Lord will provide. Cut out two waists.

Tuesday

Baked real early this A.M. Ironed. Made princess slip. Everything seems to point one way for Lloyd, seemingly the opposite for me. Must trust and obey. Want to be in the center of God's will. Cloudy and drizzly.

Wednesday

Extras here for meals. Spent eve. singing. Much comfort in parting songs. "On Jordan's Stormy Banks I Stand" and "When Shall We Meet Again?" Searching the deepest recesses of the heart. Sore toe. Wretched.

Thursday

To Uncle Abner's. Hard to think that next year we cousins might not be together. Such a feeling of lonesomeness. Things are becoming real. Tears come in spite of Lloyd's assurances. A place called Nebraska.

Friday

Toe kept me awake again. Aunt Mary opened it, applied poultice and heat. Some better. Made Uncle Ben's shirt. Started cutting carpet rags.

Saturday

Made calico yoke dress for Baby. Took up bedroom carpet. Want to be in a condition where God can talk to me and make things real. Cannot bear to miss the mark.

Momma's Diary – November 1928

Sunday

Real cold today. Commotion in church because of sparks from stovepipe. Meeting not as stirring as last Sun. night. Waiting for things to be thus.

Monday

Miss T. called home by death of her Papa. Little did she know, only yesterday, what awaited her. Want my heart to be open. Search me; sift me. Oh, to be willing.

Tuesday

Lloyd is in a mood. Restless again. After thinking matters understood, new and troubling questions rear up. Talk of Nebraska again. Cares perplexing. Cut out boy's shirt. Think it cannot be that we might still move in spite of everything. Potatoes turning brown already.

Wednesday

Finished fall cleaning today. Heavy snow by eve. Are to put from mind. Not to know. Can but trust the One who carries all. Bunions underfoot. Tramps in the barn.

Thursday

Thanksgiving Day. A very beautiful day. Lloyd shot wild turkey. Had good missionary meeting tonight. Studied South America. Clara puts on no meat.

Friday

Tinkered. Feeling poorly. No pep. Fell to weeping. All deemed settled a year ago. That door closed. Must become willing again if we want victory. Cleanse me. Longing for that sweet, sweet peace.

Saturday

Finished Martha's hood this morning. Washed hair this p.m. Lloyd wonders why things do not open up. Oh, that he could stay busy. Cannot say all that comes to mind. Dear Lord and Father, not my will.

Momma's Diary – November 1929

Sunday

Everything is different. Their Sunday School hour is much too quiet. Conference news brings much sorrow. Very cold. Reminds of winter. To every question, Lloyd says, this is Nebraska. Young girls tonight sang "Must I Empty-Handed Go." Feeling strangely. Homesick for Father.

Monday

Unpleasant wash day. Too much wind and rain. Couldn't put clothes out till eve. The house here is small and unnatural. Sod. Lloyd says: Are to make do.

Tuesday

Spent good part of day hunting for table and chairs at reasonable price. Everything too high. Came home without. Awful headache. Baby has tooth. Finished cape. Nine (9) o'clock and Lloyd is still separating.

Wednesday

Made a lot of noodles. Coughed quite a lot last night. Long to be settled. Why could we not wait till spring? Lloyd says we will understand it better by and by.

Thursday

Oh, to be thankful in a strange land. Too far West, this Nebraska land. Misty today. Tempted to doubt. No sweet Canaan. No Beulah Land. Did little cooking. To church. Subject: "Six Steps to the Throne." Coughed up dark red.

Friday

Scrubbed kitchen with broom. Rec'd 24 page letter from Illinois. So much news. Deaths of Tobie Yost and Mildred McB. Sad and lonely hearts left behind. Remodeled bonnet for Clara. Stays scrawny. Bugs in the sugar.

Saturday

Everything still torn up and in confusion. Hardly know what to do. No room to put things. Disconsolate.

Chapter 8

"They're here!" James says, calling to her from the dining room.

"What?" Charlotte says, not that she doesn't hear. "Who do you mean? They can't be."

"They're bringing things." James says each word like it's an effort. "I didn't recognize the car."

"Kenneth?" Charlotte asks. "It's not even ten." She grabs her 9:30 list; there's not time to peek in the oven, lift the foil, see if the red button on the turkey has popped up. "Is the table done?" How could Kenneth do this? The lettuce isn't washed. She should have known.

"Gloria is carrying something covered. A large tray." James sounds unsteady. "Did you ask her to bring something? Holy Cow! Kenneth is guiding someone on his arm."

"What are you talking about?" Charlotte asks. She comes from the kitchen, wiping her hands on the small towel attached to the waist of her blue and yellow bib apron. Sometimes Gloria brings home canned pickle relish or green tomato salsa. "Lord God of Hosts!"

"Oh, no," James says, holding three forks poised upright, gaping past Martha's fern, centered in front of the picture window.

"What in the—?" Normally, Charlotte would take off her apron before going to the front door, but there's no time for normal. No last trip to the bathroom mirror to check that everything looks okay. Goodbye, holiday feel. Forget thankfulness. She'll put her foot down, make sure everyone stays out of the kitchen. Kenneth will have to entertain his surprise by himself. She'll make gobbling noises at his ears, if she has to.

Mother comes down the hallway, fastening the belt on her dark green polka-dotted dress. "I believe they're here," she says. A shoelace flops ahead of her on the carpet.

"And how," James mutters. "Get a pitch pipe and we'll sing 'Now Thank We All Our God' as they walk in."

"Tie your laces, Mother," Charlotte says. "We don't need you tripping."

"Oh, I forgot my sweater," she says and hurries back to her room.

Charlotte opens the front door and says, "Come in, come in, everyone. Whatever do you have there, Gloria?"

"The fatted calf." James is still muttering behind her. The entryway flooring creaks under his weight.

Charlotte gives Gloria a quick hug, but with the way Gloria grabs to balance the tray, Charlotte doesn't need to be overly enthusiastic. James pats Gloria gingerly on the shoulder—"Take that baby inside, I guess"—shakes hands briefly with Kenneth. "New wheels, eh?"

"I want you all to meet Mr. Armburgey," Kenneth says.

Charlotte manages a smile and shakes hands with a wobbly man. His hands are clean but shaky and cold. Does he have Parkinson's? His forehead shines fiercely; his gray shirt is buttoned all the way to the top under his shabby brown jacket. Charlotte almost misses greeting her niece, Meg, standing at the edge of the front step, one hand in her jeans pocket, the other fingering the iPod around her neck. Whew! Where'd she get that outfit? The front door stays open so long that James has to call out, "Don't let the box elders in." Then everyone bunches up in the entryway with goofy smiles, looking unsure if they're at the right place.

"He lives at Sheltering Arms," Kenneth says, as if Charlotte hasn't understood in a glance that this elderly man is from a different world. "We play checkers every Tuesday night."

"How nice," Charlotte says. Her voice comes from another room, as if it's been strained through a sieve. "What's that flour in your beard, Brother Dear?" she asks. Apparently, it was too much bother for him to tell her in advance the exact nature of his Thanksgiving surprise. One year he brought raspberry truffles! His guest stands smack-dab next to him, their arms entwined.

Mother greets the elderly gentleman cautiously, as if she went to high school with him but can't remember his name. "So glad to see you all," Mother says, still fiddling with her belt. "Did you have any trouble getting here?" She gives Meg a kiss on the cheek, pats her on the arm. "You look cold. Are you chilly?"

"No trouble at all," Kenneth says. "A slowpoke or two in Janesville, till we got going. Such a beautiful drive. We followed our noses. Yum, Charlotte. Definitely not porcupine in the air."

"What time did you leave?" Mother asks, backing up against the coat closet.

No trouble at all. Charlotte hears a buzzer and excuses herself to the kitchen. No unexpected guest will be cause for overdone turkey. Porcupine, indeed. Did he say Amburger? Charlotte hasn't started dicing and slicing salad garnishes. She needs to finish the white sauce for the potatoes. Where is Caroline when you need her? "Might bring something extra," Kenneth had said. And what's with Gloria? You'd think she'd understand the complications. Oh, they're both oblivious; they think nothing of having homeless people eat with them spur-of-the-moment. And Gloria's patterned polyester blouse. Who would wear swirling dabs of dark green and silver, splashed with streaks of black lightning? Let Mother try to cover for her darling firstborn. She'll find some way to act like they've been blessed with an angel, all unaware. What if this man can't keep his food down? He's thin as a string bean.

Charlotte hears Kenneth laugh and say, "I told Mr. Armburgey I was sure you'd have an extra chair." *Oh, that is so hilarious.*

"Such a happy surprise," Mother says. "You know that Gene and Sue can't come, don't you?"

"No, I didn't," Kenneth says. "Well then, all the more reason, Cecil."

Charlotte can picture Kenneth sweeping his hand with assurance, maybe grabbing a chair from the table and sitting on it backwards.

"Thank you, thank you," this Mr. Amburgerey says in a loud voice. "I don't want to cause any trouble."

"We're glad you could come," James says. "Here, let me take your jacket."

Charlotte stops ripping lettuce leaves apart. Well, at least James can be civil—he's backed her up all these years—but she'd plunge Kenneth's head into a bucket of grape skins if she could. She scoots back into the entryway and tries to get James' attention, motions that he needs to put an extra board in the table. He looks clueless. They're all still standing.

The loud voice sweeps and booms. "Such a warm day for this time of year. Such a surprise. Surprisingly."

James stands there with a hand extended, like he's the butler, but the man makes no effort to remove his jacket. Then James says, "We had warm weather this time last year, too. Oh, sorry; let me help you," he says to Gloria. "That must be heavy."

"Sure, okay; thank you so much. I just need a flat surface," Gloria says. She looks as helpless as a school girl, her long brown hair coiled and piled on top of her head like a lazy snake sunning. "Maybe the piano bench."

Charlotte remembers the milk heating on the stove, hears Mother ask, "Whatever did you make, Gloria?" What does she expect, a cold turkey? Charlotte will have to change the table seating arrangement; there's no time for an extra board. James had been taking such care: the way he stood back from the table and lined up the water glasses exactly. This Mr. Arm-whatever is something else, looks and sounds like a lighthouse, tall and erect, with a voice that sweeps the room. *Invasion by voice.*

Meg tells Gloria to take the cover off. There's a nervous rustling and then Mother exclaims, "A gingerbread house! Look at this, Charlotte." The others hover like they're at the manger.

Charlotte places one set of glasses back in the hutch. She has only eight of the crystal glassware etched with golden leaves. A gingerbread house. Of all the nerve. *Invasion by dessert.*

"I've only made one other one," Gloria says, smiling like a mannequin, still clutching the tray. Her face glows; the tops of her ears flame through strands of hair. "Some of the icing ran down on the window frames. I kidded Kenneth that the house was crying. It took me several nights, but I had a ball. The dough has to chill before you bake it. Then the wall and roof pieces have to harden."

"Believe me, what came from the kitchen didn't always sound like a barrel of fun," Kenneth says. He laughs and squeezes Gloria with his free arm; she quickly shifts the tray to her other side. The newcomer teeters unsteadily.

"Come look at this, Charlotte," Mother says again. She sounds like she's spotted the first bud on the clematis vine, right in the living room. "Peppermints, colored sprinkles. Take a minute, will you? Gumdrops! White chocolate chips. My, my, my. So much work." Then she points to James, standing frozen ever since the cover came off.

"Where can we put this? Don't be so helpless. The utility cart? That would be just the right size." She heads for the kitchen as if she's in charge. "How did you get everything to stick together, Gloria? Oh, be careful. We don't want this house spilled all over Charlotte's carpet." Mother acts like she's Mary, leading a giggling lamb.

"Melted white candy wafers made the 'glue'," Gloria says.

Charlotte whirls around the table, moves place settings closer together on one side. *Nine* people. "Don't steal that cart, Mother. I need it for the serving dishes." No, that makes it too crowded on the side. She'll have to add an extra spot at her end of the table.

"Put it on the washing machine, James," she calls loudly. "No one will bump it there."

"You must have worked on this for a week," Mother says to Gloria. They stand awkwardly at the entry to the kitchen, as if afraid to take the next step. "Did you follow a pattern or just make it up? Oh, ginger cookies are my favorite." She gushes on, as if she's switched roles with Gloria. "Can't we move something on the counter, Charlotte?"

"I need the table space for carving, and the pies are still cooling." Those pie crusts can't be bumped. Rope, crimped, and fork-scalloped. If only Father could see them. James didn't have time to take a picture because *somebody* came early. *Some bodies.*

Charlotte moves back and forth, in and out of the kitchen. Mother opens the folding doors to the laundry room, and then Gloria scootches the tray with the gingerbread house onto the washing machine lid. She stands back, adjusts a tiny candy cane, beams, wipes the palms of her hands back and forth. Did she lick off a finger? She puts an arm around Mother, as if they're conspirators. They slide out of the kitchen, back to the living room where James does his best with the chit-chat. Kenneth's school has a problem with overcrowding. Meg's college in Minnesota is on the quarter system and they're finished for the fall. That off-white lace camisole peeking through her hot pink shirt screams for attention.

Why doesn't James just tell everyone to sit down? He leans against the love seat with its back to the entryway. Charlotte carries the floral centerpiece from the end table onto the dining table. What a crowning glory! Even if the table is crowded. The elderly man hasn't moved past the entryway, swivels slowly, stumbles on the small throw rug, and whispers loudly, "Where's the bathroom?" Kenneth promises to show him and gestures vaguely down the hallway.

"Do you want to use our checkerboard or did you bring your own?" Charlotte calls out to Kenneth. He rubs his left ear lobe, a gesture she knows all too well. He must think it looks sophisticated, but really, he looks anxious. Did Gloria pick out those red suspenders for him?

"We'll just sit and visit awhile," Kenneth says. "After dinner we may need a couple of games. I like to play take-away, but Mr. Armburgey's best game is give-away." As if they'd set an arrival time in advance, Caroline and Chad emerge simultaneously, one from the long hallway, the other bounding up from the basement. Belinda is left crying at the top of the basement steps. There are more hugs, more introductions. Chad has on his shiny silver shorts that come below his knees. Flip-flops! Well, you have to make allowances for teens. The stranger's loud voice cuts through the house like a beacon. "Car-*rie*," he says. Everyone's caved in to Caroline's nickname, but Charlotte will resist to her dying day. She has a right to name her daughter.

"How are you, Kid?" Kenneth says to Chad, who looks like he's had a short night with his hair sticking straight up on one side. He slept through all of Charlotte's early morning trips to the basement to bake the pies. Now he takes a second, startled look at this unexpected old man. Okay, so his name is *Armburgey*, not burger. He's almost as tall as Chad. The man's dark spotted hands and cheeks, his wrinkled face, make Chad's skin look like a baby's. Except for the dried pimples. Charlotte has to keep on him all the time about using that anti-acne medicine.

"Sorry, I'm late, Mom," Caroline says to Charlotte. "What can I do to help?"

"Why don't you visit with Gloria? Show her my new baskets on the porch. Tell her about teaching in Appalachia. Oh, I know that was a year ago." Charlotte hesitates. "It's too early to fill the glasses with ice." It looks like the long night's sleep has done Caroline some good. But she wears that orange turtleneck, like she's cold. And her hair—if only she'd try to look more attractive, she'd have no trouble making a catch. "Check back in thirty minutes or so. You know how I am about working by myself in the kitchen. You don't want me getting nervous, do you?" That's the key: tell a joke at your own expense. Charlotte doesn't need to apologize for shooing Gloria out to the screened-in porch. She could have had the decency to ask what

Charlotte planned for dessert. James looks like he has things under control again, and Kenneth's keeping an eye on his friend. What did Kenneth expect? Cranberry juice and a Danish?

Several years ago, Charlotte made an allowance about carving the turkey. They didn't have to do everything by the book. When she was little, she'd loved watching her father do the carving at the table. But James had protested when she expected the same of him. It turns out, it's easier to keep the mess in the kitchen. She can do it herself: dispose of extra skin, twist off a stubborn wing with her hand. She rechecks her list of last-hour jobs. Thank heavens she decided on escalloped potatoes; she'd be rattled, trying to mash them and make turkey drippings into gravy at the last minute. Water into wine, Father always said. Meg scoots by with Chad, heading for the basement pool table. Is that a studded belt? Those aren't in any more. And riding on her hips, not her waist. If Chad didn't straighten up his room, well, Meg's probably seen worse. Mr. Armburgey's voice penetrates again. It's enough to make the china cups, waiting on the far end of the kitchen counter, rattle in their saucers. *Invasion by invasion.*

Gloria and Caroline linger by the laundry room, and Gloria explains how she had to keep the dough chilled. Mother should be able to see right through Gloria's attempt to upstage the pies. Oh, what's happening? Charlotte catches the tail end of Mother insisting that Mr. Armburgey sit in her hickory rocking chair; James must have dragged it out from her bedroom. She's going on about how the chair belonged to her momma and came from Arthur, Illinois, when Mother and Father moved to Wisconsin in the '60s. Like the man cares. The chair must suit him, though, because his voice softens into, "Fine, yes, very comfortable. Comfortably." Charlotte can't keep up with all the chatter, but when she places the butter plate and jelly dish on the dining room table, Kenneth is telling James about going to a convention for middle school principals and sitting beside a deaf-mute on the plane ride back from Detroit.

Charlotte arranges slices of white meat on one end of the platter—it looks moist enough—and places dark meat and a bulky leg for Chad on the end. No, scratch the leg; it takes too much space. But he'll ask, if it's not there. Back it goes; make room. Make do: the theme for the day. That's the key. She covers the platter with aluminum foil to preserve the heat, snips and rinses a few clumps of fresh parsley from the pot in the breakfast alcove. Everyone says she's the garnish queen. Thank goodness for James, keeping the conversation going in the living room, explaining one more time what he knows about Gene's absence. Or doesn't know. Kenneth tries to joke: "Less to worry about if the undertaker's not here."

She hadn't expected everything to be perfect—it never is—especially with Father gone. But Charlotte will still do her best, make the occasion as pleasant as possible. Mother will be impressed when she sees how Charlotte keeps her composure. Mother doesn't always approve of Kenneth's choices—Charlotte's sure of it—but Mother won't say anything negative. Give Charlotte forty more minutes; they can sit down early, rather than wait until one o'clock. That's better for Chad anyway. He must be starving. That's the key: flexibility. As long as Kenneth doesn't dominate at the table—talk world politics or something with Caroline—they should be okay. *If* Mr. Armburgey keeps his voice down. And *if* Chad doesn't crack his knuckles.

Where is this Mr. Armburgey's family anyway? Surely he has a son or a nephew who takes an interest in him. He looks so fragile; if he fell, he could break a hip right in front of them. Charlotte should have put that throw rug away. Maybe she can sneak over and stick it in the closet before they leave. He must be hungry, so thin like that. *Oh, no, not an alcoholic!* Maybe he doesn't get decent food where he lives. Probably not with candlelight anyway. Maybe he'll eat his heart out, right along with Mother. That bony frame of his will take on fat before their very eyes. At Charlotte's table. And Mother won't need to look so sad about the ones not here.

Chapter 9

Sometimes the way light shines on a room, people try to predict what will happen, whether for good or ill. On this day of thanksgiving the warm early morning sunlight coming in the picture window at Charlotte and James' house has shifted to partly cloudy and tentative. It's not ominous but something to watch.

When Martha peeked out her bedroom window at the sound of car doors this morning, she was having trouble with her hair. The bare maple tree in the front lawn seemed gaunt; a strange car sat in the driveway. Now the chandelier above the dining table has been turned on. James loves to play with the wall switch that dims and brightens the room. Four extra globes of light hardly seem necessary, but they must add to Charlotte's idea of festivity.

For Charlotte it's no small miracle that the food is all prepared. When she determines to rise above petty annoyances, she's a marvel to behold. The stranger, Mr. Armburgey, sits between Kenneth and Gloria on the side of the table facing the wall. No one could miss it when Gloria gave Kenneth a loud kiss before they sat down. Mr. Armburgey's head stays erect, his forehead shiny, his jacket securely on his shoulders in spite of James' best efforts to establish order. Those three can look at the painting of the old man giving thanks for his bread.

Carrie sits beside her mom at the kitchen end of the table. She doesn't mind being part of the cramped solution to the unexpected guest. Her stomach growls again. Someone else filled the water glasses, and so far, there's been no reprimand for her extended absence. Who knew that Gloria would slay the *shoulds* on the porch? Or that she'd had trouble knowing what *she* wanted to do with her life? Courage has begun to build again in Carrie; one day she's down, the next, up. She wishes she'd used more caution, though. What if Gloria spills something to Mom?

Charlotte can't wait for people to begin eating. Preparing food is like wrapping Christmas gifts and anticipating the squeals of delight. Every dish waits to make its statement: take, eat, enjoy. And don't forget to thank the creator. She brushes a piece of lint off her deep cranberry blouse. *Isn't anyone going to comment on the beautiful table setting?* It will never look the same again; there was no chance for James to take a picture either.

"All righteee," James says. "Are you going to be safe there, Martha, between those tykes?"

Chad and Meg grin. They don't look anything like cousins, but they've always hit it off, from rollerblading to loving U2. They've been talking about colleges while shooting pool in the basement. Chad will never play on television in the big money, sudden death 7-ball, but he can be a shark with his bank shot into the side pocket. He knows to use the same smarts when he drains three-pointers: feet planted, quick release. Meg has insisted that Chad could be a big fish at a liberal arts college, but he has other ideas. If they get to State in March, that will force some Division I schools to take notice.

Martha reaches for a hand from the grandchild on either side of her. "My, you're still chilly," she says to Meg. *Why doesn't the girl cover herself better?*

Meg is bracing herself for a long meal with lots of boring talk. Who ran into whom at the grocery store. Who was the latest to get overcharged by a dentist. There'll be news of Grandma's third cousin once removed who's died—so unexpected. And Meg's dad will be at his worst, telling weird jokes that aren't funny. Uncle James—entertaining as ever with talk about his precious cows. Mastitis ranks right up there. Meg's kept her iPod around her neck, and if she needs to, she can get up and use her Flip camera, crank things up a little. She got it on an experimental deal through the college. You turn on the audio pickup and nobody'll know. Charlotte's already given her the once-over. Scrutiny-mutiny. What did she expect, a Pilgrim outfit?

There's a little snafu when Charlotte forgets to light the candles. She can't really blame James; he's done double duty already. While circling the table to light the dripless tapers, she notices pinkish, cream-colored devices curved around the backs of Mr. Armburgey's ears. *Please, God, not a shouting match.*

James calls on Kenneth to say the grace—Mr. Armburgey quickly puts down his fork—but Kenneth defers to Gloria with "We take turns and this is her week." Chad can't believe it when Gloria keeps it short: "For all these gifts of food, family, and friends, we thank you, God. Amen." He groans when his mom suggests that sometime during the meal each of them should mention one thing they're especially thankful for. He has enough on his mind. If someone posted pictures on Facebook from last night's party, he'll be in it, deeper than the cows. And when his dad adds the bright idea for everyone to say one wise thing that's stuck with them from a teacher, Chad knows he's going to barf. Why can't family just hang out together, instead of have a program?

Carrie wonders if the requested teacher adulation is for her benefit but knows it may be to keep the conversation polite. As if to answer, Charlotte says she's thankful Caroline's back home, which prompts Kenneth to ask about her teaching plans. Carrie focuses on spreading jelly on her dinner roll and says, "I don't think I'll go back." Kenneth's eyebrows twitch, not sure if she means Appalachia or teaching. Gloria seizes his hesitation and says the food is "marvelous." Carrie, just as quickly, asks if the chives on the green beans survived the early snow. Charlotte has been staring at the centerpiece—no one has commented—and has to admit she didn't cover her chives in time.

"James, why don't you go next?" Gloria says. "What are you thankful for?" She dabs at potato juice with a dinner roll, makes a stack on her fork of one bite each: turkey, potato, green bean.

"My turn already?" he asks. He's watching Mr. Armburgey use his knife to slide sweet potatoes onto his fork. "I'm not very handy with words."

"Oh, come on," Kenneth says. "You farmers act like you're the lowly of the earth: too shy to speak, not a penny to your names. All the time there's more equity out back than I'll ever know."

Carrie has smothered a laugh. *Lowly of the earth.*

"Did I say something wrong?" Kenneth asks, pulling on his ear lobe.

"The word 'lowly' came up yesterday," James says. "That's all." He uses his spoon to scoop up the jiggling carrot salad.

"So you were talking about farmers?" Kenneth asks. "By the way, how'd you come out with the insurance company after the fire?" He covers his growing pile of nut meats with a piece of turkey skin.

James avoids Charlotte's eyes at the other end of the table. "I think it was lowly macaroni. Looks like we'll do all right with insurance for the machinery. Well, not sure about the New Holland Haybine. It always costs more to replace. Not sure what to do about the crib. Another grain bin would be nice."

"You could have been talking about the Amish," Gloria says.

"Or women," Carrie adds. "But no, actually it was Appalachians."

Mr. Armburgey helps himself to more candied sweet potatoes. They remind him of the way his wife used to fix them, back when he was still a car dealer, before everything turned sour. He swivels his neck toward James. “Kenneth says you’re outstanding in your field. Kenneth said that on the way here. Very humorous. Humorously.”

“Cutting-edge humor as always, Dear Brother,” Charlotte says. She watches her mother, who’s watching Mr. Armburgey chew vigorously. The man is adorable really, the way he eats with such gusto. How many rolls has he had already?

“You’re a dead giveaway, Dad,” Chad says. “You should wear a cap to the table—lots cooler—cover up your tan line.” He cuts off meat from the turkey leg. Better not grab the whole thing like no one’s around.

“It’s all in the clothes,” Kenneth says.

“A farmer is a farmer is a farmer,” Carrie says, grinning at her dad.

Gloria practically leaps at Carrie’s words. “Do you read Stein?” she asks.

“Stein who?” Carrie responds.

Charlotte sits back, reaches for the mother-of-pearl pin at the top button of her blouse. They’ve only begun, and they’ve already escaped how many dead ends?

Kenneth pokes around in his salad bowl. “Ever wonder why bill caps are so popular?” He had to insist that if Meg wanted to drive the new Prius, her cap had to come off, her iPod couldn’t be around her neck. “We ban them at school, but everyone must secretly want to be a farmer.”

"Amen," Carrie says, feels her mom look at her sideways. "Are these potatoes Kennebecs? Very good." Definitely not Yukon Golds, not reds. Mom shrugs.

Chad stretches his head high above his grandma's and says to Meg out of the side of his mouth, "Bill caps, the new prayer hats." That gets him a glare and a quick slice across the throat from his dad. Chad shrugs his shoulders and says, "I didn't mean anything bad. The English call them prayer caps. That's all. Good food, Mom."

The last thing Martha wants is a repeat of last night, but everyone's eyes have shifted to her. She scoops a spoon of cranberry salad mixed with potato juice, hesitates. "None of the things people count as precious should be laughed at. Momma always said, 'Judge not, that ye be not judged.'"

"Isn't it fascinating? What's considered meaningful keeps changing," Kenneth says. He hates trivial dinner talk. "Fads come and go, whether it's a denomination's rules or pop culture. What's hot at your school right now, Chad?"

Chad has turkey in his mouth. He shakes his head. Uncle Kenneth is like all school principals. They try to be buddy-buddy until there's trouble; then they stick it to you. He probably doesn't want to hear about getting creamed for playing euchre in the Commons during study hall. They were just using pretzels; it's not like they had money. And it was last period.

"A head covering isn't a fad," Martha says, "you know that, Kenneth. Some outsiders think that if we dress plain or keep to our ways, we're dumb or something. No one really wants to be lowly, but if that's what the Savior asks, then it has to be."

Meg squirms. *Well, hello, Grandma.* Dumb is how it looks. Silent women, following stupid rules. She picks at her food. Why does Charlotte put nuts in everything?

"It's unfortunate, isn't it?" Gloria asks. She wishes she could give Martha a hug right now. "I don't know if I'm an outsider in your eyes, but I try to be open to people of all traditions. 'Once a Mennonite, always a Mennonite,' you know."

Martha nods. "There's humility with the plainness; that's what's intended. More *demut*, less *hochmut*." What else was it she wished she'd said last night? "Time to put away pridefulness." She readjusts the linen napkin on her lap. My, my, all this laundry for tomorrow: matching tablecloth and napkins. Such a to-do.

"Here we go, folks," Charlotte says. "Must we? What can we pass for someone?" That's the key: take charge. She has no idea how the potatoes got so runny; she knows she added flour because she spilled on the counter and had to clean it up.

"I didn't mean anything bad, Mom," Chad says again. He cracks his knuckles on one hand, stops himself. He makes one little comment and gets the evil eye. "More gravy. Please."

The talk flounders until Gloria's eyes whoosh like the jags of color on her blouse. "You have practice this afternoon, Chad? On Thanksgiving?" Her eyes close.

"That's what I thought," Martha says.

Gloria quickly adjusts a hairpin. She doesn't mean to cause trouble; this family is so touchy. She's never understood why Kenneth and Charlotte give each other such a hard time. At first she tried to smooth things over, but she's learned not to interfere. "Getting back to teachers, my high school English teacher promised us, if we read *Hamlet,* we could make it through whatever life threw at us. 'To be or not to be, you know.'"

"It's not that simple, Mom," Meg says. "It could be: to eat or not to eat." She arranges dabs of leftover food on her plate, first an oval, then a star with five points.

"I want to go back a minute," Kenneth says. "Outward forms, like the prayer covering, are never sacred by themselves, right, Mother?" He turns his body to her, gestures with both hands. "We know that *life* is always sacred—no one here would argue with that—but when it comes to coverings, the ways we express what's precious, that should always be evolving, right?" He ignores Gloria who's leaned back behind Mr. Armburgey and is staring at him. "Otherwise, how does the Spirit move among us?"

Martha keeps her head down, squeezes her lips together. *How can this be happening?* "Yes, individuals change; we can't tell others what to do."

"Do we have to rehash this?" Charlotte asks. "No, we do not. Tell us about your school, Kenneth, or—I don't know—talk about people who mispronounce milk."

"Yeah, where is your *melk* of human kindness?" Carrie asks, poking an elbow toward her mom.

James grunts. "These sports announcers who refer to *Wes*consin basketball; they never get it."

"Ah, yes, people are strange," Kenneth says. "School kids, too. We have the usual middle school kids doing crazy things to get attention. Impulsive behavior, underdeveloped brains. Most of it's still pretty tame: messing with pepper spray, doing skateboard tricks on school property." Charlotte probably doesn't want to know how heroin in Madison, straight from Chicago, inevitably finds its way out to rural areas.

Chad keeps eating. That one night, someone brought jimsonweed seeds. Justin's pupils got so big, he looked like a monster; then he started picking fights. Chad ended up in a cornfield when the police came.

"Remember that one teacher I had, Mom?" Meg asks. "Sixth grade. Mrs. Emberley. She'd get so excited when we understood something, like plate tectonics; she'd hop around the room, clap her hands, and say, 'You got it; you got it.'"

"I had a teacher—short, biddy thing—," Mr. Armburgey says, "who pointed to her neck and said to me, 'You're a pain here.' Never forgot her."

"My English teacher does the dumbest stuff," Chad says. "Writes 'a lot' on the board every day. 'It's two words,' she says. Teachers are retarded. Not you, Carrie."

Meg laughs. "That same teacher who jumped around would say, 'Don't look at the clock.' It was always at the back of the room. 'If I catch you looking at the clock, you're outta here.'"

Relief spreads through Charlotte. This is more like it. Of course, this family can still have fun together.

"I was telling James about the conference I went to," Kenneth says. "A seminar on family dynamics, how it shows up in the middle school system. Pretty interesting, Charlotte." He strokes his beard. "The oldest child has a slight but significant edge in IQ."

"Pfft," Charlotte says. "You with the straight A's."

"No, no, that's not important," Kenneth replies. "But listen to the reasons for the differences. They found two key elements: the oldest child's role in the family, and the benefits that child gets from being the surrogate teacher for the younger sibling. That's why most families have the responsible one and the one who sneaks out."

"Forevermore," Martha says.

If Chad disliked his uncle before—. Holy crap! *Keep eating. Do not look up. Do not speak.*

"I still say, I could whip you on the golf course," Charlotte says, "but you won't put yourself in that situation." She figured that out long ago; the things Kenneth's not good at don't count for anything. He probably doesn't remember that school kids told him he threw a softball like a girl.

"It *is* fascinating, how stereotypes work against a person." Carrie feels the color rising in her cheeks. "I wasn't supposed to be good at math because I was a girl. I had to fight to get enough attention to be selected for Math Bowl."

"Really?" Charlotte frowns. "Well, it's the same with golf, I guess. I was supposed to like doing cross-stitch."

"You don't have to believe a negative stereotype to be hurt by it," Carrie says. "Like for Appalachians."

"Or the Amish." Everyone jumps in. "Farmers." "Housewives." "Teenagers." "Liberals." "Any woman." "What about the men?"

"Right. Any stereotype that hurts," Carrie says. "It can make you so mad, that you don't do as well—like on a test—as you would otherwise."

"I will never write *a lot* as two words," Chad says.

Carrie laughs. "That's called stubbornness."

Kenneth nods. "Ministers can be stuck, too. When a church wants to do things the way it's always done them, everyone stays stuck."

"Dry bones," Carrie says. "Not just Mennonites or the Amish. Most denominations."

"Right," Kenneth says. "Even your Faith Community group, Charlotte. I'll bet everyone goes along, goes along, until something out of the ordinary happens. Let's say, people want to have a weekly potluck, instead of sitting in rows to hear a preacher."

"You mean a potluck instead of church?" Martha asks. "No preaching?"

"Not at our church." Charlotte shakes her head.

"I'm just saying, hypothetically," Kenneth says. "First, the potluck looks trendy, a variation on the usual worship service, then it becomes a pattern."

"Boring," Meg says. "Weekly breast-beating around the table. Who has cancer and needs prayer. Who won a gold star promotion."

Charlotte smiles ever so faintly, but it's suddenly very quiet. Even Kenneth has his head down. That pink outfit on Meg is so last year's style.

"No way, *I'm* going to sit and be bored. *Or* look odd," Meg says. She touches her cell phone in the pocket of her pink shirt. Sometimes she can tell when someone is texting her, even when it's turned off. Maybe Sonja—.

Gloria glances at Mr. Armburgey. He must feel lost with all this talk. She'd tried to caution Kenneth: would his friend fit in? She wanted Kenneth to call Charlotte and tell her he was bringing a guest. He said he probably would, but then later he claimed he didn't know if Mr. Armburgey would come, didn't want to bring it up if it might not happen.

"'My thoughts are not your thoughts, nor are your ways my ways, says the Lord.'" Martha pinches her lips tight.

Mr. Armburgey's spoon clatters on the fancy china. He doesn't catch all that gets said; the young ones talk so fast. But how could you not agree with that sweet little woman across the table?

Meg folds her arms in front of her. *The woman has issues.* Spouting Scripture like it's the last word.

"Oddness can take many forms," Gloria says. "What's odd for me—or boring for you, Meg—may not be for others. That's huge. Right, Charlotte? Most people don't want chickens in their front yard." She grins at Kenneth. "Most people trust in their bank accounts. But it's not a priority for everyone. Some people thrive on a chance to be bold." She smiles at Carrie; her mouth spreads wide.

Chad wants to put his fork down, crack all his knuckles.

"We need to get an Eating Rights Act passed, so that slow food makes a comeback," Carrie says. "Safe food that doesn't ruin the environment. Food without chemicals; no more apples that look too large and bright to be true." She turns suddenly. "Like you, Mom, with your gardening and canning. This good food."

Charlotte looks at James, raises both eyebrows.

James remembers the guy's joke at the corn growers' association. Slow food is making love to a spouse; fast food is quick sex in a phone booth.

"We try to be ethical in our food buying, what little we don't raise," Kenneth says. "We buy Fair Trade, of course, whenever we can—tea and chocolate."

Meg fiddles with her phone, spins it on the table. "Yeah, one year you bought a heifer for me for Christmas," she says. "I was not pleased."

"Well, I vote for having money in the bank," Charlotte says. "Even if the bank owns our machinery. Where would we be since the fire? Even before." She stares at Gloria, then Kenneth; they have no idea what those different heads cost for the combine. They're so caught up in their super-spare lifestyle, so proud of their dinky black-and-white TV. Now a Prius? How inconsistent can you get?

Kenneth rubs his hands together. "But in the end, your assets aren't worth diddly, Charlotte. I mean the end-end. The moth and rust end, where you can't take anything with you. Oh, a big account can get you favored status at the bank, I suppose. A lower interest rate to replace that hay mower. Do you have a ditch mower, too?" He waits, but James keeps picking at dead skin on his palm. "Well, anyway, praise from the men in pricey suits. But when you're dead, you're dead. I don't mean to be negative here. Just adding some realism."

Carrie watches her mom get up quickly from the table. Kenneth is so right and so annoying about it. Why would anyone want to respond?

Mr. Armburgey grips the sides of his chair and leans forward to push back, but the legs stick on thick carpet. *Such a peculiar family.*

Suddenly Charlotte is back from the kitchen, asking if anyone needs more water. She'll focus on people's needs, maintain an even keel.

"I'll take a hill a' beans over nothing," James says. He doesn't care that Charlotte's glare could darken the chandelier. Kenneth is not going to have the final word. "Money keeps my dreams alive, even when times are tough. People who say money doesn't matter still talk about it all the time."

"So true," Carrie says. "We all need to dream. Even if it means starting small." She and Gloria talked about it on the porch, about pursuing what drives you, even if it feels reckless. But Carrie needs to maintain a balance: push her folks, but stay on their side. It *can* be both. Once-and-for-all, classroom teaching is not the only way, truth, or life.

"So, let's say that money keeps our illusions alive," Kenneth says. "We can all agree with that, right? I don't mean to throw water. The fire's out, right?"

"Very funny," Charlotte says. "You don't know what it's like, waking up in the middle of the night and James jumping out of bed. He can smell smoke like—like nobody. I hadn't even heard the storm moving in."

"A certain percentage of lightning strikes *will* hit barns," Kenneth says. "This just happened to be your turn."

"Pfft," Charlotte says. That's what James says: percentages.

"That must have been very scary, Mom," Carrie says. "It's not very reassuring to be a statistic, is it?"

Mr. Armburgey twists in his squeaky chair. "You people have the darndest problems."

"We strain at gnats, don't we?" Martha asks. Mr. Armburgey blinks.

"Where's the love?" Chad says in a high voice. It's way stupid to think you'd ever have too much money.

"See these?" James asks, stretching his hands over his plate. He turns them over, hands that are thick and crusty, tough from carrying buckets, putting out feed, managing without gloves whenever possible. *The old man is right.* Suddenly James pulls down on the bottom lids of his eyes so that the whites of his eyes look exaggerated. "See these?" he asks again.

Carrie gasps. "Dad! That's gross."

"James!" Charlotte says. "This is Thanksgiving dinner, not a monster show."

"Did you ever hear of a blind farmer with stumps for hands?" James asks. "What would I do?" He picks at more dead skin on his thumb.

"You rock, Dad," Chad says. His leg jiggles against the table; water splashes out of his glass.

"Don't talk like that," Charlotte says. A tiny drop of spit hits her own water glass. "You could bring trouble on us all, saying things that shouldn't even be thought." She stops, sits sideways. Heaven knows, she'd be a lousy caregiver if James were confined inside. It's bad enough when he talks about early retirement.

"We flirt with disaster every day, act like trouble can't find us," James says. "At least, I do. *Did,* until the fire. I'm thankful it wasn't worse." He pauses. "Did I say that before?"

A muffled "Yes," leaps out of Chad's mouth. "You always harp on the same stuff."

"We expect life to go on the way it is," Gloria says; her eyes close. "Until the unexpected happens. Or until we can't stand the routine anymore."

"Farming's full of change," Carrie says. "That's its nature. Now I hear the trend's back to open grazing again. Reversals. Like what Kenneth said about outward forms."

"Yup, leave the cow piles in the field," James says. He picks at his other hand. "I like doing things the same way. No surprise means a good day."

"What do you ever do for fun?" Meg asks James. "I mean, do you have a life?"

Mr. Armburgey's voice booms. "Kenneth says you farm by the seat of your pants."

James braces his hands on the table edge, teeters on the back chair legs. "Okay, okay. Go ahead, laugh at the poor farmer. Most of the time farming's fun. Except on the days when I want to get out. What's wrong with that?"

"Nothing," Carrie says. "But just because you start one way doesn't mean that's where you'll end up."

"Holding out your hands like that, James, reminds me of Daniel," Martha says. Everyone hushes. "When he was sick, he'd say, 'What can I do anymore?' He felt so helpless-like. Useless really. That was his big surprise." She rubs her thumb along the edge of the table. "He loved to go to work. Physical labor was good for the body, he always said. He couldn't stand watching Jim Henry try to learn the ropes. But everyone's time comes." Then she adds, "It's not what we have in fifty years that counts; it's how we live now."

Meg clutches her cell phone. *Grandma is prehistoric*. Covered with wrinkles; full of trite phrases.

"Come on, folks," Charlotte says, "we can do better." Has Kenneth always looked the other way when Meg wastes food like that?

"I'm counting on a pandemic," Gloria says. "I used to think it would be bird flu. Then I decided I had the wrong creature."

"Oh, my," Martha says.

"Sweet," Chad says. He taps his fingertips on his water glass. Gloria is as crazy as his English teacher. He did everything exactly the way she said—quotation marks, signal phrases—and she still had the nerve to write, *Follow the directions.* No teacher worship from him.

James watches Gloria fiddle with her hair again. She is one strange duck. Where does she go when she closes her eyes like that? "Sounds like you're looking for an excuse."

"Maybe I am," Gloria says. "Will be." Her eyes stay closed while she gathers her thoughts. "I didn't mean to imply that it's *good* to acquiesce to life's hard knocks. But I'm not going to fight for bottled water either. *That* would be suicidal."

Martha stares at the floral centerpiece. *Take deep breaths. Think about something else.* How much *did* Charlotte spend?

Gloria hasn't moved. "I suppose you've heard of Virginia Woolf?"

"Virginia who?" James asks.

"Never mind," Gloria answers. "She said someone has to die so the rest of us value life more. In her case, she walked into water."

"Goodness," Martha says. "Tried to walk on water?"

"No, no," Gloria explains. "*Into.* Intentional."

"Thanks for the uplift, Mom," Meg says.

"You are so right, Meg," Charlotte says. "*Must* we talk about death? On Thanksgiving?" James should know better, holding his hands out like that. This is the holiday to help Mother forget. "Chad, have you told your Uncle Kenneth what you're up to in a couple more years? *Your* dream."

Chad looks startled, gulps water, and says, "I'm going—. I'm going to be a dentist." When the laughs die, Chad makes it clear there's money to be made with a round ball. "Wait till you see my line of tennis shoes." He glances quickly at Meg. "I want to go East. That's where the media can start a buzz. I'll walk on for a year, if I have to."

"What's wrong with our state system?" Kenneth asks. "Lots of good teams right here in the Midwest—Madison, Iowa City. You want an education, right? Not just on the side."

Chad hesitates. "I want to get away."

"Too lowly here in the Midwest," Carrie says. Her dad snorts.

In the strained banter that follows, state loyalty takes over. They outdo each other at naming Wisconsin's treasures: "cheese curds," "fifteen thousand lakes," "ten thousand Amish," "oh, more than that," "World Dairy Expo," "the Packers," "Aldo Leopold," "thirty to forty thousand black bears," "could be more," "Cheese Days in Monroe," "Harley-Davidson," "*deep fried* cheese curds," "Fightin' Bob Fest," "the mustard museum," "endangered cranes," and, somewhat softly, "Leinie's."

James tells the story about the time he dropped Chad off at the dentist's office for a routine cleaning and went back later to pick him up, only to find Chad still outside the building. "I tell you; I had to drag that boy in. Practically sat on top of him."

Amid more laughter the mantel clock chimes la—la—la—la, and sunlight breaks through the clouds. Meg walks around, casually holding her Flip camera in front of her. Her mom asks, "You're taking *my* picture?" and Martha adds, "Oh, for pity's sake; what are you doing that for?"

"Recording your voice," Meg says.

"Whoa, where'd you get that gizmo?" James asks. The girl is decked out like a gadget store.

It's Mr. Armburgey's turn to be startled when Martha suddenly peeks around the floral centerpiece and leans her small body toward him. "Mr. Armburgey, what are you thankful for?"

"No, I've had enough," he says, holding one thin, spotted hand over his plate. "Very tasty, though. Tastily."

Charlotte glances around the table. Chad's still eating. Are those thirds? If Mr. Armburgey leaves the table—he's a dear one, all right—and wanders through the house, he might snoop in closets, call for help from the bathroom. He must not have learned: the pleasure of eating comes in savoring the flavors, not bolting toward the 18th green.

"Mr. Armburgey," James says, "what are you thankful for this year?" It's like he's talking to a vacuum salesman outside the picture window.

Mr. Armburgey looks at Kenneth, sees nothing to make him pause. "Same thing as last year." He does an Uncle Sam impersonation, pointing a bony index finger at Chad. "The United States Army saved us all." No one dares look away. "The Man had us ready to drop the bomb. Hiroshima kept us safe, sure as shootin'."

"We've talked about this before," Kenneth says to his mother. "Mr. Armburgey here is a veteran. He trusts the military." Kenneth awkwardly reaches for Mr. Armburgey's shoulder, pats his stiff jacket.

"We've agreed to disagree; we're friends, you see." Kenneth's hand settles on the back of Mr. Armburgey's chair.

Mr. Armburgey points at Chad again. "Join the Air Force, young man. Or Special Forces. That's the way to zap evil. Be the main Man's instrument. You want to fly away, right?" He hesitates. "You could go on mercy errands." He taps his spoon on the table in the direction of Chad. The candle flames lean toward Chad, right themselves again. "You'll make your family proud. General Eisenhower was my man."

Chad dutifully looks at Mr. Armburgey, even though it feels like a discarded bone from the turkey leg has leaped to his throat. Who said anything about flying? This man with a neck like a giraffe is scary. He's talking the real deal, way beyond Justin's GameBoy with guys getting light-sabered and stuff.

"President Eisenhower was a good man," Martha says. "Daniel voted for him. He thought we were safer." Is that girl's machine still on?

"I like to remind Mr. Armburgey," Kenneth says, "it was Eisenhower who said: 'War is the worst waste of financial, human, and natural resources.'"

"Isn't it funny—," Carrie begins, "strange, I mean. People latch on to different ways to be safe, or saved. Religion, the military." She can't resist. "And of course, money."

"For some, it's education," Gloria adds, raising her eyebrows at Kenneth and spreading her mouth in a wide smile.

"It's refreshing when we can disagree like this," Kenneth says. He winks at Charlotte. "Some people think you should just keep it to yourself."

"I never said that," Charlotte says, touching her mother-of-pearl pin. "I get tired, though, of the same topics over and over."

"It's hard to talk about sensitive subjects," Gloria says, nodding for everyone, "unless you're with like-minded folks. Good for you, Mr. Armburgey. Saying what you think." She pats his arm and mumbles something about pacifists at the table.

Mr. Armburgey licks the leftover jelly on his knife.

Meg can't resist taking a peek at her cell phone. "Oooh, I have six new messages."

"It's hard for people to be civil today," Kenneth says. "Politicians on down." He looks at Meg. "You turned that other thing off, didn't you?"

"Politicians on up," James mutters.

"Fragile people happened," Carrie says. "Fragile people have to yell. And take dogmatic positions."

Gloria nods; her eyelids close. "So true. Folks don't want their blood pressure to go up. They'd rather talk with people who think the same way. I don't mean just politics. Families, too."

"Most of us live in our safe, made-up worlds," Carrie says. "You don't have to be president to have a glass bubble."

"You people sure have the awfullest problems," Mr. Armburgey says.

Meg giggles; this is far better than most classroom discussions. "It's true; some kids in college won't finish reading an assignment if they disagree with the writer."

Charlotte sighs and watches Chad slowing down on his last bites of stuffing. "Don't you just love that sausage in there, Chad?" She nods for him. Mr. Armburgey didn't mean any harm. He couldn't know how she hates those TV ads: *"We'll make him a man."* You never know what's going on inside a young boy's head when he sees parades and appreciation days. And the National Guard comes around recruiting in school. It's not that Charlotte doesn't value freedom; it's just that Chad has much better things to do.

"The hand of the Lord protects us every day," Martha says to Mr. Armburgey. "Each and every one of us." She likes Mr. Armburgey's dignity, the way he holds his head up. She has to remind herself not to slump in the shoulders. "The Lord's mercy falls on the just and the unjust."

"With all due respect, Missus," Mr. Armburgey says, returning Martha's lean against the table. His voice softens. "It was the United States that intervened, the hands and legs of my comrades. That and Mr. Einstein's brilliance. Some of my buddies didn't make it. I still—."

"We've been over this many times, Mother," Kenneth says again. "Mr. Armburgey knows that we believe in forgiving our enemies." He spears his last two salad croutons; one pops off his fork onto the tablecloth. "Nothing prolongs war like needing to justify the first thousand deaths."

"Nobody wants to go to war, but somebody's got to do it," Mr. Armburgey says.

Smiles freeze on faces. Gloria looks stricken with an unnamed fever. James stretches and clasps his hands behind his head. In front of the picture window, dust particles dance in the light.

"Out of the strong comes something sweet," Martha says. She leans back in her chair and folds her arms across her layers of dress and sweater. "Just like for Samson. Honey out of rotting flesh." She pictures Mr. Armburgey as a young man, bent over a comrade, offering water. Maybe something stronger, something to stop the pain. Maybe he'd say his rosary. His fallen comrade would open his mouth like a wounded bird, beg for mercy. This Mr. Armburgey would cradle his buddy, put his own life at risk. It's right there on his face.

"All the time I was across the ocean," Mr. Armburgey says, clearing his throat, "doing things I didn't want to do—. There's no pussyfooting with an enemy." His hand shakes; he grabs the edge of the table. "The Allies were too slow. No rhyme or reason as to who made it out. I told Cora, time and again, 'God must have had his eye on me.'"

A dab of escalloped potatoes teeters on the lip of the bowl. Charlotte wishes James would reach over and scoop it up with his finger. She starts to motion, stops.

Martha's nod begins again, slower and more prolonged. "God's eye," she says, "like a parent watching." Daniel must have felt forsaken, too. She'd gone off to the Missionary Sewing Group that day.

Mr. Armburgey shakes his head; his eyes are red, watery. "I never had a parent who thought I was worth more than a toad."

Kenneth gently takes hold of Mr. Armburgey's jacketed arm, looks into his eyes and holds his gaze. He'll never understand what Mr. Armburgey went through. Something sacred out of the profane. He'll never convince him that violence multiples evil, that war is self-perpetuating.

Mr. Armburgey's voice becomes tender again. "'Everything's going to be okay, Cecil,'" he croons softly. "That's what I kept telling myself. I don't know why I said my name like I was somebody else." He fumbles with his napkin, dabs it shakily across his forehead. "I thought sure I'd be a goner."

Gloria takes his other hand. "You were ready to die, weren't you? The ultimate sacrifice."

Dear God, please! Make everybody stop. Charlotte gets this same feeling when fans are booing the refs mercilessly over a blown call.

Chad cracks all his knuckles on one hand. *What a dude!*

"That must have been awful, Mr. Armburgey," Carrie says. "Knowing you could be next. I don't know what that's like."

James fiddles with the end of his toothpick. "We all decide every day, what's acceptable risk. Could be putting in another crop of corn. Could be knowing how to handle an ornery school kid, I suppose. An ornery cow."

"Could be a friend," Carrie says, "messes us up."

"A companion," Martha says. "Up and gives up."

Charlotte focuses on the painting behind Mother: the elderly, praying man with his bowl and bread. *Lord, don't let this go on.* All the times she's had to remind James to be careful. Rollovers, runovers—she can't let herself think about all the things that can go wrong on a farm. Never wear loose-fitting clothing around that spinning shaft on the manure spreader. Never, ever, let Chad near the grain bin when that machinery is on.

"If life were a storybook—Carrie and I were talking about this earlier—we'd expect bad things to happen with lots of conflict. But we'd also know that order would be restored somehow," Gloria says. "That's huge." Her eyelids flutter.

"Why is everything huge, Mom?" Meg asks. "Life isn't a storybook. Things don't always work out. Even I know that."

"I know. I'm just saying—." Gloria closes her eyes. "We'd expect."

"How true. Order doesn't always get restored," Martha says. Will this meal ever be over?

"Stop," Charlotte says, standing. "I mean, wait, everyone. I need a break." Her voice shakes and for a minute she thinks she's going to cry. "Listen up. We're taking a break for fifteen minutes. Do whatever you need to do. Everyone get up and stretch. Go outside. Kenneth, show Mr. Armburgey where the bathroom is. Someone check on Sayeth."

Low murmurs and raised eyebrows greet her. "Are you all right?" James asks.

"Yes, I'm fine; I'm fine," Charlotte says. "Terrible things don't *always* happen." In a minute she'll plug in the coffee pot; she ground the beans this morning. "I need to walk around a little." She motions idly. Three beautiful pies will restore appetites. "Be sure to come back on time."

* * *

Charlotte wasn't inventing a new spoke on the wheel. Everyone knows the value of timeout for an unruly kid, of halftime to drink fluids and diagram a new defensive scheme, of resting the eyes at the computer. When things get tense, it's common sense: do things differently for a bit. Sure, Charlotte had to raise her voice a little, but that was a perfectly human reaction. No, she didn't want help in the kitchen. She's better off removing dinner plates and loading the dishwasher entirely on her own.

So it turned out that Martha visited with Mr. Armburgey on the loveseat after he used the bathroom. And Kenneth made a quick trip to inspect the corn crib with James, while Meg and Chad fed Sayeth and worked on the puppy's fetch technique. Carrie and Gloria sat down at the table again, after they added ice to the water glasses and refilled the water. Talking came easily, everything from the routines of work at Re-Use-It, to Gloria's high school home ec teacher who told them that ladies should walk lightly on the stairs.

Everyone kept one eye on the time and came back obediently, as directed. It was easy to pick up again, once seated. But the tones were lower, and there were more stolen glances toward the kitchen, making sure all was proceeding smoothly.

"That's prime toothpick art there." "How many fire trucks did you say came?" "No, Dorinda's with a study group overseas." "I wonder, too, what all the seasonings were." "A little too heavy for me." "Trapped in the corner, off-balance, but still drained it." "The bottom is just cardboard, covered with foil, then a layer of vanilla icing." "One teacher broke a foot, another got pregnant—put on bed rest—another had strep for a week." "No, a 20GB carries only five thousand songs."

When you consider everything, the meal *has* moved along. Mr. Armburgey stayed put; no cranberry salad dripped on the tablecloth. The candles got a workout with all the hot air, but that's why Charlotte buys dripless. There's little that can be done about the subjects that come up. Kenneth would be worse, if he knew there was an off-limits list. For his part, he wants to ask Chad if he's heard about the Amish woman who went up to President Bush during his re-election campaign and asked him if he was George W. Bush. But it's not worth raising Meg's ire.

"I don't mean to interrupt," Charlotte says, coming from the kitchen. "Well, actually I do." She stops the utility cart beside Caroline. "Look at these pies, folks, before I cut into them."

Ooohs and ahhs rise in a chorus around the table as everyone stretches to see. "Oh, I wish I wouldn't have eaten so much." "I won't be able to sing this afternoon." "Look at those perfect crusts." "The average stomach capacity is eight cups." "I'm going to be sick." "Anyone for a gastric rupture?" "It's only once a year." "Sick like a dog." "I need four stomachs like a cow." "It's a choice, you know: to stuff or not to stuff." "Coming home means eating too much." "How prodigal is that?"

"Mom, the apple pie looks gorgeous," Carrie says, "but I'm not a bit hungry."

"Exceptional," Mr. Armburgey says. "Very exceptionally."

Chad stretches his arms over his head and swings his torso, touches his right hand on his left shoulder, his left hand on his right shoulder. His back bones crack. Ooohs and ahhs make their rounds again. "Need some help, Mom?"

"Oh, no, no, but thank you." How nice of Chad to offer. Charlotte pushes the utility cart back to the kitchen. No one needs to see her get the first piece out.

Carrie follows and offers to serve the coffee, but Charlotte sends her back. "It's not quite time. We want hot coffee *with* the pie, not before. Tell Gloria about the dulcimer you bought. Keep talking, everyone," she calls out. "Be nice now."

Face blotchey, Carrie admits to falling in love with the shape and beauty of dulcimer wood. "Multiple loves. I couldn't decide which one: walnut, maple, pecan, all indigenous."

"You make it sound so romantic," Gloria says. Her mouth spreads wide. "They say falling in love is an act of the imagination."

"They do?" Kenneth responds.

Chad has a hang-dog look on his face; his stomach has been churning ever since he sat down again. "Sex is all in the head?"

Meg laughs, then covers her mouth.

"Beauty is in the eye," Carrie says.

Chad wonders how Meg puts up with her mom. The woman is total emo. Carrie isn't much better, naming a dulcimer "Diana." That's as goofy as Dad naming his cows. Chad's going to duck out before they start singing this afternoon. No standing around the piano for him. Sometimes his family gets all googley-eyed about a cappella singing, like they're having group sex or something.

The sun's light through the picture window moves like a spotlight across Mr. Armburgey's shiny forehead, over to Martha's prim hair bun. She's saying to him, up and over the floral centerpiece, "My, my," and "What a pity." Mr. Armburgey had told her in the living room how he spent his life savings caring for his wife Cora when she needed to be on a respirator. How she eventually died when they couldn't afford the home health nursing service. No money to rent oxygen tanks. And during those long years in the used car business, there was no insurance. "Zapped," he says now. "My benefit check from the military goes directly to Sheltering Arms."

Martha shakes her head, makes her trademark clicking noises. Mr. Armburgey is repeating himself; he lost his house, lost his business, lost his wife. Martha's losses have been small, compared with his. Well, it depends. But she still has her three children, even if they annoy her at times. She still has the house on Township Road, even if she can't live there. *The loveseat that Daniel made, it's still hers.*

"I couldn't save her; I couldn't," Mr. Armburgey says again. "Zapped." He leans his head farther across the table and says more quietly, "Death is something you never forget. It doesn't matter who or what: a life companion or an enemy."

"You try to forget," Martha says, "but it's impossible." She speaks softly, but is careful to enunciate. Mr. Armburgey will read her lips and understand every word. "I'm not sure I've forgiven, either."

"We old people have to stick together," Mr. Armburgey says. "I'm not proud of everything I did. But wrong isn't always wrong."

Martha nods and says, "We lowly old ones, we know how these things go." She follows the movement of her empty glass as she slides it around on the same spot of the tablecloth. "It's wrong to be too rigid about what's right."

"Whoa, whoa, whoa," James says.

"What are you two talking about?" Kenneth asks, tugging on an ear lobe.

Meg casually tilts the camera, makes sure the red button is pushed in.

Carrie watches Grandma and Mr. Armburgey. Something mysterious has happened. A desire for something beyond reach, something that might not happen but still is worth stretching for. Carrie would die for such a moment again. Those times of solidarity with Ryan: a bottle of Chardonnay, a bowl of portabella mushroom stew shared spur-of-the-moment. The loveliness of love, of companionship. A meeting of minds and hearts that had nothing to do with sex. Or very little.

Chad taps his drinking glass with his bitten-to-the-quick fingernails; Meg recognizes the rhythm and beats it out with head nods. They grin at each other. How weird, if Grandma were to get married again.

Kenneth's ears feel like they're burning. What kind of intimacy is this? Mother's green eyes, Mr. Armburgey's cautious smile. Strangers a couple of hours ago. Friendship has flourished in spite of the obstacle in the center of the table. Gloria smiles knowingly. She's seen it again and again, like when two people come from vastly different circumstances, hear a poem read, and smile shyly over words. Neither knows the particulars of the other's life, but each knows something of what matters to the other, because each understands the poem.

"Sometimes you have to do what you would never choose to do," Mr. Armburgey says.

"I've done that." Martha reaches in her dress pocket, finds an empty candy wrapper from when she last wore this dress.

Charlotte has slipped into her chair at the table, drawn by a magnet; this is no funk. The cut pies sit waiting.

Chad watches with fascination: who cuts back door, who gets blindsided.

Kenneth ignores his glasses, slipping off his nose again. Someone has to sort through this, take control. "Now, Mother, when did you fight in a war?"

"Did I say anything about war?" Martha asks. She's formed the name, IKE, with broken toothpicks. She opens her mouth repeatedly, as if exercising her jaw muscles, then closes her eyes, just like Gloria.

"What did she say?" Mr. Armburgey asks.

Kenneth shakes his head sharply. "She didn't say anything." He takes on his middle school principal's voice. "Who's being rigid,

Mother?" He's not going to let her get away with this, whatever it is. Duplicity? Probably not. Inconsistency, for sure.

Martha looks directly at Kenneth. "It could be unmerciful not to let a comrade die," she says. She stretches a corner of her handkerchief away from the rest of it that's balled up in her hand. "Aren't you going to serve the pie, Charlotte? Or do we get some of the gingerbread house first?"

"Well, of course, if someone—," Kenneth says. He stretches his red suspenders and holds them with his thumbs hooked.

"Did she say *not* to let a comrade?" Mr. Armburgey interrupts. "I didn't quite get it all." Things were going well—just the two of them—until Kenneth barged in.

Charlotte sits on the edge of her chair, caught between enjoying Kenneth's befuddlement and recognizing another sign of Mother's deterioration.

Chad's never seen old people like this. Grandma's in a zone; feed her the ball.

Kenneth mumbles something about hypothetical situations, but Martha will not be stopped. "You feel helpless, when someone is suffering," she says quietly. She wishes she could reach across and grab Mr. Armburgey's hand, but she can only rub her thumb back and forth on the tablecloth where it drapes over the edge. "You want to do something to stop the pain."

The sky has clouded over again and the chandelier seems much too bright. The center fronds of the living room fern stand guard, upright, caught between curving toward the shifting light and holding still from the energy at the table.

Charlotte glances again at the old man in the painting. Is he giving thanks or does he have a headache? He sits there, hands clasped, bowl and bread in front of him. She's always felt reassured by him, thankful for something, even if she can't say what. She used to think he was a Mennonite patriarch—white beard and all. The painting was much too common, but James brought it from his parents' home and wanted it somewhere. Teresa called it homey, so the painting stayed.

"Mercy is very complicated," Gloria says. "Doctors playing God. Relief workers distributing bags of rice and flour." *Oh, no, Martha's lower lip is wobbling.*

Carrie nods. "Doing good never works only one way."

"Cora died when we ran out of money," Mr. Armburgey says. His voice has taken on a rasp.

Kenneth grabs Mr. Armburgey's arm. "There now, Cecil, now, now." Kenneth turns his principal's gaze back across the table. "Let's not confuse apples and oranges, Mother. Not all suffering is the same. You and Mr. Armburgey speak from completely different worlds. For starters, where are you getting these comrades?" He looks over the top of his glasses.

"We all have comrades," Martha replies. She feels like she's six years old and arguing with one of those smarty-pants Weaver boys.

"You go, Grandma!" Chad says. Grown-ups get themselves trapped in crazy corners where nothing they say makes any sense. They're so sure they're right. "I'm stuffed; that's all," he says when everyone turns to him. *Omigosh!* He shouldn't have taken that last helping of stuffing; he's going to be slow at the shoot-around. Coach'll yell.

"I've had to call the vet far too often for an infected cow." James pauses; out of the corner of his eye, he sees Kenneth's body tense up. James clasps his hands like the old man in the painting, rests his arms on the table. "Plural cows. I know what suffering is. That sounds corny to some of you, but if my cows are sick, I'm sick. One time Doc left a syringe and lethal doses. I couldn't do it. Could not. I had to pay him to come back."

Meg groans, hits the STOP button.

Kenneth throws his hands in the air. "I give up. Mother can't distinguish among fruit; James thinks all mammals are of equal value."

Chad gives a fist pump and claps his large hands above his head. "Yessss! Bring it on."

Carrie can't help but smile. Chad's so immature; he's funny. Sixteen years old, going on twelve. Kenneth? Does he ever listen?

"Let me tell you. I'd milked those cows for three years, every day, twice a day. They're family. Comrades." James rubs his folded arms, moves one hand up inside his short-sleeved shirt, scratches. "I know cows. I know which ones need to be first into the parlor, which ones want to be last, which ones don't care." Kenneth will never understand. *That's his problem.*

"When Jesus was asked why he spoke in parables, he said that if he told the truth directly, people wouldn't believe him," Martha says. She stuffs her handkerchief back into her sweater pocket.

"The Pharisees had no time for Jesus' stories," Carrie says. "He broke all the social etiquette rules. All that *lowly* company."

"Yes, like the bent woman," Martha says. "Oh." Did she mention that last night?

"Mercy!" Charlotte says and clamps a hand on her mouth. That's Mother's word.

"For that matter," Carrie continues, her face flushed, "most of the Christian church today doesn't think much of Jesus' teachings, when you come right down to it. They sure don't practice it. Right? Look at all the hatred and intolerance that comes out of buildings with crosses."

Kenneth blinks. The girl has a head on her. "Yeah, ministers call them 'difficult texts' and set them aside."

"Whoa!" James says. His toothpick windmill has a large gap.

"Yes, that's enough," Charlotte says, standing. She'll borrow Kenneth's school voice again. This *is* her house, her table. Things get out-of-hand so easily; Mother speaks in riddles and James gets sentimental. Caroline—who knows what's with her. "Every time we talk about religion, we ruin any chance to be festive. What kind of pie would you like, Mother—apple, pecan, or pumpkin?"

"No, thank you; I'm full," Martha says. She didn't mean to get her children riled up. But Mr. Armburgey's story—. Well, he's a dear one. You can tell, he's been through the ringer, too.

"Mother," Charlotte says, "I *made* these pies." She waits, one fist propped on her hip, the parent-to-recalcitrant-child stance. "These aren't from that Donut Hole in Borgmann."

"I'll have my piece later," Martha says, her lips tight. "I want some of that gingerbread house, too." She smiles faintly at Gloria, turns over her dessert fork, balancing the tips of the tines on the table. "That was always Daniel's idea, that we had to have pie."

"Pfft," Charlotte says.

"Gingerbread house?" Chad asks. "With candy canes? I don't want pie either, Mom. Not now. I'm gonna be sick."

"What?" Charlotte says. How could this happen? Chad thinks he can get away with it because his grandma did.

James holds up his hand like a stop sign. "Better listen," he says to Charlotte. "Stomachs are fragile. Right now our hearts are all pumping extra blood just to keep up."

"Coach won't want guys slipping on chunks that came from a dead bird."

"Chad!" James says. "We don't need pictures."

"Look who's talking," Chad says.

"You're right," Charlotte says. "Of course, we can wait." The key to entertaining is to let people have their whims. "You can have pie after practice, Chad. Bring Nicole if you want."

"We'll probably go to her mom's place." Chad's lifted his chair farther away from the table and sits with his long arms hanging between his legs; a pale look has replaced the once-hungry wolf.

"Nicole?" Kenneth asks.

"Don't leave the table," Charlotte says to Chad. She doesn't mean to sound like she's begging, but you have to be direct sometimes.

"I'll kill off one of each, ma'am," Mr. Armburgey says, stretching his long neck to get a full look at the pieces of pie on the cart.

"Well, aren't you a dear," Charlotte says. Can you believe this dear old man? It's as if James has found a higher power on the chandelier switch. Kenneth's still rubbing his beard—his philosopher pose—catching hairs between his thumb and index finger. "Which piece would you like first, Mr. Armburgey?" she asks.

"Just put them all on one plate. One of those fancy plates there will be dandy. Dandily. Pile them right up," he says. His eyes shine; his forehead shines; the room shines.

Charlotte laughs louder than she intends. "You don't want these flavors running together." Kenneth remains oblivious. "I have plenty of dessert plates," she says. *She* will set the conditions. Mr. Armburgey's never learned: pleasure is in the taste *and* the appearance.

Everyone holds their breath; James would not want to see pie consumption added to the forbidden topics list.

"Pile them up," Mr. Armburgey repeats. He knows what he knows.

All right then, if Kenneth doesn't care about out-of-control pie, Charlotte will defer. She'll make do again. She expertly slides a spatula three times and hands Mr. Armburgey an ungodly pile of pie: dutch apple supporting pecans, with pumpkin jiggling on top. It's a miracle, the way it all stays on one plate.

Martha slowly begins to talk again, like having been on pause and then given the all-clear sign. "Those who aren't miserable, don't understand misery." She pats Meg's arm.

Meg replies ever so faintly, "One person's stuffing may be another's misery."

Charlotte looks at Meg sharply. You can't trust that girl.

"Very tasty, though," Meg adds. Her absent cousins, especially Sonja, won't believe what they've missed.

"That's so true, Martha," Gloria says. "You never know about others unless you let them show you what they see. Could I have just a teensy-tiny piece of pecan, Charlotte?" There's barely space between her measuring thumb and finger.

Carrie waves her hand like a barrier. "I'd rather have a piece of apple later. There's tomorrow, too." She glances quickly at Dad. "I'll remember what you said, Gloria. Let others show you what they see."

"Remember when Daniel asked if that piece of cake was a sampler?" James asks. "Where were we that day?"

Martha covers her nose and mouth with her hand, stifles a laugh. "Oh, we were all invited to Ruby and Delbert's for Sunday dinner. That was years ago. My, my, how can that be? Two other families were there, too. Jake and Maggie and—oh, I don't know who else. Ruby had cut those pieces of cake, and Daniel thought they were awful tiny."

"Father didn't really say that," Charlotte says. "A sampler."

"Of course, he did," Martha says. "I was there; I remember some things."

"It doesn't matter if Father said it or not," Kenneth says. "It's attributed to him, so he said it."

"Amen," Carrie says.

"Well, forevermore," Martha says.

Kenneth pushes his glasses higher on his nose. "Eating is the first learned pleasure, so let me be the first to say thanks to you, Mother. Thank you for life." He extends an open palm toward her, pats his protruding tummy with the other hand. "Born of a woman, every last one of us. And that's no unbiblical cord."

Amidst the titters and snorts, Charlotte says, "Nicely put, Brother. The first part." She's starting to plan a very quiet Christmas. One dispirited person at a table is enough. Two or three: that's a killer. Holidays still cause too much trauma for Mother. It'll be just the five of them at Christmas. Unless Chad wants to bring Nicole. Six. That would be just the right number. Let Kenneth spring for a Christmas ham at his house, if he wants.

Kenneth sighs when he accepts a piece of pumpkin pie. Sometimes you have to let caution go. "So why *did* the chicken cross the road?"

Meg groans.

"To get to the other side, of course." "That's what chickens do." "In my day we didn't ask why." "Yeah, the chickenness of the chicken." "Huh?" "Some say, the road erupted, forcing the chicken to see from the other side." "And God said, 'Thou shalt cross.'"

"That's enough," Charlotte says. "All of you." Her voice softens. The man's eating like he can't get enough. "What's your vote, Mr. Armburgey? Which pie is the best?"

"Pecan. It's always been my favorite. Sure as shootin'. Yours is top of the line, too."

"Well, aren't you a dear!" Charlotte says. She walks behind him, places both hands on his shoulders, and pats his jacket. "It's been such a delight to have you here. Unexpectedly."

"This pumpkin pie is very good, far beyond imagination," Kenneth says. "I think I'm falling in love."

Suddenly, Charlotte gasps and puts her hand flat on her chest. "The coffee." How could she have forgotten? She heads for the kitchen, calling out, "James, why didn't you say anything? Caroline! Someone should have reminded me."

"I got busy way down here. All this heavy talk," James says. He picks up a broken toothpick, digs between his front teeth for a lodged pecan piece.

"I can make a pot of tea later," Carrie says, "to go with the house."

"We can't throw out a full pot of coffee. I don't waste my pennies; these are genuine Guatemalan beans."

"Carrie, have you told us what you're thankful for?" Gloria asks. "And you, Meg?"

"Thanksgiving in Wisconsin," Carrie says.

"Cousins," Meg says.

"That's it?" Charlotte asks.

Meg shrugs. "I wish Sonja and Dorinda were here. To share the pain." She grins. "Isn't that enough?"

"Yes," Martha says. "It is. We need the whole family together—all the cousins—not just when there's a funeral. I want everyone at my place for Christmas."

"Mother, let's be realistic," Charlotte says. "You're not moving back in a month. But we're all agog—did I use that word correctly, Kenneth? We're waiting, Mother. Aren't you going to say some little smidgen of thanks?"

Martha stares at the centerpiece. "The meal was delicious, Charlotte. So much bother you went to. I don't know how you do it. I'll be grateful to go back to softer chairs, though."

"The coffee," Charlotte says. "Won't anyone?" She doesn't mean to beg. Okay then. *No coffee. They're on their own with the gingerbread house, too.*

Chapter 10

Charlotte isn't sure how it happened, but out of nowhere she and James are getting into Kenneth and Gloria's fancy blue Toyota Prius and riding along to the cemetery. Everything was going according to plan in the kitchen with Gloria and James helping Charlotte clean up. She didn't mind a little help with the mess. Caroline was talking with Kenneth in the living room, so that looked promising. But when Chad left for the shoot-around—he suddenly said it started an hour earlier—and when the dishwater for the pans was so dirty it had to be changed, Kenneth came to the kitchen entryway, stuck his head around the corner, and said, "We've got an idea. Instead of singing around the piano—everybody's pretty stuffed—how about if we all go visit Father's grave?"

"What?" Charlotte asked. She turned halfway around from the sink.

"Calm down," Kenneth replied, "it's not going to hurt." He leaned his shoulder against the door frame, one thumb stuck inside a suspender.

"Why? Everyone? We'd have to take two cars," Charlotte said. She ran her fingers along the lip of the potato baking dish, felt for crust on the bottom.

"Gotta be back before four," James said, drying the serving spoons with a tea towel. "Three-thirty to be safe."

"Yeah, Carrie said she'd help you with the milking." Kenneth just stood there, looking nonchalant.

"Still have to be back," James said. "Cows don't care whether it's me alone or a team of workers. All they want is relief."

"I know, I know," Kenneth said. "What do you think?"

"Was this Martha's idea?" Gloria asked, her hands in the pre-wash pan, using a plastic scraper on the roaster.

"No, not really," Kenneth said, moving into the kitchen, nosing around. "I brought it up; Mother's okay with it, though. What's for supper?" He lifted a piece of aluminum foil on the leftover turkey.

"What about—?" Charlotte asked, tossing her head in the direction of the living room.

"Mr. Armburgey?" Kenneth asked. "I'll check again."

As it turned out, neither Mr. Armburgey nor Mother went along. She offered to teach the man how to play Chinese checkers instead. At the last minute Caroline stayed behind, too, when Meg said, "No way; too bizarre," as if playing Crazy on her phone were perfectly natural.

"You old folks, you go on," Caroline said, with a wave, "we'll stay here with the youngsters." That got a smile out of Mother.

So here Charlotte is, riding along in the back seat with Gloria in this car that still smells like the factory. No wonder Kenneth couldn't afford raspberry truffles! The four of them must look like two old couples out for a Sunday drive on Thursday. James sits in front with Kenneth and gawks around like he's a little kid in a cockpit. There's nothing special about the seat coverings, no leather trim. Plenty of leg room, though, and no hump in the floor. Whew! It's a relief to get off her feet; she should have worn support hose today. Kenneth is so proud of his keyless system, says he's saving the earth from the noxious fumes of his beat-up Malibu. Why would anyone want to know at the push of a button what your battery is doing?

"What's that?" Charlotte asks. How long has Gloria been talking?

"I said, it's a relief not to have to sing songs about being washed in the blood."

"You mean, not going to a regular church?" This must be all Gloria and Kenneth think about. They sound like they're movers and shakers, but really they're stuck with being different.

"No, at your place. This afternoon."

Charlotte stares at Gloria. "I'm missing something." They've always looked forward to singing "Wonderful the Matchless Grace of Jesus." James and Kenneth rumble along on the bass and the women keep climbing to those high notes at the end for *Praise His name.* It's exhilarating.

"Oh, you know, sooner or later, we sing songs about how sinful people are," Gloria says. "*Whiter than snow,*" she sings, "*yes, whiter than snow; now wash me and I shall be. . . .* That kind of thing." Her soprano sounds purposely sappy, trapped in this quiet car.

Kenneth stretches his neck to see Charlotte in his rearview mirror. "You like that? Those words?"

She shrugs; Kenneth knows she didn't like being hammered every Sunday: "Repent, for the evil days draw nigh." She looks out the window at harvested fields; some farmers leave so much stubble. Soon there will be fresh snow that stays and covers the brown. "I go more by the melody," she says. The inside of the car seems to shrink.

Kenneth drums on the steering wheel with his thumb. "Don't you think it's interesting what we keep from our heritage and what we discard? Some people say our children will come back to the values of their grandparents." Then with an exaggerated boom he sings, "*Onward Christian soldiers, marching as to war.*" Drumming again, he says, "Sounds like a pagan sacrifice. Oxymoron heaven."

"Never thought about it," Charlotte says. If she's going to play dumb, she might as well go all the way. Next thing she knows, Kenneth will sound off on his no-pie-in-the-sky theory. Right when people were coming through the visitation line, she heard him tell Father's minister that heaven might be a made-up concept. Some fancy word about helping people feel better.

"An eagle!" James exclaims, pointing. "Top branch. See it?" He twists in his seat to see if others have spotted his find. "A bald eagle."

"Neato," Kenneth says.

"Such a majestic bird." Gloria's head stays craned out the back window. "So wonderful that it's no longer endangered."

Charlotte taps the seat in front of her. "Do you know you're getting a good-sized bald spot in the back, James? A budding eagle look?"

"Ouch," he says and slaps his hand over the bare spot.

Kenneth adjusts his rearview mirror again and asks, "So how's it going, having Mother live with you?"

James acts like there's a gnat bothering him in the front seat.

"Okay, I guess," Charlotte says. "Not ideal, but what option is there?"

"Do you think she's happy?" Gloria asks.

"Well, sure," Charlotte says. "I guess. Why wouldn't she be?"

"Comfortable, at least," Gloria says. "Sometimes I wonder if it was hasty—the move—but she was so distraught after Daniel died."

"She puts on three layers of clothing, says she's not used to air-conditioning," Charlotte says. "That was summertime. I'm sure it's hard for her, adjusting to everything. But would she be content anywhere?"

"She seems more—how shall I say?—confrontational," Kenneth says. "That's not the right word, but she has a streak in her. Do you remember that from before? I always thought she was so quiet. But in the living room when you were cleaning up, I was explaining to Mr. Armburgey—just by way of background—that the Anabaptists weren't always nonresistant. She acted offended when I repeated that one group of the original Anabaptists was militant."

"Here's your turn," James says. "Militant?"

"Isn't it another mile?"

"Turn here," James says. "Here!" That's the same voice he uses when he's irritated with Chad. "You could ask Martha."

"Whether to turn? I'm sure I've used John's Creek Road before," Kenneth says. "That's next, right? Oh, well." He sighs. "Ask her what?"

"Ask Martha if she's happy," James says.

"Good idea," Gloria says. "Why not talk about it with her?"

"I'm really hot," Charlotte says. "Could we have some air back here?" She watches Gloria gather up her hopeless hair again. It must do something for Kenneth. "Mother doesn't talk about her old house so much anymore. That's a good sign."

Kenneth makes a show of twisting dials. "Anyway, my point was that Anabaptist groups have always had variation. But Mother pooh-poohed the idea that the first ones were radical. Any historian will tell you, they resisted the institutional church and disagreed with other Reformers."

"Now take a left," James says. "I didn't know that."

"Here?"

"That's what I said," James replies, pointing.

"This sure is different," Kenneth says.

"That's *your* thing," Charlotte says.

James coughs and shifts on his seat like his hemorrhoids are bothering him.

"Good one, Charlotte," Kenneth says. "It's like everything else; there's not just one kind of conservative, or one, clear definition of progressive." He looks at James but barely gets a nod. "When people know one Mennonite today, they think they know *all* Mennonites."

"They're all Amish anyway," James says so quietly that Charlotte barely catches it.

"How's that?" Kenneth asks. "Oh, right. Everyone who's odd is Amish. You got it; I'm Amish." He laughs loudly, snaps his suspender. "Anyway, there never was one definitive Anabaptist group, just an amalgam of multiple groups. That was my point. Of course, people who have the power in any branch claim that *they* are *the* pure deal. Well, Mother didn't—."

"Kenneth, aren't you on the wrong side of the road?" Gloria asks, craning her neck to see in front of the car.

"Just a tad," Kenneth says. "No center line on these back roads, so it must not matter." He laughs again, slaps his thigh. "Oooh, it still hurts to laugh; I'm way too full."

"One time I popped over a hill," James says, "and there was an Amish guy right in front of me; his team was pulling a wagon loaded with hay. Lucky for me, no one was coming the other way."

"I'll say." Gloria settles back in the seat again, flips the trash receptacle.

"The Amish won't be out working on Thanksgiving Day," Kenneth says.

"Buggies could be out," Charlotte says. "Mother says they used to go visiting on Thanksgiving if they didn't have company."

"True, so true," Gloria says. "Slow down a little, Kenneth." She puts her hands on the sides of his seat, pulls back.

"In spite of the jokes, the Amish remain a model for us," he says. "They understand, it's not more money we need; it's fewer wants."

"Hmpf," James mutters. "I know some who are never satisfied. An Amish millionaire is not one of your oxymorons."

"They don't flaunt it, though," Kenneth counters. He rubs his beard, scratches a little. "Way ahead of their time with farming, the way they care for the soil."

"A laughingstock for the big ag boys," James says.

"Did you know," Charlotte asks, "that when Mother was growing up, her grandfather would come all the way from Illinois to visit them in Nebraska at Thanksgiving? She's so taken up with reading her momma's diaries."

"What an undertaking—a trip like that back in the '30s," Gloria says. "It must have meant a lot."

James points. "Next turn. There's the sign."

Charlotte sighs as they turn into the cemetery lane. "Why are we doing this? Who goes to a cemetery on Thanksgiving?"

"Why not?" Kenneth says. "I haven't been back since the burial. Weren't we talking about spontaneity this noon? Yikes! This lane needs to be graded." He pats the dash of the car. "Mother didn't like it that I didn't come over Memorial Day weekend."

"You can't live your life by what she doesn't like," Charlotte says.

James half-turns. "Or what *anyone* likes or doesn't like."

"True, so true," Gloria says. "That's huge."

They climb out. Four people, four car doors. Charlotte likes the sound: thump, thump, thump, thump. All the same note. You can tell it's solid. Good for Kenneth, allowing himself a little creature comfort.

"Oh, I love cemeteries," Gloria says. She raises both arms like she's at a praise service, moves gracefully on her tiptoes. "All flesh is as the grass." Her blouse zigs and zags with her movements.

"Good grief," James says under his breath.

Charlotte reaches for his hand on the uneven ground. "Don't look."

"I see people are still dying to get in," Kenneth says, walking past a fresh grave.

"All these people, freed from their earthly cares." Gloria stops twirling, comes back. "My favorite cemetery—rows of tall cedars all around—is in St. Paul. It takes my breath away. Literally, I get goose bumps. That's where my sister is buried. It's been a year now."

"Don't you think we should tell them?" Kenneth asks. He gently puts his arm around Gloria's waist, holds her back.

She whirls away, her arms outstretched, throws kisses to the sky, then stops at a grave, reads the wording on the tombstone, straightens. "The cemetery where Rhonda's buried has gorgeous, stately tombstones. So peaceful. I couldn't dance, though; not then." She looks back at Kenneth. "Tell them what?"

Charlotte leads James in the direction of her father's grave. "Let's get this over with before anyone else comes." She's here to honor Father, not get caught in a one-woman show. "Are people going to leave their vases here all winter?"

"No one will see us," James says. "Everyone else is smart enough to be watching the Lions and Cowboys on TV."

"Why did Father choose this tiny cemetery?" Kenneth asks. He walks on the vehicle path, two tire tracks with a row of brown grass and weeds in the center. Then he cuts across, walks carefully between rows.

"Not sure I know," Charlotte says. "The folks picked out their spot a couple years ago. Oooh, that one's sunk way down."

"Maybe no vault," James says.

"Why would you want your picture on a tombstone? Does that last?" Charlotte pulls James along. She reads names quietly: "Malichky, Severance, Krogulski. It's like Father didn't want to end up in a cemetery full of Mennonites."

"Yeah," Kenneth says, "you'd think he'd want to be buried with his own. Not that it matters where your bones are. Or if you still have bones. Did we tell you? Gloria and I are planning a green burial."

"Hey, over here's a Yoder," James says.

"Look at this," Gloria calls. "An infant, only lived three days. No name. 'STUMPF INFANT.' And another one, the same family. Only twelve years old. 'John Michael. Under His Wings.'"

"Look at that," Charlotte says. She points to a jack-o-lantern, the mouth and teeth melted, the whole pumpkin sagging. "Why would anyone—?"

"Keep the evil spirits away?" James offers. "There it is," he says softly.

They stop at the foot end of Father's grave. It goes through Charlotte, the ache, just like other times. ROPP in big letters. Mother's name, too; the year of her death left blank. Etched generic flowers on light gray granite, circled by leaves forming a wreath. Their own names: Kenneth Lynn, Charlotte May, Gene Daniel. Gene's favored status. Not that Charlotte wanted to be tagged with Martha for a middle name. May is bland enough. Charlotte puts her head on James' shoulder. He nestles his cheek against the top of her head.

Kenneth stands with his thumbs hooked in his red suspenders. "Father must have liked the view." They all swivel in the direction of rolling countryside, clumps of bare trees, brown stands of prairie grass. The air is heavy with gray clouds. "We want to have our ashes scattered in a wooded area. Or maybe a wildflower meadow."

Gloria puts one arm around Kenneth's back, the other across his belly. "It's *so* peaceful. We should have brought flowers," she says.

"The centerpiece?" Kenneth whispers loudly.

Gloria slaps him on the arm.

Charlotte stiffens and pulls away with James. Well, Gloria could have brought the gingerbread house.

"What shall we sing?" James asks. "Just kidding."

"It's beautiful here in the summer. You should see it early in the morning when the grass is wet, before the sun gets hot." Charlotte looks back toward the entrance gate, its large metal frame, silver against the dark blue sky. The Prius shines like a new toy.

"Let's sing something joyful," Gloria says, "something Daniel would like. 'How Great Thou Art'?" She wanders away when no one responds.

"Maybe Meg's right," Kenneth says. "It does feel odd today. Here's what we never told anyone: Gloria and I used to have dates in cemeteries."

"You what?" Charlotte asks.

"When I was in grad school and Gloria would come for a weekend, we'd scout around. Iowa City has some great ones."

"I'm scared to ask what you did," Charlotte says.

"Oh, we were tame," Kenneth says. "We liked the novelty of it. I've wondered recently if Gene sells biodegradable caskets. Any of the soft woods like poplar. Bamboo or willow are good, too. They come with wooden hinges and handles."

"The Amish use pine, but I have no idea what Gene sells. I'm not shopping." James checks his watch. "My favorite cemetery is over on Township Road beyond Martha's house. There's a gravesite there that has a red gas can by a tombstone. I'll bet anything that guy's favorite saying was, 'Give 'er the gas.'" He imitates a noisy motorcycle starting up.

"James," Charlotte says, "what's gotten into you? Maybe we're all spooked." Tomorrow this will all be history. Teresa said to give her a call. "Yes, Father would have liked the way these hills tuck into each other. I miss him so much. It's strange, how all of a sudden, he's gone and that's it. You know it will happen sometime, but still—. I can't call him up anymore, tell him about the everyday things." She sighs. "He was wonderful."

"He wasn't perfect." Kenneth crams his hands into his pockets. "Always telling me not to dawdle."

"So why did you want to come?" Charlotte asks. "Just to say bad things?" She should have known better, should have been satisfied with the meal. No bonding will ever happen between her and Kenneth. That ended when they were kids and hid in the arbor, sneaking grapes.

"Saying someone isn't perfect doesn't mean he's 'bad,' per se," Kenneth replies. "I'm being realistic; that's all. I don't need a perfect parent. Most of our memories come from our needs, you know. Need a wonderful parent? You can have one, as soon as he's dead and the shock wears off. 'Memory makes the heart grow fonder'—that kind of thing. The best times take over, and people wonder why they hadn't been best of friends."

"Kenneth." Now it's Gloria's turn to chide. "Why wasn't that the case then for Mr. Armburgey and his parents?"

"Good one," James says. "Did Gene ever tell you the joke about the two badgers that met in the cemetery?"

"James!" Charlotte twists out of his arm. "Don't you dare. Those weren't badgers, either."

Kenneth folds his arms across his chest. "Woodchucks probably. All I meant was, you don't honor someone by pretending he was a saint."

Charlotte shakes her head. He always puts a negative spin on things. Sometime he'll wish people had better things to say about him.

"So what's your favorite memory of Father?" he asks.

Is he serious? His face is open—no smirk—like he wants to know. She begins cautiously. "Math, for one. I had trouble with story problems, but Father was very patient; he helped me reason things out. 'Now don't jump to conclusions,' he'd say. Or, 'You're guessing again.' But he never laughed at me." Charlotte looks for permission to go on; Kenneth hasn't moved. Gloria is still oohing, bending, mumbling. "He bragged about my typing, too, said I was a whiz. Compared with Mother, when I told her I did so well on the last typing test that I got called up to the stage in Assembly, she said—listen to this—she said, 'You should be glad someone noticed.' I'll never forget that. Like I didn't really deserve it."

"Yeah, Father was a good teacher," Kenneth says. "When he took me out on back roads to learn to drive the stick shift, I'd get halfway up a hill and he'd make me stop. Then he'd tell me to start again in first gear. Sometimes I'd roll way back and end up at the bottom before I could get going. You're right; he never made me feel dumb."

"I can't change *my* memories of *my* dad," James says. "Not everything's made up." He jams his fingertips into his back pockets. "I can still hear him say, 'What a *stupid* thing to cry about.' It didn't matter whether I got mad when my big brothers made me sit in the middle of the back seat—they got the windows—or if I had tears when our collie, Skippy, got run over." He rubs his arms slowly. "Chad thinks I don't show emotion; well, you didn't do that around my dad.

Not us boys. So no, I don't buy this whole make-up-whatever-you-want deal, like it's a hamburger place where you choose your toppings."

Charlotte takes James' hand and rubs it. He's her rock. He may not have deep thoughts like Kenneth, but he's solid gold.

"Yeah, I know what you mean; I'm not cut out that way either. Gloria is the expressive one. That's a good one about the hypothetical hamburger," Kenneth says, grabbing Charlotte's arm like he knows she's going to try to walk away. "I still think—."

"Not another sermon." She won't let him get on his soapbox again. "I came here to honor Father. When he came home from the hospital, I expected him to get better. I was always upbeat for his sake. I didn't know he could leave without really saying goodbye."

There's no stopping Kenneth. "I still think we make up what we need. It's not only parental memories. If you want a vengeful God, you tell stories from the Old Testament: 'God smote the Philistines.'" He waves his arm for emphasis, makes his voice a trumpet, then quiets. "But if you need fairness, you create a just God, someone who keeps things even. Or *wants* that for everyone. The new dispensation."

Charlotte pulls away. "Where *were* you those days, those long, last days of Father's? All taken up with your trip to Russia, right?"

Kenneth barely hesitates. "At least I wasn't making up cheeriness."

"Did you see that one?" Gloria comes back, stumbling, babbling. "That person was ninety-nine. I wonder if he was heartbroken that he didn't make it to one hundred."

Charlotte hasn't moved. Cheeriness? Could Gloria be quiet, just once?

James turns his hand sideways to look at his watch again. "We've got to get going. Seriously." He puts his arm around her and they head for the car, in step somehow, in spite of the uneven ground. His sweat comforts her.

"Come here, everyone," Gloria calls out. "This is how I want to be remembered." She motions big for them to come.

"Read it for us; we'll trust you not to make it up," James says. "It's three-fifteen. We'll be okay if we go directly."

Gloria looks entranced, her hands clasped behind her. "We need to come here again when we have more time, Kenneth." She slowly moves toward the gate. "Oh, this has been wonderful," she says, swaying slowly. "*Will the circle be unbroken,*" she sings, *"by and by, Lord, by and by?*" Her lilting voice carries easily across the headstones. "It's been a taste of heaven." She half-runs to catch up, skips, spreads her arms like wings, lifts her face to the sky again, as if there are no ruts to watch for.

Charlotte and James wait by the car, staring at each other. He flops his hands onto the roof; his wedding ring clanks. Neither one needs to say anything. When they get back to the house, Charlotte will set out snacks. Fresh fruit. Nothing heavy. Oh, the cheese curds; they were fresh yesterday. She'll do the best she can for Mother's sake. Tomorrow she'll call Teresa, unload. But right now she must get into this car again.

Gloria joins them with "Sorry, I'm so slow. If Rhonda had done the preventive stuff, she might—. Oh, well. Can't change that now. She lived her life the way she wanted. She thought doctors ran unnecessary tests for the money." Her seat belt finally clicks. "Don't you think it's funny, how medical clinics try to add homey touches?"

"Never thought about it," Charlotte says. James fidgets. "Are we idling?" It's unnerving, not knowing if the engine's running.

"Where I go for my wellness checks," Gloria says, "the room where they do the mammograms has a wallpaper border with old-timey white-frame houses." She dabs her forehead with a tissue. "A farmhouse with pastel flowers growing along the white fence. Isn't that great, James? Farmsteads bring comfort."

"Having a mammogram must be like coming home," Kenneth says, smiling at Gloria's laugh. "Being with family."

"Why aren't we moving?" James asks. "I can walk across the fields if the rest of you need to soak up more cemetery air."

"You're right," Kenneth says. "Sorry. Those cows can't wait. Watch this." He shifts into reverse and points to the back-up camera.

"Nifty," James says, barely glancing at the fuzzy image of a fence that runs behind the cemetery lane. "When *my* cows come home, they want attention."

"Kenneth and I are at our best, too, when we keep on schedule," Gloria says, "but it's been *so* much fun to do something unplanned. There's nothing like a cemetery to take the ho-hum out of life."

Charlotte can feel Gloria's eyes on her. *Do not turn to meet her glance. Do not say anything more about death.* Maybe Gloria will be worn out and close her eyes for more than three seconds, give Charlotte some privacy.

They drive slowly on the bumpy lane. Kenneth's chin juts out, as if keeping the right tires on the ridge is everything. "Don't you wonder, James, what it will be like when you don't have to get up to milk those cows anymore?" he asks. "I'd get tired of always being tied down."

"To be honest, I don't want to think about it," James says. "When I'm forced to think about change, I like it even less."

"But change can be invigorating," Gloria says.

"If I put James' shirts at the opposite end of the closet from where he expects them, he gets upset," Charlotte says. "He wants the short-sleeved, light ones first, then the dark; then all the long-sleeved: light ones, then dark. Then the sport coats. Then suits. Never put anything dark to the left of light. That would be upheaval."

Kenneth turns onto County Road X, and James tries to grab the wheel. He points the other way with his thumb and says the obvious, "You're going the wrong way."

"Let's try this," Kenneth says. "I never like to go back the same way I came."

"It'll take longer. You're messing with my cows."

"He's messing with you, James," Charlotte says softly.

"Do your cows get ornery?" Kenneth asks.

"*I* get ornery," James says. Charlotte hears him fiddle with his metallic wristwatch; he leans back against the head rest. A little tuft of hair sticks up above his bald spot.

"Oh," Kenneth says, "by the way, what I said back there about creating your own God, I hope you understand I'm not against religion. I just think we should be aware of what we do." He shoots a quick look at James. "Did you notice all the tombstones with crosses?"

"Not that many," Gloria says. "Some."

Charlotte can only hope that James' eyes stay closed.

"It's strange, how the cross comforts people," Kenneth continues, "even though it represents violence and death. A house, I can understand."

Here they go again. Stuck in a car with these two; it might as well be a prison—a real one. No need for fake handcuffs. James turns his head towards the window. How many more digs does Kenneth have? *Too cheery, huh?* And he lives with Gloria?

"Crosses represent many positives for people: salvation, Christian identity," Gloria says. "It's like if James put a picture of a red barn on his tombstone." She covers her mouth and laughs. "Not that he would."

"Must we?" Charlotte asks.

"No, of course not." Kenneth gestures toward the silent James. Then he tilts to look in the rearview mirror. "It's like we were saying at dinner; everything starts with the imagination." He pauses, but Charlotte refuses the bait. "Too often, people are afraid to talk about controversial things. It's as if they're afraid there may be holes in their thinking. I've had to get over that." He half turns. "Admit I have blind spots, but stand by my beliefs. And still stay open," he adds.

In spite of herself, Charlotte nods. It's so quiet, they could all be extras in a silent movie. Imagine, *Kenneth* admitting anything less than total certainty.

"And Charlotte, just so you know—Father was very supportive of my trip to Russia. He was glad I bought a new camera and wanted to see my pictures when I got back."

Gloria suddenly interrupts with "Let's focus on what's ahead. What plans do you have for the rest of your life, Charlotte?"

"Huh?" *Is this a trick question?* "Do you know something I don't know?"

"Oh, no, no, I don't mean anything bad," Gloria says. "Sometimes I look ahead to the next five years or so." She redoes her hairpins. "I'm usually wrong when I anticipate what might happen, but it helps me think about my goals. I did a lot of journaling after Rhonda died. Any special projects or travels coming up for you?"

"Not really," Charlotte says. "Farmers don't travel; we have cows." Gloria smiles but looks like she expects more. "Well, I hope Chad makes it through high school and college. Safely. I want to help James, you know, support him so he can be the best farmer possible. That sounds run-of-the-mill, I guess." There's no way Charlotte's going to bare her soul, talk about how strange that will be when both kids are gone from home. Or try again to explain the ache left from Father's passing. *You live and then you're done.* Oh, she knows there's more—.

"No, no, that's good," Gloria says. "So many people run away from the everyday; they think they have to do something spectacular to make their lives count. Cemeteries remind me to make every day one that's out-of-the-ordinary." She pauses. "I don't mean dramatic, but worthwhile. Full of *good* living." Then she shifts again. "What about Carrie? Do you think she'll go back to teaching?"

"Oh, sure," Charlotte says. James suddenly sits up straight and checks his watch. "I just don't know where." *Wait.* What's that look on Gloria's face? "She needs more time, we think. It takes her awhile to work through her questions." Charlotte raises her voice. "Did Caroline talk with you, Kenneth, about teaching jobs?"

"Not a peep."

"There's still time, I guess," Charlotte says, sighing. "She makes me nervous, though. I'd want to know. She seems content to just do whatever. What about Meg?"

"Oh, you know." Gloria throws up her hands. "She's a college kid and thinks the world will come to her door. Like Chad, I suppose. She does excellent work on anything she puts her mind to. But then, out of the blue she'll say, 'I'm tired of this.' She'll leave you in the lurch. Like with the gingerbread house. She gets bored so easily. She was going to take Special Studies credit for volunteering at a women's shelter but then changed her mind and said she'd probably do it anyway, just for fun. She's a hard one to figure." Gloria leans forward. "Where are we, Kenneth? Do you know?" Their car sits at a stop sign. "We're idling, aren't we?"

"James, do you know where we are?" Charlotte asks. Kenneth sits perfectly still, chin in hand, looking straight ahead. *Men!* "That's not Chad behind the wheel. Help us out, James. We all want to get home." She pounds the back of his car seat with her fist.

He motions with his left hand.

"I thought so," Kenneth says. "Three more minutes, right?"

"Don't talk to me about cows being the worst," Charlotte says.

"I come by it honestly," Kenneth says. "What's your excuse, James?"

"Too much exposure to bovines. It'll take five."

"I wonder what Martha and Mr. Armburgey have been doing," Gloria says. "How many games of Chinese checkers can they play before *they* get bored?"

"They've been keeping Meg and Carrie busy, I'll bet," Kenneth says. "When Mr. Armburgey gets to talking, it's hard to turn him off."

"Well, Mother certainly has her share of odd stories," Charlotte says. "What was that phrase yesterday? 'Rich toward others.' She said it a couple of times. 'We need to be rich toward others.' Where does she come up with these things?"

"I never thought I'd hear her admit that gray exists," Kenneth says, shaking his head. "'Wrong to be too rigid.'"

"It must be hard, having her world turned upside down," Gloria says. "Not just Daniel gone, but being uprooted from her house."

"Pfft. It's not like she's living with strangers," Charlotte says.

"Strangers and pilgrims," Kenneth adds.

Say nothing. Charlotte will not let on. So Meg isn't the perfect daughter after all.

"Martha's gone through a lot of changes," James says, covering a yawn. "Give her credit. Upheaval throws most people off kilter. Do you know where we are now?"

"Almost," Kenneth says.

"Just so we come close," James replies.

Kenneth slows the car to turn in their driveway. "Good integration of black cow spots on your white dairy sign." He turns to Charlotte and winks. "How'd we do time-wise, James?"

"Okay, but barely. I gotta change clothes and get the feed mixed. Whoa! Is that a light on in the shed? Don't tell me Carrie has gone ahead."

"Wouldn't that be good?" Kenneth asks. "Maybe she's enlisted Mr. Armburgey."

"Holy cow!" James says.

"Udder madness, eh?" Kenneth grins at himself.

"She doesn't know your feed formula," Charlotte says. "You worry about impossible things just like Mother."

"I showed her the sheet yesterday," James says. He grabs the door handle, acts like he's ready to spring.

Kenneth slams on the brakes and they all lurch against their seat belts.

"Holy cow!" James says again. "What was that for?"

"Get your cap on," Kenneth says. "You'll feel better."

"Martha could be giving Mr. Armburgey a tour of the cows' quarters," Gloria says, "with Meg taking pictures and recording everything."

James jumps out and half-runs to the shed.

"Poor guy," Charlotte says. "Let's hope everything's okay." She yawns, wonders if anyone dipped into the pies. Such a shame to have to reheat all that coffee.

Chapter 11

The house is quiet at last, but something is not in place. It's not as cold tonight, what with all the oven use and people. Martha knows that all did not go well on the cemetery outing. No one said exactly. James was in a rush. "Glad we went," Gloria said, "really, really glad." Charlotte and Kenneth shrugged and changed the subject.

Has Chad come in yet? That's often the last thing Martha hears before sleep comes: his red Geo slowing to turn in the driveway from the county road. Charlotte insists that Martha can't hear a whining motor from her bedroom. There's no point in arguing. *Martha is a watcher of the night.* Her heart races if she lets herself think about Chad in a ditch somewhere. It's not that she wants to dredge up trouble. That's just the way her mind works. With his bedroom in the basement—his "digs" that he's so proud of—and with the basement stairway at the far end of the house, he can come and go as he pleases. And to think that Martha's presence makes it all possible.

When she eats a big meal with too much richness, even if it's in the middle of the day, she has more trouble falling asleep. She made matters worse by nibbling on ginger cookies and peppermints from Gloria's house—they all got their appetites back when Charlotte was gone—plus a very thin slice of apple pie later. It was all Charlotte could manage, to share the dessert spotlight. She's such a wonderful cook—those were the lightest, buttery dinner rolls—but she ruins it by practically begging for compliments. Somewhere along the line, Martha failed Charlotte, failed her fragile, little, bleeding heart. So tough on the outside. These modern magazines say it's up to the parents to instill confidence. So different from Momma—full of caution.

Meg with all her paraphernalia! She wanted Martha to listen to "Amazing Grace" on that contraption you put in your ears. And credit cards already. Does anyone save up before they buy these days? Chad thinks he should have his own television. Where do they get these ideas? They want everything glittery like they see fake people scrambling for. Recognition—oh, how the young want to be noticed for every little thing. Chad's fast breaks and Meg's Dean's List. It's all good, but youngsters are so needy these days. Some of the older ones aren't much better. If Martha gets remembered for holy living, kindness even—what *will* they say at her funeral?—that's the only human reward that matters.

Kenneth will probably remember this as the Thanksgiving when Martha questioned whether killing was always black and white. Of course, any kind of strife makes for enmity, but since Daniel's death, it's hard to see things as simple good or bad. "The Lord giveth and the Lord taketh away. Blessed be the name of the Lord." That's true, but a lot goes on between that giving and taking. *Daniel.* What did he have to look forward to? More pills, more doctoring. More feeble, geeble, heeble. The burden of growing old. Martha tried to help by reading devotions from *The Upper Room*. But that only took ten minutes. How long can you look at the ceiling tiles and have the will? If you want to walk out and get your mail but don't have the wherewithal, what kind of life is that?

The digital clock reads 12:14. She turns the face with its bright red dots away. Toss and roll. Maybe she's dozed already. She readjusts the pillow between her knees.

That was a story and a half about Mr. Armburgey's aunt. Martha wished she hadn't asked what he meant. He almost coughed and spit his way to heaven's door—or wherever he intends to go—till he got the story out. That aunt must have had a very sharp tongue if she convinced him he didn't want anything to do with heaven, because she was going there. He didn't have one good thing to say about family. But what a good man he is. His forehead, all smooth and shiny, like a youngster's. Those dark spots on his cheeks seemed out of place. He made it worthwhile staying home from the cemetery. Well, she didn't want to walk on uneven ground anyway.

It's been years since Martha's played Chinese checkers. Mr. Armburgey wouldn't give an inch. Every time he made a move, he'd bend way down—squeak, squeak—to the piano bench. Martha had tried to get them to put the game board on something higher. Nothing doing. She surprised Carrie, the way she could jump marbles. Meg even made a point of telling Kenneth. Dark blue was Martha's best color. That Mr. Armburgey caught on slicker than a fox in the hen house, the way he went on offense. Meg tried to protect all her marbles, but she didn't win one game.

Half the time, she wasn't paying attention. She and Carrie went back and forth about polar ice melt, and pre-emptive strikes, and whatnot. They sounded like two men. It's not right to be so hard on people, on church leaders and such. Even on our president, even when he's wrong. One time when Carrie said, "There's more than one way to look at that," Mr. Armburgey chimed right in; he knew twenty-six ways to skin a cat. He's a character all right.

Another time he tried to give Martha a high five when she finished second to him. She was slow to catch on why he held up his palm; then when she finally understood, she couldn't reach his hand. Felt silly, jerking her body up toward him and missing. He was a gentleman, though, the way he half-bowed his head in her direction when they finally left. He told Kenneth it was getting to be too long; he said it directly. Even then, he had to practically stand at the front door like a dog begging to go out.

Martha always looks forward to seeing Kenneth again, but then things don't go the way she expects. She forgets how he can be. If he doesn't get finished on one topic, he'll come back to it later. He must have hit on every touchy subject under the sun. No wonder Meg has a contrary streak. Martha was stuck listening to Kenneth and Carrie go on about goodness and high expectations. Meg, too. After what had already been said at the table. They all agreed you're more susceptible to depression if you have high ideals. You're more likely to criticize because you expect others to have high standards, too. Well, well, well. Martha thought the ones cleaning up in the kitchen would never get finished.

Meg acted so sure—no problem with confidence for her. She knew all about young people committing suicide because the world is so cruel. She sounded like she's read the encyclopedia on people who end it because of questions of faith. "Spiritual battles," Kenneth called it. Well, he had one thing on the money: wondering how a person could believe you wouldn't be missed! The devil would have to get inside you, to think like that.

Meg had her own way of looking at all kinds of things. Whoever heard of eating being a drag? She did think to ask Martha—that was good of her—about the marble roller that Daniel made for the grandchildren when they were little. That girl used to have a whole head of curls when she was a little tyke. And she showed Martha pictures of her college friends on her phone. That one boy's hair, every color of the rainbow, stood straight up. And talk of shame. Meg said it can be used to keep discipline, especially in religious groups. Carrie seemed to agree that shame is used against women, claimed it happens all over the world, a way to make sure the abuse never comes to light. Talk, talk, talk, so different from Momma's "Too much talk can make things worse."

Martha was taught to fear the wrath. But God can't be as vindictive as the preachers made Him out to be. Poor Daniel. She did her best, the best she knew how. Charlotte would never understand.

Why didn't you—? Kenneth would want to analyze everything. *Here's what you should have done.* The neighbor lady, Mrs. Siegel, came to check, although it's hard to believe. Sleeping with his mouth open and tongue hanging out the side? The coroner had to come, because Daniel died at home. Mr. Haggarty thought Daniel had had another stroke. Martha insisted there be no autopsy, no mutilation. For awhile there, she thought she'd have to make a scene. *Not over Daniel's dead body,* she would have said. Charlotte was on Martha's side, for once. Gene was the broken one. Kenneth backed down; he couldn't get over it that his tour group left without him. "Terrible timing," he said.

What could Martha have done? Stayed home from the Women's Missionary Sewing Group. But there was so little she got to do for enjoyment those days, what with Daniel sick and all. Things always up and down. How could it be so wrong to leave the house and sew comforters for the needy? She'd tried to get some broth into him, hoped he'd sleep with his eyes closed instead of staring at the clock. How many times, she helped him sip apple juice because he didn't like to use a straw. She held his hand and stayed by his side, even when he didn't seem quite there.

A sliver of light from the outdoor pole light enters through the crack between the window shade and the sill wall. Martha folds her hands on her stomach and then quickly unfolds them. That's a pose funeral directors fashion for lifeless people. Her son, Gene. Who would have thought he'd choose such a profession? Such a tender one, disfigured in the neck by that boiling oil. Her own carelessness. Why didn't he call today? Was it too much to say "Hello"? While they sat around in the evening, all tuckered out, Charlotte said, "Something's going on." Well, what do you say to that? Carrie asked if they had a dial tone for sure, and James said he'd already checked. He told Charlotte that it wasn't too late; *she* could call Gene. But she pooh-poohed that and said, "Gene knows our number." That was the end of that.

Daniel never accepted Gene's career. Touch dead bodies? It didn't matter that he wore gloves. Sell Wilbert Vaults when the Good Book says moth and dust shall corrupt? Daniel made feeble jokes about Gene not ending up a dentist, but anyone could see the funeral business bothered him. He'd say, "Sam Whittaker had a stroke at fifty while embalming a child." Gene would come right back with: "Death is part of life. You don't have to sell bread and light bulbs to serve people." Daniel would snort. Too much emphasis on false preservation, is what he thought. "Let the body decompose," he said. "Wrap me in a white shroud. No sense, doctoring up the body." But they did anyway, when it came his turn.

Daniel claimed he could smell the embalming fluid seeping through the walls at Gene's place. Why did it matter? Their family room was always toasty warm. Martha would live there in a heartbeat, even if there are toxins. But that will never happen with Sue. Nothing big between them, just different ways of doing. Gene agreed that Daniel's hands looked too white when he lay in his fancy box. Such stillness. *All flesh is grass.* His fingernails too clean. The black hairs on his fingers looked like tiny wires, combed down. Otherwise, though, he looked natural enough. Martha was half afraid his body would turn dark overnight.

If Gene had been here today, they would have talked about old-timey things more: Daniel's Sen-Sen in his shirt pocket, the adding machine at the store, four-party lines, even rotary phones. Gene spent more time with Daniel—the others were in school already—and he knew all the delivery men. Gene would have told the story of how Daniel called on Harley Williams to say grace that Sunday noon—Gene might have been ten or so—and Harley said in his deep voice, "Gosh, man, I can't pray." *Gracious, me oh my!*

Lots of things would have been different. Gene has a way of keeping Kenneth and Charlotte from snipping all the time. It's good they didn't try to sing after dinner; they needed Gene's tenor. Meg brought up Sonja's name a couple of times, so they must keep in touch. Charlotte usually mentions Daniel's gray jacket, the lightweight one he wore to the store. She teases about how Martha threw the jacket in the trash. Well, it had gotten thin at the elbows. But Daniel rescued it and wore it even more. That was after it had been stuck under a plastic bag of cantaloupe rinds for a day. *Mercy!* How Martha had to scrub her way back to forgiveness.

Charlotte shows no interest in Momma's diaries. It's probably just as well. Momma could make it sound like "Bugs in the sugar" was all her fault. She never attained the perfection she yearned for. She'd get all red in the eyes if she said an angry word to Poppa. Even if she murmured against him. Not that it happened often, but she'd mention Lot's wife being punished, a pillar of salt. Well, you can't measure your days by what shows on the surface; you can't keep score. But *to be counted as righteous,* like Momma said. Even be like that Mother Teresa woman—all *her* good deeds.

If only Martha could think of something dull—squeeze the day's talk out of her head—maybe she could get to sleep. The hexagon pattern of the beige and blue tile in the kitchen. The piece of toast she'll eat for breakfast. She'll butter it carefully to the edges, spread the jelly evenly. Chad piles on raspberry jam like it comes from a cow. Oh my, it's nearly two in the morning. Martha doesn't mean to go on like this. She loves her family, every last one of them. But it's hard when they're all so different. What can you do but wash the wounds that come along? Try not to be the cause of more pain. Was that a door? She turns, holds herself still, balanced on one elbow, but hears nothing more. Chad needs someone to lay down the law. James has been much too lax, the way he lets basketball rule. Martha shouldn't be the one listening for Chad's car in the driveway.

When the call came after the cemetery-goers were back, that Chad had lost his dinner and had to leave practice early, Charlotte seemed mortified, as if the abundance were all her fault. Well, it's true; they didn't need sausage in the dressing. But she didn't make Chad take those extra helpings. Then she complained that Chad went to Nicole's on a weak stomach instead of coming home. She acted surprised that anyone had nibbled on the house while she was gone—it's good she didn't see Meg—and wanted to send half of it home with Kenneth. What was he supposed to say? Such a shame—the house, like an abandoned step-child, left out back on the washer. Charlotte kept saying she was too full for supper, but after the others were gone, she snitched on cold turkey all evening.

Poor Carrie. It was good of her to stay behind, even though she looked like she wanted to go to the cemetery. Carrie's seen something that's hurt her. She seems half-scared. It could be that Ryan fellow, or her job. But not go to church at all? You can't live like that. If Martha had a chance to talk with her alone—such a clear complexion and those blue eyes—she would. Last March when Carrie came home for Daniel's funeral, Martha hardly spoke with her. Too much else going on. But afterwards, Charlotte said Carrie wasn't herself, almost pulled out of the drive into another car on the county road, made comments about wanting to stay and help James put in the crops.

If only Carrie could explain herself better. She and Kenneth kept mentioning this Merton fellow but never would say his last name. "Paradox," she'd say, as if everyone understood what she meant. Or, "Nothing is as it appears." Meg went right along with it, so maybe it's the way young people are. Gloomy talk: every civilization falls. *Goodness! Topsy-turvy, mopsy-murvy.*

All Kenneth's talk about Anabaptist groups. Martha wonders if he started in on the factions when they went to the cemetery. It's sad that none of Martha's children has found a home with any of the Mennonite groups. Kenneth and Gloria would fit right in with that church in Madison, if they halfway tried. Gene and Sue need to stay Presbyterian, of course. Charlotte would never admit it, but she must feel, too, like she still belongs somewhere with the Mennonites, just like Gloria said.

How can God's children be so divided? The educated ones sit on one side; the wealthy ones take to their own. Some get into politics, right side or left. Some groups try to outdo each other, more daring or whatever: a woman in the pulpit. There's too much restlessness. But the conservative ones are the ones growing. Kenneth says the liberal ones won't last—simulate or something—too much like the rest of the world. Well, he's one to talk.

Doesn't he know he's made his point often enough, about not building up treasure? Martha agrees with him—no question there—but she couldn't blame Charlotte for leaving the room. Everybody's just trying to get by, whether they're dirt poor or filthy rich. Kenneth comes across as extreme-like. Is he going to give his state pension away? Of course, everyone's going to lose everything. The Bible is very clear: not to store up. Maybe he talks big because he's afraid. *Like Daniel, in a way.* Kenneth sees his shortcomings but can't really change. His beloved dream of people living together equal-like and sharing everything. That's his heaven, all right.

He could use a dose of common sense, acting all embarrassed when Mr. Armburgey spilled it about Kenneth writing poetry. What's so terrible about putting pretty words on paper? Meg saw Kenneth rubbing his ear; she's like a little mouse in the pantry, knows right where the cheese is. Daniel used to call Martha his very own poet; he liked it when she rhymed words, even if it made no sense. *Sixteen grape seeds, sitting on the sill; along comes a south wind, gives a salty spill.*

Martha couldn't help but remind Kenneth that he used to clip poems from magazines and keep them all together in a notebook. He got red, even though you can't see much of his cheeks with that beard. Can't he laugh a little? Everyone has times they'd just as soon cross off. Whole days sometimes. He tried to change the subject, asked about the whereabouts of the roll-top desk. He knows good and well: the antiques are stored in the attic on Township Road. He was right there and helped get some of those heavy pieces up the stairs. She didn't want the renters' children coloring on the old secretary desktop or using the cherry dry sink to store their toys.

Gloria will think twice before she brings another gift that takes so much work. Her timing is always off, just like her hair. And all those fancy writers she talks about. Flannery—what kind of name is that? Charlotte usually gets over her squabbles with Kenneth, so she'll probably forgive Gloria, too. Mr. Armburgey changed their day all right. Martha won't mind if Kenneth brings him along for Christmas dinner. She could knit something for him, short notice—a neck scarf—so he'd feel included. Charlotte warmed up to him considerable. Considerably. Too bad he wasn't the one to come in carrying the house. And to think, he was an instrument of war those years ago.

Nowadays, people don't feel the horror they should about bombs and such. All the violence on television must make it seem like a commonplace. "Just don't let it happen here" is as far as most people go. It's enough to make Martha long for that other shore. *Oh, to be with Daniel again.*

She should have gotten up long ago to use the toilet. Easy now. Swing the legs slowly. No more run-ins with vertigo. She tugs on her blue slippers with the long socks that come halfway up her legs and makes sure she's solid before she takes the first steps. Oh, the aches. It was her knees for years; now the pain in her hips is getting worse. No surgery for her; she'll stay far away from that. What with the risk of blood clots and infection, she'll make do.

That spring day in her flowerbed when she couldn't get up. She was transplanting the pink geraniums she always winters in the basement; she'd bent down as long as she could but finally had to get down on her knees. How surprised she was—panicky-like. She couldn't get up, couldn't push off either leg to stand. Tried rolling to one side—must have mashed some of the brand new flower starts—had to rest and catch her breath. *Both* knees seemed to give out on her. *Lord, what had she done?* Finally, she pushed herself up with both hands braced in the dirt. She thought sure her arms would buckle. She pitched forward, staggered-like. Later, she couldn't explain it to Daniel, but it was the awfullest feeling. Seeing ahead ten years and knowing the time was coming when she wouldn't be able to dig in the dirt anymore. Now those ten years have come and gone. And here she is, pining to get back to the home place.

Since it's so late, she'll let herself read just one week from Momma's diary. Some small solace, some encouragement to be an instrument of peace in this world of woe. Even in her family. *Lord, give all your children what is needful. Every last one. Poor though they be. Mr. Armburgey, too.*

Momma's Diary - November 1930

Sunday

Blessed by Samuel's sermon. Trusting, trusting. Almost like home with Father here. Feeling more at peace. Subject tonight was "The Way of the Transgressor is Hard." Many (16) went forward. The Lord shall wipe away every tear.

Monday

Washed. Made Baby polka-dotted dress this P.M. Papered part of kitchen. Are surprised that Father is staying so long. Far from home for most of a week. He reports that Alta is poorly. Sang German this eve. Such blessedness.

Tuesday

Are as busy as bees. Beginning to feel more settled somewhat. Had quite a time deciding about paint. Bought a new and much desired kettle.

Wednesday

So glad that Father tore out partition. Varmints aplenty. Learned that Mrs. Branch fell and broke four ribs. Must learn to be a better neighbor. Missionary meeting tonight. Studied Guatemala.

Thursday

A never to be forgotten day! Seven cousins arrived from Illinois. News of Ira Mast, called home. Many sweet memories brought to mind. Nice time singing. How glad we have the piano. "What a Friend We Have in Jesus."

Friday

Everyone busy. Different opinions when it comes to babies. Mattie made custard pie for dinner. Much colder. Brrr. Have not seen bugs today. Hope and pray.

Saturday

Help from cousins and Father until Monday. Finished outdoor work. Bulbs to the basement. So glad. Had a fine time this eve. Such laughing! "Five-legged cow with apples in the milk."

Chapter 12

Carrie sits in the kitchen nook mid-morning on Friday, eating toast and drinking coffee. The aroma of a fresh pot filled the kitchen when she and her dad walked in from milking. No more of that tragically reheated coffee from yesterday. She stares absently at the five clay pots of herbs: parsley, rosemary, basil, thyme, and cilantro, sitting in the bay window. Beautiful. They'll get decent light; there's a good chance Mom can keep them alive all winter.

It was a relief to play Chinese checkers with Grandma after the cemetery gang left yesterday. She had that cute little habit of holding together the tips of her thumb and index finger after every move. Her hand hovered over the board like a butterfly, looking for a place to go next. She and Mr. Armburgey went through their sacrificial duel about which chair to sit on. He wouldn't budge from where he sat before dinner, harrumphing every time he reached down to the game board. It was sweet, in a way; maybe they passed notes in grade school and want to make up for lost time.

Everyone was on their own last night, getting whatever leftovers they wanted. The apple pie was as good as it looked, a meal by itself with ice cream on top. Later, Mom announced she hadn't been a bit nervous about the meal. *Oh, my!* Gloria's advice before the meal had renewed Carrie's hope. Be your own person; stay calm and face the puzzled looks. By evening, though, she'd lost her nerve; she couldn't bring up her proposal. Now she's mad at herself. All kinds of excuses had seemed legitimate. It wasn't the right time. Mom was worn out. Dad was nostalgic; it was important to honor that. Besides, she wanted to talk with him alone one more time. Now she has no choice; she *has* to talk with Mom this afternoon.

Carrie has to be more specific about her plans. When she comes back at Christmas, she'll have everything written out on paper. She'll show them she can put her math to work. She needs to get beyond reading testimonials on the internet, jotting down ideas on scraps of paper here and there. She'll list all the equipment, a small garden tractor, small seeder. The big stuff, too: a high tunnel, over five thousand dollars. Drip irrigation system, another ten thousand. There's no way to feel complacent about borrowing on Dad's name. Maybe he'll be willing to share small implements. She's always thought of business people as hard-nosed, rip-off-the-public types, while farmers are settled back, stuck in their ways. Those stereotypes don't help. She'll do more research, figure out her competition, know where to establish markets. Next spring, she'll plant blueberries and raspberries.

Tailgate marketing, like in the South, isn't going to cut it up here. Everybody says word-of-mouth's the most crucial.

Yesterday, before Dad got home from the cemetery, Carrie had gone out to the shed, looking for the ingredients to mix feed. She snooped around but then backed down, didn't have the nerve to start on her own. He wasn't very happy when she asked about the stack of pesticide containers in the corner and wondered whether they'd been rinsed. She couldn't believe he'd be that careless. Mostly, though, he was relieved she hadn't started any augers. After the cows adjusted to their twenty-minute delay—no undue balking that she could see—he settled down.

They talked again this morning; she made it clear she's serious. Such a delicate balance. She can't come on too strong, but she can't waffle, either. He played it cool, like he was ready for her this time. Basically, he was non-committal, but he agreed to keep talking. He said to come back and work for a CSA for a year. Someone else's CSA. Maybe it *is* too much to take on herself. How do you ever know until you try, until you're given a chance? He seemed open, though. But can she count on him when she approaches Mom?

She made the mistake of talking about canola. Dad hooted, said that's what they raise when they can't raise anything else. He slid the barn door shut so hard, the whole frame rattled. It got worse. She brought up cycles again. A farmer raises canola and soybeans, presses the oil, distributes it to restaurants. The owners collect the used grease from cooking, filter it, sell it back to the farmer who uses it in tractors and trucks. Why can't he get excited about the connections, see that everyone's situation improves?

He didn't want her help treating the ringworm. "Don't want you to get it," he said with a sly grin. Did he think she'd be in the way? He'll scrape off the crust, spray with blukot, force humongous pills with a plunger, watch to make sure each pill goes down, wait for the final sign: the cow's tongue in its nose. He said a hoof trimmer was coming later to get a stone out of another cow's foot. Was he purposely trying to protect himself from her questions? Maybe he just needed time alone. He'd paid no attention when she pointed out the natural cycle: pasture land, to milk production, to some child's lunch. And why was she talking about dairy when it's not her thing? Well, that's all he wanted to talk about last night.

He had turned off the TV and shut off two basketball gurus who were analyzing the first-half performance of nineteen-year-olds. He launched into a long story of how difficult milking used to be. How the old stanchions were made of steel and wood, not brightly colored plastic and metal. How the cows nearly smoothed the wood away, rubbing their necks on the inside part. How he got filthy dirty when he had to milk a cow that had stood out in the rain, the rainwater mixing with the dust in the cow's coat. Then he motioned all over his body, made circles in front of his face, moved his hands up and down his arms, to show where he'd been covered with mud from slinging one arm up to the cow's spine and pressing his body against the cow, all the time reaching under with his other arm to wash the udder.

She reminded him that taking care of her girls wasn't a piece of cake either. Sometimes there were as many as twenty calves—back when she was in junior high—each in a separate pen so they wouldn't pass on respiratory problems. The worst thing was to hear her dad say that one of them had johnes. He'd let her think the calves were entirely her responsibility. She cleaned the pens with the manure fork and that long-handled scraper with the blade on it to pull straw out of the corners. She mixed milk replacer with water and fed each calf separately. That calf crunch mixture, a scoop and a half of molasses, corn, oats. They loved the leaves of fresh hay, always needed more clean water. Then it started all over again, forking out more wet straw and manure from the pens. She'd loved every minute; it took two months before the calves were ready to feed on their own.

They reminisced about vets, too. Dad still likes the one in Brodhead best; the Amish use him, too. He can handle an ornery heifer better than most. Carrie remembers the guy's little black suitcase where he kept his tools. One time Dad let her watch in the shed when the vet tranquilized a cow with a twisted stomach. His clippers buzzed, then he cut right through the hide with his scalpel, right through the inner lining. The cow had bucked a little and Carrie had backed up. The vet's arm disappeared inside till he found the stomach that was out of place. She knew he was straightening the pink flesh, suturing it to the cow's inside where it belonged. She'd watched a thin line of blood run out on the shed floor.

Somewhere in all that cow talk, Carrie said she wanted to help with the milking in the morning. Her parents had looked at each other, as if she'd asked permission to stay for an after-prom party. "Get up at four?" Dad had asked. Carrie assured him that was her plan. She'd meant to get up on Thanksgiving morning but slept right through her alarm. He's always said: early morning rising is a matter of training the body. He probably still wakes up five minutes before his alarm goes off. Mom had to tell Carrie to go to bed if she wanted to get up early. Mom's daily instruction, her ever-available advice. Carrie will need to let it roll off like Dad does. And yes, she'll have to train herself to go to sleep early. Physical labor will take care of that. Daily exhaustion from pulling weeds before the heat of the day, making deliveries to restaurants and small grocers before noon.

Now her mom tosses a couple envelopes on the nook table in front of Carrie. "This mail came in the past month or so," she says, rolling up the sleeves on her striped aqua-and-white shirt. "It didn't look like anything important, so I didn't forward it."

Carrie brushes crumbs from the table into her cupped hand, drops them into her empty cereal bowl, and sorts through the return addresses. A couple of credit card offers, a fantastic rate on a car loan from a bank in Monroe. An envelope touting a free hands-on demonstration for an unnamed but exciting product that included state-of-the-art technology—an eight-billion-dollar industry!—and the opportunity to become a business partner in an emerging company. She leans forward; Grandma is right: the back of this kitchen nook isn't very comfortable. "Nothing to purchase," she reads. "No sales pressure. Call toll-free to reserve a seat. There's still time! A two-night, three-day resort for simply attending. A six-figure income." They make everything sound so easy.

Carrie wipes her table knife and slits open another envelope. This came from The *Right* One: The Relationship Professionals. "Stop waiting . . . that special someone . . . compatible singles . . . trained consultants . . . background checks . . . a sensible, safer method. Please take a few moments to complete this personal profile." She laughs and reads the last sentence: "There's never been a better time to take charge."

"What's this?" Mom asks.

"A joke," Carrie says, handing her the letter. "It's like the websites that use sappiness. All the people working hard to make others happy."

Mom puts on her glasses and skims the letter. Then she lightly touches Carrie's shoulder. "Don't you ever want a man to put his arms around you? Yes, this letter's ridiculous, but Ryan—." She pauses, then rushes ahead. "I see his picture—your picture with him—is gone."

"You were in my room?" Carrie glares at her mom, shoves her bowl toward the edge of the table. *Go ahead, wait on me!*

"I've had to store some extra linens in the bottom drawer of your dresser, since your grandmother moved in."

"Thanks for asking!"

"I should have." She stacks two dirty juice glasses inside a cereal bowl. "What about Ryan, Caroline? You still care about him, don't you?"

Carrie looks again. There's a gentleness in Mom's voice. Carrie tears her paper napkin into long strips. Will she ever get over him? "At one time I thought Ryan and I loved each other. I imagined it, I know now. I created him to fit a certain image. What I wanted." Carrie rips the letter in two. "Then I found out he was someone different than I had made him out to be. I didn't understand his need to get away."

"I'm sorry, Caroline. Sometimes it takes longer for things to work out. He might still come around."

"Yeah, right. Well, I'm not looking to settle down, if that's what you mean." *Wait! That's not true!* Carrie puts her elbows on the table, rests the heels of her palms in her eyes. She's considering a choice that will tie her down; Dad says, "Like a slave." About to settle down with a marketing plan that includes a production schedule, an estimate of costs and yields. She's pushing hard for a decision to cozy up with pest management, weather extremes, nitrate contamination.

"That's fine; there's no hurry, Caroline." Mom busies herself, stacking dishes in the dishwasher. "I'm curious where you are on religion, though. If you don't mind my asking. Kenneth makes it sound like religions are made up or something."

Talk about a double-barreled attack! How did Carrie let herself get stuck in the kitchen nook, being grilled by Mom? Carrie needs to be the one asking the questions. "No, I don't think religions are made up. There's some kind of spiritual connection that meets a human need for many people. Believing in something beyond yourself and this world—it's real. But all of life is sacred, for me, not just Sunday morning." She hesitates, sees an opening. "Land is sacred. We need to take care of it, protect it."

Mom closes the dishwasher door with a bang. "Oops, I didn't mean anything by that. Sure, we make a living from the land."

"Oh, it's much more than a living. Food is sacred. What goes on in the kitchen is holy. Your cooking." Carrie crumples her napkin, squeezes it. *Wait!* "But that's me. I don't know about Kenneth. If he means that much of modern Christianity doesn't have much to do with Jesus, well, yes, I believe that. The church would make an excellent mission field. But often it's hard to hear what Kenneth's saying because he's so annoying."

"I quit listening."

"He hates intolerance. That's his big thing. He—. Yeah, he's intolerant of being intolerant. Well, sometimes he talks like he has a messianic complex, too. He's sure; if you can't get along with others, say with Muslims or Mormons, gays or Goths, if you can't accept anything different from yourself—*any one*—then you're out of step with Jesus."

"He acts like he *is* Jesus."

Carrie laughs. "That's what I mean. That bumper sticker: 'Honk If You *Are* Jesus'. He needs a shot of Grandma's humility—that's how I've got him figured—what Grandma says we're losing. Her *demut.* It's ironic that Kenneth's personality gets in the way of following a man who never isolated himself from any human being or group of people."

"Well, aren't you something. That's the most sensible explanation I've ever heard for Kenneth." Mom looks at Carrie like they've just been introduced.

"Get past his packaging—there's no glitter—if you want to see the truth he's getting at."

Yesterday it was the wink that did it for Carrie. Right after Grandma said, "Everyone's stupid and smart about things—just stupid and smart about different things," Uncle Kenneth had winked at Carrie, like he thought she'd be amused, too. Then when she admitted that trying to create a better world might be a way to make herself feel better, he winked again. What was that about? The all-knowing Master Winker. She wished she'd shut up. But something in her kept on trying to impress him, even when she knew he wasn't going to give her any satisfaction.

Carrie slides out of the nook, pulls out the rolling shelf, and throws napkins and banana peels in the trash. She stretches and yawns. "I need some exercise. Mind if I do some spading, spread those leaves on your garden? I saw there was a pile of them under the tarp."

"Oh, I wasn't going to do any real work today."

"That's fine; you did more than enough yesterday. I'm the one who needs to do something physical. Okay if I do whatever I see needs doing?"

"Well, no, of course not. I mean, yes, if you want." Mom's eyes blink like she's trying to think of what Carrie could mess up. "I wanted to vacuum, straighten up inside."

"Rather you than me."

"Do you mind taking Sayeth with you? Use the tie-down if he's in your way."

"No problem."

Escape! More time to think. Carrie uses the tarp to drag leaves to the garden, spreads them, works them into the soil. Sayeth runs around in his circle. Okay, where do things stand? At least Dad didn't say a flat-out "No" this morning. If he were completely repulsed, he wouldn't string her along. He said he didn't want to buy more land; he'd decided a couple years ago that two hundred acres was enough. Why did he keep talking about Chad so much? When they were in the barn looking at the new uniloader, he said Chad hated helping him stack the big rectangular hay bales, even with the bale fork. Chad claims he's allergic to dust, but he's never been tested.

Her boot shoves the spade into garden soil. She'd tried to be cautious. "If farming's not Chad's thing, you can't expect him to care about improvements." Then her dad said what she'd suspected. "I always thought if I had a son, he'd love farming, like me. I even said that to him once. I told him he'd be a heck of a farmer someday." Dad had made a show of stretching out his hands, saying what long fingers Chad has. Carrie almost felt sorry for him; how deflating to have Chad show no interest, how irritating that Chad would rather go to the weight room at school than build muscle by working at home.

Dad seemed to want to talk about anyone but her. "This Snyder guy, Bo," he said, "making good money—so he claims—working at the Swiss Colony plant. At fifty years old he started as a line worker. Now he's a forklift operator. Sold his small herd of twenty cows.

People in church talked up a storm when he called it quits." Then Dad mentioned a guy who moved to California and started his own company, making some kind of chip for computers. He was a millionaire in no time, but that wasn't good, either. People yacked about him making too much money too fast. Wait till they start in on Carrie: "That Lehman girl." Maybe she'll always be "James' daughter."

Whew! It's muggy for this time of year. She felt it already when they walked to the milk parlor. She'd watched Dad wash the udder, sanitize each teat with an iodine solution, then use another sanitizer to kill the bacteria. He worked carefully, methodically in his prized herringbone parlor. The cows, as dour as ever in their slanted stalls, looked down with disdain. When he put the milker unit on the cow's teats, she remembered how clumsy that apparatus was. He made a point to explain how the suction reduces when there's no more milk coming. "See?" he said, pointing to the cow in the next stall. "It's like a massage, the light suction, so the udder doesn't get harmed. Ready to do one side of the parlor, while I do the other?" he teased.

How could he stand that routine, twice a day? He moved effortlessly from cow to cow, never hurrying, prodding with a long stick out the open window when it was time for the next four cows to come in from the holding lot. The same thing, over and over. Maybe no different, though, than checking for bugs on the green beans every day. Her stomach kept growling with discontent. Why couldn't he break his ritual of never eating anything before he went out to milk in the morning? Even a granola bar would have helped.

When they left the milk parlor, they watched silently again. A hawk, probably the same one they'd seen the other day, tried repeatedly to lift what was left of the pheasant. Claw feet carried the carcass twenty feet into the air, then dropped it. At last the hawk flew off. Not a word from Dad, not even a "Whoa there."

Carrie pauses, rests her arms on the spade handle. She's going to have to build up her muscle this next month. But more to the point: she needs to find the perfect opening with Mom. She had one a little bit ago, and all she managed to say was something about seeing farming as more than making a living. She wanted Dad there. It's chicken to wait till she's back in Ohio; she doesn't want to say it over the phone. Her mom was kind about Ryan, and she seemed to listen about Kenneth. Maybe she's the one who needed a good night's sleep. It didn't sound malicious that she was in Carrie's bedroom. Besides, the roll of money is none of her business. But still, how will the two of them ever share kitchen space?

She throws leaves on Sayeth, watches him jump. She tosses his red, plastic bone, growls at him, slaps her thighs playfully. There's no glamour on Wisconsin farms. She'll be a rural misfit, a hick for New Yorkers to laugh at. Not that they'll care or even notice. There's no novelty as a female farmer either; Wisconsin has oodles. She'll be odd only by her mom's standards. Carrie is who she is. People are driven to do daring things. Gloria understood. Passions are meant to be lived out. Carrie can't help it that she loves the smell of earth after it's been frozen and thaws again. When the breezes are *right.* If she finds herself compromised, trapped in a borrowed tractor—a helpless female—or stuck alone with a wrench under a broken trailer bed, she'll figure a way out. She needs to be back here, not just dream about it. The land calls her back. She's a boomerang.

She had told Ryan about their family bonfires on holiday evenings. How, with the cows milked, her dad would use rotting logs to build an enormous fire. They'd drag plastic folding chairs out to the site, take blankets if it were New Year's Eve, stay up late singing everything from "Home on the Range" to "If I had a Hammer." "Jesus, Keep Me Near the Cross," too. Dad would sip occasionally from his thin-necked canteen, and they'd all tell stupid jokes and riddles. *A little boy ate too many green apples, died, and went to heaven. What was his telephone number?* She hadn't cared that 812-GREEN had too many digits. It was the best riddle. Chad would fall asleep, and Mom would carry him into the house. Then it was just Carrie and her dad, sitting in that biting, cold air. Heaven on earth. Is that when she first heard him say, "Kiss the earth or die"?

Yes, these are her kind of people: Midwestern, rural, practical, "use-it-up, don't-waste-that-crust" kind of people. Good people at heart. Mostly religious people who find meaning in where you park your car (your buggy?). Not first in line; not on someone's grass after a hard rain; not where you can't back out if you need to leave suddenly. People who find satisfaction in the daily task. The everyday. Extra-mile people. Trusting kind of people, sometimes to the point of gullibility (why would your neighbor want to harm *you*?). Dependable people, even welcoming inconvenience (why *wouldn't* you expect your neighbor to want help when water seeps into his basement?). She comes from earnest people. Church-going people who measure their worth in regular attendance and bigger irises than last year. Perfect. Yeah, that's big. That must be why the Mennonites split, if someone doesn't measure up or conform to church standards. Grandma said that her kind divide to start new congregations in different parts of the state—*spread the word*—rather than sit in a pile and build super big buildings.

Grandma, the one who's lived her life for others—wore herself down, caring for Grandpa for one thing—and ended up harming herself, although she can't see it. Serving, serving, serving. Making casseroles for grieving families, knitting baby blankets, like the invisible hand of God. How did she get by, only having three children? She studied her Sunday school lesson on Saturday night, even though she couldn't teach the class the next morning. It *had* to be a man, *because the Bible says so.* Because the men in charge said so. That big breakthrough when Grandma got gunsmoke grey shoes instead of the usual black ones. Those times she prompted Grandpa to tell stories about being called slackers and yellow-bellied parasites toward the end of World War II. How their house and others' got egged. Grandma, always caring about edification for the grandchildren.

So different from Carrie's mom, off the hook from anything that smacks of simple apparel and head coverings. Jerked over, flown the coop, kicked the traces. She'd be unsettled by Ryan's assessment that Anabaptism probably lingers in the genes. But she's found some balance—her own—far from Grandma's model. She's happy to be involved in Labor Day golf tournaments that raise money for

Children's Services. It doesn't have to be *only* one way. That's what Carrie will say. Life is about change.

So what's the bare minimum? Five or six acres. Seven would be better, but ten is a stretch. Some of that will lie fallow because of tractor paths—no more than five hundred feet long, max—between strips of field. Dad's right: there's no way she can be ready to start with the next growing season. She'll go online, check out local CSAs, work at one for a year, while she gets her own set-up in order. She can do the preliminaries like planting green to reverse soil impaction. Buckwheat next summer; rye or oats in the fall. Well, there's all that cow manure, too. It'll take at least three years to transition her acres to organic. Eventually, she'll have to hire part-time help. She'll end up borrowing lots more before she can make any kind of living wage off six acres. What if she fits in too well and becomes superficial? That's funny. Imagine her attending church regularly, sending donations to the needy overseas, smugly satisfied with doing good to the earth.

She knows this much: she wants to wake up excited about the day ahead. She wants to love what she's doing. Yes, Mom, *love.* Start onions and cucumbers in a greenhouse. Transplant tomatoes into the earth when the ground's warmed up. She'll find her own happiness. Will that be caving in to North American values? Listening to her Self? Well, she's doing it in an unorthodox way. No, she's not a hopeless romantic. Naïve? Maybe. She can't predict all the things they'll throw at her. Unprepared? She'll figure it out. She'll be The-One-Who-Came-Back, not half as ridiculous as those letters in the mail. She has to believe.

Chapter 13

The day after a major holiday celebration is always a letdown for Charlotte. Not that she's depressed—she hates that word—but she catches herself thinking too much, replaying conversations. Anyone who's hosted extended family members, stood guard against the Kenneths of this world can understand Charlotte's need to relax. She's done the slaving to please others. Of course, she enjoyed it, too. But now satisfaction and fatigue roll together and demand some catch-up time. All that energy she expended, all those surprises she took in stride—little toads in the hostas.

It'd be nice if Mother could acknowledge how well everything came off. That unexpected guest turned out to be quite the charmer. Charlotte showed she doesn't put food preparation ahead of people. Today she's humming, halfway singing: *"O Love that will not let me go."* Sweet words from her childhood days. *"O Light that follows all my way."* Yes, Gloria is strange all right, so excited about her cemetery fix. If only Charlotte had thought to reply—she's never quick enough—

that having too much money is never a problem for anyone running a family farm.

A night's sleep has definitely helped, but nothing would pick up Charlotte like a round of golf. A chance to get away and walk off some of that extra food. She had trouble with the top button on her jeans this morning. When Father died on that unseasonably warm day last March, Charlotte was out golfing. How could she not? She'd survived the winter and they had a burst of early warmth. Golf stays in your blood. She's not the kind who wants to hit balls farther each time; that's such a male thing. And she's not sucked in by these premium balls that claim extra distance and "sensitivity around the greens." Pfft. No, there's something restorative about golf—much as Charlotte loves to cook. Getting out early in the morning, even on nippy fall days, and walking over manicured grounds is energizing. *"O Joy that seekest me through pain."* She's given up trying to explain it to Mother. Sure, her shoes get wet sometimes; that's to be expected.

But Caroline's here, and James frowned when Charlotte barely mentioned calling Teresa. It's like he's jealous sometimes. Doesn't he know it's better to process Kenneth with a family outsider? He seemed preoccupied about Caroline. "Don't try to force things," he said, when Charlotte suggested pushing Caroline to call the local principal. Why would it hurt to check if there's an opening?

Charlotte often feels caught between her daughter and mother. Both are impossible at times, although Charlotte loves them both, heaven knows. But one is completely old-fashioned and the other doesn't care that her clothes make her look like she's living in the wrong decade. Charlotte can't seem to make either one happy.

James won't let on, but Charlotte knows he's thrilled with the way Caroline takes an interest in the dairy. That talk about farming last night probably did him good. Something was a little different, though, when he came in from choring this morning; he kept clearing his throat like he'd picked up a nervous habit. It reminded her of the first time Chad had a break-out game and James couldn't show his pride. He holds himself so tight sometimes. It's okay for Caroline to ask questions, but she's way too full of advice. All those sons back in the '70s who took their fathers under. You never know about children. Still, it's better for Caroline to be fixated on cows than hung up on the poor.

She must be desperate for exercise, wanting to spread leaves. The garden doesn't really need them, but Charlotte's not going to stop her. It won't hurt. That e-mail message about a delay on the order of pillows at Sears is disgusting. These businesses do anything to try to avoid giving you the sale price. No message from Gene yet. *What is going on?* Yesterday, the silence was irritating; he could have squeezed in a call sometime, asked how big the turkey was. Today the silence seems unnatural; it's hard not to wonder.

Charlotte vacuums the living room carpet, finds a stray crouton and a dried-up bean, right next to a table leg. That's it for cleaning today. Normally, it's satisfying to straighten up messes. Give her tarnished brass and she'll make it look like new. Give her a closet to organize and she thrives. But not today. What is Mother doing in her room so long? She said she wanted to write a letter. Charlotte divides leftover turkey into two-cup portions for freezing, perfect-sized containers for turkey divan or a gumbo soup. All too soon, winter will be here for good; no golf for four whole months. Arrgh!

Charlotte could take Caroline shopping, but who wants to fight crowds at the mall? Pre-Christmas sales aren't what they're cracked up to be anyway. Caroline seemed to listen this morning. Did her eyes get watery, or had she just yawned? It sounds like it's over with Ryan; maybe that's just as well if he was feeding her radical ideas. But Caroline's still having a hard time. It's tough, being young and thinking you need to put on a strong front.

How well Charlotte remembers when *she* lived to see James; she couldn't stand to be away. Even going to church with him on Sunday evening was exciting. She loved his Old Spice; now she can't get him to try anything new. They'd ride home together when it was dark out, and she'd put her head in his lap. His one hand on the steering wheel, his other pulling her tight, caressing. How could you not be crazy about that? It's like Caroline's afraid. Weird. Some kids only think about sex; Caroline acts like it never enters her mind. *Pleasures of the body don't make you evil, Little Girl.*

Charlotte taps on the kitchen counter—ugh, this lethargy. It's too early to fix the soup for lunch. The cheddar cheese curds with pesto have lost their squeakiness, but they have to be finished up. Some kind of cheese is a must with turkey-noodle soup. She could go outside and help Caroline, but Charlotte doesn't feel like getting dirty. Some of her perennials didn't get much mulch and Caroline would probably do the heavy stuff. But no, Charlotte's varicose veins need rest. When she was growing up, she hadn't liked outdoor work, never dreamed she'd end up loving to garden. What was it she'd tried to carry as a teenager? They never bought big bags of compost, so maybe she was pushing manure on a wheelbarrow. Her father yelled at her. "Don't lift that yourself; you'll hurt your female organs!" Maybe Kenneth had egged her on that time, told her she couldn't do something, so she had to try.

Where *will* she and James go for their winter vacation? It's hard to think about going South when it's still so unseasonably warm here. Caroline acts upset that they don't come more often. What's there to do in that dinky apartment? Stare at bare mountains? James needs to say something soon to Simp, though, if they want time off in January. Otherwise, Simp acts put-upon about doing the milking for a week, not that he doesn't get paid well enough. She'll check Chad's schedule for an open Friday night. Mother could cook for him for a week, especially if Charlotte had casseroles ready in the freezer. She'd ask Chad to make sure the oven always gets turned off. He can be trusted; last year was just a fluke. Mother keeps hinting about him coming in late at night. Charlotte and James sleep soundly most of the time, but they'd hear that. Chad always bangs into something or accidently slams a door. Maybe this *is* the year to go to Pensacola; they could stop off with Caroline for a night on their way down.

Charlotte looks idly out the bay window, watches Caroline walk over stubble in the field beyond the garden. *What is she doing out there?* She walks slowly, looks down like she's lost her watch. Now she stops, looks off to the north. She's found that hideous, gray sweatshirt with the blue letters BAND that have gotten all crinkly from the dryer. *Oh, good, that must be Gene calling.*

It's Teresa, wanting a recap. "Did they like the stuffing?" Teresa's always accepted Charlotte's family—bless her heart—seems amused by this Mr. Armburgey. Charlotte doesn't want to start in on all the things Kenneth said; Mother might show up. Inevitably, the conversation steers itself toward golf. It *is* Friday. Charlotte flounces on the couch and says she can't. Caroline's time with them is so short, leaving already tomorrow afternoon. Yes, it *is* a gorgeous day. Charlotte lowers her voice and confides that Caroline's relationship with Ryan is on the slide. Yes, it's too bad. Teresa agrees that Charlotte's done the right thing to ask directly. Then Teresa adds, "You've been a role model, going after what you want." And then later, "But you've spent all week taking care of everyone else."

Teresa might as well have smacked Charlotte. She's told her before that it doesn't matter what a parent thinks; that's not the *only* factor. "You're right," Charlotte says. "Let's do it. This may be our last warm day. I'll take you on at Windy Acres this afternoon. One more outing before the snow and cold take over. I can be there by one. One-thirty?" Teresa has it handy living so close; she can get to the course early and do her stretches. "No, no. Mother's happy to have Caroline around."

When Charlotte hangs up—she can't believe she said yes—Caroline has come back inside and sits at the computer. "Doing research for Dad?" Charlotte asks, pausing behind Caroline's shoulder.

"No, well, maybe. I finally remembered to check my e-mail. This is stuff about organic farming. Vegetables. Being a peasant."

"Peasant?" How old-fashioned can you get? There's a small, bare spot on the back of Caroline's head—doesn't she care? If she didn't cut her hair so short, it wouldn't stick up wrong after she sleeps. She had such beautiful shoulder-length hair in high school, exactly the blonde shade Charlotte always wanted.

"There's an old tradition: an organic farmer is called a peasant." Caroline's eyes stay on the screen.

"Listen, Caroline, don't go giving your dad ideas. Organic sounds good, but it's way too expensive." She won't even turn to look at Charlotte. "When we were young, we didn't understand how complicated everything was, either." Caroline mumbles something about General Mills threatening to use the organic label, and then blah, blah, blah. Charlotte moves to the side of the computer to get Caroline's attention. "I meant to ask if you wanted to do some shopping while you're here. We could make a quick run to the mall before lunch, if you'd like. Maurices has nice clothes. Or Nancy's downtown is even better."

"Do I need something?"

"You need to get out of the house. It's not natural, a young person coming home and not getting out to see anyone else. Besides, it's always good to look around, keep up with the styles."

"I have stuff I never wear here in my closet."

"You should get rid of that old stuff. It's ridiculous to wear a sweatshirt from high school." Charlotte puts both hands on the computer desk, leans down. “Caroline, you need to get a job where you can dress up and feel good about yourself again. That secondhand store isn’t the place for you.”

“I agree, about Re-Use-It.”

“Then do something about it. It’s so frustrating with you. Don’t just dilly-dally. Oh, I know it’s confusing. But you can be so aggravating. Sometimes I think you’re worse than Chad; teenage boys are supposed to be one-syllabled.” Charlotte watches the word SUSTAINABILITY flash on and off the screen, like it’s too hot to stay in one place. “If a person feels good about how she looks, she’ll actually look better than if she thinks she doesn’t look good. Your aura. It’s been proven.” Charlotte knows better than to dress young like some mothers do: tight halter tops, cleavage, high heels. She’s not desperate like that. “You could do so much more for yourself, Caroline. You need to look confident.”

“Lots of good sidebars here,” Caroline mumbles, reading from the screen. “I *am* doing something. ‘How to Start Your Own Berry Patch.’ ‘Ten Steps to a more Fruitful Relationship with Your Banker.’”

Charlotte straightens and backs away. “Oh, well, good. That’s good, Caroline.” Who knows what she means. “Are you hungry for blueberries? I have some in the freezer from Troyer’s; they got them fresh from up North.”

“I was checking on prices for *plants*. I’m kind of on a fast from clothes shopping.” Caroline scratches the underside of her chin with her thumb. “You’re right; I need to take stuff to Goodwill. But I can’t think of anything I need, not at the mall.”

What a daughter! You say something to be helpful, and she just tries harder to be contrary. Does she really want her fingernails that short? "By the way, Teresa and I are playing nine holes this afternoon. Want to come along? Get some more exercise? You could be my caddy. I saw you walking outside, like you were stepping something off. Did you lose something?"

Caroline grins at the screen, then shakes her head. "Oh, no, I'm fine here."

"You'd be welcome to come; I was just kidding about the caddy part. It'd be fun to do something together." Charlotte doesn't know how some mothers do it. Maybe it's all show, the ones who make it look like they're tight with their daughters.

"Yeah, sure. Me, too. I haven't had time to get much reading done. Dad'll probably need help with something. Fix some loose boards."

"Oh, didn't he tell you? He has a board meeting at one. He wants to see Mr. Starling again, too." Charlotte hesitates. "I'm not sure what all Chad's planning. You're not mad about me being gone for a couple hours, are you?"

Caroline turns to look at Charlotte. Their eyes connect ever so briefly. "Oh, no, I'm fine with that. Go for it. Grandma will be here."

Charlotte opens the refrigerator door but forgets what she's looking for. It really makes no difference to Caroline whether Charlotte's here or not. Some mothers and daughters are too different to be close. *Get over it.*

Charlotte opens lids, reorganizes. Put that stuffing near the front, so it doesn't get forgotten. The evening meal will be a snap: cold turkey and other leftovers. Everyone can warm their own plateful in the microwave. She had thought about shepherd's pie—something lowly—but she'll do that for lunch tomorrow. Oh, she could cook some corn; there weren't many beans left over. Or succotash, that would be special. Maybe open a jar of dill pickles for Caroline; there wasn't room on the relish plate yesterday. There's plenty of pie. *What is it with Gene?* Maybe she *should* call him.

And why doesn't Chad get up? She forgot to ask when his practice is today. Well, things have been hectic. Poor kid. She hopes he's not still sick. That must have been embarrassing in the gym. She could cook some pasta for him, if that would be better. It's so important that the team gets off to a good start. Chemistry issues always pop up. James says they need to practice inbounding under their own basket. Well, Chad knows to stay on the good side of Coach. That's disgusting when some parents call the newspaper and complain about the coverage. Always looking out for their own.

It'd be nice if Kenneth and Gloria could come to one of Chad's games. It's not that far to drive, not for the only nephew. Who could ever make sense of Gloria's cemetery dance? And her comments in the kitchen when they were cleaning up, that her *life* told her what to do, once she figured out the truths and values that made her tick. It sounded like gobbledy-gook. Then while Gloria was yacking away, James almost threw out the turkey carcass. What was *he* thinking? Charlotte came that close to not having broth for this noon's soup. Maybe they can eat a little early; she should try to leave the house soon after twelve-thirty. She's so lucky to have a golf partner who doesn't let the calendar hold her back. "Keep your head down, your left arm straight. Play it as it lies." Who thinks that applies only to golf?

Charlotte gave Kenneth a little surprise of her own yesterday. He looked right at her—he is so determined to drag things down—and asked, "Do you ever feel down-in-the-dumps?" She'd happened into the living room and had to say *something,* so she could leave again. Her answer must have sounded silly, but it's definitely true. The only time she feels a little anxious is when she's in the new Piggly Wiggly, miles different from Father's store. She catches herself, wandering up and down the aisles—oodles of cereal boxes, five brands of the same basic spices—and she feels a kind of malaise spread over her. Is that the right word? She's overwhelmed. She has to study labels and compare ounces. Sometimes she just grabs the first thing. But it catches her off guard every time. It's like the boxes and jars are sassing her: *too much, too much.* Well, you can't give in to that kind of mocking. You can't. Or pretty soon you'll put a pillow over your head.

Chapter 14

It comes like an answer to prayer. Martha starts plotting as soon as she learns that Charlotte has given in to her golf itch. Even before lunch, Martha checks for the basic ingredients: flour, cinnamon, raisins. She has to be sly, not call attention. The coconut is too high to reach, but not if Carrie helps. She knows Charlotte bought yeast recently because Martha had to remind her that she was low. Martha goes to the picture window, stands beside the fern, and watches as Charlotte drives away. Two squirrels chase each other on the big maple tree, running diagonally, disappearing on the other side. That squirrel nest still sits up high, stronger than rain and wind.

Martha nabs Carrie before she can get caught up in whatever it is she does at that computer. "Will you help? I want to surprise Charlotte, make cinnamon rolls."

"That's great, but what if Mom has something else in mind for breakfast?" Carrie glances on the counter for one of Charlotte's lists.

"She can change. There's nothing sacred about pancakes on Saturday."

Carrie hesitates, but soon they're melting butter, measuring sugar. Carrie plays along. "We're the Local Resistance Movement," she says. She finds the hard-to-reach ingredients, says she remembers that Martha always wrinkled her nose when she looked up high in a cupboard. What a peculiar thing to remember. When James leaves for his bank director's meeting, the yeast is rising—he promises not to tell—and Carrie has mashed the cooked potato.

"I can't knead worth anything," Martha says, working the dough in the big bowl on the kitchen table. "Not with the counter this high. My arms give out." She touches her hand to her chest. "Something goes too fast, and my wrists are no good anymore."

The phone rings and Martha heads for the portable. Maybe it will be Gene. Kenneth is on the other end, chipper as ever. Martha is glad to know they arrived home safely, got there by eight-thirty. He wants a rundown of what everyone's doing today, so Martha sits down on a kitchen chair, uses her free hand to support the elbow of her phone receiver hand. This will take awhile to cover Chad's practice, Charlotte's golf, and places in between. Kenneth says Mr. Armburgey would like more games of Chinese checkers. Martha can't help but smile. "Yes, I enjoyed meeting him, too." Dropping his voice, Kenneth asks if they've heard from Gene. "No, nothing. I'm concerned, too. We all are."

Questions about Martha's health follow. She gives short, direct answers. Couldn't Kenneth see that she was doing well yesterday? No, the headaches haven't been excessive. Only the occasional pain above the eye. Yes, she's taking her blood pressure medicine. Finally, he runs out of questions—should she volunteer that she sometimes has to strain?—and Martha can hang up. She sighs and says, "It's good you were here to keep the dough going; you greased the bowl and everything. Kenneth forgot to cover some of his bases yesterday."

"Do you think Mom will invite Mr. Armburgey to spend Christmas with us?" Carrie asks. She folds the sides of the dough into the middle, pushes it down and away with the heels of her hands, flips it over, pushes again.

"He wasn't invited the first time," Martha says. "My, that dough looks nice and smooth. Did Charlotte teach you?" Martha puts her arms on the counter, leans forward. "That man had us all befuddled, didn't he? But what a kind man. He made me wish I could be as free to say what I think."

"Grandpa was never the talkative kind, was he?" Carrie pokes the dough with her index finger, watches the indentation fill again. "Did you always hold back?"

"With Daniel, the fewer words, the better." Martha pats the dough, elastic to her touch. Smooth, oh, so smooth. "You must bake bread a lot; so nice and springy. Is there anything more wonderful? So mysterious, the transformation with yeast. Like churning cream into butter. Hard, hard work but very rewarding." She pokes again with her thumb. Would she dare? "I counted on Daniel. Never worried when he was around," Martha says. "That all changed when he took a turn and left."

"Left you?"

"That dough's plenty good. Let it rest; it'll do its work," Martha says. She must be careful, not start down a road where she doesn't want to end up. "Use that same bowl; no need to dirty another one. Won't Charlotte be glad when she walks into the smell of cinnamon rolls?"

"Or upset." Carrie snaps the lid shut on the bowl. "It's good she went golfing, although she acted half-guilty. She's not the first woman to struggle." Carrie rubs sticky dough off her fingers, runs cold water over them.

"There's a balance. Everybody looks for it, gets put to the test. Not just women." Martha hesitates. "Are you doing all right, Carrie? At peace and all?"

"Oh, sure." Carrie looks away, out the bay window. She rubs dried dough off the rolling pin and scrapes away stickiness with her thumbnail on the large wooden cutting board. "Little things bother." She digs under her fingernails.

"Set that over by the big window, on the ledge there. The sun can warm it. You look like something troubles. Is that so?"

"Just, you know, wondering where's the best place. Where can I be myself *and* do something worthwhile. Seeds into plants—that miracle transformation." Carrie pours out a handful of raisins. "Want some?" Martha shakes her head. "What was that like, when you and Grandpa fell in love?"

"I can hardly remember." Martha smiles faintly. "Daniel had an automobile; very daring for his time. He shaved off his beard and promised we wouldn't have a big batch of children."

"You said something—. How do you mean, you should have worried? Did Grandpa get cranky?"

Martha rubs the spot above her eye. So much pressure at times. Is this how Daniel felt? He surely stopped to count the cost. "We all knew he was sick; he was never the same after his stroke. First, he had those tinglings; then one day his right arm was numb." She rubs her own arm through her white sweater over her long-sleeved blue dress. "He thought he must have slept on his arm wrong. It wasn't painful, so he thought it would go away. Then the stroke came. But that wasn't—. He died when it got to be too much." She runs water in the sink. "I might as well wash up these dishes. Momma always said, 'Redd things up.'"

"I suppose you're never ready for death," Carrie says, "even when you know it's coming." She stands with her hands propped behind her on the counter.

Martha glances at Carrie's smooth forehead, her blue eyes. *No, she's too young.* Martha promised herself, not to. *Not ever.* "One thing led to the next. Long ago he had the gout so bad. Oh, you probably didn't know. And his toenails—terrible, ingrown sometimes. But when his sphincter gave out after the stroke, that was too much." She shakes her hand in the dishwater, watches the sink fill with suds. "Oh, I say strange things sometimes. Ask Charlotte if that's not so. When you get to be my age, things don't always come out right."

Carrie takes a long drink of water. "You're not *that* old."

"It's humbling, old age. Wouldn't it be something if we knew how we looked to others?"

"It's a cosmic joke at any age. When I think I've said something clever, I probably look stupid instead." Carrie grabs a tea towel out of the drawer. "But with Mom it's hard to take; she acts like she has everything under control. She knows exactly what everyone else should do. Does Chad really need pasta before a practice?"

"Your great-grandfather, Poppa Lloyd, was like that some. He cared about how he looked—not that he acted puffed up—but he never quite got it the way he wanted. I don't mean physical appearance, but what others thought of him. It *is* a mean trick: right when you think you look your best, you're like as not to look your worst." Martha points to the woods. "Have you noticed? The trees look like they're dreading cold weather."

"I'd rather have it hot, too." Carrie rubs a fleck of dough off her faded jeans, brushes her black knit shirt. "I think Mom's ashamed of me, the way I look, my winter clothes." She dabs at a plastic bag with the tea towel.

"Oh, no, not you. Me." Martha points with her soapy thumb. "Charlotte's never been one for the old ways. I'm not sure she wants me to go along when she shops for groceries. I slow her down. Even whether to go to their church. They have some ritzy friends, you know. Sometimes she tells me I'll get too tired. I feel like a tagalong."

"She wouldn't want you to feel like you're in the way; I'm sure of that."

"We shouldn't talk about her." Martha swishes the paring knives in the rinse water, puts them in the drain board.

"I have a bad habit of writing her off. Mostly, I try not to let her take over."

"You can't hang onto malice, Carrie. Not toward Charlotte or anyone." Martha swirls leftover crumbs down the sink drain. "For one thing, you don't *really* know your mom. I didn't know Daniel; not the depth." She shudders. "I have to let things go, if I want Charlotte to tolerate me. She doesn't see that tin foil can be wiped clean and used again. Aluminum foil, she calls it. I have to tell myself: it's hers to throw away. She doesn't mend things either, not even socks. I can't let the upset eat at me. It's too hard on a person."

Carrie runs cold water and flips the switch on the garbage disposal. "Sometimes when her pushiness gets to me, I remind myself that she gets irritated with me, too. That puts me in my place." She runs a hand through her short hair. "How about a cup of tea?"

"Oh, no thank you, but you go ahead." Martha stands silent, fixed on the woods. The trees look stark, putting on a brave front. Carrie's cup of water clanks against the glass microwave plate. "They say, we're all wounded by life," Martha says. "I tell myself I have it better than most. You know, I—." Martha stares. Only the oaks are hanging on. The other leaves, stripped away. Men as trees, walking. That blind man in the story from Mark. He reached out and was touched. *She can't.* She promised herself. When the man's sight was restored, Jesus told him not to tell. The microwave dings.

"You must miss Grandpa a lot."

This is too hard. Martha shouldn't have to lose the respect of a grandchild. Daniel shouldn't. She must focus on Carrie. "If you were the last one to offer someone a smile—squeeze a hand—you'd do it, rather than feel guilty afterwards, neglectful."

"What is it, Grandma?" Carrie asks. "You look like you don't feel well." She puts an arm around Martha's waist. "Let's sit down. We have time to talk. Tell me stories. About Grandpa, or Poppa Lloyd. Unless you need to rest in bed."

"I can rest on the couch just as well. You haven't said much about your job." Martha hangs onto Carrie's arm. This must be Gethsemane, bartering sorrow for an ounce of understanding.

Carrie sets the timer. "There, now we won't need to keep checking if the dough's doubled." She dips a tea bag into boiling water. "Re-Use-It? Not much to say there. You sure you don't want to share this tea bag?"

Martha lingers, looks out the window again. Not a tree sways in the woods. Oh, to be that resolute.

"You used to make up the best stories; you'd tell me ones where the little girl was named Carrie—well, you said Caroline then—and her mother's name was Charlotte. I thought I'd entered a magical land where a little girl lived who had the very same name as mine."

"If only our lives were made up. Then we could change the parts we don't like." Whatever Martha says, she'll have to live with. "You must have other things you need to do."

"Come on. Let's sit down."

Martha settles in the middle of the chocolate brown couch. She rubs the suede covering. "I've never liked this couch," she says, pulling her dress down. "I like the soft fabric, but the seat is too long for my legs and I feel like a little girl."

"Here, let's prop you up a little." Carrie puts extra pillows behind Martha. "Now you won't slump. How's that? Too much? You still look pale. Would you rather sit on your rocker?"

"No, I want to be here beside you." Martha doesn't mean to beg. "I miss sitting beside Daniel. Isn't that silly for an old woman?"

"Of course not."

"Have I ever told you? You take after your father's side in the face. Your Grandmother Lehman. Maybe I *will* have some of that tea. The cinnamon smells so good. I shouldn't bother, now that you're sitting down." There's a force leading Martha, as surely as a flashlight in the dark. But there's also a blinking yellow light in the corner of her other eye. Did Jesus waver, the night he was betrayed? He could have gotten away if he'd half tried. Did Daniel—? "This Ryan fellow. What happened?"

"He left," Carrie says from the kitchen. "Not much to tell there either."

"But you expected him to stay in touch?" Martha asks when Carrie reappears.

"Yes." Carrie's lips curl unnaturally, like she's repulsed by a sour taste. "It was unrealistic. I was the one, looked stupid, didn't have an inkling. Hey, look what I found." She holds up a chocolate bar.

"Charlotte's fancy stash!" Martha blows on her cup of tea. Much too hot to drink, but the cup feels good in her hands. "Is that Free Trade?"

"*Fair* Trade. Want some? Here's a bowl for your tea bag. I'm going to get fat in only four days. I love Mom's cooking, but when I let myself start eating so much, I have trouble controlling it. This chocolate is totally unnecessary. Here."

"No, thank you; oh, maybe one square. Had you made a commitment? You and this Ryan?"

"Not really. Well, *I* had, in my mind. I was excited, thinking about my life as a we."

"So you thought he was, too?" Uhm, the chocolate slowly dissolves in Martha's mouth, sticks to the roof of her mouth.

"Yeah, crazy how that works." Carrie sips her tea between bites. "He never said he wanted to be together forever."

"I'm sorry." Martha puts a hand on Carrie's arm.

"I thought we'd show the world, the two of us. How to be in a relationship without being attached in a suffocating way. How marriage can be. Well, I don't know." Carrie squeezes on her eyebrows with her thumb and finger. "My mind ran way ahead."

"I was always glad when Daniel came home from the store. We could finish each other's sentences, but it didn't matter. I was ready to wait on him. I never dreamed—." Martha shifts on the couch, pulls her dress down again. "You don't think Ryan will come back?"

"I doubt it. He was the one, talked about holding people lightly. Detachment. 'Close, but detached,' he'd say. I thought he meant not possessing someone, soul and body. Not assuming rights to the other's time and energy." Carrie puts her head down. "It turns out, his detachment wasn't the same as mine."

"So it feels like betrayal?" The cup teeters in Martha's hand. She has to be careful not to spill on Charlotte's couch. "He didn't talk it over?"

"No, not really. Well, yes, betrayal of my dream life. I was naïve." Carrie whispers the last word like it escapes in spite of her. "Forget plural. It's back to I for me."

Martha blows on her tea, glances at Carrie, blows on her tea again. Does Carrie know she has a hole in the toe of her sock? "He treated you badly, that's for sure. It seems we always expect more of others than they can give."

"It's only in romance novels where one person's need matches another's desire to fill." Carrie tucks a leg under her, licks a finger. "Even when he first left for the Middle East, I thought he'd come back. I never dreamed he wouldn't write back. I rationalized for weeks."

"He treated you like you were second-class." Martha pauses. "That feels awful."

"You know?"

"Oh, Carrie. This may be betrayal, too." Martha sighs. Surely Judas counted the cost. "Daniel would probably tell it differently. But it's my story, too. Part of it."

"If it's yours, then it may be mine, too." Carrie crumbles the chocolate bar wrapper. "Maybe that's why we step on each other's toes in families; we can't separate what's whose."

"How true; there aren't neat lines to separate. You last saw your Grandpa Ropp when you were home for Christmas, right? A year ago." Martha shivers, puts both hands around her cup. Maybe she's the one who gave Chad the tendency to blurt.

"Right. I was out playing Ultimate Frisbee in March; it's kind of like football with lots of aerial skills. But fancier: body rolls, behind-the-back catches. And the movement is non-stop. No tackling, but lots of teamwork. We call our own violations, don't need referees. It was a co-ed league that Ryan helped start. But anyway, I came back to a phone message: 'Call home.' Grandpa hadn't looked well at Christmas—thin in the face. But I didn't think that much about it."

"Charlotte thought he'd get well." Martha tugs at her dress.

"Mom's such an optimist; she won't let herself think about problems. That's why she pampers Chad; she thinks she can make him stay out of trouble." Carrie leans to the far end of the couch and sets her cup on the end table. "Well, that's my theory. I'm not so sure she really thought Grandpa would ever get back to feeling good. He'd lost a lot of hair, lost his color."

"She thought he'd get well," Martha repeats. "That's what she always told him." Martha licks her lips. She might as well be sipping lemon juice concentrate. *What if Carrie doesn't believe her?* Daniel always said: *Finish what you start. Or don't begin.* "Daniel wanted to die. He said as much." She grabs Carrie's arm, hangs on to her wrist. Carrie feels *cold.* "He did it himself," Martha says suddenly. That isn't how she was going to say it. "Please understand; he was sick."

Carrie pulls away ever so slightly. She squints at Martha like she's trying to locate a street that's folded up in a map. "You mean, by accident?" She reaches for Martha's hand.

"I wasn't good enough to help him live. He lost his wish to live. His desire." *Cold on cold. There's no stopping now.* Her head feels hot but her hands are cold, just like Carrie's. "I was at the Sewing Circle, our church women's Missionary Group. Gene had called that morning, just checking in. I was in a hurry, and I left the cap off the pills. I saw it first thing, the pill bottle, when I got home. I didn't take enough care. When I saw it, I put the lid back on right away and put that empty bottle way back in the cupboard. Later, I stuck it behind the glass canisters in the pantry. I was shaking so bad, I almost dropped one." Martha's lips tremble. "No one ever asked." She rubs her index finger back and forth under her nose. Of all the times, not to have a handkerchief in her sweater pocket.

"Oh, Grandma!" Carrie scoots closer, rubs Martha's arm.

Martha's fingers curl inside Carrie's hand, tight as a fist. She shivers. *Cold against cold.* "Don't judge. Please." She hands Carrie her half-empty tea cup, rattling like a house afire, motions toward the end table. She'll be cold the rest of her life.

"Where's your lap robe? Here, let me get it." Carrie untwists her body, stumbles in her hurry.

"Oh, thank you." Martha tucks the multi-colored cover under her thighs. The work of Momma's hands, those long years ago. She wants to lean into Carrie's shoulder, doesn't dare.

Carrie looks like she's spooked, her eyes wide. "You haven't told anyone?"

Martha slumps away on the couch. Carrie won't want to sit by a leper. "I was ashamed. Daniel did what he thought he needed to do. He lost the wish." Her eyes search Carrie's face. That frown may stay there forever. "It was too much for him. 'What good am I?' he used to ask. He tried his best, up until the diapers. I hear those words every day. He passed them on—'What good am I?' Words as common as my dresses." She shudders. "No, I haven't told; I didn't want others to talk bad."

Carrie scootches her body closer, puts her arms around Martha. She mashes Martha's hair bun, bumps her shoulder. She tries to pat Martha's back, settles for rubbing her shoulder. "This must be a, a boulder. For you, all alone. You used to talk about the eternal verities."

Martha goes limp and digs once more for a handkerchief. "No more stock phrases. It's too late." She finds a hankie in her dress pocket. "It's like Mr. Armburgey said. You have to forgive." She wipes her nose, puts both hands under the lap robe, holds tight. Pink, orange, black, bright pink, purple squares; whatever scraps Momma had. "Forgive myself for not being at home. I can't. For being in too much of a hurry. Not saying a kind word when I left. Not even a peck on the cheek. I knew he'd be there when I returned. Maybe that's the hardest."

"Oh, no."

Martha's gray, old woman's shoes stick out beyond the cover. Dark laces that are too long. "The neighbor, Mrs. Siegel, came to check and said he was sleeping. I don't think she really looked. Well, I don't know. It's hard to believe. Maybe he did it after she left. I don't know. We paid her good money to check. Daniel did what he had to do. It must have been his Lion's Den. Only, there was no one to whip the wild animals into submission. He must have hoped I'd come home early; I stayed almost three hours." She wipes her nose again. "I feel so guilty. Unworthy. The church preaches against selfishness."

Carrie holds Martha's hand like a fragile cup, fashioning a saucer with her own hand. "You don't think the neighbor checked?"

"I doubt it. Looked in is all, didn't want to disturb. I can see how it could happen." The clock chimes: la—la—la—la. "Human error. I can't judge her. We all do the best we can. Now I'm telling; I'm telling someone. I said I never would." Martha covers her face with her free hand. *Don't try to make it better.*

"I don't know what to say. Oh, Grandma. How awful. You knew he was feeling bad, but you—. You never imagined—?"

Martha can't say more. This is too much to tell one so young. "Never. Not the depth. Maybe I should have. His upset over Mrs. Fortwright those years ago. Maybe a sign. I knew he had the severe leanings, but—. I wasn't good enough." She fingers the lap robe, squeezes the bumpiness inside the fabric.

"I'm so sorry you have to carry this, this huge—." Carrie's hand lingers in the air, like it has no place to go. She looks more at a loss than Mr. Armburgey.

"No one wants to get old. He left me all alone."

"Mom doesn't know?"

Martha shakes her head.

"He was always such a joker."

"He was reaching for something. I'm sure of it. Sometimes I made things sound better than they were, just to help out. I said there'd be graduations, weddings to look forward to—the grandchildren. He'd had troubles before. I knew it. Downhearted."

"Disconsolate." Carrie sucks in a long breath, lets it out slowly.

"Yes. I tell myself—." Martha shakes her head from side to side. "He wasn't afraid to die. That's a good thing. Dust to dust. That transformation. He knew—." She raises her thin hand with its blue veins, holds it empty in the air. "He must have counted on a merciful God. Impartial-like." She stops to gather herself. "Maybe we all do. Compared to how partial we've been. We hope we'll be treated better. Daniel couldn't see any point in the hope the rest of us tried to give him. Charlotte would come in, tell him he looked good, when he knew I'd hidden the mirror. He did what he had to do for himself. Did I say that?"

Carrie puts her hand on Martha's, squeezes their fingers together so hard, it hurts. "I'm so sorry. I wish I knew what to say. How to help."

"I shouldn't have been in such a hurry. It was my fault. Gene didn't know I was getting ready to leave; he was so good about calling. My hair was down like a loose woman when the phone rang. Then I had to hurry to be ready in time. I'd stay with Daniel every day, if I had it to do over. Every minute. The Home Health nurse had made it clear; 'Always put everything back.' I tried to be mindful, but so much needed looking after."

"Oh, Grandma." Carrie shakes their clenched hands. "If he wanted to do this, he would have found a way, whether you were at sewing or not. How could he—?" She pauses. "You can't blame yourself. Well, you can." Now Carrie leans back on the couch, wipes her nose with the heel of her hand. "It doesn't change anything. The blame."

Martha can only shake her head. *This is all wrong.* Carrie doesn't believe her grandpa would do this. It was selfish to unburden.

"We probably all say things that hurt." Carrie's eyes open wide. "Yesterday. All that talk. You sat there. You haven't told anyone?"

Martha holds her body stiff. Shiny blue and dull red squares. Gray shoes. "Not till you. At first I was—what do you say?—stupefied. I went around silent. Charlotte? I can't tell her. I go back and forth. I should. But she thinks the world of Daniel. I don't know what she'd say."

"I don't blame you. It doesn't go over well, trying to tell her something she doesn't want to hear." Carrie shudders. "But—. Don't you think it'd be better? Holding it in can't be good."

"You won't say anything, will you?" Martha clutches at Carrie's arm.

"Oh, no, I have enough of my own."

It's just as Martha thought; all she's done is upset Carrie, ruined her image of Daniel. "Kenneth was busy making arrangements with the preacher. I intended to tell, but everybody was preoccupied. Gene was heartbroken; I almost blurted it to him. Charlotte was having a crisis: which of Daniel's suits to use. She and Kenneth got into a snit over which tune to use for "God is Great" at the meal after the funeral. It was all so petty. She corrected me every time, insisted it was to be called a memorial service."

"I can hear them. It must have been a nightmare."

Martha tries to sit up straight again, blows her nose, and leans her head against a pillow. "After the funeral—that's when I thought I'd tell—I worried so. They'd all be angry with *me*. Hold me responsible. Charlotte would never forgive *me*. She'd say I should have done something, any number of things, differently. She'd have had plenty of ideas. Or else she wouldn't speak a word to me ever again. And Kenneth, he had his packing to do. Then he was gone." She puts the soaked hankie back in her pocket. "I didn't want to hear his questions. There may have been old pills in the medicine cabinet, too. Well, I know there were—those white ones, the anti-depressants from way back. Some doctor—can't remember his name—a specialist of some kind. Daniel stopped taking them. He didn't like the way they made him feel. I don't see how he was strong enough to get up by himself, but—. Oh, I don't know." She can't say how she pictures him. Trying to get up, scratching at the sheet, wretching, reaching. His eyes must have bulged. Shaking. All twisted up. It's too much to think he might have been peaceful.

Carrie changes her position, her legs yoga style, facing Martha. "I've heard fantastic stories about people rising from their deathbeds to do one last, impossible task."

Martha shakes her head. "He was too weak." *Don't say more.* "Charlotte started in on me, said I looked like I'd seen a ghost. She insisted on taking my temperature and fussed about me not eating. How could anything look good? I was the one deserved to die. The scourge. Neglectful. If Daniel needed to be forgiven fifty coins' worth, I surely needed to have five hundred wiped away. All I wanted was to be left alone." Wrapped in a sheet, lips covered with hyssop. "Oh, Carrie, try not to judge. Kenneth flew from Madison the day after the burial; he'd already missed two precious days with his tour group to Russia—his spring break."

"Yeah, he joked around about how he'd be dead soon, too, because he stayed behind to bury his father. Some obscure scripture."

"You heard that, too? My, my." Martha shakes her head. "I've wondered if Daniel had it all planned out, waiting for me to fall into error. Well, I don't know. After Gene's call, Daniel asked for the tumbler of water. 'Closer,' he said, harsh-like. I told him he had enough with the plastic glass and the straw. He just stared at me, so I did what he said. Why couldn't he talk about how he felt? Oh, he tried, I guess. I couldn't listen. I thought I was, but I wasn't." Martha has slipped again, the gap widening between couch, pillow, and her back. Her neck has no place to go.

"Why can't any of us? Listen? I'm sure you did. But it's like whatever we want—what we most need—family can't give. Or not give enough."

"I don't know. Family's good for some things." Martha hesitates. "The preacher says, 'All things work together for good to those who love the Lord.'"

Carrie shudders, like she's completely disgusted.

"We had just refilled Daniel's prescriptions. When he first started taking those pills, some kind of 'blocker'—channel, no, some other name—he had asked the doctor what would happen if he forgot to take one. Doc Murphy kind of laughed and said that missing one pill wouldn't matter, but taking too many would be a different story."

"I'm so sorry, Grandma. What an awful thing. I can't imagine going through that." The poor girl looks as bad as when she first got here. "My troubles look like little melodramas, made-up TV shows."

Martha grabs Carrie's arm again. "You won't tell, will you? I don't mean that Daniel planned his demise from the moment the doctor said that—the doctor's not to blame. But when it got to be too much—those diapers were like unto pestilence—Daniel got more and more despondent. It's easy for me to say that he lacked the grace. I thought I needed to get out of the house. The Sewing was my respite. Did I say, I stayed away all morning? No one begrudged me that; it was only once a month. Charlotte was a big help, caring for Daniel. But when he didn't rally the way she expected—he tried to tell her he'd had a good life—she shushed him up and told him he didn't dare give up. Like that was a cardinal sin."

"Please don't blame yourself, Grandma." Carrie scowls, like she's been marked for life by Martha's weakness. "Maybe Grandpa did the right thing. Maybe some day he'll be held up as a model."

“Oh, no,” Martha says, shrinking back. These young people and their ideas. “The church is very clear. Life belongs to God, from conception to natural death.”

“That’s true, but—.”

“He’s not a hero. Don’t try to make him out that way. Oh, Carrie, no; that doesn’t help.” Silence hangs between them; everything changes when you tell. What if Carrie can’t help herself and spills it somehow? She’d never get it exactly right. “I can’t tell anyone else. Not the preacher at my home church. Daniel’s reputation would be ruined. Not that minister at Charlotte’s church—did I tell you he has the warmest handshake? I don’t know what either one might do. Ask me to stand up in front of the whole church? Like Momma?” Martha covers her mouth with her hand. That’s what she was afraid of. One thing leads to another. Her eyes fill with tears again. “I see Momma looking down. She’s sad-like, shaking her head, wondering how I could have gotten in such a fix.” Martha’s body shakes even though Carrie’s arms wrap around her. “You won’t make me tell, will you?” she asks, muffled in Carrie’s shirt.

“Oh, Grandma. Of course not. What could you have done? Here, let me get you some tissues. Why can’t *this* life be good? Good, like you. Like you *are*.”

Martha shakes her head, wads tissues in her hand. “I shouldn’t have told Daniel so much about Momma’s demise. I should have kept it in.”

“What do you mean?” Carrie pauses like she can’t believe there’s more. “My great-grandma?”

"Momma's death was long and drawn out—bedfast over a month. I shouldn't have bothered Daniel with it. 'Help me to walk,' Momma would say. I'd remind her that the pneumonia had taken all her strength away. 'No, I mean help me to walk,' she'd say. Then when I must have looked puzzled, she'd say, 'Walk to Jesus. Pray for me. Shout it out. Beg, please, on bended knee. You have to help me. Walk to Jesus. Plead for me, won't you?' On and on. I shouldn't have told him all that. I see him—still to this day—staring at the ceiling, looking at the clock, thinking it was to be his lot, too. To linger."

"Oh, Grandma. This is—. Don't take this the wrong way, but you know what I hate? People run around like crazy; then they die. We die. What's the point?"

"There's good too, Carrie. Don't give up. There's beauty, too. You have to throw yourself into the good." Martha can't bear to have tipped a young one the wrong direction. A granddaughter! All because of a selfish need for comfort. She's gone on too long. "Promise me. Promise you'll find the good and grab on to it. I'm just a weak old woman."

"I—. Oh, no, don't worry about me." Carrie folds her arms tightly in front of her like she's wracked by shivers. "Who knows what's *good* anyhow? Grandpa couldn't have been thinking straight. He wouldn't want this, for you to suffer. There has to be a better way. Why can't we have choices? You hear about older people, refusing to eat or drink."

"I've thought of that. He said food didn't taste good anymore. But how would you *will* your body to stop? Most people say, 'If God wants you to suffer—old age or cancer—then no one should interfere.'"

"Most people?"

"Most people I know. My oldtime friends, the few still living, are up to their necks in righteousness. Ruby looks like she's guessed. I used to be the same way. You can see it in my pictures—ten years ago—there's a hard look in my eyes. A sternness. Like Momma. I knew right from wrong. But the Lord could have punished Daniel, left him in a coma, vegetable-like, if the pills hadn't finished the job." She dabs her eyes. "I don't know about Charlotte. Sometimes I think she might have sympathy. But I can't be sure. She adored him."

"It'd scare the heck out of her, I'll bet. She'd—. I don't know."

Martha wants to snuggle into Carrie's arms. *Hold me*, she wants to say. "Oh, Carrie, Daniel always said you were the smart one. He had no idea you'd be such a comfort. You've looked so drawn down, disheartened. I wish I could help, but I can't bring back the verities."

Carrie takes both of Martha's hands in hers. "You've honored me with your trust. I don't know what it's been like; no one has any idea." She looks back toward the kitchen, as if a buzzer might have gone off and neither of them heard it. "People don't like ambiguity; that's why they make up rules, wise sayings. As if every situation's the same as the next. Artificial verities."

"A lot of us think we're planted; we're solid. But when we're holding onto something, it may slip away, or get pitched. Then what?"

Martha lifts the lap robe. "Charlotte thinks this is done for. That must be how Daniel felt."

Carrie sits up straight and pulls back from Martha. "You're not finished. Don't even think that. Don't say you don't matter." Her eyes look like blue fire, and there's a tightness in her grip. "Sorry. I didn't mean to yell." She looks down; her lips tremble. "Sometimes I feel the same way. Like there's nothing for me. Or like no one appreciates what I *could* do, if I had a chance." She looks scared, stares out the window at the bare maple.

"Carrie, will you forgive me?"

"What do you mean? I said you weren't—."

"I need to hear the words."

"I'm sick of all this shame. You. Me. Mom." Then Carrie studies Martha. "You're serious."

Martha nods.

Carrie's hands take hold of Martha's arms, squeeze. "I forgive you, Grandma, for whatever weaknesses. Perceived. Imagined. Your humanness."

"I needed a human voice." Martha waits, looks past the fern that needs turning, then back to Carrie. "Your mercy is like unto God's. No one will ever understand how Daniel jolted me out of complacency. My Damascus Road. Thinking I could only reach God through a man, wearing an outward sign."

"Oh, Grandma."

"When I go to visit Ruby, I see she's ashamed. I let her down, not holding to the old ways like we were taught. But God looks on the heart." A car slows on the county road. Chad? No, it sounds like a pickup. James' truck. Martha straightens, stuffs the tissues under the lap robe. "I used to think we could earn God, that I could pray and know to do what's right. Then I'd deserve God. Now I believe it's simpler; we have God, if we want."

"Oh, Grandma, you are so wise. The old way, Ruby's way, happens in cultures all over the world. Second class for women. Sometimes though, to be fair, it happens the other way, too. Women treat men badly."

"Yes, and I know women who treat other women badly."

Silence sits with them until the side door opens. "Anybody home?" James calls out. A cap lands on the dryer. Martha and Carrie look at each other. They wait as heavy steps come through the kitchen. James stops when he sees them.

"Hello," Martha says. She clears her throat, hopes she doesn't look too bad.

"Oh, sorry," he says. "I didn't mean to interrupt. Gotta change clothes." He turns away and slides down the hallway as if he's in someone else's house.

"It's okay," Carrie calls in return. "I'll punch down the dough, Grandma." The clock chimes on the half hour.

"I can finish the rolls," Martha says, "if you want to help with the milking. All the hard parts are done."

"Are you sure?" Carrie asks. "I might sneak in a walk yet. Then help Dad."

"Yes, go, by all means; the days are so short anymore. You know what I mean. Less daylight. I'll punch down the dough and rest until it rises again. I can roll it out and do the cinnamon."

"You don't mind? Filling the pans?"

"Not a bit." Martha waves to Carrie to go on. It will be a relief to be by herself. *What has she done?* She wants to go to her room and close the door. *Lord God of Hosts! All heaven and earth shall pass away.*

"Thanks, Grandma." Carrie comes back to put her hands on Martha's shoulders, gives her a tender kiss on the cheek. "Let's talk some more tomorrow. Love you."

Momma's Diary – November 1931

Sunday

Sermon topic: "I go to prepare a better place for you." Oh, to be acceptable on that day. Awful headache. Wind turning. Quite a number of confessions, nine (9) reclaimed this eve. One poor young girl.

Monday

Dust storm. Smaller wash. Oh, to be willing. Think it is one way, then see it is not. Sewed. It seems we cannot make headway. Potatoes spoiling. What will it all come to? Already two long years. When will we know?

Tuesday

Hold fast. Hard to say goodbye to Minnie and family. Such a lonesome feeling already. Lloyd says: are not to retreat. Not ours to choose. Sore finger. Lloyd tries salt. Bugs in the pantry. Are not to ask.

Wednesday

Finished hood. No one from Illinois. Try me and see if there be any wicked way in me. Lloyd has the grippe. My help cometh from the Lord.

Thursday

Did not venture out. Finger, no good at all. Disconsolate.

Friday

Saturday

A feeling of somewhat sadness comes over. Must scrimp. Jeremiah 31:11. Claim the promises. Redeemed and ransomed. Every day is one day closer. Dare not waste paper. Dora here to lance finger.

Momma's Diary - November 1932

Sunday

To church. Very good and larger attendance. The preacher R.D. Spanker and family here. Stayed for supper. Not much prepared for company but got along. Talk on non-conformity this eve. Very nice.

Monday

Beautiful wash day. Rec'd Uncle Ab's postcard photo. Wanted to write a letter but could not find a pencil. So little burdened for the unsaved.

Tuesday

Ironed. Put log cabin quilt in frame. Are longing to see things in deeper reality. Lloyd says not to dwell on months ago. One year, living day to day.

Wednesday

To Women's Missionary meeting this A.M. Not much going. Too much gossip. Soiled. Sad differences. Work for the night is coming. Made apron & petticoat. Father arrived near to sundown. Not near as spry.

Thursday

Crowd at church not as large, due to inclemency. To really and truly fill my place is my desire. The Lord knows whether or not. Must but follow. Nothing dare remain covered or hidden. Heavy rains tonight. Large hail.

Friday

Painted chairs and a few more other things. Worked on coverings and cut out garments. Father to stay one more week. Dare not overwork.

Saturday

Father and Lloyd on long trek to city. Very weighty matters. Objection not understood. Deepest distress and anguish. Babies and I alone.

Chapter 15

Carrie doesn't want to admit how much she needs to get away, be by herself. She thought she knew this morning, but now the roar in her head threatens to explode. She meets her dad outside the shed and mumbles something about going for a walk. "Something came up and—. It took more time than I expected." She reaches down to pet Sayeth, yipping at her ankles. She looks up, looks away, looks anywhere but at Dad.

"Go ahead," he says, as if he's used to being stranded. "We have extra feed from this morning. If you can help finish up, that'd be good."

"Oh, I just need a half hour or so. Be back soon." She suddenly gives him a hug, as much as she can throw herself around coveralls.

"Mind taking Sayeth? He'll be a wimp—run *away* from the cows—if we're not careful. There's a leash inside the back door, if you're going on the road."

Carrie claps her hands for Sayeth to follow to the woods. There's little room to walk on the side of the road in daylight, let alone at dusk. Her boots scuff on the gravel driveway. If only it were a day later and she were on the bus with hours to think. *She has to do something.* She snaps her thumb and finger for Sayeth.

Grandpa. What went through his head? *Her* grandpa. This is something you read about in books or hear on the news. *No, not Grandpa!* The man who scooped peanuts into his hand, jiggled them, and then ate them one at a time, fist to mouth, fist to mouth. She takes a shortcut, brushes aside brown prairie grass bent from early snows, waits for Sayeth—where is he?—whistles. The air has taken on a late afternoon chill as the sun hides on the back side of the woods. She can see her breath: warm air hitting cold.

How could he? Did he think he was the only one in the world? *Disconsolate.* Carrie blows out, watches her breath; the mist blends and disappears in the cool air. Did he down a handful of pills and then realize it was too late to stop? His hand shaking. She never knew him very well. A grandfather figure, old-fashioned and stodgy, except for playing jokes on people. One time he hid Mom's putter, put it in a corner of the basement behind a plant stand. She was beside herself, had walked past that corner countless times. Did he joke to cover his distress? Must everyone? Pretend. Even Mother Teresa felt despair at times.

Carrie jams her hands into her jeans pockets, burrows her chin into her red sweatshirt, rubs it against the zipper. Didn't he know how much pain he'd cause? Grandma left alone. What was he thinking? *He wasn't. Maybe he was.* Which would be worse? His desire gone. Grandma called it the *wish* to live. When it's gone, does obligation take over? Carrie trips on barbed wire—leftover downed fence—sidesteps scat. Maybe he realized he'd never find a doctor he could trust. No cohort. No spiritual guide who wouldn't condemn him to hell. He'd probably never heard of the Hemlock Society. But he took care of his own needs. Eight months ago. Eight months of not knowing. Mom still doesn't know. What would the Master Winker think? What if we all could say *when,* like arm wrestlers? "Give up?" *Say when.*

This woods, filled with mid-sized trees and spindly saplings. A few oaks and evergreens. Everything looks bigger up close. They used to come out here to find a Christmas tree; sometimes they tied two together to fill in the sparse branches. Sayeth whimpers like they're off limits. "Come on. Get over it." He hops after her, snoops at damp earth. A fallen log stretches across the ravine; it's covered with bracken fungus that's lost its color and hardened. She puts on her thin, brown work gloves and sits down. She's going to soak her jeans. Who cares? Her life is small. Her wrongheadedness, petty. The fat roll of money. How easily she stuck it in her jeans' pocket, stuffed it under a used Kleenex, pulled her sweater down over the bulge. Only later in the restroom at Re-Use-It, she realized she had three hundred dollars in her pocket. A trifling, compared to this.

Imagine! Holding another's secret of this magnitude. Taken into Grandma's silence, her shame. She's made it worse by not talking. Hasn't she? Now one silence demands another. A chain. Carrie's supposed to act like nothing happened. The natural order of things: an apple falls. Did Grandpa think he was protecting Grandma by not getting help? No one dreamed he—. What torment to violate himself! Like no one else mattered. People do it all the time. Why not Grandpa? If a person's mentally competent, and death is imminent, shouldn't he be able to say when?

Carrie gets up, brushes dirt off her backside, follows the small creek bed, picks up litter: plastic wrap from a cheese slice, a flattened water bottle, half a page torn from the Sunday comics. Hunters. Who do they think they are? She crams trash into her hoodie pockets, stomps her boot at a squirrel, watches the gray blur run away. The rich smell of decay—maybe leftover hickory nuts.

What could Carrie have said to Grandma? She felt stupid, speechless. What inane things *did* she say? Grandma might feel worse for telling. She squeezed Carrie's hand like it was keeping her from going under. At the time of the funeral, Carrie had barely talked with Grandma beyond the usual greetings. She can't picture her. It was all a blur; she'd gotten in late the night before. If Grandpa was going to do it, he was going to do it. What could Grandma have done? Maybe it's not right to try to talk someone out of it. Maybe that's selfish, pleading for someone else's existence, so you don't have to be the one, run over by a truck.

Grandma's shame must burn inside her, a churning. Not a boulder—did Carrie say that? Carrie can't know what it's like; no one has any idea. Grandma looks so meek and innocent, incapable of carrying more than a ten-pound bag of flour. Only a few days ago, Carrie thought of her as old; that was about it. Sure, she had the heart problem—they used to joke about it—and she complained about her joints. But something happened in that living room, in the telling. Grandma's a person, not to be lumped with an age group. They're tied forever, far beyond bloodlines.

Carrie kicks dead lichen off a rock—powdery, no longer brittle, dull, and gray. The bright orange of its springtime look, long gone. Is shame what connects people? The Grand Equalizer. What if Mr. Disappearance felt shame? *Cut the crap!* If he was going to go to the Middle East, he was going to go. There's no comparison.

She backs up to a poplar, stands on one leg, balances the other, bent against the tree. *Obligation.* Is that what life is? You *have* to suffer when there's no quality left? What kind of God is that? What kind of sadist would mastermind that kind of conclusion? Woohoo to the loving God, the ultimate mystery. The one who wants good things for people, rolling out a feast of life, like Mom's spread yesterday. Yeah, right. Pay now or pay later. Die now or die later. That's it? What happened to the thumbs up? Why isn't there a widening of openings at the end, not a shutting down?

What's Carrie to do? Pull back in fear? Betray Grandma's trust? Never. It has to be hers to tell. What was she saying about her momma? A secret not yet handed on. Carrie props the other leg, leans her hoodie back into the poplar. *She can't stand it.* Her scream would bring people running, send Sayeth for cover. Why can't reasonable people figure something out? Guidelines or something. There has to be a better way. Where are the right-to-die people? They didn't all move to Oregon. If families could band together when life's terminal, resist the automatic push to revive in the emergency room—. Oh, yeah, the slippery-slope people would yell. But why couldn't it be legal? Moral.

Carrie snaps her fingers for Sayeth, starts walking again. She used to know this woods well. She loved spotting the first wildflowers, hunting for mushrooms. She scrambles around a fallen tree top, hears small critters head for new nesting places. So hunters have the right to trash, do they? And property is just a human construct, intended to protect those who have, from those who don't. *Don't be so hard on everybody.* Everyone has a place; hunters are helping keep the deer population down.

She has to get back to help Dad. He'll be steamed, even though he looked calm. A spring! She drops to her haunches. *It's still here.* A thin stream of clear, fresh water seeps out of nothing, runs over small rocks, finds its way. It has to come from somewhere, hidden away. A gift of ancient, geologic forces. Is this the same spot she remembers? Natural springs are drying up, but not here, not on this farm, not yet. Sayeth scratches in the leaves, buries his snout, tumbles sideways, picks himself up. His version of excitement: a natural dam of leaves, shoved up by the rain, short sticks piled high.

Grandma said not to judge. How many times did she say that? Is she *obligated* to forgive? How do you ever? Out of love or duty? From the burden of sorrow? Her story the other night about Grandpa helping the man left with the five boys. *Generous!* Yeah, right. Carrie won't ditch Grandma; she asked for mercy. "We are who we protect." Where did Carrie hear that? Heaven hinges on how we act toward a common, frail person. Something like that. A sweet story about a disguised Christ. Not Carrie, though, bumbling for words. But she forgave Grandma.

Carrie pokes at more algae, fungi. It's everywhere. We are *what* we protect. The earth. Fresh-water springs. The soil that blesses seed into food. She's running out of time. Friday is almost gone. How did this happen? She's let too much time slip away. If she'd been serious, she'd have gone to the Ag Extension Agency and gotten a soil testing kit. She has to get a soil sample before the ground freezes! But no, there she was, making rolls with Grandma inside the house. Waffling. Sure and not sure. Waiting for something else to happen, someone to push her one way or the other. *Well, something has happened. Someone has acted.* Grandma needed to hear words; Carrie needed to hear story. They're linked forever. No, Mom, she hadn't lost anything this morning. Well, yes, she had, but she didn't know it was this. Now she can say: it's time. It *matters* that the water table doesn't get depleted by irrigation. Yes, she's wasted time, but she still has time. *She'll carry through.*

"Come on, Sayeth. There's work to do." Carrie clicks her finger and thumb. Dad'll be ticked. He'll figure she's been chewing on some woman problem that Grandma couldn't help her solve. Jeez, it's practically dark. No way to avoid deer scat now. She'll track in. It's not going to be pretty tonight, but here she comes.

Chapter 16

A casual observer, untuned to the clatter beneath the surface silence, might anticipate a quiet Friday evening at the Lehman homestead with more time to recover from the stresses of a major holiday. More harmless exchanges, as when Charlotte came home renewed from golfing. “What’s this?” she asked her mother at the sight of seven aluminum pans full of cinnamon roll dough rising.

“Carrie and I decided to surprise you. I’ll take care of getting them baked and make the icing.”

“How nice.” Charlotte rearranged the pans on the counter, covered them carefully again with her mother’s thin tea towels embroidered with domestic activities. “Kind of late in the day to start such a big project, but thanks. It won’t take me long to mix up the frosting.”

"I'll do it." Martha wavered ever so slightly. There was no reason not to hold her ground, no reason Charlotte always had to correct her for calling it icing.

No reason, indeed, to deny anything individual, unless it interferes with the perceived good of the whole. Family members can come together, rub shoulders, laugh, and deflect blows. The calm façade can continue for the sake of surface unity, until one person's desire gathers enough heft to come up against another's expectation. Then voices rise, questions ripple in the clash to establish a different order. Some parts of some voices may need to be subsumed again.

It's no surprise when Charlotte pulls a bag of corn from the freezer and places her new magnet with the teeny-tiny letters on the refrigerator side: TODAY IS THE BEST DAY OF THE REST OF YOUR LIFE. It's no big deal either that she came up short, score-wise; she whacked Kenneth out of her system with each long drive off the tee.

Everyone fills their plates with leftovers, and the mealtime talk steers clear of past pitfalls. But an electricity with the lid on remains in the kitchen. Martha and Carrie exchange glances in the nook, share caution about what they might give away in a longer look. A part of Martha feels unburdened—the Lord sent an angel—but was the visitation wise? She won't let herself think on it too much, or it will show. What's done is done. Maybe Carrie will give a sign, a warm smile in the hallway.

James stays on edge, too. Carrie's time is winding down. He watches her accidentally drop a piece of turkey on the floor, throw it in the trash, and not say a word. Chad stays quiet, except for complaining that Coach works them too hard at practice. Charlotte reminds him to be smart and keep pushing fluids to restore his body. She predicts that Stockville will be a pushover next Tuesday, but James shakes his head. She doesn't understand how overconfidence can lead to upsets. Carrie imagines the Monroe team gobbling up tiny Stockville for a practice meal.

One topic leads to another—golf to hunting—and then the talk turns to food. James hopes Simp has gotten his buck, and Charlotte reminds him that she didn't like that deer salami Simp gave them last year. He reassures her, he's asked for sausage, but he also cautions that processing takes time. That reminds Martha of the years she and Daniel helped with the meat canning that Mennonites organized back in the '40s and '50s. She makes the moment sound dramatic when the mobile meat canner pulled into town. Daniel and the men cut the meat—sometimes they'd slaughtered and donated their own beef—ground it up and cooked it in a big kettle, careful to keep it stirred. The women toiled in the kitchen, washing two-quart jars. Years later, when they canned the beef in twenty-eight ounce cans, Daniel's favorite job was gluing labels on the cans: Food for Relief: In the Name of Christ.

Through the chit-chat Chad is plotting the next hours, calculating how much time he'll need to hang around before he can duck out. Justin is The Man when it comes to getting out of the house. Chad considers passing some time by scooting down the hall to his old bedroom. Carrie used to go ballistic when he'd mess with stuff in her room. He has to wait awhile, though, before he can start dipping into the freshly baked rolls.

The leftover leftovers get put away, but before Charlotte settles in the living room, she takes a good look at the furniture. Maybe Teresa is right: the dark green leather loveseat and the new chocolate suede couch look odd together. In the store Charlotte was sure they'd be fine. Everything would fit with other earth tones: the tan carpet, the flecks of pale green and burgundy in the beige drapes. Martha sits on her platform rocker, moving slowly back and forth, the same way she used to sit with Daniel on the wooden swing. They'd go back and forth between her clematis plants, not needing to say a word—their special place.

And then, right when James and Chad decide which basketball game to watch—a team with two hot-shot freshmen starters or a coach who has a short leash when his players miss defensive assignments—the phone rings.

"Hello," James says and immediately looks at Charlotte. He makes small talk with Gene about the Thanksgiving get-together, sounds polite enough about them not having been able to come. Charlotte has gotten up, waits for the phone handoff, when James says, "Sure, she's right here." And to Charlotte, "He wants to talk to your mother." Charlotte grabs the phone anyway, hesitates, and then silently hands the phone to Martha.

"Hello?" she says. How is she supposed to carry on a decent conversation when there are so many ears in the room? Chad picks up his new *ESPN the Magazine* and disappears. James eyes the game.

Carrie starts making a list of spring greens: spinach, lettuce, Swiss chard, kale, Asian, chicory. Beside each, she jots down assets and liabilities. Oh, duh, there's a chart that compares them all.

Martha makes it through the usual greetings and belated holiday wishes. She pictures Gene in his expensive-looking brown loafers with the little tassels. "What's that?" Her head whips up. She adjusts the phone; it has such a small receiver that it sometimes slips on her ear. "Do you mean it's serious?" And then, "Oh, I'm so sorry. I'm not familiar with that." Her eyes dart around the room, looking for a place to hide.

Charlotte stands nearby listening, idly checks the thermostat setting. Martha's voice rises. "You say she's in the hospital? Her heart? But she's so young. Oh, my, how do you spell that?" Charlotte edges closer. There's a long silence and Martha's head stays down. "Yes, I understand it must be very hard for everyone." Charlotte tries once more to straighten the picture to the side of the piano. "Meg does?" Martha's free hand smooths the unfinished embroidery in her lap. "Yes, we surely hope so. No, you can't be too careful. A treatment center, you say?" Charlotte is right there again. "Yes, well, give her my love. Yes, I'll be sure to tell them." Charlotte stretches out her hand. "Wait now. I believe Charlotte would like to say something."

Charlotte clutches the phone. "What is it? We've all been worried to death."

Carrie can't stand to be present at one more overheard conversation, goes to the computer nook, and double-checks websites she looked at this morning. Where was that one for CSAs in south central Wisconsin: realfoodgroup or farmfreshatlas? She wants to compare prices on seedling trays, too. How much trauma can Grandma handle in one day? This sounds like one more thing that could derail Carrie's plans for tonight. What is going on? What forces aligned against her? She hears Mom announce to the whole room, "Well, that puts food in a whole new light."

"I don't really understand," Martha is saying. "Anor—?"

"Anorexia," Charlotte says. "It's Sonja," she says to Carrie. "An eating disorder," to her mother.

"How could she have a heart problem?" Martha asks. She hardly knows Sonja, the one who didn't want to go to college. "Not much more than nineteen." One time she spelled Sonja's name wrong on a birthday card. Sue pointed it out that she'd used a y instead of a j. Martha knew better; she just forgot.

"She's been starving herself," Charlotte says, "to the point of developing an arrhythmia. She's going to be all right, Mother. Don't you worry. Oh, and James, Gene apologized for not telling you the other night. They weren't ready. For one thing, they hadn't reached Dorinda yet in Spain with her Study Abroad group."

Then Chad's back again, balancing with Belinda on the couch arm. Voices scramble over each other. "She's afraid she'll be fat." "Basically, she thinks she *is* fat, so she starves herself." "Isn't it about perfection?" "Lots of girls think guys want a pencil to go out with." "Thinks she has control when she doesn't eat." "Skinny as a rail." "They often lie about what they're eating, how much they're exercising."

"Meg knows about it," Martha says. She runs her hand over the smooth rocker arm, forward, backward.

"Meg does?" Carrie asks.

"How long has this been going on?" James asks. He watches Belinda, grooming herself, extending her tongue sideways, cleaning her back. That rough tongue that makes everything better.

"I didn't ask," Charlotte says. "Are you sure about Meg?" She turns quickly. "So it's not what you said, James, about a suicide."

Martha rustles in her sewing basket, comes up with nothing. Sonja used to love her pineapple fluff; sometimes that's all she'd eat. A couple years later, she wouldn't touch it.

"She always loved ballet," Carrie says. "I used to be jealous; she was so limber. Not that I wanted a ballerina outfit or wanted to twirl around on my toes."

"You say Meg knows?" James asks. Martha nods her head. "I'll be darned."

"They probably text each other," Chad says. "Girls know all the gossip; *they* get it started. Someone else makes it ten times worse, passes it on." He motions to his dad to change channels. It's hard to imagine *making* yourself vomit. No, that's bulimia.

"Gene didn't tell *me* that Meg knew," Charlotte says. "But he wants you to know, Mother, Sonja's going to be all right. She's getting the very best treatment." It's natural that Gene would want to tell Mother first. Meg probably hasn't told Kenneth.

Carrie slumps on the couch. She doesn't remember even talking with Sonja at Grandpa's funeral. Did she talk with anyone on that visit? Over the years she might have made stupid comments about overweight people, some thoughtless putdown about body fat at a family get-together. Mom's the queen of glib, but maybe Carrie's no better. There was that cluster of overweight girls in high school that stuck together, probably to protect themselves from the slurs: "Double fatty with cheese."

"What can they do for it?" Martha asks. "Are there pills? When did Gene say this happened?"

"Tuesday night was the worst," Charlotte says. "This treatment center has a very high success rate. They'll teach Sonja to look at food and hunger differently. Gene said they may want family therapy."

"The whole family?" Martha asks. She rubs her knees; she can tell when cold weather's coming on. Daniel used to bring candy home from the store: licorice, lemon drops—rewards for the youngsters' good behavior. Other times, they used food to punish. No dessert until the children finished their school work.

People talk over each other again. Chad clips his fingernails. "Not pills exactly, but medication for depression or anxiety, if that's part—." "Forevermore." "Family's often the last to know." "It may take a year of counseling." "Get the heart treated first." "Just like any change: you have to have the will." "Lots of pressure, stigma." "Girls take things way too serious." "Here we were, stuffing ourselves." "Love her; we can't do it for her."

Martha never told Gene how guilty she felt when she let him stand on a chair to watch her make donuts. She should have paid better attention with the hot oil; she had turned her back. He was just a little boy, and he ended up with neck burns. It could have been most anything that distracted her. Now he has to wear turtlenecks. Well, this settles that. She won't be telling *him* about Daniel any time soon.

"I can't believe none of us knew," Charlotte says. "Chad, please stop that clipping."

"Okay, okay. Makes sense to me that Meg knew," he says. "Girls talk way too much. They'll rat on you to save their own necks."

"Is that what Meg was doing at the table with that thing of hers?" Martha asks.

"That was only yesterday," James says. Belinda has found her spot on his legs. "We never know what kids are thinking. Right, Chad? Gene and Sue must be worried sick."

"Huh? Yeah, I guess," Chad mumbles. "Wow! That guy made a monster dunk, completely faked his man."

"Kids can be cruel," Carrie says. *What is going on?* The mood is all wrong. Mom's totally distracted. Grandma must be exhausted. *Grandpa! She can't let this derail her.*

"Do you understand for sure, Mother? Sonja is sick, not bad."

"Well, of course, Charlotte," Martha says. "I didn't say anything about anyone being bad." Oh, she should have kept in touch better. Does Gene blame himself? He's such a successful forty-two-year-old, prominent-like. The doubters thought Sun Prairie didn't need another funeral home.

Then the questions start in again. "How long did you say?" "Didn't Sue have a sister—?" "That was *Gloria's* sister." "Hits you like a kick in the gut." "What did Gene say the other night?" "No, not purging." "A kick in the belly button." "Food's not always the answer." "All families have their baggage." "Why *not* our family?"

"I wish we were all closer," Martha says. She looks at Carrie as if she's sailing for Bolivia tomorrow.

"There's still time," Carrie says. *She won't let this stop her.*

"Not with you in southern Ohio," Martha says without looking up.

"I'm working at that," Carrie says. And more quietly she adds, "We made progress today." Blood rushes to her neck.

"Yes, what *was* that about?" Charlotte asks, looking from her mother to Carrie. "James said—." The clock chimes la—la—la—la.

"Still time," James says like a distant echo. His hand looks huge on Belinda's back. "Have any of you noticed how thin Belinda is?" She stretches her neck away from him until he resumes smoothing her fur. Her eyes close.

"Stories. Just telling family stories," Martha says. She pulls the brightly colored lap robe more tightly around her. *Once today is enough.*

"So you're keeping secrets, too?" Charlotte asks.

"Some, yes," Martha says. "We have enough to think about for tonight. Too much. Some things are better left—."

"Right," James says.

Carrie stares at her mom's corner curio shelves. Wooden carvings: the dark red elephant from Africa, a monkey from who-knows-where. Secondhand knowledge of what's foreign, the inexplicable.

"Don't you have secrets, Mom?" Chad asks.

"Pfft. Nothing like this."

"I'm telling you," James says, "look at all this hair Belinda's shedding." He holds her up with one hand, her feet dangling; he clutches loose hair in his other hand.

"James! Don't dump that on the floor," Charlotte says. "I'm not doing any more vacuuming this week—fingernail clippings or hair. She always sheds a lot; you just don't notice."

"Not like this," James says. Belinda jumps down and stares back.

Just as quickly, Chad's on the move. "I've got stuff downstairs—. Mind if I take a roll?" Enough of family bonding. He and his boys are going to have some fun tonight.

"Help yourself," Charlotte says. "Just one, though. Check Sayeth's water. Okay?"

"Even the cat's spooked," James says. He grabs Belinda, huddled by the drapes, and carries her to the basement door like she's dripping. "Can't tell me, this is the usual amount." He goes to the back door, slaps cat hair off his pants' legs. A current of damp air seeps in.

"Well, I have something to say, Mom. Something I want you to think about till morning," Carrie says. "I know we've had enough turmoil, Grandma, but I've run out of time. I want to move back to Wisconsin."

"What? Finally! Oh, I'm so relieved," Charlotte says, clasping her hands. "There's still time to call Kenneth in the morning."

"It's not what you think, Mom. Don't give me an answer tonight."

Charlotte looks from Caroline to James. *Oh, no.* "What's going on with you two?" James fiddles with his pen, rehooks it on his shirt pocket. "There are too many private conversations around here."

"I've asked Dad if I can rent six acres to grow organic vegetables," Carrie says. Her cheeks feel flushed. "That's my goal, but for now, next spring, I want to work at a CSA."

"You what?" Charlotte's neck twists back and forth between her husband and daughter. They sit there with matching, shy smiles, although James' looks decidedly forced. He's clearing his throat again.

"Mercy!" The platform rocker doesn't move.

"It'll be a new division." Carrie grins and waves her hand in the air to suggest a banner stretched in front of her. "The organic vegetable component of Lehman Enterprises. We might have to get a new sign out front: Designed to Bring Safe Food to a Table Near You." She looks at her dad; he won't back out now, will he?

Charlotte places her hand flat on her chest. "You want to move back to Wisconsin to *farm*? That's as ridiculous as someone saying it's not going to snow anymore this winter. I mean, it's not crazy *to come back*. That would be wonderful. But it's insane for any young person to want to farm. Not come back to teach? I thought—. What about your education? Mother, do you know about this? Someone tell me what's going on."

"This is all news to me," Martha says. She presses the back of her hand against the spot above her eye. *Lord have mercy!*

"You know there are men out there who won't want you in their way, Carrie," James says. "That's the way they'll see it. Some of them are built mean. They'll stare, say crude things. Hateful. You'll have to prove yourself."

"I won't try to show men anything," Carrie says. "But I won't go away, either. I'll just do my thing. By the way, Dad, I've bookmarked some new websites on your computer. Moses is really good—mosesorganic. Nothing to do with tablets, Grandma. It stands for Midwest Organic and Sustainable Education Service."

"James, what's been going on in the cow parlor?" Charlotte asks. "You haven't let her talk you into going completely organic, have you?" Mother makes her clicking noises. Caroline sits there, rubbing her chin with her thumb and fingers, like she's doing an imitation of Kenneth, minus the beard. "Next thing, you'll tell me Meg's been consulted. James? It gets old, being the one who keeps people's feet on the ground."

James shrugs and says, "It was hers to bring up."

"This has nothing to do with milk," Carrie says. "That's Dad's part. He'll have to decide about that. Oh, I bookmarked the Cornucopia Institute, though; that's a farm policy think tank that tries to keep factory dairy farms honest about what's an organic cow. But that's strictly for you, Dad." She leans forward and faces her mom. "I'm sorry, I haven't had a chance to talk with you before." Mom keeps her eyes on Dad. "From now on when you think of food, think vegetables. Well, dairy, of course, but I've just upped the FDA recommendations: three veggies every meal. Maybe only two at breakfast."

Mercy!

"You're not a gambler like that, Caroline," Charlotte says. "It takes a certain personality." Why didn't James talk some sense into her? He's always been too soft with her. Back in high school it was like he was secretly glad she didn't have a boyfriend; no one was good enough for her. Charlotte can't let her make another mistake, even if she wants to come home. She must still be on the rebound; it's so easy to jump at anything. "If you're saying what I think you are, you wouldn't have one free minute from mid-winter through fall. No social life. Is that what you want? You haven't thought this through."

"It's all I've been thinking about for ten months. Definitely the last five." Carrie tucks her legs under her, rubs the bottoms of her thick socks.

"Your mom's right, Carrie," James says. "The planning never ends—laying out the fields, using spreadsheets. Machines *will* break down. You'll have to scrounge around, find used refrigerators."

"I've already checked," Carrie says. "All that equipment's available online." She was afraid he'd flip-flop like this.

"You're talking hard, manual labor," Charlotte says. "Listen to your dad. Farming's nothing like those zucchini that took over by themselves when you were little. Is that what you're going by?"

"I know, I know. I'm not afraid of hard work, Mom. You'll love my lists. I'm just asking you to think about it overnight."

Charlotte glares at James; he should have nipped this. Caroline keeps right on talking like she doesn't hear. Or else she doesn't care what others are trying to tell her. Reseeding the buffer strip along the stream? Is this what she was driving at this morning about blueberries? "A hoop house?"

"It's a metal structure—well, it can be plastic—it's less expensive than a greenhouse." Carrie's done her homework; she'll impress Mom. "The frame is metal—or PVC pipe. You cover the frame with plastic instead of glass. That way you can roll the sides up or down to vent air and control the temperature."

"Do you know about this, James?" Charlotte doesn't care that she's still glaring. "None of this is cheap."

Carrie goes right on. "You have to be careful that it doesn't blow away or blow over; make sure it doesn't cave in if you have a lot of snow. But the main thing is, a hoop house extends the growing season for five or six months."

"Forevermore," Martha says. "Here in Wisconsin?"

"Yeah, and another neat thing: you can grow food right in the ground. Or you can make raised beds, or use pots. Lots of choices."

"No break, huh? You want to wear yourself out like your dad?"

"I'm really sorry, Mom, about springing this on you. It's not the way I wanted it to be. I thought sure we'd talk last night, but everyone seemed tired. Well, *I* was worn out. Then today got away; everyone had their own things to tend to. Life kept interrupting." She can't look at Grandma.

Charlotte rubs her knees; all that getting up and down to size up putts takes its toll. Now this. It puts Sonja's problem in a whole new light. Caroline rattles on about organic ways to stop beetles and worms. She says some methods work, some of the time. She'd be satisfied with that? Charlotte never dreamed things could get so out of control. And that picture to the side of the piano is crooked again.

"Don't worry, Mom; this isn't a jump off the deep end. I suppose it sounds like it." Carrie looks steadily at her. "It's something I want to throw myself into, something that matters. We're not powerless. We decide every day what we're going to put in our bodies. Food is political, Mom. I want to make it easier for folks not to eat so much processed food." She hesitates, hates to pile it on, but tomorrow may be worse. "I was wondering, too. Could I live here?"

Charlotte stares back. "You're really going to move back?" Thank heavens, Caroline took off that old sweatshirt. "I don't mean that it wouldn't be wonderful to have you here. But it takes more than spunk in a man's world. Is that what you want? Ridicule? Oh, they won't say it to your face. But you'll know it." It's so hard to put the brakes on when a young person has let herself go wild, dreaming. How will Charlotte ever explain this to Teresa? "Tell her how it is, James."

"Like she said, she wants to work at a CSA for a year," James says. He speaks slowly, makes a tent with his fingertips. "She can learn the ropes and see for herself."

"I plan to pay rent for the land. If that's what's bothering you, Mom. But I'll have to borrow on Dad's name. I need your support, both of you. And Dad, I've thought about planting trees on the big hill for a windbreak." Carrie shakes her head quickly. "Oh, that's down the road; I don't mean now."

"You're going to do all these start-up jobs while working for a CSA?" Charlotte asks. "Time doesn't grow on trees, Caroline." It's not easy to provoke Charlotte to sarcasm, but this child—. She makes Chad look sensible.

"Sometimes you have to be bold and reach for what you can't see exactly," Martha says. Her rocker is moving again. "Or what *you* can see, but others can't."

Charlotte stares at her mother. Was she listening in this morning when Teresa said that—nearly the same thing—on the phone? She couldn't have been. But there she goes, twisting things again.

"Momma and Poppa Lloyd moved us all to Nebraska before they moved us back to Illinois. That wasn't easy, till they got everything figured out—where they were to be." Martha nods at Carrie. "It's all in the diaries, how Momma learned to trust." Her lips pucker in a tight circle. "It takes some people longer than others to make the right move."

"You've said that before," slips out of Charlotte. Then she says more certainly, "Besides, that was long ago. That Nebraska deal."

"That's true, Grandma," Carrie says. "There's nothing like going far from home to get a better look at what you left. And really, Mom, it's just like you said at supper. You have to see your putt going in the hole *before* you hit the ball. *Visualize* the way you want it to go, then hit it. Even back in high school, our band director, Mr. Kowalski, told us we had to pretend we were a marching band before we could play like one."

It's obvious to Charlotte: those two have been plotting. Caroline! Those clear, innocent eyes. *Moving back?* She definitely takes after James' mother in the face, right through the cheeks. This next generation is so determined to shake things up. Well, the key still is: don't get rattled. This afternoon Charlotte had a string of bogeys, but she remembered to think about the next shot, not the last one. Then she came home to cinnamon rolls on the counter. Definitely a surprise, but nice in a way. Then Sonja. Now this. This one's big enough to count as a quadruple bogey all by itself.

"Sometimes I hold out my hand," Martha says, "and I don't know who or what will touch it." She smiles at Carrie.

Charlotte can only shake her head. *There Mother goes again.* But maybe this CSA step is necessary; James might be stalling. Caroline needs to see the responsibility for herself. And she'd be at home.

Into this whirlwind of confusion Chad comes tearing up from the basement and says Justin's been in an accident. He has to go.

"What do you mean?" James asks. His recliner foot rest bangs down. "Who called? Where?"

"County Y. That bad intersection with 88." Chad grabs another roll. "I'll be back."

"You still have curfew," James calls out.

"Gotcha."

Before anyone can say more, he's gone. Charlotte lifts her hands in resignation. What can a parent do? If a child wants to do something, he's probably going to do it. *Or she.*

"Just think about it overnight, Mom. I know it's a lot to take in, but consider it. That's all I'm asking."

"I'm going to have to call it a day," Martha says. "I didn't put in one stitch tonight, not that it matters." *Mercy me!* These young ones. She shouldn't be living here and have to hear all that transpires. *Only one life, 'twill soon be past.* "If the house catches fire, let me know."

"Mother!"

Carrie gets up to give Grandma a hug. The dear woman looks like a gust of wind could knock her over. "I hope it hasn't been too much—your heart and all. I'm glad I was here today, really glad."

Those two! "Don't forget your pill, Mother," Charlotte says. Then strangely, she gets up, too, gives her mother a hug and a pat on the back. "It's been stressful tonight, but we'll all be better tomorrow. James, I'm going to bed. I've had enough." Where did Chad say he was going? Well, things can't get any worse tonight when you've already been hit in the head this often. "You'll need extra sleep, Caroline, for that long bus ride tomorrow night." And right then, Charlotte turns and gives Caroline a quick hug.

"Heck of a day!" James says. He got by without being asked about Mr. Starling at the bank. He checks the indoor-outdoor thermometer by the kitchen sink. "Whoa! Temperature's dropping; supposed to rain first."

"'Night, Mom. 'Night, Dad. I'll wait up for Chad, take Sayeth out one more time."

"Be sure to get the lights," Charlotte says, heading down the hallway.

"Where shall I put them?" Carrie asks. Okay, bad timing for one of Uncle Kenneth's jokes.

Charlotte comes back in her satiny-looking, maroon bath robe and says, "You're welcome to take turkey sandwiches along on the bus, Caroline. There's bread in the freezer."

"Thanks," Carrie says. "I'll fix them tomorrow."

*   *   *

After water faucets run and toilets flush, the house quiets down. Carrie changes into her blue flannel pajamas with the yellow sunflowers, adds her old green, fleece housecoat. What an evening, is right! It didn't go very well, but what did she expect? Grandma gave a major assist, even though she must feel like Job. She's a marvel, all she's gone through; she's had to stretch herself so many times. Now her granddaughters are pushing her. All her years of living by the official word, knowing you die when the One-Who-Counts-Every-Hair says so. *Grandma's secret!* An honor to protect.

She must wonder what she did to *deserve* Gene's news. A granddaughter with a serious illness. Yikes! What confusion got in Sonja's way? What demons? More of the world's extremes: starving or stuffed. Is it the family's fault? Fam spam. *Keep it together, girl!* There's still time. Her body might be out of whack. It could be a chemical imbalance or some psychological component. Does someone always need to be blamed? Some *thing*? The hand that life dealt? "Society's fault" means nobody's fault.

Uhm, good cinnamon rolls. Carrie sinks her teeth into the soft dough. They're never as fresh the next morning. Grandma might be surprised to know that Ryan taught her how to knead dough. But that's past; Carrie has to brace herself for tomorrow. Two bits, Mom is hashing things out with Dad. Well, she's overdue for her own private conversation. She'll think of sixty-seven new objections. But tonight Carrie did it; she made it through the first round with Mom. Now she's even more sure. *Grandpa!* She still can't believe it. But he helped her, in a terrible way. This is what *Carrie* must do. Must needs do, Grandma. She'll grab and hang on for the ride. The truck is moving.

She catches the last of the local news: rain, turning colder, snow possible. Is Sonja attracted to a perfect body like the commercials show with their toothpick models? And Chad! She can't believe Mom and Dad let him go out; they barely asked questions. How can they trust him like that? He does as he pleases. Friends come first, not family. Did the folks really buy his story? That was crazy. She'd like to hang out with him, but she'll be low on his list. By the time she gets her acres set up, it'll be time for him to leave home for his college dream.

Mom's right; Carrie won't see much of friends. But who's here anymore? Most of the cream leaves, they say. She doesn't care about going out anyway; she's never really fit with her generation. Give her solid and old, not new and glitzy. She's too much of a snob to be friends with people who watch mindless TV shows that pretend to replicate reality. She'll get old fast, though, hanging out with Mom and Dad. But she has a mission: pull weeds, aerate the soil, welcome back lots of birds when the land is healthier. Easy now; she's no Rachel Carson.

She could go to the computer while she waits for Chad, but she's kind of wiped. She couldn't tell what Dad thought of a hoop house and didn't want to ask directly in front of Mom. He had to be extra cautious because of her. If he still drags his feet in the morning, Carrie's in trouble. It definitely goes better when she doesn't talk about alienation; neither parent gets that. And she showed she could compromise—the CSA.

If she doesn't go with the hoop house, she'd definitely want a high tunnel to extend the season for greens. Dad will know if a neighbor has a bed raiser and irrigation drip liner she could borrow. Maybe she can rent other equipment, too; it's best to make the beds and lay down the plastic all in one pass. But that's a year and a half away. Getting rid of soil compaction from the combine is a big deal, no matter what Dad says about his chisel plow turning the soil over every fall. If the land behind the house is best for Dad's crops, she's okay with going closer to the pond for her acreage. Better for irrigation, for sure. She doesn't know the first thing about laying pipes. It's crazy how much help she needs, but between the internet and Dad—. Maybe it *is* insane. And this Mr. Starling at the bank; Carrie needs to meet him when she comes back. She'll take case studies with numbers, if Dad thinks that will help.

Carrie turns off all the lights, except the low beam on the kitchen stove hood. She's exhausted. Is Chad in trouble? He has his cell phone, doesn't he? She wouldn't know where to look for him. The folks went off to bed, like they're used to it. Oh, Sayeth. Out with you, pup. She steps off the porch into a heavy cloud cover. No stars to count or wish on tonight. *Grandpa!* She snaps her thumb and finger; Sayeth waddles back, damp from the grass.

Should she write Chad a note? As in, would writing a note be a *good* thing to do? The best thing to do? Or only an average, sensible thing? Perhaps a waste of time. What would she write? Where's the love? Let's take a buzz on the uniloader in the morning? Carrie walks past the night light in the bathroom, wonders if Grandma's asleep already. All's quiet with Mom and Dad. How strange, to live here all the time.

She double-checks the setting on her alarm clock—cows waiting to be milked—slips into bed, and turns off the bedside lamp. *Not a gambler.* That beats having Mom think Carrie's too impulsive. Two bits: she'll make one more push for Carrie to reconsider teaching. *Stay calm. Trust yourself. Make it up, if you have to.* Otherwise, life is too depressing. *Grandpa!* What a day! *Be bold and reach for what you can't see exactly.* The bottom line: she needs to be part of making the land better, growing the good stuff, getting Wisconsinites hooked on squash, obsessed with when they'll sink their teeth into their next eggplant. *Get real, Carrie.* People will still drive to the nearest roadhouse, still order a couple of beers to chase down their onion rings and greasy cheeseburgers, still defy the odds and live until they're ninety. Some will. Don't try to make sense of it.

Chapter 17

Mercy, mercy, mercy! How often must Martha say the word? Where will she ever start to sort out this jumble? *Mumble, rumble.* It's too much. She can't think straight, can't put two sentences together. Such exhaustion. Every bone. If only sleep will come. Too, too much. *Bless Gene and his little Sonja. Supply their needs, Lord; supply their every need. The whole family, Lord. Give Carrie—. Give your children—peace, Lord.*

* * *

Martha wakes during the night; the rain beats against her bedroom window. She fumbles, turns the alarm clock toward her: 2:18. *Goodness.* It seems like she's slept longer. Deep, deep sleep. How wonderful. If she gets up and goes to the bathroom right away, she won't wake up as much and her mind won't start in so bad. The house is cold, but the night light from the bathroom beckons. Rain beats on the bathroom vent. Wind pushes against metal. Oh, sweet rain. James will be glad. Carrie, too? Soil for her crops?

When Martha was little, someone told her—one of the Weaver boys in Illinois—that rain, especially hard rain, goes into the ground and travels all the way to China. And China lies at the center of the earth. For years she believed it as gospel truth—*as the waters cover the earth*—until her teacher in the one-room school, Mr. Kurdsoft, the only man teacher she ever had, showed them a map and told them where Illinois was in relation to China. From then on she disliked him. Why couldn't rain go through soil and rock, pool itself into oceans below land, and emerge again in another country? She kept the idea as hers—Daniel got a chuckle—while living in the midst of Wisconsin farmers who said their corn and beans soaked the rain right up.

She still likes her view. Rain is part of a cycle that falls on one part of the world and reappears somewhere else. Everything is connected. It takes a day or so before a Wisconsin storm moves on East. Then the same system may reach Carrie in southern Ohio, oozing down from the Upper Midwest before it drifts out to sea. Carrie. Is she really going to come back?

No, no mulling. Go back to bed. Go back to sleep. Tomorrow will be sufficient.

Martha covers herself, tucks the top quilt under her chin. This winter she'll get stronger; she'll insist on fixing liver and onions. That's what Daniel always wanted when he felt weak. Come spring, she'll go back to her house on Township Road. She'll go right back, all on her own, to that wooden arbor that Daniel made. She's not that old. Right back to her clematis plants. The loveseat. Her loveseat. If the chief end of man is to glorify God, then Daniel did his share. He lived an upright life, for the most part. As good as anyone. He did what he needed to do. And Martha shouted out to heaven for him. *Mercy!* That's what a life companion is for, to help the weak one enter at the gate.

She must not dwell on eternal rest when God has given her this family, here and now. What do you say to a grown child who's grieving over his own? Oh, he'll mend, but Gene must be broken, if not grieving. Sonja, as fragile as one of the blossoms on Martha's tuberous begonias in a wind storm, but old enough to make her own decisions. Had Gene ever given her extra allowance for cleaning her plate? She'll need some propping up. And Carrie—! She's determined to stand up tall like the first daffodil, sticking its neck out in spring. She doesn't know what she's getting into. James and Charlotte will have to decide what they can muster. It can't be easy, the way money is. Martha must rise up, pitch in more, even when not invited. She's been too tangled in her own strings. She must stretch out her hand once more and hope that God will see fit to take hold.

Momma's blank days back in '31. "Think and wonder." Was her finger too sore to grip a pencil? Her spirit too beaten? Is that when they lost everything and went back to whatever it was in Illinois that Poppa Lloyd wanted to get away from? Maybe everyone retreats sometime, goes back on something they once held dear. Looks the fool to some, but finds a way to survive. Going back doesn't have to mean defeat. If Carrie can make a go of it—*come home!*—Martha can surely make do on her own again. There must be more ways she can help than just making rolls and listening to Charlotte rattle on about that sharp slope on the seventh hole.

Oh, Daniel. *Such trouble, stubble, rubble.* Life humbles everyone. You go along humming and humming. Then thump. Or, thump, thump. Who was it said yesterday that church people expect too much of themselves? Gloria, the family songbird? Or Carrie? That girl listened this afternoon. And talked, too. And now—who knows? Oh, Lord, don't let this be another wild goose chase. *Bless her heart;* she wants to do what's right.

No, no reading of the diaries tonight. Remember the hugs. How Carrie held her hand this afternoon.

Chapter 18

What a lousy night! Did she sleep at all? She worked so hard, *trying* to sleep. What was James mumbling? "Not yet! You gotta wait. Wait for the next one, then pull." Simp must have been helping him with a calf. Caroline? It's a relief to be awake, going through the motions. James and Caroline sit there, not saying much, drinking coffee in the nook. He's telling her about how much hunting has changed. He and his brother used to share a beat-up old Winchester rifle, but Simp has a digital scope and uses a computerized GPS. Is that the second pan of cinnamon rolls that's over halfway gone? Charlotte takes a look inside the oven; it's not any dirtier than it was before Thursday. She'll sort through the silverware instead, put the best set away in its box.

She made James tell her everything last night. He kept getting sidetracked about Chad—the way he took off. The word from the bank is that Mr. Starling hem-hawed. It's not going to be easy, getting loans. But James is willing to let Caroline give it a try; he knows some guy with a CSA over near to Stockville. And there's another one in Brodhead. He's right; there could be advantages. She'd be a back-up for the hired man and the chores. It's not unusual for adult children to live at home these days, and it'd probably only be temporary. The whole thing came as such a shock, though. How was Charlotte to take it in stride, when she's still recovering from Thanksgiving? James insists he didn't know a thing about it in advance; when Caroline hinted at something that first afternoon, he thought she was kidding. It's certainly not the way Charlotte raised her. But what can you say, if that's what she wants? James insists the dairy part won't change. And he says this might be less expensive than an eating disorder.

Who knows with Sonja? She's always been super thin, but Charlotte never thought a thing of it, what with inherited body build and metabolism. Sue is small-boned and thin as a wheat cracker. It's disturbing, though, that none of them, except for Meg—Meg?—knew Sonja very well. Charlotte remembers all the nieces' birthdays and sometimes adds a gift card for Target or The Gap, but still—. James kept saying, "Sun Prairie's only a couple hours away. It can't be that hard to go to the undertaker's." It's not like Sonja's died. It's not *that*, although somehow it feels like it. That punch, that doubling over to the stomach. One of their own has flirted with the body's systems. But she's safe; she won't become a statistic on the wrong side. They'll focus on the positive, have more family get-togethers. They don't have to make each time be a big deal.

It's so hard being a parent these days, especially when you're dealing with kids who act before they think. Somewhere Charlotte got the idea that anorexia is a spoiled rich kid's disease, but that doesn't have to be the case. Just so Gene isn't taking it all on himself; self-blame is so easy. She's heard everything from parents being too controlling to too permissive. Well, it can't be both. Half the time, folks don't know what they're talking about when it comes to other people's problems. Some folks talk bad about parents of athletes, like they all raise kids with one-track minds to get filthy rich and build Mom and Dad a mansion some day.

Charlotte looks for the shepherd's pie recipe she's used before. Oh, she forgot; it calls for leftover *mashed* potatoes. She's not sure she can improvise. When Chad wakes up, he'll tell them what was going on last night. Yes, it *was* sudden, and it *is* strange that he didn't call from the emergency room. It probably turned out to be nothing, but that doesn't mean Chad's a goof-off. And he's not *that* competitive. James thinks he's a ball hog sometimes, takes off-balance shots when he should pass. Well, you have to trust the coaches and let the players play. And you can't force someone to like farm work. It always comes down to that for James. It'd be nice if Chad were more like his dad, but he's not. If farm work is boring, it's boring; you have to accept it.

Finally last night in bed, she and James were just repeating themselves. They had to get some sleep; these cows—they might as well be roosters—are always standing, come morning. When James turned out the bedside lamp, Charlotte snuggled into his arms. No hard feelings, just different ways of seeing. Their bare skin, his tender touch—it all ended in exhilaration. No groping, like clumsy, oversexed teens. No fumbling, like oldsters with leg cramps. Just soft, skin-to-skin enfolding, letting bodily sweetness overcome all that's up in the air.

But James is still James. On the prowl this morning, he wanted to go down and rouse Chad. Before that, he made sure the Geo was here with no dents. While James and Caroline were out choring—she said *she* slept fine—Charlotte got down a couple boxes of Christmas decorations. Mother won't understand; what's the hurry, she'll ask. There's something dazzling about opening a box of tree ornaments, finding objects that haven't been touched for eleven months. Sometimes distraction is the best course; just get your mind on something completely different. Where is that new Christmas tree skirt she bought at half price? Charlotte won't bother James right now to reach to the top shelf for garland and the extra strings of lights. But Christmas cards—she needs to get started with that. What a kick that one year when she signed them, "James and the three Cs." Everyone's smiles were perfect on the family picture that year, too.

When Caroline finishes her coffee, Charlotte will show her the new crèche; it's olive wood from the West Bank. These tiny ones have the most amazing detail. She had to push the clock to the far end of the mantel to make room. And she moved cups and saucers to the top shelf of the dining room hutch—it's temporary only—so there's room at eye level for the crèche fashioned from thorns, the one she bought last year from Nicaragua. She found a spot beside the computer where she could squeeze in a tiny Ecuadoran nativity scene. That's not going to work—she can hear James already—but it's made of bread dough and has to be somewhere in the kitchen. When that gingerbread house is gone, there'll be one less thing.

Mother has washed her hair and walks around like a queen with her hair wrapped up in a towel and balanced on top of her head. "I'll get it," Charlotte says when the phone rings. "It's probably Gene." Her thigh catches on the edge of the table. "Hello?" Her eager question mark slips away. "James," she says, motioning for him. He looks puzzled but follows her into the living room. "It's Justin's dad," she says quietly and hands him the phone. Charlotte stands at the picture window and rubs her arms. The bare maple tree glistens; lavender and bronze mums along the front walkway fling drops of water whenever a gust of wind shakes them. A chill wind has come inside.

Justin's parents want them to come over—Chad, too—over on the west end of Borgmann. The police found a couple of six-packs, still full, in a cemetery somewhere close to Stockville. James mumbles something about Justin's uncle being on the police force; he recognized the car, though it got away. Charlotte has to remind James not to jump to conclusions. This is not the other shoe. Kids'll be kids. No word about Justin's accident. Charlotte changes clothes, hears James open the basement door and head for Chad's room. His steps are heavy, loaded with purpose. There's a low rumble of voices. They have to make sure this doesn't turn into a nightmare. Why drag in Coach Lucey? Chad's picture sits on their dresser; he's only seven with his front teeth missing. He sports his Bucky Badger pajamas and that adorable, ready-for-anything look.

Suddenly, James is back, splashing Old Spice on his neck and chest. "Chad says it's all a misunderstanding."

Charlotte picks at the chenille bedspread, watches him in the dresser mirror as he changes into tan Dockers and the blue plaid shirt he wore to the bank meeting. "What'd he say about the cemetery?"

"They were looking for a Black Angel statue like Kenneth saw years ago in Iowa City. The stone turns white if you kiss a girl and it's true love."

"Good grief. Kenneth told Chad that? What about the beer?"

"A dare for the Stockville team."

"Huh? What about Justin?"

"Accident didn't happen."

"Omigosh. Just a crazy prank?"

Chad stands at the kitchen counter, eating rolls and drinking milk. His blue gym shorts hang below his knees; his bill-cap sits backwards. Flip-flops again! He probably doesn't know it's turned colder. He looks half-awake and stunned at the same time. Mother nods to Caroline and like one body split in two parts, they head for the living room. They wouldn't have to make a big deal of it, like they're getting out of the way of the inquisition. Lunch is covered—it's barely nine o'clock—Charlotte will decide for sure when she's back. If those two get their heads together and try something on their own, well, what if they do? Charlotte had thought about brownies; she doesn't know why she has that mix in the cupboard. Maybe Caroline can help Mother understand that all parents go through times like this. If they have to monitor Chad more carefully, they'll do it. But they can't let him get kicked off again. Coach won't want that either.

Charlotte puts on her jogging suit jacket with the cranberry and aqua diamond shapes, slings her long purse strap over her shoulder, and waits by the side door. James sticks his nose in the living room long enough to say they're going to the Walshes'. "Be back in time to take you to the bus, Carrie. No problem. Bring Sayeth in, if it starts to rain again."

They'll figure it out with Chad; they have to. The key is how you respond. When you hit the ball into the rough, you have to come right back with an unbelievable shot that nestles right up to the hole. You do. They will.

*　　　*　　　*

Carrie feels guilty watching, but she half-follows Grandma to the picture window, stands back discreetly. She's pretty sure Chad hasn't found out that he's invited to Nike's summer basketball camp. He suddenly sits up straighter in the back seat as the van pulls onto the rain-slickened highway. There goes Carrie's chance to talk more with Mom. What are circumstances trying to tell her?

"Enough grace to live," Grandma is saying, "it doesn't come easily." She reaches to the center of the fern, breaks off a long frond that's brown on the tips. "I've been wanting to get rid of this dead stuff."

"Here, let me get those," Carrie says, dropping to her knees to pick up tiny brown leaves. "Chad still has his long arms, his peripheral vision. It'll take a lot to break his view of himself: basketball super-hero-in-waiting. Quick hands, I guess. Dad says he moves his feet and doesn't just reach in to swipe the ball. But he needs to set more picks for others."

Grandma lightly shakes the fronds. "There's no joy, seeing someone else flummoxed. Charlotte's the one I worry about. Children hold us up like a mirror."

"Oh, it won't be the end of Mom's world either. She'll get her dignity back."

"Whatever this is, she'll need to do more than grab Chad's chin between her thumb and fingers. Hold still; you have leaves in your hair. I've tried to tell her: his car comes in late. But I can't say much; I don't really know."

"Did Coach say what would happen if Chad got into trouble again?" Carrie asks. Grandma's eyes look heavy, like she still carries burdens. Is she ready to say more about Momma?

"There may have been a threat; I don't know. That was before I moved here. Coach Lucey was always extra polite to Daniel and me when we went to Chad's junior varsity games. He called us Mr. and Mrs. Ropp and made sure we had decent folding chairs in the front. I'm afraid I've upset the balance in this house."

"What do you mean?"

"Another body creates more tension."

"Don't say that. You know how Chad talks about his dates with you last summer at the Tastee Freeze. He wouldn't say that if he hadn't enjoyed it."

"He'd wolf down his double-dipper before I'd eaten half my small cone. But still, an extra person can tip the scale."

What's Grandma saying? This house is too full already? "You're not responsible for everything, Grandma. We don't even know what's going on with Chad." Carrie picks up her seed catalog and notes, looks for other things she's left lying around. "I need to pack a few things. It won't take long; I'll be right back."

Things are unraveling before they've been put together. This morning when she and Dad walked in from the milk parlor, their boots made heavy, dark marks where they cut across the grass. They stood outside the back door and talked some more; his mind was on cows 312 and 79, both supposed to deliver next week. It's always about the cows. He kept to the usual subjects: how small farmers get the shaft, how the subsidy is essential.

Carrie fills her backpack; clean underwear goes in the side pocket. She checks the roll of money one more time. She must have miscounted this morning, only half awake and not wanting to keep her dad waiting. She'd riffled through the roll of bills and had come up short. Sometimes two bills can stick together. But this is incredible; she's still missing a twenty. *Count once more.* Who would pull a trick like this? Mom might snoop, but she wouldn't take money, not even for a joke. Would she? Well, it serves Carrie right. The money's been a nuisance the whole trip. Maybe she left one of the twenties in her apartment. She nearly missed finding the wad in the first place, tucked in an extra zipper of a donated purse. It would have been better to let some bargain shopper deal with the dilemma, maybe get a reward. All she cared about was not giving the money to Manager Milt. Not after all the money he's taken from her, never paying a decent salary. He doesn't have to leer like that.

So, what's to do yet? There's no need to take extra clothing to Ohio. The less she has to move back here in December, the better. If these work clothes show up in the laundry, Mom won't throw them away, will she? Reading material is packed. Carrie can wear an extra sweatshirt on the bus, in case it's cool. Fix a couple of sandwiches yet, check e-mail.

"What time does your bus leave?" Grandma asks. "I should remember."

"Three-thirty." Carrie knows the next question that's coming. "It'll take fourteen hours," she adds. "I wonder what Mom intended for lunch." She looks on the counter for a list. "I don't see a menu anywhere, but I'm sure she has something planned." She looks inside the catch-all drawer by the refrigerator, finds grocery store coupons and odd scraps of recipes torn from magazines. "Do we have license to *help* her, two days in a row?"

"No, not license, but we'll do what we can."

Carrie opens the refrigerator door and stares. It's like snooping in Mom's purse. Containers of leftovers sit in neat rows. Not alphabetized, though. "I see hamburger thawing, but that doesn't tell us much." Okay, sandwiches to go. The turkey still smells all right, and she'll use peanut butter and jelly for the other one. "So Grandma, how are you handling this news about Sonja?"

"I slept better than some nights. It must have been our talk. With Sonja, I don't know how to feel. Remorse mostly. The trouble's been done. I can't make any of it different."

"I feel helpless, too. But for the two of us, I'm glad we talked. Knowing about Grandpa has given me more resolve."

Grandma steadies the towel on her wet hair, pulls out a chair at the table. "I was afraid you'd wake up and not want anything to do with me."

"Oh, no, I'm amazed at what you've gone through all by yourself."

"Don't you think your plan is going to be too much work?" Grandma scratches at the palm of her hand.

What? Why can't anyone trust her? "I'm *choosing* the work; that makes it only half as hard. I wish I could start with ten acres, but that's too much."

Grandma makes clicking noises. "You're not feeding the five thousand. I worry about you—the investment."

Carrie puts the sandwich fixings back in the fridge. She can't afford to lose Grandma. "I can live simply, just like I do in southern Ohio. I don't need much for myself. And I've saved some money from when I was teaching." She pours a cup of leftover coffee, sits at the far end of the table, one arm folded on top of the other. "I want to leave the land better than it is now. I don't buy this idea that farmers can take from the earth indefinitely and call the result wealth." Grandma looks like she doesn't have a clue. She rubs her cheek, touches the corner of one eye, steadies the towel. "Do you believe in signs, Grandma?"

"It all depends."

"How do you know when things are pointing right or left?" Carrie tilts the chair legs forward. "Like, suppose I found a brownie mix—fat chance in Mom's kitchen—would that be a sign we should make brownies? I've had so little time to talk with her; it worries me. Now this Chad thing'll have Dad more upset." Grandma doesn't seem to be paying attention; she's walking again, restless, looking out the bay window. "It feels like whenever a door opens, the wind messes around. Nothing's where I left it."

"It'd be an awful lot of responsibility," Grandma says. She turns to Carrie, arms folded, towel perfectly balanced. Her brown and orange dress with the tiny paisley pattern looks serene, in spite of tails swishing every-which-way. "So much hard, hard work for you. And the expense." She pulls her tan sweater tighter.

If Carrie says anything more about the holiness of growing food, Grandma may think she's gone over the edge. "I've always loved being outside, driving tractor. You know that." Okay, that sounded accusatory.

"But you can't do this on your own." Grandma's eyes dart around the kitchen, as if she's desperate for someone to show up and help her talk some sense. Now she sits with a glass of water, neck erect.

"I'll need to hire help later on; I know that." She and Grandma connected so well yesterday. What's happened? That dumb towel makes her look stiff, uncompromising. "Right now there's a growing market for organic vegetables that are raised locally." No, that's the wrong tack; Grandma doesn't care about market conditions.

"You're really serious?" Grandma fingers the belt buckle on her dress, presses on a spot above her eye. "So young, a woman by yourself."

"Oh, Grandma, I thought sure you'd understand. I know it's different from your generation. But Dad's excited; I know he is. He just can't show it. One time when we were talking, he said, 'Holy moly.' I thought the jar of milk was going to slip right out of his hands. He's good with me paying three hundred an acre for rent; I'll make sure he doesn't lose money." Grandma's lips tighten, like she knows better. "Do you think I'm taking advantage? He has the land and some clout with the bank." Grandma keeps staring, like she's watching a hole in Carrie's head grow larger. "Dad agrees; we need a buffer zone between my organic acres and his farmland with the chemicals. It'll take several years to make that transition, though. We might need some run-off, diversion ditches to keep his chemicals from seeping into the vegetable fields." She's babbling. These are points she had ready for Mom. "You said something last night about taking risks, about reaching for what others can't see."

"I know; I understand. I'm surprised is all." Grandma goes through her routine: rubs her chest, her elbow; touches the corner of her eye, the towel. "Blind men walking."

"What's that?"

Grandma shudders and reaches to steady the towel. "I never thought about you this way. Out of the whirlwind." Now she rubs the fingertips of one hand into her open palm. "I half believed Charlotte; you'd come back and teach."

"So what would be a sign for you? You said it depends."

"The unbelievers were the ones who asked for a sign."

Carrie slaps her hands together. Grandma's shoulders jerk; the towel tilts. "That's it! I'm a believer. I don't need rainbows or fleece." Carrie slumps back in her chair. "That doesn't mean there won't be obstacles, but things are never *only* bleak. Or *only* rosy."

"Did you have this all figured out when you came home?"

"No, not really. Well, yes, I had hoped, but I wasn't sure. I've bounced all over the place. First, I had to convince myself; then I had to figure out how to approach Dad. But now, knowing about Grandpa, and then thinking about Sonja—." Carrie stops. "I've changed my mind so often, it's pathetic. I'm like everyone else, trying to figure out a little slice of life, find a rationale, some meaning to live by. I want to come here and be connected to something important. Not that I think I'll save the planet, one vegetable at a time. Well, for that matter, it's not that I want to live right *here*, either." Carrie points and adds, "Not right in this house." She laughs nervously, waves her hand vaguely. "But close by; maybe a trailer." Okay, she ruled that out the other day. "Here's what I really don't want. I don't want to have a job just to make money. That's not well-being."

"Well, this is surely something all right," Grandma says. "I need to lie down awhile, dry my hair. There's a lot going on for this old heart." She takes tiny sips of water, licks her lips.

Carrie watches Grandma linger at the disarray of magnets on the side of the refrigerator. Carrie had counted on her, but she doesn't approve. *Oh,* please*, not a heart attack. Not that sign.* Maybe it just takes Grandma time to adjust, like most everyone. Okay, focus on what needs to be done; maybe Trudy sent an e-mail. Too bad the apples are gone. Ooh, the bananas are soft; no chance to be Banana Boy on the bus. "Who's that?" she asks sharply.

"What?" Grandma asks, coming back quietly in her blue slippers. She has a way of sneaking up on you, just like Mom said.

"That guy." Carrie looks out the bay window at a man in camouflage pants, bright orange jacket, and an orange cap with the flaps up. "He's just standing there, looking into the woods. Where's Sayeth? I forgot all about him."

"It looks like that same hunter." Grandma's towel slips; her hair falls in damp strands. "Charlotte will throw another fit."

"That's the guy?" *If only Dad were here.* Carrie goes to the closet, grabs her red hoodie, hops on one foot to put on her boots. "Where's the phone book?"

"Carrie, what are you doing? You're tracking up the kitchen."

"Someone's gotta get rid of him." She flips through the front pages of the phone book, writes down a number on a bright pink Post-It note, scoops up a clump of dried mud on the floor. "I'll clean up the rest when I get back. Don't touch it. You go lie down."

"He has a gun, Carrie. A rifle." Grandma dabs at her hair with the towel. Her eyes are wide.

"I know. But that doesn't mean he has a right. He needs to leave." Carrie grabs the portable kitchen phone. *Please, God, let this thing work outside.* "Did you hear me, Grandma?" she asks again at the side door. "Don't clean up after me."

"Caroline! He's not worth it." Grandma follows her, but Carrie slips out.

Sayeth is yipping, tugging on his tie-down. Why hadn't she heard him? She dials the number, walks a few steps, stops. The phone works! She explains the situation, exacts a promise, starts walking again. Yes, Grandma, this could be foolhardy, but she can't turn back now. She can't be all talk and no show. By the time she gets to the muddy field, the man has moved out to the round hay stand. He keeps looking toward the woods, stands slightly slumped and silent, rifle at his side. *He knows he shouldn't be here. The nerve.* "Hey!" When he half-turns to look, Carrie holds up her hand like a policeman. *Okay, ignore me.* She leaps over a puddle of standing water, imagines Grandma watching from the window, her hair undone. She'd be better off kneeling beside her bed. Carrie's never done anything like this in her life.

"What are you doing?" she yells. The man's turned his back. "Hey! You!"

"What does it look like, lady?"

"You have no right to be here." She moves around slowly into his line of vision. He looks like he's in his fifties, like life's been hard. Scruffy beard, shaggy eyebrows. A lowly one.

"I got permission," he mumbles.

What did he say? "No, you don't. The land is posted." She's sure Mom said that Dad posted it last year when he got tired of hearing shots fired during the night.

"Neighbor gave me permission." His voice is rough, like the crook in his nose. Probably a break that never got set properly.

"What neighbor?" The guy's bluffing. *Keep praying, Grandma!* Carrie would never confront someone holding a rifle in Appalachia. But here, on *this* land—. "What's his name?" Her voice quivers at the end. It wouldn't be a neighbor woman.

"Who do you think you are?" the man asks. He grins—teeth missing—like he's thinking about how easy it would be to grab her and sling her over his shoulder, tie her feet together and drag her out to the road, like a doe.

"Cop's on the way," she says, clutching the phone. If that officer doesn't get here soon, this could go down as her last misguided attempt to save the world. What if the dispatcher was negligent and didn't transfer her call?

"Big talk, little girl. I got my license. You don't scare me none." The man hacks and spits a load. "Your daddy's a nice man."

Why did she think a cop would come and come quickly? *That was stupid.* They probably have reduced staff on a holiday weekend. Should she dial again?

"Pretty enough," he says, staring, as if her silence eggs him on. He pushes his cap back, scratches his forehead. "Kinda on the skinny side, but that could be fixed." He leers. "Your daddy ain't even home."

In spite of herself, she looks back at the house, sees a small head in the bay window. Grandma's holding her spot. Sayeth has quieted. Then she hears a car. It goes past, backs up, slowly turns in the driveway. Dad? No, it's a squad car. The crunch of tires on gravel. Someone in uniform gets out, acts like he doesn't want to get his shoes muddy. She motions to him to stay left to avoid the worst. Her mouth won't open. Sayeth is yipping again; Hunter Guy couldn't care less.

The sheriff's deputy breathes heavily; his mouth hangs open like he's doing an ad for a nasal decongestant. The butt of a pistol rides on his hip. "What do we have here?" he asks, like everyone's being congenial, mildly amused even, assessing livestock at the county fair. He turns his foot sideways, studies the soppy mud on his shoes. Does he expect her to clean them? Then more briskly with a wave of his hand, "You need to move on," he says to the hunter.

The man looks away. "I got my rights."

"This farmland is posted," Carrie says, as if the deputy might not have gotten the full message. "We take walks out here; the dog runs. We don't want anyone with a rifle messing around."

"Gotcha," the deputy says, checking the side of his other shoe. "Don't make any trouble now, you hear?" He slaps the hunter's shoulder. "You know you can't hunt wherever you want."

"How much you going to fine this guy?" Carrie asks. He might be out of work, but that doesn't mean he doesn't have a loaded mattress at home.

The deputy shrugs. "Eh—warning's good enough."

Carrie can't believe it. She stands like her dad would, legs spread, arms folded in front of her. "There's gotta be a fine; I'm sure it's well over a hundred. Maybe two. He's trespassing; this is my land." The deputy won't call her on a technicality, will he? "Otherwise, he'll come right back. He already has."

The deputy looks at her like he's trying not to laugh.

"Feisty little thing, ain't she?" the hunter says.

"Go on now." The deputy slaps the hunter on the back. "Don't you go making things worse."

Hunter Guy guffaws. If nothing good comes from this, Dad won't believe she could be so stupid. Mom—? "He'll be right back here—I'm telling you—if you don't write him up. He'll go terrorize someone else."

"Terrorize?" the hunter says; he snorts and spits a stream of dark juice. "Can you believe this crazy girl?"

"That's what trespassing with a gun amounts to," Carrie says. She can't help it that her voice shakes. She leans forward to stare at the deputy's badge number. "There *will* be a fine, right, Officer? Officer Grockel." Maybe she's learned a thing or two from hearing Trudy's stories about standing up for herself against the system.

"Okay, lady," the deputy says. He pulls out his pad of tickets. "I'll take care of this."

You'd better, she wants to say. He could go through the motions and then tear up the guy's ticket. They seem to know each other. Is she taking advantage of a person with no power? No, she's expecting the rules to be applied. Is she rationalizing? Well, she's standing her ground against a man with a rifle, on her land, her dad's land. The hunter stuffs the ticket in a pocket, shuffles away, muttering, "Yeah, yeah," at the reminder that he has ten days to pay. *Don't come back,* she wants to say. Okay, he's not a fifth grader.

Carrie shows the deputy the drier path back to his car. Should she make small talk about football? Ask if he had a nice Thanksgiving?

"Supposed to snow tonight," he says. "You have yourself a good day now."

"You too." Carrie releases Sayeth, watches him chase a squirrel. "Time to grow up, pup." And time to face Grandma's music, see if there's a smidgen of common ground left. The hunter had asked, "Who do you think you are?" Yeah, it's about time someone recognized her.

Chapter 19

It's palpable; everyone's trying. They stand around in the kitchen, bumping into each other—"oh, excuse me"—doing their bit parts to get lunch ready. James offers to make the hamburger into patties, and Charlotte lets him. She found some hamburger buns deep in the freezer. James shapes the balls of meat in his big hands. Slap, slap, whomp. They all give it their best shot: getting their family legs under them. Carrie enjoys the repeated questions about having chased away Hunter Guy. No one needs to point out that she must have been half out of her mind. She says she's met the two worst hunters in the county in only four days' time. Chad tries to slip away to the basement, but James stops him. "Nothing doing, unless you're going to feed Belinda and coming right back."

Five minutes later, Chad makes another run; he grabs the pad of pink Post-It notes, heads down the hallway, and walks right into Carrie's bedroom. She follows and finds him standing at her dresser, writing a note. With one eyebrow raised, he grins and places a tightly-folded twenty dollar bill on her dresser. "Charge interest?" he asks.

"What's up?"

"You didn't notice? I had to keep up my rep. You always claimed I messed with your hair stuff." He pulls off the Post-It, sticks it in his jeans pocket.

Carrie pokes him in the ribs. "You stinker! Sure, I missed it. When did you—? I should have known." Thank heavens she didn't confront her mom. "Hey, how's it going?" She doesn't want to pry, but he *is* her brother.

"Could be worse. Parents have all the say, unless Coach finds out. Long story. Just having some fun. Trying anyway. No stones got defaced; no flags stolen. But just 'cause Uncle Kenneth ran around in cemeteries doesn't mean it's a good idea for me to check it out with my guys. Girls—they are so easy—hard up for a little smooch."

"Oh! That story he told about the guy from Europe who brought his wife to the States, testing for true love? Then he murdered her."

"Yeah. That angel statue in Iowa City that turned black from one measly kiss," Chad says.

"So you did your own little dramatic reenactment? Girls, but no violence?"

"Yeah, girls, but no action. Dad didn't even give me credit for being clever. You'd think we threw raw eggs or something. No social life for ten days. Two whole weekends! No cell phone. That sucks, big time. There goes Nicole. Mom says it could be lots worse. Well, yeah.

If Coach finds out about the keg the other night at Justin's. We didn't know older kids were going to crash."

"Hey, we all do stupid."

"I tried to tell 'em: Nicole and I came here when things got hot. So much for that. Dad says I'm a screw-up. He's one mean, old farggher, just like his old man."

"Not quite. He's actually got a soft streak."

"Hnnh. Not for me."

"If it helps, that wad isn't really my money. Stupid things don't mean stupid people."

Chad raises an eyebrow. "What the—? I swiped stolen money?"

"It's a long story, too," Carrie says. "Not stolen, exactly. It's found money. I'm giving it to one of the women I work with; her daughter needs cosmetic surgery. The doctor had said the lip scar would go away, but it hasn't. She's twelve and self-conscious. The dad's out of work—so it'll help a little. I brought the money along to keep it safe. That was dumb."

"Cool."

Carrie tucks the roll of money in the purse with the long strap that she'll wear around her neck. Fourteen more bus hours of tugging to make sure it's still there. "The dumber thing is, I live in an apartment where anyone could force the door open with a hard shove. Don't tell Mom. Okay?"

"Sure. No sweat." Chad chews on a thumbnail. "Sorry, I haven't been around much. Dad said I should apologize. Like that makes it real. He said I might be lucky to get another chance. What's that about?"

"Oh, you weren't here. I want to move back."

"Here?" Both his eyebrows shoot up. "No kidding?"

"For real. I'm going to raise vegetables to sell. Want to help?"

"Me?" He looks toward the door. "You know what happens when Mom wants me to dig potatoes."

"It's something that grows on you."

"Not me," he says. "Hey, uhm, about the twenty; maybe keep that under. Right now, if anything else comes out, the folks'll kill me."

"Sure, don't worry. We'll play the old, 'I've got your back if you've got mine.' I haven't really said where I found those twenties."

"Works for me," Chad says, backing out of Carrie's room.

She closes the blinds. One more month and she'll be back? Well, heck, yeah.

*   *   *

Charlotte moves quickly from table, to counter, to refrigerator, still wearing her shimmery two-piece jogging suit. Everything's looking up in spite of the gray sky. "Please" and "after you" roll off lips. They'll share this lunch, even if they have to stumble through it. Charlotte's totally worn out: Caroline's bombshell last night, Sonja, this hunter thing, Chad. No time to make a shepherd's pie. It's down the drain with the leftover salads that had moved on to the runny stage. Caroline might have wanted to talk tomatoes this morning, but James is going to have to be the one to follow up on the way to the bus station. Charlotte doesn't have one extra ounce of energy left.

She and James agreed: no talk about Chad in front of the others. They're going to have to work on his lack of respect—typical adolescent outburst. He can't really mean that he hates them all. He wanted to say something hurtful, and he punched the right button. That's the kind of thing you absorb as a parent; you don't let it get to you. "What if Grandma knows?" he mimicked. It's going to be a *long* ten days for him. But Nicole isn't his only chance. And he still has his music. And they'll let him drive to school—no need for Charlotte to play bus driver again—as long as he comes home right after practice. If word leaks out about the keg, they'll tell Coach they've already put the clamps on Chad. You have to be smart about these things.

There's been no time to call Gene. That will have to wait until Caroline leaves with James; Charlotte can't possibly ride along. It's not just her varicose veins that are killing her. It's everything. She'd intended to call Kenneth, too, but not now. What was it he'd admitted on the ride back from the cemetery? She can find out later exactly what Meg knew about Sonja. There's no need to listen to Kenneth's vast knowledge of teenage behavior, even if he was right about the second child.

Suddenly Mother says, "You could make yourself at home and stay awhile."

"Mom wants to be like Mr. Armburgey," Caroline says, tearing apart lettuce to add to the hamburgers.

"The man loved his jacket," James says.

"What's wrong with that?" Charlotte asks.

"That's right. As long as he was comfortable," Mother adds.

"Absolutely," James says. "Wear your jacket all day, Charlotte; wear it to bed. Won't never bother me none."

"James," Charlotte says. There he goes again. He knows she's at her limit, but he can't help himself.

"You go, Mom!" Chad says. "Give him the cold zipper treatment tonight."

Charlotte tries to smile. Chad has a point; James says some pretty dumb things. Thank heavens, he'd calmed down by the time they got to the Walshes' this morning. On the way home it was Chad's turn to unload. It's hard to set that aside. He said they're the stupidest parents; they tell him to bring his friends around, but then they act like idiots when he does. James wants so much for Chad to like him, but he tries too hard. Buddy-buddy won't work. If only James could relax. You can still be respected, even if your son doesn't want you for his best man someday.

When James calls on Caroline to say grace before they eat, she acts surprised. Thank heavens she was here this morning. She has more nerve than you'd think, the way she saved them from this hunter nuisance. She makes the prayer snappy, just like Gloria the other day: "Bless this food. Help us to know what matters and what doesn't."

Charlotte looks around the table. "That's it? No Amen?" *What a strange daughter.*

"Never enough grace," Mother says, but she smiles at Caroline. No, she beams. You'd never know she was upset about Caroline taking on that hunter. Ever since yesterday afternoon, there's been something going with those two. It's no fun being the last to know, but James insists people—even family members!—have a right to keep some things to themselves.

The talk at the table comes out in little bursts. Comments about snow being in the forecast fall like duds. Out of nowhere Mother says she can't think of one good reason why people need to clap during a church service; it shouldn't be entertainment. Well, Charlotte doesn't like the way Coach Lucey claps his hands at a game—like he's putting a lid on a pan—but she doesn't need to talk about it. Caroline asks about the whereabouts of the old sugar bowl, the one made of Depression glass. What made her think of that? Mother says she keeps her candy in it on a shelf in her bedroom. She wanted one pretty dish from Momma close by.

Maybe sitting at the formal dining table stifles the talk and makes comments scatter. But Charlotte decided not to squish five bodies into the kitchen nook again; she tried to keep it casual with the multicolored placemats. Maybe it's the red beets that aren't quite cooked enough; Charlotte knows she set the timer. James gives his elaborate explanation of how his mother taught him to cut through a pickle—"fork tines straight *down*"—rather than using the side of the fork. "Same deal with these beets," he says. "What?" he asks, when Charlotte slyly looks at Chad and shakes her head. Next thing, he'll challenge someone to a peel-off. He loves to take his spoon around and around on an orange and acts triumphant when it all comes off in one piece.

Mother sighs and says, “I can’t believe how much trouble’s been knocking on our door.”

“Maybe we should name all the disasters that *could* have happened but didn’t,” James says.

“Please,” Charlotte says. “Let’s not get started on the calamity list.”

“That’s so true, James,” Mother says. “No car accident, no temperamental bull, no gun going off. We have much to be thankful for. Much, much.”

James asks Caroline again what she said to convince the deputy to write up the hunter. She acts nonchalant. “I wouldn’t leave,” she says. “I didn’t trust him. He acted like I should be satisfied if he just got rid of the guy.”

“I bet you stuck a flower in the hunter’s rifle,” Chad says. He grabs a midget dill pickle and holds it like he’s smoking a cigar.

“Not quite. When the deputy said, ‘I’ll take care of it,’ I knew he wouldn’t. That’s when I leaned forward and looked at his badge. I said his name, ‘Officer Grockel,’ like I knew all about him. Like I’d be sure to let others know.”

“And here I stood at the bay window,” Mother says, “praying the whole time.”

“Well, we’re very glad, Caroline,” Charlotte says, “that nothing bad came of it.”

The name Grockel sends Mother on a tangent about their old neighbors on Township Road. Then she and James get sidetracked about where Lulu Brocklemeyer is buried. Like it matters. Who cares which county road runs past the Holy Guardian Angels Cemetery? Now they're talking about the Saugerman Cemetery. Chad squirms.

Then boom, Caroline brings it up, as if she can't wait anymore. "Are you feeling okay this morning, Mom, about my plans?"

"It's hard to know what to say. Things have been so hectic."

"Anyone want that extra hamburger?" Chad asks. "Sorry to interrupt."

"It's yours," Charlotte says, not taking her eyes off Caroline. Her whole face lights up when she talks about anything to do with vegetables. "I don't know if it's the right move or not. But farming seems awfully important to you." She looks at James for help. "I won't stand in the way. The CSA gives you time, gives us all time."

"I'm not sure there *are* right moves and wrong ones anymore. Who's to say?" Caroline adds. She looks around the table as if it's hers.

"Takes some of the heat off me," Chad says. He crunches into a bite of burger, hunches over his plate, salsa dripping from one side of his mouth.

"The good news is, you're coming home, Caroline," Charlotte says. Her jacket swishes as she goes to the kitchen to get more water. The truth is: sometimes you just throw up your hands and hope for the best. "How about some ice cream and strawberries?" she calls out. "Let's get rid of that house, too."

"Whoa now," James says.

"Ice cream on Saturday noon?" Chad asks.

"Don't get ideas," James says.

"Give us this day our daily ice cream," Caroline says.

Charlotte brings a carton of Butter Pecan. "Who wants what? We have Moose Tracks, too."

"Bring it on, baby," Chad says, motioning with his spoon stuck upside down in his mouth. "Any coconut, Mom? Extra syrup?"

Caroline carries the remains of the gingerbread house to the table. "It's mostly crumbs. No tiny jelly beans or M & Ms left. Here we go again, eating more food than we need. One scoop of each for me, Mom."

"How many scoops are acceptable risk for you, James?" Charlotte asks. "Say when."

Caroline snorts and then covers her mouth. "It's nothing. When to say when, like arm wrestlers. How people decide to give up or keep on."

Mother picks a candy cane off the house, looks like she's inspecting it for quality. "While we're dreaming—." She extends the hook of the tiny cane toward Caroline. "I've been thinking. I still have *my* house, and I still want to move back. Why not with a granddaughter?"

Caroline gasps. "Grandma! Me?" She puts down her spoon, sits back, and grabs a clump of her short hair. "I never thought of that. Would you really? I mean, could we?"

"Mother!" Charlotte says over the top of James' "Holy moly."

"We can move next spring when the school year's over. The new house for the renters should be finished by then. But I'll have to convince my children. They're not the easiest bunch to get through to."

Mother breaks off a tiny piece of peppermint, puts it on top of her scoop of ice cream. "Who else wants some?"

James moves his ice cream bowl to the side, puts his arms on the table. "Let's not rush into things here."

"Awesome!" Chad says. He pulls the last cane off the house.

"It makes sense!" Caroline says. "It does. Your house on Township Road isn't far to drive back and forth." She beams at everyone. "Could I live here until then, Mom? Dad?"

"We can't decide everything today," Charlotte says. "We've had so much going on. You're always welcome here, Caroline; don't misunderstand. You too, Mother. But I've got whiplash, trying to keep up. Ugh, stale ginger cookies. I should have made coffee, so we could dunk them. Don't feel obligated to eat anymore of this." She'll definitely pitch what's left of the house before she does laundry on Monday. "Oh, would you like tea, Caroline? Help yourself if you do. You'll need some kind of social life, you know." No twenty-five-year-old could be content going home to her grandma every night.

"Here," Chad says, "I've got a bite for everyone." He reaches around the table, places a small piece of broken candy cane on everyone's ice cream, and points. "Mom, Dad, Carrie. Grandma. Broken for you. Me. Is that how it goes?"

"Thanks, Chad. Very cool." Caroline squints at the mantel clock and says to her dad, "We need to go in fifteen."

"Just a minute." Chad points again around the table. "Father, son, and all the female ghosts."

"We're given people to help us through different stages of life," Mother says. "No reason it can't be family."

"Oh, Grandma," Caroline says, "that's so sweet." She gets up to hug her, squeezes her arms, mashes her hair bun. "Oops, didn't mean to do that. You're the last piece in the puzzle." She puts her hand to the side of her mouth and whispers loudly, "We don't really need to get signed permission."

James crunches into his piece of candy cane. "Not the last piece by a long shot. There'll be lots more hitches." He shakes his head. "Whose land is this anyway?"

Caroline giggles. "I told the deputy it was mine."

Mother half-turns in her chair and says, "You're right, Carrie; we wouldn't be breaking any laws. You can have the big bedroom upstairs." Then she adds, "The renters haven't said anything about the furnace giving trouble."

Charlotte presses a finger to her lips. *Sometimes you just have to shut your mouth.* "We all need to slow way down." Is Caroline serious about moving back for good by Christmas? Charlotte will have to hustle to get ready, what with all the shopping and decorating. She turns to James. "Have you talked about how you'd work out the milking? You two? Wouldn't that be wonderful if you had help you could count on? We could get away, evenings. I don't mean all the time. But you could be in a bowling league if you wanted, James."

Caroline pulls the tip of her candy cane out of her ice cream, sucks on it, and points around the table. "Mothers, daughters, and two Holy Ghosts. Help us to know what matters."

Chad lifts his bowl to his lips, slurps leftover, melted ice cream.

"Don't get all giddy on us, Carrie," James says. "You, too, Charlotte. Carrie can only be one place at once. Things aren't going to be perfect. It's still us."

"You're right, Dad," Caroline says. She alternates a spoonful of ice cream with a long suck on her candy cane. "Better yet: none of us *has* to be perfect."

Sometimes you just have to close your eyes. Whose house is this? Mother sounds like she's the boss. Caroline acts like she has money *and* land, looks like she has everything settled. Ah, youth! But it is exciting. What would Caroline be like, running a business? Teresa goes to that Saturday farmers' market in Monroe and says it's great.

"Did you hear, Mom?" Caroline asks. "I said no one has to be perfect."

Charlotte nods. "Well, of course." Wouldn't that be something if Caroline wanted *her* to help? Charlotte could pitch in, sell produce in a pinch. She and Caroline might even—. But that's way down the road. What would Gloria think if she saw Charlotte toting a money box around? Her new five-year goal. "Oh, James, wouldn't it be wonderful—? This is *not* a hitch. We could—." He's frowning again. She tips her bowl to scoop the milk that's left. "I'm beginning—." She puts her bowl down, takes a quick glance at the painting of the old man praying over his bread and bowl. "I can't believe I'm actually going to say this." She points at Caroline. "It's probably time. I give you credit, *Carrie*. You know how to stand your ground. *Carrie.* I'll try to call you right from now on." Everyone acts like they're holding their breath. Gradually, heads come up, like when a meal's grace is silent and no one knows how soon to look up.

James makes a production of clearing his throat. "Next thing I know, the cows will start milking each other. What say, we hit the road, Carrie?"

Mother clicks her tongue. "Forevermore!"

Carrie licks cookie crumbs off her fingers and thumb. "Thanks for everything, Mom. My name, especially. Good lunch, too. Those were your beets, weren't they? All that good vitamin C. Bye, Chad," she says as his dirty dishes clatter into the kitchen sink. He comes back to give her a quick hug. "See you in a month. Can you believe it?"

Chad cracks his knuckles and says, "Watch your twenties."

"And you, watch your fingers," Carrie says, as he heads for the basement, takes the steps two at a time.

"What was that about?" Charlotte asks. She shakes her head; she'll get it out of him sooner or later. Wouldn't that be something if Chad and Caroline—Carrie—became friends. *Oh!* Charlotte looks quickly at James. If Mother and Carrie—Caroline is gone—both move out in the spring, that frees up Chad's old bedroom for him. That will not go over well at all. James shrugs like he's thinking the very same thing.

"Oops, forgot my sandwiches," Carrie says, decked out with her backpack, her purse strap dangling around her neck.

"That would be so wrong," James says. He lets out a loud laugh.

"Let me give you goodbye," Mother says. She holds onto Carrie like there's glue on her fingertips. "Blessings, blessings."

"Give us a call when you get there," Charlotte says. "Is that all you brought?" Her daughter, her firstborn. A farmer, Carrie, has taken her place. Better to have her come back home, changed—her hair isn't quite as short as when she got here—than to be stuck away in the South, pining all by herself.

"Thanks, Grandma," Carrie says. She bends for one more kiss. "We'll be the new odd couple. Just watch." Then she wraps an arm around Charlotte's waist. "Bye, Mom. Keep those magnets straight."

"Bye, dear," Charlotte says, giving Carrie a peck on the cheek. "There's lots to work through yet; it's not all final, you know. I suppose you'll give notice soon?" Who knows if it'd be safe for Mother to live on Township Road again. Caro—. Carrie wouldn't be around much in the daytime. But maybe it's better if it's just James and Charlotte at home for Chad's last year of high school. "Your ticket?"

Carrie points to a pocket of her backpack. "I have the whole bus ride to figure out how soon to give notice. Whenever it is, Manager Milt will be ticked, because of the Christmas rush coming on. Hey, everybody. I can tell Acey Banger I've got a new landlord in Wisconsin. Two of them. A house to live in and land to dwell on. Bye, everybody. Christmas'll be here in no time." She waltzes out the door like she's eaten five packets of sugar. James raises both eyebrows, shrugs, follows like a sheep.

"Can you beat that?" Mother asks. "I never thought—."

"She sure has changed," Charlotte says. "Nothing at all like when she came."

*   *   *

It's a relief to have Carrie on her way. *Mercy, mercy, mercy.* Out the door before anyone could ask too many questions about Martha's sudden inspiration. Was it selfishness or the Lord's will? She'll call Ruby next week and find out when the school year will be over; she'll make sure the renters' new house is on schedule, so they can move out. It's Ruby's boy, doing the carpentry work. Oh, dear, is that the wind picking up again? They've had so much lately. *Slow down. Slow way down.* She stretches her legs on the bed and sucks on the last of a butterscotch. She needs to remember to buy some hot cinnamon candy the next time she's at Troyer's.

It's not that moving back to the house on Township Road is a new thought, but Martha never dreamed she'd have the chance to do it like this. She'd always figured she'd have to put on a brave front about being safe, living there all alone. She tested Carrie with all those questions this morning. Then the sea parted; the water turned to wine. Just like that, the offer popped out. All unpremeditated—for the most part. And on a Saturday, the most ordinary of days. She made a connection with Carrie yesterday—*Thank the Lord!*—a meeting over failure. If only Carrie doesn't change her mind. Oh, there are differences—the poor girl's not even sure if church is the place to go for answers—but the walls are starting to tumble. What a gift from a young one, even to consider it.

Martha runs her hand over the half of the bed where Daniel would be. If only he were here to talk things over. He'd know what to think. Momma? She'd have plenty of questions. *Relax now; stop this pounding.* She feels like she's been riding in a car with Daniel, pushing her feet against the floor to supply extra brakes. He was a different person behind the wheel, especially when it was just the two of them. He'd tailgate cars, pass when there was barely enough room before the oncoming yellow line, dart in and out between delivery trucks on Route 88. Most of the time it was a white car, got him started.

Martha may never know the details of Chad's latest mess. That's all right; she doesn't need to know. Charlotte put on a good front when they came home. But then the scales fell off. If Charlotte felt an inkling of relief—the thought of having Martha out of the house—she never let on. She may still come up with a roadblock or two, but they'll get past it, if it's supposed to be. Charlotte said it! *Carrie!* That barrier came tumbling down. *Glory be!* Martha will have to watch and make sure Charlotte doesn't backtrack.

Martha's going back home! Goodness gracious, sakes alive. You learn to be satisfied with what you have, but the yearning never stops. Martha will do everything she can to help Carrie make a go of it—*coming back home!* They'll eat mashed potatoes every night, if that helps. Carrie seems like the type who would keep things tidy, not leave tracks like she did this morning. Martha won't make demands. People don't have to be the exact same to live together, but they have to *want* to live together. Be united over something bigger than thinking the same way about every little thing. They'll need a reverence to get through *each* day, ordinary or not. And they'll need respect. No different than anybody else: Mennonites or not, families or otherwise. Very risky, though, for James—all his talk of hitches—relying on one so young.

The truth is, Carrie's much too modern for Martha. Her talk about loving the earth like she's devoted to it. It's sobering. But there's more that binds than drives them apart. Martha might not always have the right words or the right answers, but she can be herself with Carrie. And to think Daniel may have played a part. An instigator like Mr. Armburgey, in a way. If Martha ruined Carrie's image of her grandfather, she didn't let on, didn't act a bit skittery. Those warm hugs.

Martha will send Sonja a card; "Thinking of You" probably fits better than "Get Well." She'll write to Gene—there's so little she can do—and tell him she's praying for all of them. Did she even say that on the phone? She can't bake a cake for him—the black walnuts are reserved for James—unless Charlotte approves and delivers. Martha didn't even think to ask Gene—last night seems so long ago—if he had any business right now. She doesn't know if a dead body would help him get his mind on something else, or if he'd just mess up, replacing all that blood. Well, he's a father before he's a mortician. His heart must be bruised like a big, floppy, red poppy with some of its petals torn.

Maybe Martha can teach Chad to play Chinese checkers, so she stays polished up for Mr. Armburgey. She can slip in a word or two to the wise, if she needs to. Yesterday Carrie kept saying: "There's still time." She has no idea—how time can drag on. And how it's gone in a second! *But what a gift!* As long as Martha has a day or an hour—*one life to live*—she'll make the most of it. All she is, that she doesn't yet know she is.

Someone still needs her! Isn't that what everyone wants? To stand on the side of good. To know that your life means something, that what you say and do—what you choose—matters to someone else.

While Carrie's out running around on her little tractor, flicking Japanese beetles off bean plants, Martha will fry up as much chicken as Carrie can eat. She'll bake it if that's better and use oil instead of lard. She'll keep that girl fed and watered, even if it has to be mostly Swiss chard and lima beans. Next spring, she'll ask Chad to paint Daniel's decorative windmill; by then Chad's basketball year will be history and he'll be glad for an excuse to get away from the cows. Charlotte might even offer to help spruce up the home place when the renters move out; she'll find projects. Only six months to go. *Matthew, Mark, Luke, John, and all the apostles.* They'll all help find a way. So long as that spot above Martha's left eye doesn't take a turn for the bad, they'll see it through. All that they are, that they don't yet know.

Epilogue

Abide with me, fast falls the eventide; the darkness deepens; Lord with me abide.

The plain white meetinghouse on the west side of County Road H is hot, the kind of summer day when you can smell the corn growing and people's backs stick to church benches. Carrie sits with her family while the song leader guides them through all five verses and slows their already slow pace to the final *O Lord, abide with me.* It's weird and strangely comforting. Grandma would like the mournful harmony of voices, would probably see no incongruity with singing about eventide at mid-morning. *Help of the helpless, O abide with me.* She might call it a fitting self-description: *Swift to its close ebbs out life's little day.*

Carrie had attended this church several times with Grandma, but it was a better arrangement for the Beachys to pick her up on Sunday mornings. It wasn't the plainness: the wooden floors and wooden benches; the creaking didn't bother Carrie, either. It wasn't the absence of stained glass windows. But Grandma agreed, what came from behind the wooden pulpit was what she'd heard for over forty years. Not verities exactly, but a way to handle the mystery of uncertainties. She hadn't seemed upset when Carrie said it didn't connect with her world. Grandma had simply nodded, almost seemed relieved, and said, "That's all right."

They'd lived together for most of four years. They'd made it work, although Grandma didn't like it when it became a habit for Carrie to go back outside again after supper. Dad had helped put up the hoop house at Grandma's property on Township Road, not far beyond the trellis where Grandma's clematis plants flourished again in their deep purple. He's still breeding to improve his herd, but he provided all the basic know-how when Carrie set up her record keeping. And yes, Carrie's found kindred spirits who also understand that healthy soil leads to healthy plants that lead to healthy people. Her friends have pointed the way: earthworms make the best aerators; red plastic lets more light through than black.

But now Grandma's body rests in a beautiful oak casket that Gene donated. Carrie's steady path of soil building has come across a large field stone. She's refused to look at the body. It's not that she thought Schneiders would do a bad job; she just doesn't want to remember Grandma as pasty-cheeked and still. The overwhelming smell of flowers in the cool funeral home was enough to endure. Carrie's not denying that death has come—Mom tried to imply that—but Carrie prefers to think of Grandma's hands moving a needle in and out of cloth. A slight grin comes when Carrie remembers the time they made cinnamon rolls that Thanksgiving before Carrie moved back home. The sadness and power of their conversation that followed in the living room. They never spoke of it again. One time Gene said offhand, "We should talk sometime." But they haven't. Not about that.

Carrie and Grandma often talked about flowers. Ruby gave Grandma castoffs to replenish her house plants, and she always had starts of spider plants on the window ledge. Around this time two years ago, Carrie helped Grandma revive her iris bed. Carrie did the digging and Grandma used the old butcher knife to divide the plants and decide which ones to discard. They started a new bed, too, with cow manure from Dad. Mom insisted that the bed be kidney-shaped, not rectangular. The best part came this spring when the new plants outdid themselves, and Carrie convinced Grandma to let her take some of the yellow and lavender ones, chemical-free, to sell at her stand. When she returned home, she gave Grandma the cash—had to insist on it!—and watched as Grandma slowly folded the ten and six ones and said she really didn't need the money. But she smiled and gave Carrie a hug like it mattered.

No one knew this past Sunday would be the last time Grandma would walk into this church building on her own. If she'd been short of breath in the past weeks, she hadn't said it and Carrie hadn't noticed. Maybe she'd missed the signs, but she won't give into self-blame. She helped Grandma achieve two big wishes: live in her own house on Township Road and not die hooked up in a hospital. Soon her body will be buried near to Daniel's, the dirt will be heaped high, and they'll all troop back to the church building again to eat salads with frothy whipped cream. Mom all but guaranteed there'd be ham and cheesy potatoes. "The family invites everyone to return to the church for a light lunch provided by women from the Missionary and Sewing Group," the young minister announces. Mom's kept herself together, busy with making sure Grandma's navy blue dress with the teeny-tiny dots is clean, taking pleasure in the casket spray of red and white roses, the gold ribbon that scrolls out: *Mother, Grandma.*

Now the man's stumbling through the obituary; Gloria squirms and looks like she wants to scream, "Put some life in it." On Tuesday Carrie had left home as usual, no inkling that the day would produce anything unexpected; no thought but that she'd come home to another warm meatloaf or chicken-noodle soup. Grandma never let her down—hot cereal for breakfast! She'd gotten really good at fixing a potato crust for her spinach and onion quiche, a bit of bacon thrown in for flavor. But life intervened with its predictable unexpectedness. Charlotte had called Carrie around noon to say she'd found her mother on the floor close to the phone—gone at age eighty-two. A heart attack, the doctor thought. Gene came right away, but they had trouble locating Kenneth. He was in the middle of his July break from the school office and was browsing in an antique shop with Gloria, enjoying the freedom of having his cell phone turned off.

Mr. Armburgey sent his condolences but chose not to attend today. During the summers Kenneth has been dropping him off to play Chinese checkers with Grandma at least once or twice a month. Whoever thought the wobbly man would outlast Grandma? Carrie will miss not getting to hear stories from Grandma about which of them had the better day with their marbles. Their games seemed to have tapered off, though; Grandma sounded vague when Carrie asked what kinds of things they talked about. It's enough to know, they had their own ways of giving each other some measure of contentment, some companionship to look forward to.

What is this older minister saying now about the dead being raised incorruptible? When will he pay tribute to Grandma's understanding of goodness and mercy, her generosity of spirit, her willingness to adapt? No doubt he found some of her choices in recent years confusing, if not downright disturbing, to the natural order of things. What the man doesn't know! Grandma wouldn't want Carrie to judge him, though. Many times she set Carrie straight about not creating boundaries for others. "Let others see what they see; the fences you try to put around others, only limit you."

Grandma kept many things her way—no air conditioning running at night!—kept to herself those things she felt others wouldn't honor. The story of Momma's Child came out one night over pot roast, but Grandma sidestepped questions about Poppa Lloyd. Carrie had promised to take Grandma to Arthur, Illinois, but it never happened. That's on Carrie. She'll have to search out that cemetery on her own, unless she asks Phil to go with her.

She met him at the Farmer's Market in Monroe. Philip Moore. Some days it seems their produce stands were meant to be right next to each other. He's stocky but there's not an ounce of fat on him. He and his brother raise goats and vegetables; they both swear by cold frames and use a high tunnel greenhouse. Carrie met Phil the second year she had her own stand, the year she handed out recipe ideas for using herbs. The transition to organic vegetable farming hasn't been problem-proof. Flea beetles—black and very tiny—are the worst when the plants are young. And now she's keeping an eye on the occasional Japanese beetle that's shown up on her young blueberry bushes this summer. But she can't complain, not with the bumper crop of strawberries she had in the spring—excellent flavor!—and the tomatoes that look promising. Through it all Grandma stayed with her, listened to every complaint, seemed surprised when Carrie's Dad didn't want to rent more than two more acres to go with the first six.

But he came through big-time after he sold off forty acres to a neighbor a year ago. He repainted all the farm buildings and made an interior part of the crib into a walk-in cooler for storing her vegetables. Mom convinced him to get rid of the old bikes and broken down milk equipment. He purchased the compressor on his own and wouldn't let Carrie pay for any part of it. "It's yours," he said. Grandma agreed; it was his stamp of approval. Of course, he's stayed guarded about Phil; no surprise, that he needs more time there. Well, they all do. "A goat farmer?" Carrie's not jumping to any conclusions this time.

It's better to think about the four acres of pasture behind Grandma's house. Waiting to be divided up? Put up for sale? Carrie can't let her mind run too far ahead, although she knows she'd hire Gordon Yoder, an Amish farmer, to work up the land with his plow and horses. But Kenneth might want the acreage for his dream of llamas. And there's Grandma's house, old and solid with beautiful hardwood throughout. Think what a deck would add, off the kitchen in the back, looking out to the north.

The house has been terribly quiet these last three days—its reigning spirit sucked out. Carrie's been eating leftovers; she may have to move out by fall. Well, they don't know. Grandma updated her will last year but was quiet about it, much to Mom's dismay. "It's nothing urgent for any of you to know," Grandma had said. "You'll hear about it soon enough."

That was around the time when Mom was consoling her friend Teresa about her dad's sudden death. Grandma hadn't been very comforting. "We're mortal," she said.

"Get over it?" Carrie had added unhelpfully.

"Get over it," Grandma had said, her lips pulled tight.

Mom had turned away, and Carrie regretted having piled on. But there's been no maudlin wailing these last few days, and Carrie's been able to listen to Mom reminisce about how satisfying it was to repaper Grandma's outdated kitchen.

Oh, now they're standing to pray again. Is this the closing? Carrie brushes shoulders with Phil. She took the initiative and asked him to be with her during the funeral and all that follows today. She didn't want to cry, if she was by herself. Chad can't be here because his team at Drexel is spending two weeks playing basketball teams in Canada, courtesy of a wealthy alumnus. No one expects him to give up any of that to come home and honor his grandma. He's already written off most of Wisconsin anyway and loves living in the East.

Phil had planned to pick more green beans today—it's the every-other-day stretch for her, too—but he'd smiled and said the beans could wait. "I'll pick yours, if you pick mine." They have an understanding about helping each other, whether it's routine or an emergency. It's amazing how he stays level-headed about potato bugs, and he showed no dismay last winter, coming in bitterly cold weather to help replace some of the plastic on her hoop house when they had a heavy, wet snow. Mom had said, "You two go together like cream cheese and crackers. With chives," she added, as if that explained everything. She'd only registered mild surprise when Phil disappeared for a week during deer hunting season. Whatever reservations Mom had, went out the window when she discovered that a fourth pound of fresh venison enhanced her vegetable soup.

Phil surprised Carrie today, wearing a long-sleeved blue shirt with navy blue Dockers. He must have trimmed his beard, too—a good way to mark his first, and likely last, venture into sitting through a service at Grandma's church. For that matter, it's probably Carrie's last time, too—sad, in a way. When they walked in to join the family, Phil had looked tense. He can joke easily with Meg and Sonja, but Dorinda still gives him the cold shoulder. When Carrie took his hand—he'd picked her up in his old Subaru—he relaxed enough to return Mom's quick hug and shake hands with the ministers in their plain coats. What nerve this must take to enter such a foreign world. They're singing again, and Phil fumbles, holding his half of the hymnbook. She'll need to have an answer ready when he asks later about the meaning of corn and wine in Beulah Land.

Who can say what's next for Carrie? Her best comrade for these years is gone. But she's certain she was given Grandma when she needed her most, never mind whether the mystery of circumstance was by accident or intention. Who's to say exactly what they were for each other? Neither one saw the other as an abandoned shoe on the road, waiting to be rescued. Rather, they offered backbone and unwavering support. And just as surely, Carrie will keep passing on the good that's been planted. Yes, without question, Grandma's gone. But she's not missing.

Acknowledgments

I've wrestled with *Everyday Mercies*, on and off, for twenty years. During these years of multiple drafts I've heard many stories in casual conversation that have helped form my perspectives. Although I can't identify the source of every snippet or idea, I thank all the unnamed contributors.

In addition, the following people have played a significant role in shaping my novel by providing insight and by responding to various drafts: Marilyn Annucci, Lois Yoder Brubacher, Joyce Dehli, Marilyn Durham, Gwen Ebert, Judy Gingerich, Alex Hancock, Liz Hunsberger, Kathy Kauffman, Carol Lehman, Mary Mercier, Dorothy Yoder Nyce, Thor Ringler, Claudia Stine, Jeanie Tomasko, Andrea Wallpe, Kathy Walter, Bess Ann Wenham, Brenda Smith White, Cynthia Yoder, and Wilbur Yoder.

Special thanks go to Joan Connor, other members of my dissertation committee, and my graduate school classmates at Ohio University, where the trajectory of this novel first emerged.

I'm indebted also to my aunt, Emma King Risser, whose diaries from the first half of the twentieth century served as a model for Momma's entries.

And finally, I'm grateful to generous friends for their time and support in this publishing effort: Melanie Zuercher for editing the manuscript, Andrea Wallpe for technical assistance in book layout, Susanne Gubanc for cover photo, and Wesley White for advice and help with self-publishing.

About the Author

Evie Yoder Miller has lived in Wisconsin for fourteen years, most recently teaching at the University of Wisconsin-Whitewater. She grew up in a Mennonite community in Kalona, Iowa. Her academic degrees in English come from Goshen College, Goshen, Indiana (B.A.) and from Ohio University, Athens, Ohio (M.A., Ph.D.). Evie's first novel, *Eyes at the Window*, was published in 2003.

Visit her at evieyodermiller.com.

CPSIA information can be obtained
at www.ICGtesting.com
Printed in the USA
LVHW09s1337280918
591705LV00001B/127/P